GLASS HOUSES

GLASS
HOUSES

BY JACKIE BUXTON

urbanepublications.com

First published in Great Britain in 2016
by Urbane Publications Ltd
Suite 3, Brown Europe House, 33/34 Gleaming Wood Drive,
Chatham, Kent ME5 8RZ
Copyright © Jackie Buxton, 2016

A CIP catalogue record for this book is available
from the British Library.

ISBN 978-1-910692-84-4
EPUB 978-1-910692-85-1
MOBI 978-1-910692-86-8

Design and Typeset by Michelle Morgan

Cover by Julie Martin

Cover image Copyright © Klára Kobáková

Printed and bound by CPI Group (UK) Ltd, Croydon, CR0 4YY

urbanepublications.com

For Richard

Watching over us, and smiling, I hope.

ONE

THERE WAS BLOOD on the steering wheel. Etta stared at her fingers as they gripped the rim. She uncurled them, flexed them in and out, then turned over her hands to examine the grooves in her skin. She smiled – a surface wound. Just a surface wound. Her half-chewed nails had plunged into her palms.

She patted her face, her arms, her legs: everything was in place. Her neck was stiff but it moved. Her feet ached so she lifted one and carefully replaced it, then lifted the other. Nothing broken. She undid her seatbelt, leaned back against her seat and forced out a long, whistling sigh.

"Thank you," she whispered, looking up as if to acknowledge the powers-that-be who'd looked after her.

Etta wrinkled her nose. Her eyes darted to the footwell where she saw her flask smashed into too many pieces to count, drowned in a puddle of milky coffee. She reached for her phone where it had fallen, narrowly missing the liquid, but she froze before she could lift it to her ear. Her engine had cut and the radio silenced but it was more than that. She placed the phone on her lap. The silence was too loud. In the rear-view mirror she saw stationary vehicles behind her. She held her breath, cast her eyes to the side, to the stream of cars travelling as if in slow motion in the other direction. Tentatively she turned back to the front. The smashed side window of the Jeep was only a few paces ahead of her.

Not again.

"M62, yes, eastbound." She picked her way quickly over the mess of twisted metal and fragments of glass, covering her mouth against the stench of burning rubber. "Junction? I don't—"

She dropped her phone, stared at the door to the Jeep which had come away in her hand. It was heavy. She let it fall and covered her ears as it smashed against the ground. She bent down to look inside the Jeep. Her body crumpled and she sank to her knees.

A woman had collapsed face down across both front seats. Her twisted hips were wedged under the steering wheel. Dark, curly hair spiralled towards the footwell, covering her face. Etta let out a cry but stuffed a fist into her mouth and sprang back to her feet. The least she could do was help.

"OK," she said, smearing tears across her cheeks with the back of her hand, "I can do this." She hadn't done the First Aid course to learn how to put plasters on children. She'd volunteered in case she found herself in this type of situation again.

She crouched down next to the doorframe and leaned in to touch the stranger's hand which dangled over the blood-stained carpet below. More tears plumped down Etta's cheeks as she lifted the lady's hand into her palm. It wasn't warm.

"But not freezing cold," she whispered. "That's a sign, a good sign." She wrapped her own cold, yet sweating fingers around the woman's hand, breathed out and wiped a tear angrily away. "Come on Etta!" she mouthed. She had to rally herself, had to remember what to do.

She needed to get closer. She rested her knees in a gap barely big enough, in between where the door should have been and the edge of the seat.

"Can you hear me?" She positioned her mouth as close as she could to the driver's ear. "Can you tell me your name?"

Nothing.

This was the wrong order. What had she been taught? "I'm going to try to help."

She looked quickly around the car, over the driver's motionless body. She had to check the environment was safe; that was the first thing. The back seat was buckled, its cushion wedged against the driver's in front but there were no other passengers. No children. Thank God.

"ABC: AirwayBreathingCirculation," the memory came so fast, the words tripped over each other. "Can't see the airway," Etta whispered, her head shaking indiscriminately. "How can I tell if it's clear?" Still holding the driver's hand, she stretched further into the car, over the woman's back and her turquoise cardigan, pulled and torn. If she could rest her ear against the driver's torso, she might be able to hear her breathing, even feel the rise and fall of her back against her cheek. But the woman was suspended, hanging two inches above the passenger seat because the seatbelt had reached the limit of its tension. Etta shot upright, looked at her head as it dangled, and at the seatbelt in its socket.

"Mustn't move the body," she chanted. She looked into the back of the car - broken glass, everywhere: nothing she could use as a support. Around her everything was wet or broken but what was that hanging off the gear stick, resting on the carpet below?

"I have to let go of your hand," Etta said, "just a moment. I'm going to—" she dragged the lady's mottled-green tote bag over towards her, hastily unravelling the strap. A few items slipped through the open zip onto the floor as she did so. She watched them fall, shook her head, they weren't a priority. She rubbed the bag through her thumb and forefinger. "—not even a rip," she said. "Incredible. You'll be able to use your bag again." The words echoed through her ears, the pettiness of the observation taunting her but what else could she say? She guided the bag into the space between the lady's stomach and the seat. It was a perfect fit. Her body was no longer suspended and her head was in line with the rest of her spine.

"That's better," Etta said hollowly. "Never come between a woman and her bag."

She took the lady's left hand again, squeezed it as she placed it back onto the seat and held it there. She wouldn't let go. It felt the right thing to do; she didn't know why. "Can you feel my fingers?" she asked. "Can you hear me? I'm right here with you."

Now she could rest her head gently on the driver's back, her ear to her rib cage. But she couldn't concentrate with the voices outside the car: hurried, incoherent words flying, and the sound of footsteps too, people running. Fix on her breathing, Etta! Was that a tapping, a faint 'ptt, ptt, ptt'? She might have to perform CPR. Could she remember? How many breaths? Oh God! Was it five breaths and twenty pushes?

"Focus!" She pressed her ear a little closer to the driver's back gently - who knew what was broken? She put her free hand against her other ear to block it.

Ptt, ptt, ptt.

She threw a handful of the woman's curls away from her down-turned face. "You're breathing!" She squeezed her fingers under her still lips and felt damp blood, a soft brush of air against her fingertips. "Definitely breathing!" A flicker of a smile crossed Etta's face. She pulled her hand from the lady's mouth, considered the mauve lipstick stain on her fingers and wiped it on her new trousers. What next?

Broken glass crunched in the metal rim beneath her knees. She shifted position and placed one foot on the tarmac to support her weight. The disjointed chatter behind her sorted itself into sentences. Tentatively, she turned her head, the lady's hand still firmly held in hers. Her eyes rested on a wall of bystanders, their faces increasing in number like cells of honeycomb. Some were talking, others shouting. Phones rang. Someone sobbed. Etta wanted to shout but her voice barely sounded through her shaking lips.

"She needs air. Can't breathe. Space," she said, just loud enough to force a few of the onlookers to take a step back.

"Get her out!" a man shouted. "She should be in the recovery position!"

Etta shivered. She glanced at the man's puce face but quickly back to the lady whose hand she held.

"No," she said in a voice only she could hear. The driver had a gash to her head. "Mustn't move the body." She was more defiant this time, the words of the First Aid coach clearer now. "It could worsen a head or spinal injury."

She shifted her bottom to provide a better barricade between her and the crowd. The instructor had said to stay calm, to make sure no one distracted her. She reached two fingers to the near side of the lady's neck, desperate to feel a constant pulse, to be sure the breathing was continuous, that she didn't need to do CPR. The voices stabbed into her resolve. She focused on her fingertips as they tiptoed over the skin then back again. Nothing. She dug in deeper between the soft folds, crawling up and down her patient's neck, searching. There was something close to her ear. Was it a rise and fall under her fingers? There was one beat, a pause, a second and third beat in close succession. But she couldn't shake the picture of the trainer, with his tie slightly off-centre, his large stomach protruding over the top of his waistband and his white hair combed close to his head. "Don't mistake the driver's heartbeat for your own," he'd warned several times. Etta's heart smacked against her ribcage. Was that what she felt in her fingers? She pulled away, squeezed the hand she still held.

"We can't help thinking the poor soul would be better out of the car," a woman's voice sounded from behind her. "She's in an awful position."

Etta shook her head.

"You'd better be qualified!" The man's voice was steeped in irritation.

She would check for a pulse in the driver's other wrist. She followed the twisted forearm down into the pit between the seats. Please, where was the ambulance?

She cradled the fragile forearm in her hand, rotated it gently with the other and placed two fingers on the fleshy underside of the wrist. It was faint, irregular, but Etta felt movement and just when she doubted it, the pulse came again.

"You're with us!" She'd stay like this until an ambulance arrived, both of the driver's hands now clutched in one of hers. Her other arm was stretched over the lady's back, her own small frame pressed against the larger woman in an attempt to keep her warm. "We have to wait a little longer," she said. "I'm Etta, by the way." She spoke into the cluster of their hands. "I wish I knew your name."

The woman seemed almost peaceful. Her wild hair still obscured one side of her face with the other cheek pressed into the seat. Etta tried to blow some wisps to the side so she could see something. But her hair was matted, stuck to the skin by the blood which had trickled from the gash. Etta gave a small cough.

"It's short for Henrietta," she said. "Ridiculously posh, I know. My parents wanted me to have a very English sounding name." She shook her head. "They had some funny ideas."

Etta looked out of the front window, through the only section on the passenger side which wasn't blocked by a web of shattered glass. Many people were ahead of her now, leaning into other cars, pirouetting as if a full revolution would change the scene before them, barking orders, standing a step back, hands on hips or arms crossed, pointing inside bent and dented cars. How many vehicles were there? Three, four? She couldn't see past a van some distance ahead, straddling the road. A white van. Of course it was. She tutted. How many other people were injured?

"They fled from Slovakia, you see." Etta returned to the driver and squeezed her hand. "My parents. There was a relaxed sort of communism, I don't know if you know much about—" She shook her head. "Maybe I should try to guess your name." She forced herself to smile even though the woman wouldn't see. "Let's hope it's not Rumpelstiltskin."

Her eyes darted around the traffic as it trudged past on the other side of the road. The emergency services had to arrive soon, surely? She glanced over at the hard shoulder on her own side. A few vehicles nudged their way along, bypassing the barricade of cars behind her which spanned the three lanes designed to block all but the most determined, or thoughtless, from moving beyond the scene. A man and a woman waved their arms, directing cars back from where they'd come. The woman slapped a hand to her forehead and the man punched the bonnet of a white car, its driver defiantly pushing forward. How would the ambulances get through?

She looked away, shook her head. "Keep breathing," she whispered, "help is coming."

Her gaze settled on a red car, no more recognisable than if it had already been crushed and pressed into a cube by the crane at a scrapyard. A group of four or five people sat in a circle next to it, guarding something on the tarmac. Etta gasped and squeezed her patient's hand a little tighter.

"This one," she heard suddenly. She span around. The crowd which had aligned itself to the Jeep had largely left but still the man's voice found her. She heard footsteps, faster now. He ran towards the car, his arms in the air, pointing towards it as if directing planes to land.

"This is the bloody idiot who won't let her out," he shouted, as he kicked the front wheel. "She should be locked up."

Etta found herself panting but focused on the driver. "Mustn't move the body," she chanted to herself. "Mustn't move—" She flinched as someone's stomach pressed against her side, a breath of air passing over her shoulder.

"Is the patient breathing?" a soft but hurried woman's voice asked.

"How can she be with her body screwed up like that?" the man's voice interrupted, much louder, much harder to ignore.

"I'll need you to move aside."

Etta felt the light touch of a span of fingers on her shoulder and looked up to see a woman in a high vis jacket. "You've done a great job," the woman said. "We'll take over now."

Etta stepped backwards out of the car. Her legs buckled but she straightened herself, wiped a rush of tears from under both eyes and slowly made her way towards the hard shoulder. She stopped. A female police officer beckoned her over. She cleared her throat, lifted her head and smiled. The officer was walking towards her.

She pressed her finger to her sternum. "Me?" she asked.

The officer nodded. Once she'd reached Etta she walked at her side, an arm cocooning her back, a sliver of air away from touching it. The pair halted a pace inside the hard shoulder and the officer positioned herself so that it was she who looked out onto the motorway. She stuck out her hand and introduced herself as WPC Denby, called here for what they'd class as a 'serious investigation'.

"It's my job to have a chat with all potential witnesses, get an overview of what happened here, just a few questions, and your name is –?" She opened her notebook.

"Etta Dubcek."

"We're spelling that?"

Etta thought she might be sick.

"You're shivering." WPC Denby waved to attract the attention of a member of the ambulance crew, stationary in front of the open doors of his van diagonally opposite. She traced a rectangle in the air. "Or we could do this in the car." She pointed further down the hard shoulder to a row of police cars.

"No!" Etta snapped, but smiled and added, "No, thank you, better to straighten out after being cramped in that Jeep." She pointed behind her in its vague direction but had no inclination to look at it.

"Of course." WPC Denby explained that she'd follow up this little chat with a more formal statement later, after the medical staff had checked Etta out. Etta nodded and found herself belching. Before she could apologise, WPC Denby lifted her hand to acknowledge her understanding. She asked Etta what she could remember about the incident, anything at all, there were no wrong answers.

Etta stared at the thick foundation smothering the officer's acne-pocked skin on her square face. She focused on an unblended dollop at the top of her nose and said that she didn't remember much about the Jeep stopping in front of her.

"Slammed on my brakes," she said, and added hastily, "Didn't touch the Jeep. I thought I might have hit it but my car had just stalled." She pulled at the cuffs of her white shirt, rubbed her arms, remembered her jacket on the back seat of her car.

"Can you—" WPC Denby broke off to acknowledge Etta rubbing her arms, to tell her that a blanket was on its way, "—recall anything of note before the moment of impact? Any erratic driving, something about the Jeep, other vehicles…?"

Etta's mouth opened and closed again. She rubbed her arms a little harder.

"Yes?" WPC Denby asked.

"A white van."

WPC Denby looked up and down the stretch of motorway. "A minibus?" she asked. "Did you notice anything about how it was being driven?"

The man's voice again. Behind her. Loud, aggressive and directed at her.

He motioned first in her direction, then towards the Jeep. The lady she'd sat with was still in the car but crowded from her view by a troop of emergency staff.

"You'd better be charging her!" she heard him shout. He gesticulated in her direction, fingers then fists flying, staccato, movements above his head.

"Ignore him!" WPC Denby rolled her eyes. "Etta? Anything at all?"

"Hmm? No." She shook her head. "Nothing. Mind's a blank."

TWO

CARLY STOOD AT TORI'S BEDSIDE and lifted her mother's hand from beneath the folded hospital sheet. She interlocked her fingers through hers. Her mother was a bust with arms. The protruding face, hair and shoulders certainly bore a credible resemblance but where was the colour, the vibrancy, the animation? When would this representation of a person do anything other than, 'be'?

"Looking great, Mum!" she announced.

Tori's left eye slowly opened halfway.

"Nice to see you." Carly gripped her hand and brought it to her lips for a kiss. "It's 6.30 in the evening. Carly's here and it's your birthday." She looked at Tori's lopsided face. "You're fifty-one today." One eye was swollen and higher than the other. The bruising that had started on her forehead had crept lower and now extended over her nose and cheeks. "Not looking a day over fifty-one," Carly said. A hollow joke, one her parents shared every birthday, much to their glee, and the bemusement of her and Nicky. Funny how the banal family rituals took on such poignancy these days.

She lowered herself down onto one of the orange chairs, her mother's hand still held tight, and watched her lying there with her head slightly raised and one eye open and blinking. She would wake up. Carly had to believe the nurses. Her body needed more healing time. When she was ready she'd open the other eye, wince as she acknowledged the painful bruising, spot Carly and ask her why she looked so tired.

Carly tutted. That's what she should focus on: her mother's recovery. She should deal with one thing at a time.

"I've made you a birthday cake, Mum. Fruit cake. I'll tell you about it." Finally, she let go of her mother's hand so that she could lift the cake from her feet to place it precariously on her lap. She described her first ever attempts at royal icing, lifting Tori's fingers onto the top and pushing them over the bumpy surface as she spoke so that she could read the cake like Braille. The numbers 'five' and 'one' in solid chocolate replaced candles on the top and dotted around them were brick-shaped mounds of white fondant, daubed with strings of icing to give the illusion of presents.

"Looks more like I've decorated them with a bow of toothpaste," Carly said. It was time she learned from the master. She'd book her mum in for a cake decorating lesson as soon as she woke up. She squeezed Tori's hand again. Was she listening? "Why am I talking such utter drivel, Mum?"

"Hello girls!"

Carly's father rushed into the room, reaching the side of Tori's bed in two paces, ruffling Carly's long hair en route and catching his fingers in the chaotic, brown curls she'd inherited from her mother.

"Happy birthday, you!" His eyes fixed on Tori's as he placed a small, poorly wrapped box next to her on the bedside cabinet. "It's Doug here. There's a little present for when you wake up." He kissed her lightly on the lips, then on her forehead, his soft, ginger hair falling over his eyes. "Got it all by myself."

"Superb cake!" he said to Carly, with the upbeat lilt back in his Geordie accent. "We should get a photo. We can show your mum later." Carly stood up to be next to her father. "We should sing," he said.

The sound was scratchy and vulnerable, too low for Carly, too high for Doug. She could picture him at his secondary school in Leeds. The headteacher projecting the words of Church of England hymns to the back of the assembly hall of a thousand pupils and later booming out specific harmonies as he trooped down the corridor and ushered students to their lessons. But within the confines of Tori's hospital room, one long arm wedged around Carly's shoulder, the other gripping Tori's hand, he looked ridiculous.

Barely reaching the final bar, he shouted, "There it is!" Carly looked at her father's finger shaking in the direction of Tori's closed right eye. "You see that, Carly? Her eyeball looks more rounded."

"Bulging?"

"Yes, exactly. Behind the eyelid."

Carly looked at her mother's face, sunken into its pillow with every feature protruding less than it should. She looked at her eyelids, pull-down blinds to a soul without a window. "Definitely more spherical than flat," she said.

"Let's shine the light!" Doug pointed to the torch lying on the table on wheels, a magazine atop where there should have been supper. "Carly?"

She handed it to him. "You do it."

Doug spun the torch through his fingers like a juggling trick, then snatched open his wife's eyelid and shone the light directly into the socket. Carly flinched. They both saw it. It was a miniscule movement of Tori's pupil but blatant to two people who had waited for this moment for almost a month. Doug punched the air, hugged his daughter and said he'd tell the nurses as he bounded over to the door, flinging it open.

"She's reacting!" Carly heard him shout from the corridor.

"Brilliant, Mum," Carly said, close to her ear. "Can we have a smile now?" She cupped her mother's face in her hand, stared at her long thin nose, the only aspect of her face unchanged. Would one side of her lips be downturned forever more? She couldn't bear to see her without a smile. Her mum was always happy, animated anyway. "Please Mum?"

Doug held open the door for Anna who waddled into the room, announcing herself to Tori and beaming at Doug and Carly all in one well-practised movement.

"What have we got here, Tori, eh?" Her voice was loud and crisp. She lifted the eyelid, shone the torch directly at Tori's eyeball, right then left, and repeated the action several times, before taking a step back. She tilted her head to the side.

"Yes," her head tipped the other way, she pushed her bottom lip over her forefinger, "there's certainly movement."

"And both eyeballs are more spherical aren't they? Getting back into position?"

"Yes, Doug, those eye muscles are certainly on the move." Her eyes trained on Tori, Anna rubbed Carly's back. "Yep, they're tightening up." She squeezed Carly's arm and mouthed, 'OK pet?' but didn't wait for a response before striding out of the room. "Congratulations you three!" she called. "We're moving forward."

"Isn't that fantastic?" Doug took Carly's face in his hands but she pulled herself away, excused herself for a moment, and said,

"She's not with us though, is she Dad?"

– – –

Carly knew he'd find her in the cafeteria. It would be the first place he'd look with its guarantee that there would be no cameras or microphones and on this floor, at this time, rarely any people either. Really, she'd wanted a little space. She pushed coins into the slot of the vending machine, only for them to be thrown back out at random intervals. When she took her coins from the refund slot for the fourth time and slapped the side of the drink machine so hard it wobbled, her dad finally paced over, directed her to a Formica-topped table in the corner and successfully purchased the hot chocolate himself. He slid it towards her.

"I'm listening," he said.

Carly leaned back against her chair, picked up her cup, glanced at the brown ring it had left on the table and realigned it to cover as much of it as possible.

"You look smart," Doug said, "special effort for your mum's birthday? I can see that would be hard—"

She shook her head.

"The lack of visitors, I know—".

"Nicky barely visits." She exhaled loudly. "I'm ashamed of my own sister."

Doug leaned over, touched Carly's hand, told her to drink her hot chocolate before it went cold. "The few who visit bringing in flowers which live and die without your mum knowing they were even there. I struggle with that," Doug said, his eyes trained on Carly. "Am I getting close?"

Carly found herself smiling briefly. She shrugged her shoulders. She said that it was the grapes which annoyed her. What did they expect them to do? Put them in a blender and serve them via the NG tube?

Doug laughed but Carly didn't join him. She grasped her hair in her hands and held it on top of her head for a moment before letting it fall down and saying that she just wanted her mum to be human again.

"I thought that once her second eye recovered she'd look more like Mum. I know everyone speaks about her waking up: all the staff, you," she raised an eyebrow, "and her two remaining friends, but underneath that eyelid she's blank, Dad. It freaks me out. I'm scared about what her disabilities will be. I'm worried what she'll look like."

"Aesthetics, Carly. You know that."

"It's not me, Dad. It's everybody else. They'll stare and photograph her, write even more horrible things. I can't bear the thought of it."

Doug pulled Carly's face up to his with a finger under her chin. "You're strong, I know you'll cope," he said. "And you're not on your own. I'm here." He pushed the remainder of her drink towards her. Did she need anything to eat, a bag of crisps or something?

Carly shook her head, thanked her dad but asked him not to fuss. She gulped down the remains of her drink and pulled a rogue hair back behind her ear. Her father's watery blue eyes belonged to somebody much older and his characteristic stubble appeared to have greyed in only three weeks. She rubbed a knuckle under one of her eyes then the other.

"When your mum took it upon herself to text me about that bloody chicken," he said behind a fist shielding an unnecessary clearing of his throat, "and when I replied—"

"Yes, Dad." Carly looked up at her father and nodded. "When she caused that most horrendous crash - saying it every time she isn't in earshot doesn't make it any better, though."

Doug asked Carly to let him speak. "When she sent that text, all our lives changed for ever," he said. "I will do my utmost to protect her from the press." Carly wiped away more tears with her fingers then crunched the empty cup between both hands. "But it's a new world we're entering. We have to be strong and we have to be thick-skinned."

Carly gave a resigned shake of the head.

"I'll do my best to protect her from the press," he said, again. "And I'll do my best to protect you." He lifted her hands from the debris and held them in his own. "You have my word on that, Carly."

She blinked, tried to look away but Doug's gaze followed her.

"I know," she said.

THREE

ETTA GLANCED in the rear-view mirror and quickly back to the road ahead. She breathed out. It was a three mile trip door to door from school. She'd done it successfully several times before, hundreds of times, thousands in fact.

"What's the giggling all about, you two?" she asked Johan and Adriana, her eyes fixed ahead. "You are sitting face forward, feet still, no bunched up knees, I hope." She dared to glance in the mirror again, enough to see their bright faces beaming as they sat stock still in their booster seats, backs dead straight, feet dangling as close to the floor as they could reach. The traffic light was red. Etta pulled up the handbrake, gear into neutral and this time she turned around.

"Why the mirth?" she asked.

"The 'mirth', Mama," Johan said, "is because you drive so slowly. Everyone overtakes you. That lorry overtook you—"

"—a van, I think." Etta looked back to the front. Hand poised to release the handbrake she mumbled, "Not my fault everyone drives too fast." She cleared her throat. "Vans can go surprisingly fast you know. Faster than my sorry looking Kia Picanto."

Johan said that, anyway, it was the man on the bike who made them laugh.

"That bike should not have been overtaking a car," Etta said, a little crossly. Besides, it was a 20 mph zone for the area near to the secondary school and Etta felt it was safer always to drive a little slower than the speed limit. Even if everyone else thought it was fun to play beat the policeman and drive 9% faster than the law, outraged when they didn't dodge prosecution.

Johan said he hadn't done percentages yet at school, even though Miss said his class were halfway there already because they were so good at their tables, so he simply explained for Adriana's benefit that going faster than the speed limit was not allowed, that the policemen would send you to prison.

"Prison!" Adriana said, with the familiar admiration in her voice for her brother, a constant source of tales of blood, gore or punishment.

"Lots of people are in prison for driving too fast," Johan said in a tone to match the wisdom afforded by his elder status.

"Not so many, Johan." Etta raised her eyebrows as she flicked a glance in the rear-view mirror and saw the convoy of cars behind her. "Most people are very law-abiding." A car horn made her jump in her seat and she squeezed the steering wheel more tightly. "Sorry," she mouthed, her hand raised in salute. "I just want to get us all home in one piece," she whispered. "Why is that so bad?"

She inched slowly up their drive with its modest incline. "Seatbelts remain locked until I say so," she said, as she said every time they approached their home. She came to a halt, moved into neutral, put on the handbrake, checked it was secure, released the child locks, turned off the ignition and shouted, "Go!"

The pair flung off their seatbelts and raced to first place on the step.

It was an unfair game. Johan was three years older and stronger so even having to run from the far side of the drive he was always first to the door, always the one to choose the first of their two slots of fifteen minutes of television.

"Adriana, you come and make some milkshake with me and then we'll have a special reading of *a Squash and a Squeeze*, eh? How about that?"

"And again at bedtime, Mama?" Adriana's blue eyes were wide with excitement as her chubby little hand found its way into Etta's.

"Certainly." Etta squeezed her daughter's hand. Reading with children was the most important thing there was, after all. If she started her assignment straight after bedtime, if Andy could be persuaded to clear up after supper and put the PE kit on to wash, and if he didn't look too crestfallen that yet again she was leaving him alone on the sofa as she went up to their bedroom to study, she could perhaps be in bed before midnight.

FOUR

JO ALWAYS FORGOT to press the door closed to prevent it slamming. She dragged the orange chair by two of its legs to the foot end of the bed.

"Sorry for the noise, Torr, but to be honest, it's a bit bloody quiet in here. In fact," she rummaged in her bag for her phone, "I was thinking that today we needed some new sounds. Well, not 'new' exactly, some of our anthems. No more dolphins for you, my quietest client." She halted the search to look over at Tori, her friend since their primary school years. "Never thought I'd be saying that of Tori Williams." Jo shook her head, pulled her phone from her bag, wiped the screen with the cuff of her jumper and declared that today was Led Zeppelin and Meat Loaf and let's get those 'sirens screaming' and 'fires howling' because baby we are 'way down in the valley tonight.'

"Anywhere better than here," Jo mumbled to herself as she scrolled through the playlist, pausing at Sister Sledge's 'We Are Family' but deciding against it and plumping instead for Carly

Simon's, 'You're So Vain'. "How loud do we sing this, Torr!" Her voice wavered but she was not going to break down. "I bet you think this song is about you, don't you, don't you!" she sang, walking up to the top of the bed to hold Tori's hand. "It is about you, Torr, we're going to get you out of here. You're my best friend," she said. "You will wake up and we'll be out to lunch with Amelie before you know it and you'll be blackmailing me with Sauvignon Blanc to help pack a thousand heart shaped mini shortbreads into muslin bags - bags which are, let's be honest, a size too small - without breaking off any of the icing. And you'll be winning climbing awards, for the old-timers, granted, and you and Doug will be pretending you're both working so you can have your nights in together, and we'll come to you for our Sunday lunches and pretend we have every intention of leaving before dark, but bring the head torches just in case."

She looked at Tori and released her hand to cover her mouth, giving a small cough instead of a sob. It was ridiculous to think that if she prattled on in an annoying fashion Tori would sit bolt upright and say that she loved Jo dearly but if she didn't stop talking right this second she'd get a bop on the nose.

"Right," Jo said. "I'm leaving the tunes at your end of the bed and I'm going to attack those feet." 'Two Out Of Three Ain't Bad' was next on the playlist. Should she flip over this one, too? It was so sad. They always said that they wanted to rewrite the lyrics, make it a proper love song, 'Three Out Of Three was good', they'd sing, 'There ain't no way I'm ever going to leave you'. A simple change and yet so effective they'd agreed and continued to croon, I want you, I need you, into whatever piece of cutlery was to hand. Jo would let it play. Even though the tears were already streaming down her face and the track hadn't even started, because this might be the one which gave Tori a jolt.

Jo knew how to move the bed up and down to the right height so that she could sit while she kneaded Tori's feet. She concentrated on her toes in particular as Sheena Easton belted out that her baby was working nine to five. She couldn't help thinking that Tori would suggest Miss E got out of the house and got herself a job, rather than sitting at home pining for a lover to come back to her from his day job but still, it was pretty innocuous with Ms Easton's doll-like tones.

She pushed and pulled, tapped and stroked. Jo had a dream, that it would be *her* reflexology, *her* manipulation of Tori's feet which would bring her soul mate back.

"Had my hair cut today," she said, suddenly, "into the nape of my neck." She lifted one hand away from Tori's toes to stroke the hair at the back. "It's soft, certainly," she said. "And Marian's coloured the grey a rather succinct red, if red can ever be succinct." Looking away, both hands on Tori's toes again, she added, "But boy, do I look old!"

Jo's dedication never waned but she preferred to work Tori's feet, hold her hand, even sit mesmerised by the creases in the bluey-white bed linen, rather than converse with Tori's hollow face. She always started well with the semi-planned energetic hokum bunkum, but in reality she found it uncomfortable talking about her life and mutual friends. It was like talking about a party with the one person who wasn't invited.

The door opened and Doug guided the door into the frame to prevent it slamming. Jo leapt to her feet.

"Fleetwood Mac," he said. "You two always did know how to party!"

Jo inclined her head towards the drip high above Tori's head and said that his wife was at a distinct advantage now that she'd discovered narcotics, albeit a decade or three too late.

Doug smiled and thanked Jo for coming. "Again."

She cocked her head to one side. Of course! She held out her arms, taking a step over to Doug. She didn't think that Tori was the only person who needed a hug around here. She could feel the ribs in Doug's back as they embraced, neither of them willing to pull away until Doug sighed, which Jo took as their cue to part.

He strode to the other side of Tori's bed, stretched over to kiss her on the cheek, his hands on either side of her face. "Hello you."

His strawberry blonde hair was too long. Tori would be appalled at the ginger tufts sprouting from his ears. "Are you getting enough fresh air, Doug?" Jo asked.

He shook his head. "I never see daylight. I'm either here or at school."

Everything about Doug was less vibrant than it should be. Even his lips appeared to have paled to the merest hint of pink. He wasn't so much white as ivory. Jo promised she'd deliver a box of fruit and vegetables to his house every week until this sorry ordeal was over.

"Guess what I did today?" His Adam's apple rose and fell, protruding over the top of a crinkled white shirt, the top button undone, the crimson tie loosened. "Bought a new phone," he answered himself.

Jo grimaced. "Oh."

"Yep, smashed mine up.

"Not like me to destroy something perfectly useable." He hooked up Tori's next batch of vanilla Fresubin with all the carefree concentration warranted by an important task which had nonetheless become routine.

Hello my darling! Tori thought. *Please Doug, try to hear me.*

"But once I'd smashed it I panicked that the hospital wouldn't be able to get hold of me."

"Quite."

"Have you seen the yellow banners in the phone shops?"

Jo nodded.

"Two on either side when I walked in through the Phones In Force door." He interrupted himself with a belch, "Sorry you two, I'll never get used to that revolting smell, makes me want to vomit." Doug checked the point where the tube and its sickly contents entered Tori's stomach. He drew her face towards him and searched her eyes. "Do you know what they say, Tori?"

Go on! she urged.

Jo squeezed Doug's forearm, "I'll get off, I've intruded enough on your time together." She touched his hand lightly. "Vegetables!" she said, pointing her finger for emphasis.

— — —

The door closed and Doug sat himself next to Tori. "Jo and Amelie have been so good to me." He smoothed her tangled hair against the pillow. He'd pleaded with the nurses not to wash it. This curly brown hair was her trademark, bobbing up and down as she did. She hadn't washed it in fifteen years. To subject it to cleaning products would undo all the work of those six tortuous weeks when she'd first taken on the challenge for a bet.

"Her hair is self-cleaning," Doug had argued. "Please don't take that away from her too."

"Does it clean blood?" Doug's favourite nurse, Anna, had answered, pulling her fingers through it hastily. "And shards of metal, vomit and diesel?" These days Tori looked like she'd been electrocuted. She would be cross when she woke up.

"The banners, Tori. I admit, they've unnerved me." His hand rested on her forehead. "They say, 'Don't Be A Texting...' well, you know. Then I sit there for half an hour in the phone shop, with the half-pint employees all around me, self-righteous little sods, checking me out. I tell you, I thank my parents for such an innocuous surname." Doug stood up to check Tori's food was flowing from its bag through the tube and into her stomach. "Even then they're asking, is this the Doug Williams married to Tori Williams whenever I sign anything these days."

What banners, Doug?

He unpacked a mini pink drumstick and smiled, did they have blue for boys? He rolled the drumstick from one corner of Tori's bottom lip to the other, picking up dust particles and flecks of dry skin as he went.

"I was nearly sick when I found the yellow flyer in the bag with the phone. There's a photo of a car in the centre. Jeez!" He rustled the used drumstick back into its wrapper which seemed too small for it now. "This car was unrecognisable," he said. "Who's to say it wasn't your car?" He sat back down, took hold of Tori's hands and brought them to his lips, kissing them tenderly. He held them there, told her that he hadn't imagined her car to be like that at all. He hadn't seen her Jeep after the accident. It was scrapped after the police had finished with it. He'd pictured a few scratches, almost like a soft top once the crew had taken off the roof.

"Jeez, Tori, what a mess!"

There was a flash, then a bang, then red. Red metal jumped towards her and span away. Her brain rocked and then it was quiet.

Doug squeezed her hand. He shuddered. "Phones! It's all anyone talks about. 91% of the Global scum think you should be banged up for life."

Who should be banged up for life? Who was scum? Concentrate Tori! The flash of red metal came back again and again. But then, before the silence, there was something else. She heard herself scream. Just once.

"That's all right of course, until you read that 81% of the bastards have used a phone in the car. Hands-free most of them, of course. Yeah right!" Doug said, "Until the signal gets a bit iffy."

The red came back again, incessant. Each time it crashed into Tori's face faster than the time before. A bang first, then red, a crash, a scream, then blank. 'Banged up for life!' he'd said. Except this time after the scream there was something else; spinning slowly away from Tori's grasp. 'Don't be a texting...' The piece of metal twisted slowly through the air, Tori could only watch. A thud and finally: her phone on the floor.

– – –

Doug belched again and ducked under her bag of food and its repugnant smell. "I've said too much." He took two steps to the door. "Anna says you can have mint choc chip when the next Fresubin comes in." His voice was higher than usual, shaking. "That's incentive enough to get you back on meat and two veg, believe me."

Tori heard the door open.

Don't go!

Doug told her he'd only be a minute. The nurses were going to roll her when her tea had gone down.

Please Doug, stay!

The door didn't close immediately. "Hello there," she heard. "Yes...stable...certainly eating well." Doug laughed but then said more softly, "Why don't you go in? What harm can it do?"

– – –

Tori fell, pulled further back into her mind, down a peach coloured helter-skelter ride. Medical staff, holding monocles larger than a ship's portholes, loomed and faded.

Stay! she shouted. *Mum! Somebody?* Nobody heard.

The staff peered periodically as she dropped, the marshmallow walls billowing in and out as she made a slow motion descent into her single bed.

The nineteenth of July 1964, five o'clock on a Sunday morning. Tori was eight years old. The phone rang, jumping into the silence. It rang in a way it had never rung before and had never rung since. This was 'Lottie's Ring'.

On and on it rang, begging her to pick it up. She could almost hear the whisper behind the shrill tone, 'Tori. Come. Tori. Come.' Where were her parents? Her mum was always up by five, having her first cup of tea.

Tori crawled out a hand and prised the blankets away from her pink flannelette pyjamas. She swung her legs over the side of the bed to reach the floor but paused to rub her feet together.

— — —

"I see her thinking," Doug said, as the two nurses required to move Tori from her back to her side every two hours joined him at her bedside.

"I can believe it." Anna gave a nod for the rolling procedure to commence.

"I think her eyelids bulge more when she's thinking."

"There's a lot we don't understand," Anna said. In two moves, Tori looked comfortable again.

"And they flit about as if she's dreaming."

"I should say." Anna leaned into Tori, "Tori, pet, come and see us. We're all here waiting for you."

"Anything you want Tori," Doug said. "Can you hear us today?" He gestured to Steph, Anna's timid Health Care Assistant, so young, she still had a face-full of spots. "She's dreaming," he said through an exaggerated yawn. "Look."

— — —

Once Tori had stumbled to the landing beyond her bedroom door, everything moved much more quickly. Because the Lottie Ring was imploring, desperate somehow, filling the house. She took the stairs two at a time, her eyes fixed on the phone, pulling itself from its cheese wedge support where it attached to the wall. She snatched at the receiver before noticing that her auntie, who lived fifty-five miles away, was watching her from the landing above, squeezing her bottom lip with her front teeth and twisting a wisp of hair around her finger. Tori put the phone to her ear.

"Hello, love," said a familiar voice Tori had never heard before.

"Mum?" her voice was so much higher than usual, she had to check. "Mum?"

"Tori. Love—" her mother was saying something she couldn't bear to hear.

"She's dead, isn't she?" The words were hers, fallen now into a whisper, a question Tori didn't know she knew. "Lottie's dead, Mum, I can tell."

— — —

Anna and Steph had tucked in the stubborn edges of Tori's extra blanket and Doug's head had dropped to his folded arms on the bed. His eyes were shut and he was as close to Tori's face as was possible with the tubes which connected her to her 'nearly life'.

Doug heard Anna gasp and felt her hand lay itself heavily on his shoulder. "Doug, look at this!" Tori was awake, her left eye was wide open and her right eye had opened a smidgen too. She was crying.

"Tori!" He sat bolt upright. "Oh my word, Tori, hello. Hello!"

— — —

Tori thought she was shrieking, holding her ears to dull the sound. *I want to tell a different story!* Tori wanted to scream, to shout, *I don't want it to end like this! Not Lottie, no!* But again and again the phone rang. Lottie's Ring.

"Hey, Torr, don't be sad!" Doug grinned as he looked into her fully-opened left eye for the first time since 17th August. "This is a great day!" He held her face, scrutinised it for clues: were they working? Did they see? Did they know what they saw? He wiped away her tears but her lids dropped shut to meet his fingers.

"No!" Doug squeezed her cheeks. "Don't close them! Anna!" he shouted. "Help us!"

Anna pushed Doug aside. "Tori!" she said sternly, clicking her fingers in front of one eye then the other. Both were sealed again. "This is important. I'm going to nip your skin. You need to tell me how it feels." Anna took a knob from the back of Tori's left hand and pulled it up between her thumb and forefinger. Tori baulked, once, twice, three times but her eyelids remained firmly closed. Anna took a clump of Tori's hair, holding it close up to the scalp. Tori's eyebrow followed as she pulled, but her eye remained shut.

Doug winced. Steph mouthed that it was OK. "Can you open your eyes again love?" he moaned. "Please, Tori? Can you open them again?" He picked up her right eyelid with the tips of his fingers and rolled it back, even though he knew he wasn't supposed to.

"It's great progress." Anna lifted Doug's hands from Tori's face. "Gives us oodles to work with."

He perched on the edge of the bed, looked at his silent wife and sighed. His chest fell onto hers and he wrapped his arms around her, as if trying to squeeze her back to life.

Anna picked up Tori's arms and connected her hands over his back.

"Doug needs a cuddle, Tori," she said, on her way out of the room.

The couple lay like this for a few minutes: their chests squeezed together; Doug reaching behind him to re-clasp Tori's hands once they'd slid apart, so the hug could begin again.

"Knew my lankiness would come in handy one day." Doug picked up the fallen hand once more. "It's a bit of a manoeuvre joining your hands behind my back. Long arms are—" He jumped up. Had he felt a slight clutch around his ribs? Tori looked the same. Peaceful. Relaxed. He threw himself back into the exact position, placing one and then the other of Tori's hands together over his back. He'd imagined it, surely?

"Hug me, Tori, I know you can." His ribs tightened as he felt the clutch again with her left arm. One of Tori's fingers lifted and dropped onto his backbone. He gasped. He daren't move. Her hand slipped further down his back, close to falling off. Hurriedly he replaced it, his chest still pinned to hers.

"Are you OK?" he asked. "I need to know that you're OK." Again he felt the plop as her finger lifted and fell onto his backbone. "That means, 'Yes,' Tori, doesn't it?" he said, muffled, into her emaciated breasts.

'Yes,' the finger beat again.

"Yes, yes, yes!" Doug said. "Are you in pain?"

Two taps of her finger: no.

"Do you know you're in hospital?"

'Yes.'

"Are you happy?" There was no response. "Tori, are you sad?" Nothing. "Tori, please, you have to answer me that. It's the most important question of all. Can you bear it?"

Tori tapped three times in succession.

"Yes and no." Doug grinned. "That's a start." Questions, he

needed questions. "Do you like baked beans?"

'No.'

He was enjoying this. Champagne and mini eggs? Sex? The top of a mountain? Hands in damp soil? There was a flurry of positive responses.

An hour later, Doug and Tori were still lying together on her bed. Doug could feel her heart beating but the closed questions and answers had ground to a halt. Entwined, she'd fallen asleep.

He kissed her on both cheeks several times, stopped, stroked her hair and kissed her on the lips. He squeezed his arms tighter around her torso and whispered into her ear, "Can we have another chat tomorrow?" But he didn't pull away because he felt Tori's fingers inching themselves up the monumental climb from her bed covers to the hairs on his forearm. Her hand sat awhile and composed itself but once rested, her pointer finger said, 'Yes, of course.'

FIVE

ANDY PROPPED HIMSELF UP against the bare-plastered wall and wondered if he and Etta would ever become grown-ups and decorate their house properly. He juggled one of his pillows behind his shoulders and shuffled around in search of a comfier position. The unforgiving hard wall was cold on his back. Was that why people had headboards? Maybe they should go the whole hog: wallpaper and a headboard, a padded, floral type. The last time he'd ever given thought to a headboard was as a child working out the meaning to his dad's wry smile when he'd wondered why he always hung pictures up at night. He was embarrassingly old to be first working this out but then, who wants to learn that their parents still have sex? Perhaps the association was why headboards were rarely a topic of conversation in his world. Or maybe it was only people who hadn't had sex for three months who made the connection.

He clasped his hands behind his head, his knuckles scraping against the wall. He exhaled. They couldn't even run to a pot of paint. He had a crucial site meeting early in the morning. The alarm was set for 5.45am. It was all right for Etta, she slept through her own yelling and blaspheming – he didn't. She thrashed around, her arms and legs jumping out and punching, smacking and kicking him in equal measure. It would defy the resilience of all but those under severe medication. It had to stop, he was falling asleep on the job.

"Etta." His voice hoarse from lying awake. "Et, you're shouting again."

"The van!" she cried.

"The minibus," he corrected, his hands now polishing his shaven head in small circles. He explained for the umpteenth time that all the pupils had escaped, even before the emergency crews had arrived. "The police officer told you that in the official interview, Et."

"The bags are hanging from the ceiling, Officer. A seat is upside down on the motorway."

"No it isn't, Etta."

He could try to ignore her, leave her shouting but he couldn't bear to hear her in such distress. He shifted back down into the bed, moulded his stomach around her tiny back and pinned her arms into her sides with his arm across her, as he'd learnt to do.

"There are no teenagers," he tried again, stroking her hair this time, holding her still tighter with the other arm. "No cars, no minibus, no van. It's us in bed."

"Those teenagers could have fucking died."

"You're swearing," Andy said into the back of her neck. "You never swear."

"Mustn't move the fucking body," she said. "Why doesn't that man understand?"

"Ever since the children, Etta, you've never sworn." He couldn't help smiling. "I like it," he said. "It's sexy."

He knew she couldn't hear him, that however convincing she may sound, they weren't involved in proper conversation, more the murky half world of dreams and what-ifs they visited all too often. But it felt better to pretend to reason with her. When she could hear him, she was so vulnerable, so tired and so scared. He couldn't begin to tell her to 'give it a rest', even if he did secretly feel that her method of dealing with the cloud which had descended after the accident smacked of self-indulgence sometimes.

"Bastard driver!"

She was a normal, healthy mother of two who'd narrowly missed being at the centre of one of the worst pile-ups in his lifetime. The fact there weren't even more fatalities was only down to fortune. He was a road construction engineer. He saw all too often the aftermath of a serious incident and wondered at the horrors which had come before. Of course the experience would be difficult to shed.

"Bastard driver!" she said again.

"Etta?" He pulled away to get a glimpse of her face. "Who?" he asked. "Which bastard driver?" He was still at a difficult angle so he sat up, and pulled Etta up by her shoulders, "What driver? Is this the minibus, Etta?" He turned on the bedside light, gently guided her face towards his. "Etta this is important! The white van?"

Etta gasped. "Red," she said.

Her eyes were open but were they seeing? "The van, Etta?"

"Not a van," she twisted away again, "a car."

Andy groaned. Meaningless crap! He switched off the light and shuffled the pair of them back down into the bed, his feet pushing out of the other end of the quilt. He was too long for a standard bed, which was another observation he'd barely considered in his deep-sleeping past. He pulled up his feet, folded himself around

Etta's back and nestled his head into her shoulder.

"Quiet now," he whispered. He kissed her ear, the soft piece of flesh behind, and again on her neck. She stroked his hands at her waist.

"Love you," Etta mumbled. She faced him and asked if she'd been shouting again.

"Swearing," Andy said.

"Oh flip." She clasped his face in her hands and kissed his lips.

"No," Andy ran his hands up and down over her tiny ass. "It wasn't 'flip.'"

She squeezed her chest into his, her breasts rubbing against his skin, her nipples forging a track as they slid up and down through his chest hair.

"Fuck! I've missed you," he said.

SIX

TORI OPENED HER LEFT EYE and stared straight ahead. There was a change in the shadowy light, a dark shape in the distance. She kept her focus and made out the gap where the door had been wedged wide-open. The shape was the width of the doorway and half the height: some sort of table. She honed in on the top and a haphazard pile. Folded sheets? To the left was an array of tubed and twisted shapes in different coloured sections, the smallest at the front. She wanted to laugh. These weren't sheets but magazines and newspapers. The coloured shapes were confectionery. Outside her room was a newsagent's trolley bursting with snacks for those who were allowed to eat. Did they have white Toblerones? Please say they had white Toblerones!

She switched her gaze to the wall next to the doorway and saw much larger shapes. In front was something orange: a chair. Her sheet was white. Her arm was small. Where was her other arm? She couldn't move her head to look. She wanted to reach out to grab the arm in view but she could only lift her fingers. She wanted to scream. *Help!* There was a mumble from staff outside the doorway. How would she tell them she could make out their form but couldn't see parts of her own body?

It's progress, she said to herself, staring forward, determined. *I can see something. And tomorrow I'll tell them.*

Tomorrow she would wake earlier. This time it would be breakfast she'd see on the trolley. She wouldn't be able to smell it, nor be given any to taste, but she salivated at the thought of bagels and jam, porridge with honey and bananas, even a piece of toast and butter. In the future she would place an order. *Positive Mental Attitude*, she repeated to herself: PMA. Who had sat next to her and talked of a 'PMA'? She couldn't remember. She wanted to close her eyes, but she mustn't be tired. There was light in the room. It was daytime.

It's a dissilient day, she sang inside her head, *soon I will 'burst out' of this illness and go back to being Tori Williams. Alive.*

Tori had always liked fantastic words. As she lay in hospital unable to communicate with the outside world, the inner dictionary she'd compiled over five decades opened and closed itself like a musical box. *'Hesternopothia,'* she tried to annunciate clearly. Yes, she had lived in better times. *'Absquatulate.'* It was rude of her, ungrateful, but she wished she could run away at the first opportunity, desert the ward in favour of the home where she'd lived for twenty years. It was a four bedroom, 1930s detached house for which she and Doug had borrowed far too much money in their quest not to be neighbours with the children they taught.

Carly and Nicky were both brought up there. She could remember everything about them. Carly was twenty-four, a teacher, dependable, sweet nature, bit of a worrier and dressed a little scruffily - still thought she was a student. Nicky was nineteen. She'd embarked on a course in hotel and catering. Tori tried to recall the name of the qualification, an abbreviation, three letters.

Come on! This is easy! They were working Nicky too hard. She wouldn't stay the course, would leave when a better idea presented itself. Her younger daughter was fearless, would agree to anything. It was a trait which Tori found exhilarating and terrifying in equal measure.

Tori remembered their births, their bedrooms, the surprise candle-lit dinner they'd organised for her and Doug's 20th wedding anniversary, the home-made gifts and loving notes Carly still left around the house for her to find.

She could remember all this but she couldn't picture their faces.

Other people collected stamps, Tori hoarded words, furrowing for them in novels, extracting them from history books. It wasn't the intellectual puzzle, or a pompous pride, but the music, the rhythm, the bounce and the rarity of the sounds butting up to each other in the particular order which entertained her. *Dissilient*, she said again. *If I'm to burst out I have to keep speaking and then I will be heard. I must keep finger tapping. I must see more every day and I have to keep grimacing because it will save my face from freezing.* She smiled to herself. Her mother would tell her not to scowl in case the wind changed. Where was she? Ruby was the only person who shared this love of superfluous vocabulary, the only one to join in with her pointless researching. Why was she never there when Tori was awake?

For the last few days Tori had been testing herself on everything she knew: 7 x 12 = 84; how to spell *'intumescence'*. She willed the nurses to say it, a much grander word for swelling. She could recall every person in her family and the odd friend as well. She could even trace the route to her favourite client and of course to The White Horse where she met with Jo and Amelie every month. Did they meet without her? She would be at the next date.

Judging by the inane questions the staff asked every day, Tori wasn't expected to know anything so she was pleased with all the facts in her grasp. Admittedly she had no idea when to tap 'yes' when one of the nurses trawled through the days of the week, one by one, but why did it matter? She knew when it was 6.30 in the evening because that was when Carly came. She knew which of the nurses would treat her softly and which of the others had hands like a facial scrub. It appeared she couldn't smell but why would she want to smell the excrement that had to be cleaned from beneath her? The texture was enough.

What she didn't know, was when her mother visited. If she knew, she'd make sure she was awake.

SEVEN

ETTA LOOKED OVER to the tall sash window, a short distance from where she sat at her desk. The PC, her files and two half-finished glasses of orange cordial, served with a straw, filled the desk. The breeze from the oscillating fan perched in the apex of the room lifted her hair from her shoulders at the edges. "Got a pile of paperwork," she'd told her colleagues. 'Need to lock myself in the office for a couple of hours." Really, she couldn't concentrate. She'd removed and replaced a stack of twenty-pound notes from the safe three times before remembering who'd asked for them.

She watched the red change to amber and green and back again, an orange circle burning evermore brightly around the edge of the red light, the more she stared. She heard the faint beat of a car radio in the distance. The noise from that day was still there. It never really left, filtering into her dreams day and night. She shook her head, put her hands to her ears, needed to rid herself of that hauntingly melancholic sound: the absence of engine noise and in its place, the tinny sound of radio, the cacophony of bells and drums, keyboards and voices, all totally incongruous with the situation which warranted nothing other than silence.

"Tea, Etta!" Janine called as she knocked and opened the door simultaneously. "I thought you could do with a cup." She placed Etta's bone china mug on her 'I'd Rather Be Shopping' coaster. "Everything OK?" she asked, returning to the door and hanging onto its handle, prepared to either leave or stay.

"Fine." Etta smiled. "Thanks Janine. Bit tired, if I'm honest."

"Can't persuade you into a drink tonight then? We haven't done that for ages."

Etta wrinkled her nose, shook her head.

"Well, any time, let me know." She waited a moment, before closing the door behind her.

Etta looked down at the files, opened the cover of the first and shut it again. She picked up her tea, blew on it unnecessarily and wandered over to the window. She touched her forehead with her fingers. It was damp. The sun burned through the single-glazed panes. They'd been talking about replacing the windows right back when she'd joined 'Interest' seventeen years ago.

She put her hands under the brass hooks and pulled up the bottom sash as high as she could, so that she could poke her head right out into the street. The breeze tickled her cheeks and the perspiration evaporated. She closed her eyes, let the sun settle on her eyelids. Alive! She took an exaggerated breath. She was the lucky one. She knew that. Thanks to the selfless backing of her partner, she was finally studying. Focus on that! He'd been as keen as she was. True, he'd have to be more involved with the day to day running of the house and family but they hadn't waited this long to be put off by baked beans on toast (with a handful of grated cheese now he was in charge), collar-only ironed school shirts and wrinkly tutus. And hey, holidays abroad were overrated. All you needed were happy children and a non-leaking tent. He didn't mean any of this, of course. He'd have loved the relative comfort of their traditional family life to have remained intact, but he'd stuck to his word, because unlike her parents, Andy wanted passionately for Etta to realise her dreams.

She thought of the assignment on temperature waiting to be written by tomorrow, how her tutor running the seminar on sphericity, conduction and convection had looked pointedly at her, over the top of an imaginary pair of glasses, and said, "26 October, Etta Dubcek, all assignments in by 26 October."

She listened to the hum of cars slowing down. She shouldn't have been on the motorway at that time. Johan's sickness bug had put her three hours behind schedule. She should have been back home, the library card in her possession and the battered reference books already lined up on the makeshift shelf above the foldable table in their bedroom, ready for her to do her studying. She should have half heard a snatched report on the radio of the inconvenience and an update later to inform drivers that they could resume their journeys. Any more detail and Etta might have shuddered a little but only that, before continuing to tidy away dirty shoes, peel carrots, assist with homework and check Johan's temperature.

Instead she was in the middle of the carnage.

Etta didn't know Tori's name then. She didn't know that the woman whose hand she held had texted her husband to ask him to put the chicken in the oven. This was an injured driver. She wasn't a 'killer', a 'murderer' or even a 'selfish bitch'. Etta sat with a mother, a wife, a lady.

Etta sat with someone who'd made a stupid, selfish mistake.

She owed it to Andy to move on. But to move forward, she had to burst the carbuncle of guilt lodged in her brain which pressed its weight against her every action, her every thought. People were getting restless, impatient. They thought she was exaggerating her role in Tori's car, that she should be celebrating that she'd side-stepped death. Etta agreed.

Except it was more than that.

She dragged her head back through the window and closed it a fraction. Andy had said she should leave the matter there, that she couldn't be sure, that the media interest, the incessant pub chatter, the local people stopping her in the street and asking her what Tori was really like, might have influenced her. Sometimes people could put a story down to a vivid memory, he said, when in fact they were repeating what somebody had told them. Hadn't she done that with memories of her own childhood? Etta shook her head. This was different.

She walked back to her desk, placed the cup of lukewarm tea on the coaster and looked at her phone. She picked it up, checked the signal, put it back down again, then took a long, deliberate breath in and an even longer one out. Slowly, methodically, she dialled the number she'd memorised after so many aborted attempts to call.

EIGHT

AT 7.30PM THE DOOR to Tori's ward shot open and Doug strode into the room, pacing the length of it three times before noticing his daughter sitting bolt upright on the plastic chair, a magazine open on her lap. He picked it up, glanced at the cover and put it back down again.

"I thought I'd run some kitchen designs past Mum," Carly said. "That's still on the cards, isn't it?" She opened her eyes wide to remind her father that there was only one acceptable response to the question.

"Yes, yes." He commenced another lap of the room. "Bloody reporters. Jeez! Does that Steve character have any concept that we are human beings?"

Carly patted the chair next to her. "Ahem." She tilted her head to demonstrate her mother's hand resting on hers. "We've been having a chat, haven't we, Mum? I describe the kitchens, Mum taps 'yes' or 'no'. It's a much quicker decision process than it used to be." She gestured again to the chair next to her and mouthed, 'OK?' to her father.

Doug shook his head. "No." He scraped the chair away from the bed to give himself room to sit down. "I'm not OK." He stood up again, his hand slapping his forehead. "Speak Tori! Please, I can't tell you how much I need to speak to you."

Carly took her father's hand and guided him back down to the chair. "You're listening though, aren't you Mum?" She gestured to Doug to place his hand over Tori's, three hands now in a pile. She added her second hand to the top. "It's Pat-A-Cake," she said.

Doug placed his hand on top and prized open a smile before pulling away. Tori's second hand remained at her side. "Conversation appears to be over," he said, and let out a long, noisy breath. He kissed his daughter on the crown of her head before walking over to the opposite wall and propping himself against it, one leg bent. Carly joined him, resting her head against his arm.

"She's been laughing with Jo," she said. Jo had regaled Tori with stories of her clients. "A perpetual stream of conversation," she'd announced to Carly, adding that she'd never again be stuck for something to say. Jo held Tori's hand in her palm as everyone did, and at every amusing anecdote, Tori's fingers had fluttered over it. "How amazing is that?"

Doug shook his head. "Dear God," he said, without even attempting to wipe away the tears which dribbled onto his cheeks, "she's even worked out how to laugh. I asked her if I could clean my potholing boots in the front room, whether I should be in charge of the house accounts and if I should grow a moustache."

"She said no?"

Doug nodded. He told Carly that it was an emphatic 'no' – none of this tapping twice nonsense. No, these days she dug her nail into his palm. He wore the wounds with pride.

Carly linked her arm through her dad's and silently they watched Tori sleep. Carly smiled before gently pulling away. She couldn't be late for James again.

"Of course." Doug moved over to the door to hold it open for her. "Anywhere special?"

She gave her father a kiss on the cheek. "Somewhere we can talk."

– – –

Doug kicked off his shoes and lay down next to his wife. He picked up her hand, placed it on his thigh and covered it with his own. "Talk to me, Tori," he whispered. "Talk. To. Me!"

Her fingers were still.

"Are they looking after you?" he asked. "Hmm?" He shook his head, squeezed his hand a little more tightly around hers. "Do you know they brushed your hair? What do you think about that?" He waited for a response and when none came he muttered under his breath that it would be the least of her worries. "Don't you wish your mum visited?" he asked, but jumped up from the bed as soon as he said it, paced back to the wall and let his face sink into his hands.

He was exhausted. Summoning the required restraint not to lash out at the weedy little excuse for a reporter he'd come to know as Steve, was draining. His comments about the baby of the family, the absent Nicky, were below the belt.

He yanked open the door and slammed it behind him. But Georgia was passing. She mouthed, 'OK?' and when he didn't answer, she called behind her, "Stay strong! You're doing well." He tugged the cuffs of his long white sleeves over his wrists in an effort to retain some decorum and ran back into the room. He launched himself onto the bed, grabbed Tori's face in his hands and told her that he loved her more than he could bear and that he would be back tomorrow.

– – –

Stay! He mustn't go before she'd heard him speak. *Doug, hold me!* She could only communicate with him if her hand touched his skin.

But the more she concentrated on opening her eyes, the further away she span, propelled to the bottom of the tunnel.

They'd barely come to a standstill and they were being spun again, the marshmallow walls ebbing and flowing around them, pushing them upwards now. They arrived in Doug's empty classroom, the place where he taught physics when they first met. Tori was a teacher then, too. That day he'd beckoned her across the room with a wrinkle of suggestion in his nose. It had been Civvies Day. His jeans were tight, his white t-shirt clung to his nipples. A trickle of fair hair covered the partition between his rounded pecs, teasing her. He tossed his head back with careless enthusiasm. This was the way he'd always laughed with his confident ease, his smiling eyes, his positive outlook. She loved the stubble on his chin that he'd rub affectionately when he concentrated, the nod of appreciation, the 'Oh, now that's funny,' when she said something vaguely amusing.

They made love across a cluster of wooden desks. If they'd been found they'd have lost their jobs, instead they got engaged.

– – –

Doug couldn't face the prospect of Steve hiding in the rosemary bush he'd begun to loathe in his front garden, so he parked his Volvo at the end of the road and tiptoed along the cobbled pavement. With barely a crunch of the gravel he snuck around to the back of the house, retrieved his key from under the mat and nudged open the rickety patio door, decided against replacing the key in its hiding place and let himself through.

"Well negotiated, Doug," he said into the warped, mirrored wall tiles beneath the high cupboards. Tori was right. They magnified rather than detracted from the 1980s decor. There were only so many times you could paint over textured feather wallpaper and distress yellow pine cupboards. He smiled for the first time that evening.

He'd eat his spaghetti carbonara for one, have a beer or two, and go to bed. He closed the microwave door with a bang and the over-used 'reheat' operation cranked into action.

"Not the phone?" he asked himself. He spoke frequently to himself these days. It had become normal, a mere extension of the Doug Williams monologue of Tori's bedside. "Was that the phone?" This time he opened the microwave door to quieten the background noise.

In the beginning the phone never stopped ringing as friends and neighbours called in disbelief to confirm Tori's condition. It didn't ring anymore. Everyone knew what had happened. Everyone knew what she'd done. Had someone slipped through the net? Was he going to have to explain it as he had in the early days, "... regrettable, yes, but for the Grace Of God, no, she won't do that again, the girls are doing OK, we're all praying she'll pull through and that society will go easy on her..." Nobody ever admitted they were appalled that Tori had been so selfish. But the diminishing contact, the few cards to the hospital and distinct lack of visitors, told Doug all he needed to know.

He re-started the carbonara and peered through the microwave's glass door until he heard the ping. He yanked open the fridge door which was sticking, he suspected, due to a lack of wiping around the rim and retrieved a green bottle from a drawer in the base.

"Ice cold!" he said with a gasp of satisfaction, encouraged he'd remembered to unload the box of beers last night, albeit on top of the bags of salad. He should change the regular supermarket order. He'd go further than that; he'd stop it altogether. All this waste was unacceptable. Tori would be appalled. He would shop locally and be conscious of food miles. He'd tell her about it tomorrow.

Doug's head was a constantly updating list of subjects for discussion with his mute wife. Tori always liked a challenge so he'd talk with increased animation on topics that he knew would rankle. One day she'd jump up and tell him that he was entitled to his own opinion but that he was wrong.

Slumped in the crinkling leather, one-and-a-half-seater armchair, the 'loveseat', which had been delivered while Doug had been on a French Exchange, two days before the last time Tori spoke, he balanced the plastic container of carbonara on his lap and emptied the last of the beer into his mouth. Tomorrow night he would do some washing up.

"Need a fridge in here," he mumbled, as he happened upon England playing South Africa in the Rugby World Cup. He'd been looking forward to it for months but it had started without him. He'd fetch himself one more beer and then he'd sit in peace.

This time when the phone rang he sprang from his seat and jumped down the steps into the kitchen. "What's it doing in the cereal cupboard?" he muttered, as he lunged for the phone.

It was a quiet, unfamiliar voice, not the usual tone of a journalist – were they trying a different tack?

"Yes, this is Doug Williams. Did you ring earlier?"

"Mr Williams, I've, well—"

"In fact, have you rung a few times tonight?" he asked.

"Yes. I wanted to explain about the—"

"Well don't! Jeez!" he exclaimed. "Don't explain anything. Just leave us alone." He switched off the phone. "We went ex-directory," he shouted, throwing it behind him on the way to the living room. "What more do I have to do?"

Then he noticed the white envelope, the address neatly handwritten in black, lying on the mat by the front door. Tori received lots of post sent directly to the hospital, hate mail usually. The staff would pass it to Doug and he'd pretend it never arrived.

He bent down to pick it up. The postmark was Leeds but when he flipped it over, there was no return addressee. He lowered himself down onto the cold tiles of the hallway and slowly worked his finger along the gummed join to remove the thinly folded paper.

This letter is written in support, it began, *it's important you know I'm on your side.*

NINE

ETTA BREATHED OUT as she gripped the brass door handle of the police station where she'd first visited on the day after the accident. Inside the wooden-clad entrance lobby she considered the sign which demanded she switch off her phone before approaching the 'Welcome' desk. A message from Sara flashed as she took it from her bag. 'U studying? Worried bout u?' She tucked the phone into her bag.

The Traffic Officer had agreed to meet Etta at 9.30 so after racing with her children into school, she'd driven into Leeds far faster than she ever dared these days. She was still ten minutes late but it was the best she could do now she no longer drove on the motorway. She could see a thick set police officer through the window which took up much of the wall separating his office from the waiting room. She leaned through the gap where the door to a wooden hatch was pulled open. When the officer didn't respond to a light clearing of her throat, she pressed the button on top of a brass bell, screwed down onto the wide counter separating him from her. She jumped even though it only let out a miserable 'ting'.

The officer heaved himself up from the desk, rested his forearms which could have supported Etta's body weight on the counter and, after inserting the details which Etta thought she'd previously given and printing out three papers for her to read and sign, he directed her to a seat in the waiting area.

"WPC Denby will be with you as soon as she can." His eyes fixed on Etta's perspiring forehead. "What have you got to worry about?" he asked. Etta smiled to acknowledge his attempt to be jovial and as her fingertips crept up to wipe the beads of sweat from her face, he smiled too and suggested she help herself to a drink.

Etta filled a cup with chilled water from the wobbly plastic machine and stared at a poster above. A broad red cross stretched over a picture of an antiquated mobile phone and, 'Don't be a Texting Killer!' was written in capitals below.

"Why don't you just say, Don't be a Tori!" Etta mouthed.

She sat down on a faux leather sofa and prodded a dark stain on the mustard coloured carpet with the toe of her boot. It was rougher than the rest, the pile thinner where some poor cleaner must have been taxed with removing chewing gum. She looked at other blemishes, more spots showing themselves as she examined the area around her feet. She looked away but it was too late. Bang! Like clockwork: the inside of Tori's car.

Instead of this dirty yellow, now she saw a brown carpet, littered with glass and metal and other indiscernible debris from the accident. She pictured the open bag, the one she'd wedged under Tori's stomach. She'd ignored the spilled contents back then but these days she saw a sparkling phone face down. It could have been new, save for the dark blood congealed in marble-sized spots over the back. Had she added this detail? Had she altered the picture she first saw when she sat with Tori, praying for her life?

— — —

PC Denby walked over to the square table with two plastic cups of iced water and placed one in front of Etta without comment, instead gesturing to the chair for Etta to sit down. Etta pulled her legs in against the metal bar which ran around the base of the table and sat with her back straight, her water protected in her hands. The room seemed smaller than when she'd first been there. She hadn't noticed that there was no window, nor any colour.

"So," PC Denby leant casually against the back of the chair, "what did you want to see me about?" Her foundation was no less gloopy than on the previous two occasions and had she put on weight? Her stomach spilled over the top of her black trousers exposing the top of grey ankle socks when she crossed her legs.

"Thank you for seeing me again at such short notice," Etta said.

PC Denby glanced at the clock high on the wall to her left. "What I'm here for."

She listened to Etta's revised story without uttering a word of contradiction. Aside from introducing the conversation to the recording equipment, she gave no sign that it was of interest.

"OK," she said, as Etta's eyes searched the inside of her empty cup. "What would you say if I told you I didn't believe a word of it?"

— — —

It was that voice again, the voice from the accident, the same tone for scolding as consoling.

"Can you tell me the driver's name?" Etta had blustered, when she'd chased after PC Denby striding down the hard shoulder. "I wish I'd known her name."

PC Denby had glanced unnecessarily at her notebook, inclined her head slightly to one side and exhaled loudly. She tapped a couple of fingers on the base of her throat when she said,

"We're calling her Tori. Driving licence says Victoria but she has a 'T' on a chain around her neck."

And this was when Etta had cried, pearl sized tears. PC Denby didn't speak, simply waited for the tears to stop.

"I saw her purse," Etta said. "Cards, money, everything scattered over the footwell. I should have looked for her name."

PC Denby had nodded.

"When I sat with her, if I'd said her name, spoken to her, she might have come round."

And then the voice which PC Denby used now, here, in the interview room. "There are good signs of life," she'd said, "a chance of survival." In her dreams, this constant re-telling of the same story, Etta heard an aside, the officer saying to herself, "Although she might wish there weren't."

— — —

Etta looked up. PC Denby was staring.

"Sorry. You asked me what I'd say if you didn't believe me?" PC Denby nodded. "Well, I'd say I didn't blame you," she answered at last. "But if I've remembered something, however dubious it sounds, I have to tell you, don't I? It's important isn't it, for justice?"

PC Denby inclined her head, concentrating on Etta's face, her eyes rarely blinking. "Yes, you have an obligation to tell us the truth." She continued staring and just when Etta was about to break the silence, she asked if she'd had any contact with Ms Williams since the accident.

Etta shook her head. "She's in hospital."

PC Denby crossed her arms. "You've been to the hospital though, haven't you? A few times."

Etta gulped. "I haven't seen her."

The officer allowed the quiet to stretch. She asked if Etta had any contact with other members of Tori's family, Mr Williams perhaps, anybody who could compromise her credibility as a witness.

"I've had no direct contact with Mr Williams." Etta squeezed her cup until the plastic cracked.

"Anyone else?" PC Denby asked, rubbing her cheek with a finger and blowing out of the side of her mouth intermittently. Now she was taking notes.

Etta told her that she'd spoken with Tori's mother, Ruby Crawford.

PC Denby looked up from her notepad and raised her eyebrows. She wove her fingers together and squeezed them under her chin. "Ms Dubcek, you are aware that people died in the crash?"

"Of course," Etta said quietly.

"Regardless of what you feel for the family of Ms Williams, you know how seriously we take the wasting of police time, sudden amended memories appearing as if by magic?"

"I know all that," Etta said. PC Denby's head was cocked to one side, the clock ticking obstinately. She laced her fingers into a cradle behind her head, unpicked them again and lay them flat across the table.

Etta couldn't bear the silence. "But do you know how stressful I've found this whole situation? Do you know what it's like to be one second away from a similar fate and to be reminded of it every minute of every day because 'Don't Be A Texting Killer!' is all anybody ever talks about?" The words rolled out twice as fast as before. "Because everybody has a view and most people think it should be Tori who died in the crash, not the others. And everyone else is so self-righteous, like they've never made a mistake, never done a stupid thing when they should really thank their lucky stars that they've been fortunate enough to escape without anyone else knowing. I think it's very possible that my brain should blot out the horrific incident—"

"—To be returned with such precision?" PC Denby shot back.

She held up her hands to announce the pause which followed. "OK," she said. "I'm going to give you a moment to think about this. If you do wish to continue, I'll come back to take your *revised* statement." Her lips were pursed. "But," her hand was already on the door handle, "perverting the course of justice is a crime, regardless of how *stressful* you're finding all this," she said. "Think about that before you sign."

TEN

GERALD AND SOPHIE came to a halt about fifty metres from the main entrance to the hospital. Sophie had asked Gerald to wait; the sight of the press holding microphones, booms and cameras at their sides had taken her breath. Three vans emblazoned with TV company logos sat on double yellow lines forming a barrier between them and the hospital.

Gerald gave Sophie's shoulder a squeeze. "Nothing to worry about," he said. "They'll love us, you'll see."

He wet his palms and ran both over the top of his thick, black hair to smooth it around the back of his ears. He coughed and placed his arm around Sophie's waist.

"Ready? You'll feel like you're at a film premier," he said. "It's good fun." They continued towards the front entrance, each step in perfect time with their partner's. Gerald pushed out his chest. It had taken him into his sixth decade but he had achieved what many men never managed to do: he'd found his perfect woman.

"They're just doing their job," he soothed, when he felt her steps falter. "Nothing to be afraid of." She was staring straight ahead.

He'd never seen her nervous before.

They were only a few steps away from the reporters who weren't paying attention to anything beyond the small clusters in which they were talking. "Watch what happens," Gerald said. "They know me."

A small man, with round glasses and grey hair pulled back into a ponytail, caught sight of the important visitors and jumped in front of them. Other journalists mumbled their acknowledgement and an engine started up in one of the TV vans. In unison cameras were raised to shoulder height as the pack seamlessly fused together, all space sucked from the centre of the mass.

"I'm Gerald Crawford, gents," he boomed, dipping a mock cap. "For those with whom I'm not yet acquainted, I'm family: step-father to Tori Williams."

Sophie clutched at his fingers around her waist, her other arm hanging tense.

"Any news for us Mr Crawford?" a voice called out.

"Is it true Tori can communicate?" said another.

"It's true lads, yes," Gerald said. "She made sounds when we last saw her and now she's tapping her fingers to make herself understood."

Sophie nipped his thigh. "Gerald?"

Gerald smiled, tickled her waist.

A woman a few inches taller than him stretched out a slim arm to place a microphone under his chin. "Liz O'Brien, Ms," she said, "The Global. Tell me, Mr Crawford, is Tori aware of what she's done?"

Gerald raised a hand in the air in an attempt to silence the other less audible questions which poured into the atmosphere around them. Sophie, clutching ever more tightly at the other arm around her waist, would have preferred to have gone into the hospital. But it was important that the press were kept up to date with Tori's excellent recovery.

"Doug told you not to speak to them," she whispered, pressing herself even tighter against him. "I think we should honour that."

Gerald suggested she leave this up to him, he knew what he was doing.

"Mr Crawford?"

"I think Tori knows, yes." Gerald finally lowered his hand. "But the family have agreed not to talk about it in front of her. We don't want anything to detract from her recovery."

Questions span around them:

"What makes you think she does, 'know' Mr Crawford?"

"Because she's a clever girl," he said.

"How does she feel about her actions?"

"Will she ever drive again?"

"How will she recompense her victims?" the small man with the glasses and ponytail asked.

Gerald acknowledged every area of the crowd with a smile and professional nod of recognition.

"Has she texted *you* from the car in the past?" It was Liz O'Brian.

"Enough questions, Miss." He raised his eyebrows. "This is Sophie." He released his arm from around her waist and held her hand instead, lifting it into the air as if they'd won a general election. "We're going to tell Tori that we are to be married," he said, "and we hope she'll be able to join us for the wedding breakfast. We're concentrating on good news for now."

"Thank you," Sophie stuttered in a voice that belonged to her childhood. "We're going in now."

— — —

Tori recognised the popping noise as the seal around the door to the room was broken.

Doug?

She didn't feel the two damp kisses, one on each cheek. She couldn't smell Gerald's body spray nor see the white-grey stubble shaved to within half a centimetre of her stepfather's chin. But she heard him whisper, "Happy Belated Birthday," and say that she'd get her present when she was out of this godforsaken place.

"Hello," a polite voice said, "I'm Sophie."

I don't know you, Sophie, Tori thought.

"I think she's frustrated, that's why she's grunting," the woman's voice said.

Did I grunt?

"I bet she's trying to speak."

It was me who grunted! Tori tried to do it again. *Where's Doug?* No response. She tried to force the words through her lips but nobody asked her what on earth she was talking about. *Want to go home,* she said in a mind that conversed fluently with itself. *With Doug.*

"Gerald! We need a question, quick!"

"How are you love?"

Better if you could hear me.

"Can you hear us Tori? It's Gerald. I'm with Sophie, my wonderful fiancée."

"Your dad says you've improved greatly over the past three weeks," Sophie said.

Stepdad Sophie. Ex-stepdad. My dad is dead.

"We think you want to speak, don't we Gerald?" She paused. "What do you want to say?"

Tori yearned for Doug and the girls to be next to her. Nicky jabbering away, answering her own questions; Carly much calmer, holding her hand and whispering, "Come on Mum," with a different kind of force.

"I know you can hear us," Gerald said.

It's Doug I want to be here, was all Tori could think to say.

She missed her own mother. She wanted to hear her voice. Her words would soothe the chaos in her head and make some order of the gaping gaps in awareness.

Tori heard Gerald say that meeting Sophie was the best day of his life. "She owns a men's clothes shop in Harrogate, and that's where we met."

Now he was talking about climbing, that a doctor said Tori had been to the bottom of a deep mine and was slowly clambering out. "Although, knowing your need for a challenge, I suggested the Grand Canyon might be more apt." He laughed loudly, the peals culminating in a self-gratulatory, "hah!"

"Everyone's excited about you reaching the top of the mountain," Sophie said.

Tori tried to picture her, she sounded so much younger than Gerald.

"Or canyon," Sophie corrected. "And you will make it, Tori. Won't she Gerald?" Tori heard a weak cough and Sophie telling him that if he simply nodded, Tori wouldn't know. "It's a different method of communication," Sophie said. "It will take a bit of practice."

– – –

The couple perched on the orange visiting chairs, aligned so perfectly they could have been in school assembly. They held hands clumsily. The liver spots of one covering the smooth pink of the other.

"Gerald!" Sophie squeezed his hand so tightly, he gasped. "She closed her eyes! Do you think she did that on purpose?"

Gerald pouted, took off his royal blue blazer and loosened his tie. "I'm a retired carpet salesman, Sophie, I can't tell you about the workings of an unconscious mind."

"She looks more peaceful."

"Then she's better off than we are. She gets to think about something else."

"Gerald!" Sophie whispered. "She might be listening."

Gerald watched Sophie as she gazed at his stepdaughter, her sultry blue eyes, outlined with make-up, blinking steadily. He appreciated her support in such a difficult situation. "I don't normally admit this kind of thing," he said, kissing her lightly, "but the hospital unnerves me."

Sophie sighed, winding a stray dark hair back around Gerald's ear. "It's the same as any other hospital, sweetheart," she soothed. "And Tori's lucky to have her own room."

"She had to have her own room."

"Yes, of course. So it's good people are thinking about her safety."

Gerald inched closer to Sophie, their shoulders pressed together. "It's like a bloody hotel," he hissed, his Bristol accent exaggerated. "And after what she's done."

"She'll appreciate your support, Gerald." Sophie let go of his hand and sat up straight, her shoulder blades and breasts protruding in equal measure. "It's only right you're here, with you being so close." She lowered her gaze and flicked an imaginary fluff from her thigh length skirt. "Could you do the finger tapping thing?" she asked. "You have to put her hand on top of yours according to the papers."

Gerald coughed and shook his head.

"OK, perhaps if we think of some topics first." Sophie asked Gerald what he knew about mountains but when he shrugged his shoulders and said that they were generally cold, she suggested it might be easier to talk about Tori's work.

"She just throws parties," he said.

Sophie clapped her hands together. "How cool!" But Gerald looked at her and mouthed, 'Ruddy waste of time,' so Sophie suggested he reminisce instead. "You've got hours. Start when you met."

"No." Gerald patted Sophie on the thigh and stood up. "She won't want to talk about that." He strode over to the photographs and greetings cards covering the entire wall around the door frame. "These are from her fridge door at home," he said. "I recognise them from my visits."

"It's nice you're still close."

He was glad there were no pictures of him on view. He'd been lucky enough to keep most of his thick, wavy hair into his sixties but had recently taken to colouring it, becoming progressively darker in the four weeks since he'd met Sophie. She clearly liked it. "Fifty-ish," her friends had concluded when the relationship had become serious enough for him to stop being so candid and suggest the flock of girls guess his age. He'd always kept himself trim, which also helped to erase a few years.

He looked at the old print-outs of small areas of maps, peeling away from the pins which held them, with mountain climbing routes traced in red. His eyes flitted over the collage until they settled on one particular get well card of a woman loading her Zimmer-frame into a cable car, which he signalled with his finger.

He snickered. "I sent that one."

"It's funny," she said, patting her tufts of short blonde hair. She stopped, her hand poised on top of her head, and turned in the direction of a low, grumbling noise. "She's trying to speak, Gerald. Look! Her eyes are open again."

— — —

'*Discombobulated,*' Tori wanted to say. She hated being so confused. And she was certainly discombobulated today; couldn't understand why Gerald was with a 'Sophie' at her bedside when Constance was his wife.

"It's good to see your eyes open," Tori heard.

Discom… She tried to push the word from the back of her throat and when that had no success, from the pit of her stomach. She even managed to curl her toes with the effort. Or did she dream it? Could she move her toes in this prison cell, this purgatory where anybody could choose to visit and she was always at home?

She was tired of looking at the metal lampshade above. She wanted to jump up, see the sun, decide who looked at her and choose who spoke. Had Gerald told her that this Sophie was his fiancée and that they were going to get married in the Grand Canyon? What was he going to do with Constance? Throw her into it once her replacement had signed the documents? She gasped. How long had she been in this hospital bed?

"She's grunting again, Gerald. Should we call someone?"

'*Lucifugous!*' *I want to go home.*

"It sounds like, 'moan'," Sophie said.

Tori felt Gerald's hands grasping her shoulders. Were her lips parted? Was that air she felt between them as she tried to push, 'lucifugous' into the real world?

"Can you say your first words for us?" Gerald asked. "Anything at all, complete nonsense if you like," he added quickly.

"Her bottom lip, Gerald! It's moving from side to side. Do something!"

"A few words would be good for the press," he said.

Tori's lips froze, clamped together.

"Give us something to tell—"

She squeezed her eyes tight shut and hoped she'd managed to scowl as his voice stalled.

ELEVEN

THE COFFEE SHOP was a minute's walk from the police station, a tiny venue, four tables at most, squeezed above a charity book store. Here, cappuccino was served in soup bowls and sugar in a stainless steel pot. Sitting with an incongruously straight back in a sloppy leather armchair, Etta rushed through the salient parts of the Global. Andy had banned the newspaper on account of the nightmares and Sara always scoffed when she caught Etta with the paper she'd previously chastised, so she was quick to return it to the general rack of reading material for customers. By the time Sara arrived, Etta was extracting random sentences from a website in Mesoscale Meteorology in Midlatitudes and wondering how she could make them her own.

Sara gently pulled herself away from her embrace with Etta. "You sounded terrible," she said, releasing the single diamante clasp on the woollen jacket of her trouser suit where the hook was hanging on by a thread. She sat herself down on the floral covered armchair opposite, shifting around to get comfortable and eventually choosing to perch at the front.

"What happened?" she asked.

Etta leaned further forward so that their faces were almost touching and breathed out before explaining that she'd been back to the police station.

Sara offered a conciliatory smile, cleared her throat. "She didn't believe you about the other car?"

"No."

"Well, you can understand that."

"I have to do the right thing," Etta said.

Sara sank back, her long legs twisted around each other, like a gnarly tree trunk. 'Statuesque' everyone called her, 'long' as opposed to 'tall' because of the fascinating length of her limbs. She hated it, laughed with Etta that once, just once, she'd like to be the one who sat down at the front of a group photo or was asked to sit in the back of the car for the longer legged person to have the coveted front seat.

"What happens if the police don't believe you?" she asked. "Will you be charged for time wasting?"

Etta shrugged. "They certainly wouldn't use me to back up their case. Anyway—" she held Sara's gaze, "that's what I saw."

Sara picked up the menu but discarded it after a cursory glance and ordered a cappuccino for both of them as well as a plate of biscuits.

"You looking after yourself?" Her eyes were fixed on Etta who folded and re-folded a silver wrapper she'd found on the table. "You'll break down if you carry on like this." Sara took the wrapper from her and pushed it into her empty cup.

"I shouldn't really be here," Etta said. "I'm already leaving assignments until after midnight."

"You'll make yourself ill."

"I see Andy for twenty minutes before bed if I'm lucky. Usually for a row."

Sara ran her hand over the back of her straightened hair which had curled at the edges in the rain. She smiled as she took both coffees from the waitress and placed them on the table.

"Your hair's looking gorgeous," Etta said, "love the very blonde."

Sara stared. "Etta," she said, "something has to give."

Sara was clearly waiting for a response but not inclined to break the quiet, so Etta said,

"I've already exchanged twice baked soufflé for pizza."

Sara tutted. "We both know what has to change."

"You tell me," Etta whispered.

"Hospital visits."

"No, Sara. I can't."

Sara shuffled to the back of her chair and raised her hands in the air as Etta rummaged in her bag for the glasses she only remembered when she was tired, sipped her coffee and fiddled with the white chocolate biscuit.

"All right," Etta said eventually. "You can quit glaring at me." She dipped the biscuit in her coffee. "It's complicated."

She'd wanted to visit Tori. She felt a connection and needed to see that the woman whose hand she held was doing OK. But it never occurred to her that she wouldn't get past the lift doors. Security was so tight.

"I got as far as her floor," she said. "But then I hit the doors to the ward itself and there was a nurse's station beyond." Etta had intended to walk away but found herself drawn back to the noise at the main entrance, crammed with cameras and reporters and members of the public with banners saying Tori Williams should rot in hell.

Sara shuddered.

"There was this old woman," Etta said. "I recognised her face. She didn't want to answer any questions but they wouldn't let her past, kept asking the same thing: 'Why don't you visit your daughter?' and, 'Isn't that your duty?'"

"Tori's mother?"

"Yep. She's called Ruby."

"She and Tori are estranged, aren't they?"

Etta flinched. "No! The reason Ruby doesn't visit her daughter is because she can't go into her room. We had a coffee. She told me."

Sara crossed both arms across her chest and considered Etta. She shook her head.

"It doesn't make sense. She's in a coma for Christ's sake!"

Etta ran a spoon around the froth at the lip of her cup and looked at Sara over the top of her glasses to encourage her to keep her voice down.

It wasn't so simple. Tori's sixteen-year-old sister, Lottie, had died when Tori was eight years old. Ruby sat next to her and the life support machine as she faded away. Lottie couldn't be saved, even after having her stomach pumped of the remains of the bottle of vodka that she and a friend had won in a raffle.

Sara gasped, a whistle leaving her lips. "There but for the grace of God—"

"—there's more," Etta said. "Ruby's husband died of a heart attack before he was sixty. She sat with him in the ambulance watching him die. Next up was a nasty second husband who messed with her head.

"And now," Etta picked up the last segment of her biscuit and considered it before placing it back down again. "She's on her own."

"Very sad." Sara sat back, her hands behind her head. But she still didn't understand why. "If I had a child I'd be at their bedside. It doesn't seem too complicated to me."

"She thinks she'll watch another member of her family drift away if she sits at the side of a hospital bed again."

"But that's absurd!" Sara sank her teeth into her bottom lip. "How can it have a bearing? It doesn't ring true."

Etta rubbed her eyes, probably smearing mascara into dark crescents beneath. "Illogical maybe," she said, "but how do any of us know how we'll react to a situation until we get there? I didn't think I'd be here again a few months ago—"

Etta cracked her knuckles and Sara winced which was her cue to stop. She said that Etta needed time; she wasn't surprised she was a bit anxious with all that she'd been carrying around in her head.

"I assume you're still keeping the truth from Andy?" she asked, as she leaned across the space.

"—having nightmares, getting so cross, so emotional," Etta said.

"Have you told him?" Sara repeated.

Etta shook her head. "No." She shrugged her shoulders. "This is a box I can't re-open."

Sara cleared her throat. "But the box isn't closed, is it?"

Etta stared at her friend. "Sara, I can't go there." Her cheeks were hot but she was not going to cry.

"OK." Sara held up her hands. "I understand that some secrets do more harm if they're told." She rubbed her eyes with her hands, sat back and dragged her jacket down over her waistband. "But where is Tori in all this?"

Etta waited a moment then cleared her throat. "I haven't tried to visit her again."

"But you go to—?"

"—the hospital, yes," Etta said.

Sara shrugged her shoulders and waited for a response.

"I see Ruby," Etta said. "There's no reason why we can't be friends."

TWELVE

THE HEAVY GREY DOOR opened to the outside of the hospital with a lingering squeal. Scowling as the late summer sun met their eyes, Etta and Ruby raised their free arms to provide relief. Etta was the first to lower hers, realising that the flash of light wasn't from the sky, rather the blast of a dozen camera flashes a foot from their faces. Etta tutted loudly and Ruby dipped her gaze.

"We hear Tori's communicating, Mrs Crawford, what do you have to say on the matter?" The voice belonged to a skinny man who'd forced himself between two others.

"It must be very exciting," a voice offered from the other direction.

"Nothing to say," Ruby said. "Nothing at all."

"Or weren't you aware of her progress?" the first voice asked.

Etta gasped.

"They spy on me," Ruby whispered. Etta let her arm slip from the crux of Ruby's elbow, to squeeze her hand instead.

"This has got nothing to do with what happened on that motorway," Etta called in the direction of the cameras. "You have no right to invent a story." She didn't release Ruby's hand but instead increased her grip around her shaking fingers. "Walk straight ahead!" she said. "We aren't going to make it easy for them."

They paced the fifty yards to Etta's car together, hand in hand, with the huddle of press behind them like the Pied Piper's children. They only released their grasp at the final moment before dashing into Etta's car.

"Doesn't Tori want her mother?" one reporter called as she thumped the passenger window. Ruby jumped at the vibration of the glass and clung onto the sides of her seat.

"Right!" Etta said and lowered her window. "Fuck off!" she shouted as loud as her naturally high pitched voice could manage as she sped away from her parking bay, leaving the reporters huddled together like children.

"I'm so sorry, Ruby." She stifled a giggle. "I never swear, truly, never!" She covered her mouth, before adding, "Silly one-way system," to emphasise the point.

A smile crept over Ruby's face as she wound down her window. "Me neither," she said. "Fuck off you bastards," she whispered and then louder as the car drove back in their direction, "bastards the lot of you! Meddling in my life like it's your right."

"Piss off back to your own sordid little lives!" Etta's eyes watered with laughter. That felt good.

Rather than circling the block until the reporters were bored of trailing them, which Ruby confided was her usual strategy, the pair took a twenty-minute drive out to a village north of Leeds. Ruby had insisted she buy Etta a 'proper' cup of tea at the Old School Room, where a black board attached to the entrance door (the Girls' Entrance) announced that the 18th century stone building was open for Cream Teas All Day, Sticky Buns and Parkin. They drove over the recently re-painted hopscotch markings to reach the Old Playground at the back of the building where they could hide the car away from the main road. They hurried to the Girls' Entrance, pausing only for a nod of appreciation of the selection of hula hoops hanging from the handle.

"I think the press have put paid to any outside play today," Etta said, pushing open the door.

Satisfied there were no members of the press seated alone in the four corners of the ex-classroom, poorly hidden behind tall broadsheet newspapers, when everyone knew the only place anyone caught up on the news these days was via their phones, Etta and Ruby took their seats. Their square table was made from four oak desks welded together and was covered with four mats made from gingham material, such as that from an old school dress, Ruby mused. It was 11.20am. It had happened again. If Etta had left the hospital before 11 as planned, she wouldn't have missed her final seminar of the week. She sighed. She couldn't have abandoned Ruby outside the hospital. Nobody would have left her on her own with that lot, would they?

The lady who sat before Etta was barely recognisable as the one who'd shuffled from the hospital. Ruby's legs had shaken so badly, one more twitch and Etta feared she'd have hurled herself accidently into the arms of the reporters. But even once her composure had returned and her face had loosened with the laughter, once the expletives had stopped and her shoulders were back and strong, still something in her demeanour leaked her vulnerability.

"Have you always been superstitious?" Etta asked.

"I'm not sure I am," Ruby said, amicably.

"The sitting outside the door," Etta said. "You know that logically, whether you enter or not, it couldn't possibly have a bearing on Tori's recovery?" When Ruby looked blankly at her, she added,

"Do you remember, you explained why you couldn't visit Tori?"

Ruby smiled. She took a sip of her Earl Grey Tea and winced. It was hot. She put the cup back down. "I remember," she said, "but I hadn't considered the unfortunate situation in superstitious terms before."

Etta opened her mouth and closed it again. Ruby alternated a smile in her direction with a glance down at her tea, her knobbly fingers framing her flower-speckled cup. Etta followed her gaze towards the wall at the side, over to the wooden roll of honour displaying the names of former head boys and girls in an elegant, gold script. Surrounding the wooden slab were innumerable certificates of various shapes and sizes on faded cream paper behind dusty glass frames, boasting everything from the winning of the 1927 North Yorkshire Rugby Championships (Under 11 boys), to the best debut performance from an Under 14 girl in Pygmalion.

"Well done Mary Welbourne," Etta said, shaking her head dramatically, and pointing to the particular certificate. "You'd never catch me on stage."

Ruby's eyes drifted back to centre and Etta followed. She touched Etta's hand. "Tori needs to hear it first—"

Etta smiled. "Of course," she said. "I don't want to pry, then I'm no different to the people who criticise the press but believe the papers."

"—then I can think about telling other people."

Etta hurried her cup back onto the saucer. "Does that mean you're going to go in?"

"When I know she isn't going to leave us, then I'll see her," Ruby said. "Not before."

The pair sipped their tea in silence. Etta smiled in response to the waitress to show that they had all they required and fiddled with the gold edging around the handle of her cup.

A tall, young man, barely out of his teens, in tight jeans and a cable-knit jumper with only a speck of hair on his head, entered the café. Ruby bristled but Etta shook her head once she noticed the man grab a quick kiss with the waitress. Etta smiled.

"They watch me too," she whispered. "It makes me paranoid. And I have nothing to do with any of this," she added, quickly.

Ruby doused the final mouthful of her scone with further sloppy cream. She said that these were strange times they lived in and she had no understanding of what would and would not make the news nowadays.

"Sometimes I wonder if I should make something up to throw them off the scent," Etta said.

"What scent?"

"Oh, something and nothing." Etta picked up the teapot, re-filled both cups, the tea slopping slightly as it reached the top. "Something and nothing," she repeated. "Moments in our past can haunt us in these circumstances, can't they?" She smiled broadly. "They can take on great significance."

"Yes, they can." Ruby looked into Etta's eyes without so much as a glance away, as if to reach to the back and pull out the truth. "You'd rather not tell me," she said. "That's your choice entirely."

Etta took a square of Parkin, this piece dipped in chocolate, pulled it apart, examined the treacly sponge and returned it purposefully to the edge of her saucer. She pushed the rest of the plateful towards Ruby who declined with a little shake of her head and a smile which showed only at the corners of her mouth.

"Ruby." Etta cleared her throat. "Something happened, very unfortunate. Two years ago. The press got it wrong," she said, "well, everybody got it wrong."

Ruby nodded judiciously.

"It died down quickly," Etta shook her head. "There were no charges."

"I'm sorry."

"No," Etta said flatly. "Please, don't be sorry."

THIRTEEN

CARLY PULLED THE CHAIR out noisily from the top end of the bed. She cupped her mother's hand in her own as per the now daily ritual. She loved it when she had something new to talk about.

"Dad showed me a letter that came for you," she said, barely seated.

It must be 6.30. Tori thought. *Why didn't she say?*

"It's not like the others." Her hands still gripping her mother's, Carly leaned in to kiss her on the forehead.

Perhaps it isn't 6.30. Maybe something's wrong.

"Listen to this!" Carly withdrew a hand so that she could tug the page from her bag. She shook it to unfold it, gave it a flick with a finger to ensure it was perfectly flat and laid it on the bed so that she could read from it and still leave her hands free for communication. She took her mother's hand in hers again and introduced the letter by saying that it had been painstakingly crafted in inked italics, apart from the signature which was written in an illegible scrawl.

"'Sometimes I feel quite alone in willing you to get better,'" Carly read.

"You tap away when you think of anything, OK?" She squeezed her mother's hand, coughed and continued. "'Sane people I have known for years make insane judgements. They forget too easily that we make mistakes every day. Usually, thankfully, our own mistakes are not so catastrophic.'"

It's the simplest situations which are the most frustrating, Tori thought. Is it or isn't it 6.30? Why hasn't Carly told me?

"'It's a protective force field people use,'" Carly continued, absent-mindedly releasing Tori's hand before quickly snatching at it again.

"Tap once for 'yes,'" she said, unnecessarily. She paused, waited for a response, then continued to read. "'If we criticise other people's behaviour, we think we deflect attention from our own.'"

She scraped her chair in closer and lifted Tori's hand into her lap. "I know you'd say she's quite right, Mum. It's ironic that somebody like you should be at the centre of this backlash." She squeezed her hand. "Isn't it Mum?" She brought Tori's hand up to her lips and kissed it. "That's a compliment by the way," she said. "I'm saying you're a good person. Tap once to thank your favourite eldest daughter." She kissed her hand again, sighed and said that she'd continue reading without the interruption of the inane questions and hope that as soon as she felt able, her mum would join in with the conversation.

Backlash. Controversy. Aggression, Tori had heard. Disappointment. Responsibility. But, 'I was with you,' was what she repeated over and over to herself. 'No one can take that away from us.'

"Somebody held your hand, Mum," Carly said, "somebody who cares for you. Listen to this!" She read from the letter again. "'I did not know what I know now but I would do the same again, every time'. This is gold dust, Mum," Carly said. "Trouble is, we can't work out who this person is." She tutted. "It was the same person who hand-delivered this letter and called Dad," she said. "I could kill him," she muttered, into the cluster of fingers. She returned Tori's hand to the top of her sheet, stood up and wandered over to the proliferation of photos attached to the wall. She and Doug had brought them from frames, albums and the fridge doors in their homes and the nurses had turned a blind eye to the Blue-Tack. She stood now with her back to her mother and scanned the wall in search of inspiration. "Who feels this bond for you?" she mumbled. "A name beginning with 'E'." Her eyes darted from one photo to another. "Is it Ellie? Ella? Think! Esme?"

The colour red splashed in front of Tori's eyes then faded as quickly. She wanted to touch it, feel its texture. There was the crash and the scream. But the picture that lasted for any duration was the mobile phone, goading her, practically unmarked.

"No, no. Not Esme, no."

Carly shook her head, and looked back at her mother. Her eyes were open! She tapped her hands together and strode back to the bed, throwing herself back down onto the seat. Their hands entwined again she explained the importance and that she needed her mum's full concentration. "A short name beginning with 'E'," she said. "Ellie? Ella? Esme?" she asked with a significant pause between each. She shook her head.

"Emma? Emily? Could it be Edna?" She looked into Tori's eyes and asked if she'd prefer to blink. She felt the sudden tapping of her mother's finger, two firm beats, quickly into her palm and watched her eyes close. She smiled. "No," she said, shaking the cluster of hands. "Finger tapping it is then!"

The red was pulsing, the phone was no longer menacing but tiny in comparison to the huge hand which held hers. Tori was calm, warm and the hand was tight but soft.

"I'm Etta," the voice said, "I'm Tori," she wanted to say.

"Ella? Mum?"

"No. No. No." Tori shrieked, Etta! But the name soared away until its echo became only a soft 't' in the distance. "Etta-ta-ta-ta!" She clenched her fists and shouted, "The name is, Etta!"

"Ouch! You're getting stronger, those pushes against my palm almost hurt!" Carly said, repositioning her hand. "The name's certainly not Ella. I got that. Keep going, keep squeeze—" Tori's hands fell from hers. Her mouth was slightly open, her breath slowing.

"Mum? No!" She grabbed Tori's hands and clapped them together. "Erin?" No response. "Esther? Esta!" She clutched at the hands again, squeezed ever tighter. Tori's fingers flushed with pink but the nurses had said it was OK, nobody would be more pleased than Tori to feel pain again. "Eliza?" she tried, her voice starting to squeak as the remaining possibilities dwindled. There was still no reply and Tori's breathing had lengthened. Her eyes were shut, her eyeballs no longer jumping around behind the closed lids.

"How many short women's names beginning with 'E' are there?" Carly re-folded the letter into three and slotted it purposefully into her bag. The Fresubin was flowing smoothly. She pressed a damp cloth over Tori's face and combed the top few tresses of her knotted hair with an afro comb. Was she a little too rough? She pulled Tori's bedding up to her chin.

"Going to get a hot chocolate to help me think, Mum."

Outside Tori's room, Carly leaned against the wall and let out a long, slow breath. She should splash her face, use the sink in the visitors' toilets diagonally opposite. It annoyed her when people used the en suite bathroom in her mother's room. It wasn't so much that they ignored the clear signage that it was strictly for patient use, more the irony that her mother was the only person who couldn't use her own facilities. Would she ever? Tori's room was bang in the middle of the corridor, one of only three individual rooms. All the other poorly women were in wards of four staggered across both sides. The corridor was always so eerily quiet, aside from the odd beep of a monitor or the bip bop of the timer when an infusion bag was empty. Who'd have thought that Carly would come to know the difference between bips and bops and beeps and that an infusion in hospital was a sack of medication and not a bag of tea? To her left at the end of the corridor was the nurses' station. Today she'd take a right, the long route to the cafeteria. Georgia, Anna, in fact all the staff looked out for Carly and concerned themselves with her health, too. But today she didn't want to talk about it. She closed her eyes, gently stroking her temples with her index fingers.

A flash of light lit up her face and Carly turned instinctively towards the source but it had vanished before she could place it. A doctor was pacing down the corridor. Pressed up against the wall opposite was Ruby.

"You gave me a fright, Grandma," Carly said, giving her a quick kiss and a lacklustre hug. She was going to ask if she'd brought a camera with her, to remind her that they didn't have permission to use them here, but she noticed that Ruby was holding nothing more than a bunch of keys.

"Are you going in?" she said, instead. Ruby shook her head quickly. "Oh Grandma, Mum isn't going to die anymore. It's all about her recovery now." Ruby didn't answer. "I know it would help her to hear your voice," Carly said.

"Maybe tomorrow, love. It's difficult."

The bags under Ruby's eyes were large as pincushions and

embroidered with a web of thread veins. Her top and bottom jaw didn't quite meet when she spoke. "It *is* difficult, Grandma." Carly gave her a perfunctory hug. "But I know it would help to hear your voice."

Ruby opened her mouth but closed it again. She spread the bunch of keys over the palm of her other hand, chose the most traditional, a rusting heavy garden gate type key, and held it up to Carly.

"Could you help me with this love?" Her fingers shook as she spoke. "I need this key on a different ring."

Carly grabbed it, wrestled the ring from the band and thrust it back into Ruby's hand but when her grandmother simply stood still and looked at the keys, Carly tutted, turned on her heel and sped down the corridor. Before she reached the exit, she turned quickly.

"Grandma! Wait!" Carly was panting even though the distance covered was slight. "A girl's name beginning with, 'E' - short one. Can you think of any?"

"Is this a trick question?"

Carly tilted her head. "No."

"Why do you want to know?"

"Grandma, please!"

"A short girl's name beginning with 'E'." Ruby struggled to squeeze the bunch of keys into her pocket. "How about Etta?"

"Etta!" Carly said. "I've never heard of it. Is it an abbreviation?"

Finally, Ruby gave up and dropped the keys into her woven shopping bag instead.

"What made you think of 'Etta' Grandma?"

"I'm not certain." She looked Carly directly in the eye now. "Pretty name though isn't it?"

FOURTEEN

ETTA STARED AT THE KETTLE, shaking her head when she finally realised that it had switched itself off. Some inappropriate dance music squealed from the television in the living room but she chose to ignore it. One viewing of a raunchy music video wouldn't make Adriana a prostitute, she told herself, and she was too tired for any tears. She stretched up to remove the pasta from the cupboard above, dodging the fake wooden panel as it swung away from the MDF door again.

"Afternoon!" Andy removed the first of his three jackets. "Freezing out there today." He threw an arm around her waist and gave her a squeeze. "And Adriana's in there with a pair of tights and your bra on."

Etta picked up the vegetable knife and sliced at speed. "We'll have a read of *Squash and a Squeeze* tonight," she said, "get her back on track." She cubed the carrot sticks so that Adriana could build the three little pigs' brick house before being force-fed them for tea. She asked Andy how his day had been, rapping his hand gently to dissuade him from stealing any more meticulously carved carrot bricks.

He crossed his arms, his stiff jackets crackling. "Won't ever run out of work, that's for sure."

"The state of the nation's road surface was the lunch topic again today." Etta peeled an extra carrot. "I try to tell them that every bump and hole is not your fault."

"I've never known people take quite so much interest in my work." Finally, he removed the other two jackets. "I blame it on Tori's Text running and running. People don't normally care about anything in the news for longer than a day or two."

"It's because Tori's still alive." Etta scraped every last carrot stick into the steamer.

"They're certainly not praying she'll survive," Andy said, "not the people I talk to anyway."

Etta tutted, as she fished out the handful of carrot sticks from the pan which she'd intended to set aside for Adriana, producing a vibrato yawn to accompany the head shaking. "It's brought out the worst in people," she said.

Andy kissed Etta on the top of her head. He'd make them both a cup of tea.

"Come and sit down with me, Et," he said, as he carried both mugs to the round table. "I'm worried about you." Etta yawned again and Andy beckoned her over with a swoop of his arm. "I'll finish supper in a moment." He retrieved a tube of chocolate biscuits from the inside pocket of his overall. "Special treat," he said, "BP's finest."

Etta placed her biscuit on the fake-oak table without a plate, which made Andy raise an eyebrow, and he raised the other when she said that she couldn't be bothered to fetch one. She lifted the biscuit to her mouth and took a small bite.

"You're acting slightly strangely, Andy, if you don't mind me saying. Have I done something wrong?"

Andy reached across to touch Etta's free hand.

"You're making me nervous now."

"I'm worried about you." He leaned back. He was worried that she wasn't getting enough sleep, had too much on. When he added that she was making mistakes, her eyes grew wider and she returned her cup to the table.

"Don't stop there." She crossed her arms.

"With everything you've gone through, it's all perfectly understandable," Andy said. "But—"

"But—?"

"As well as your sanity, I'm worried for the children."

Etta stared at Andy and said in a voice, which cracked a little, that almost cooking Adriana's carrots hardly classed as child abuse.

"Their education," Andy said.

She pushed her tall chair backwards. "Need to get the pasta on," she mumbled. Andy reminded her that he'd finish the supper but she pushed past him and said, "No, no, couldn't possibly. I'm quite capable of feeding their bodies even if I can't feed their minds."

Only when the water had boiled and the pasta was simmering in the pan, did she drift back to the table, think better of it and sit herself down on the two-person sofa instead. Andy waited until she was seated, gathered the tea and biscuits onto a tray, and sat down next to her.

"Do you know you used 'wheeze' for 'squeeze' when you were reading last night?"

Etta shrugged. "I guess."

"And that our bouncy little five-year-old," he emphasised with a roll of his eyes, "corrected you every time and you simply said, 'Well done love', as if she was pointing out the error for the first time?"

Etta hugged the nearest cushion, unclasping her hands only to take sips from the now lukewarm tea and then re-clasping them again.

"I'm busy, Andy," she said. "All parents read to their children in a semi-comatose state at some point in their lives. It doesn't cause psychological harm. You," she said, speeding up, "can't even finish the line before the children are nudging you in the ribs."

Andy took another biscuit, tipped the packet in Etta's direction but she shook her head. "Fair cop," he said, "the difference is that I've always been like that."

Etta heaved herself up from the saggy base of the tatty sofa. She'd make them another cup of tea. But Andy stood up, too.

"Sit!" he said, and she fell back down. "Yesterday you told Johan that it was indeed 'e' before 'i' in 'friend'. He told me that Miss Root was cross with him when he told her that his mum had said it was definitely that way round."

Etta shook her head. Of course she wouldn't have said that. Johan was only seven. He'd made a mistake. "Why are you making so much fuss, Andy?"

Andy strode over to the sideboard, opened up the flip top lid and rummaged through the recycling.

"Look!" He rushed back to Etta and laid the offending note on her lap. "That's *your* writing and *your* smiley face."

Etta opened her mouth and closed it again. "He won't be harmed if I'm a bit tired sometimes," she whispered. "I'll tell him later, make sure he unlearns *'freinds'* for all our sakes."

Andy put his arm around Etta's shoulder. "It's not like you."

She dipped her shoulder to lose his hand, and thanked Andy for his offer to make supper. "The children and I are fit and healthy," she said, leaving the room before her face could crack.

FIFTEEN

DOUG LEANED BACK in his swivel chair and marvelled at the wonders of modern technology as he clicked on 'electoral roll'. 'Etta,' Ruby had suggested. It was worth pursuing. Once you compared the name with the signature, it most certainly could be 'Etta'. Of course it was bound to be an abbreviation. Although you didn't know these days, what with names which had performed perfectly well in the past with a 'y' to finish, now ending in 'ie', not to mention the inanimate objects suddenly becoming the stuff of forenames. There was a 'Box' in Year Ten, affectionately referred to as 'Boxy' or should he say, 'Boxie', as well as a Stepp (with two 'p's), and Twig which led nicely into the veritable life cycle of nature. Cloud, Ant, Petal and Stump were all proud members of his Year Eleven. OK, Stump was on the petite side of average and had been christened a very pronounceable, George Stump Harrison and Stump, with its various connotations of Stumpie, Stumpy, Stumper and even Stum seemed preferable to this excellent student. It occurred to Doug that perhaps George Harrison was not as much of a fan of the Beatles as his parents had been.

Rebecca poked her head around the door and woke Doug from his reverie. "I'll be on my way if that's OK? Busy day tomorrow, of course."

The 'of course' hung in the air, an auditory reminder that Doug's fiendishly organised PA was the linchpin in his position; the only way he was clinging onto any sense of order in this school. He couldn't bring himself to admit that beyond his visit to the hospital later, his mind was a blank.

"Absolutely." He smiled brightly. "What would I do without you?"

She gestured to the computer screen. "Definitely start with 'Etta' but I think it might be short for Henrietta? And if not, how about Georgette?"

Doug raised an eyebrow.

"And are you confident it's a woman? The double 't' could actually be a 'u', don't you think? And then you've got, 'Eua', short for 'Euen'?"

Doug cleared his throat.

"Right then." Rebecca lingered on the door handle. "Truly hope the investigation gives the info you need. But don't forget to sleep." She waggled a finger. "And eat some veg. Still looking a bit peaky."

Doug turned back to the PC. He didn't like to tell Rebecca that once he'd sat with Tori until she slept, it would be baked beans again for tea. He wished his life could be transformed, as the remaining females in his life seemed to think, simply with a head of cauliflower.

"Night, Rebecca, thanks for your concern," he said. When he didn't hear the door close, he swivelled around to see her shifting from one foot to another. "How can I help?"

"Would it be nosy to ask why you were looking for someone called something beginning with E?"

He cocked his head to the side, drummed his fingers on the armrests. "This Etta-cum-Georgette-cum-Euen," he said, "not forgetting Henrietta, or course, she might just save our lives."

— — —

He leaned back against his chair, the front casters no longer touching the carpet which would have caused Tori to tut. The first, second and even the third search for 'Etta' resulted in a blank page. He took a gulp of cold coffee, clasped his hands behind his head for a moment, and stared, really stared at the name. 'Winetta,' perhaps? He tried it. Clearly no Winettas were registered to vote in Yorkshire. He wondered if he should widen his search to nationwide but he had to start somewhere and the letter had been hand delivered. How about further along the M62?

He breathed out. It wasn't without a smack of conscience that he sat racing through a list of people with Etta as full or part of a name on the electoral list. If this Etta had wanted to be found, she'd have helped everybody by including her contact details.

Still, he didn't have much choice. Amongst the sneers and recriminations and the vilification by the press and public, one lone voice had defended his wife. How did she 'know' Tori wasn't driving badly? How could she know? Was she her passenger? And why weren't the police all over this?

'Henrietta', Rebecca had said.

Doug's stomach lurched. The results showed not a blank page, not even a full page but one, just one, result for a Henrietta, over the age of eighteen living in Yorkshire. He slumped back into his chair with relief. But when he looked closer, she didn't live in Yorkshire but in Rochdale in Greater Manchester. No matter, he'd call her anyway. He hadn't got any other leads.

"For Christ's sake," he shouted, closing down the PC with a slap of the keys. "Of course she's bleeding ex-directory." He cleared his throat. The sound of him cursing on school premises made him feel oddly self-conscious, in stark contrast to the mild-mannered, sweet talking persona he assimilated on walking through the school gates.

But why could nothing ever be straightforward?

SIXTEEN

NOBODY COULD EVER accuse Gerald of being mean, he congratulated himself, as the employee in the top hat and tails opened the enormous, gold embossed door to Octavia's for him and Sophie. Sophie gave a twitter of a giggle as the gentleman's white-gloved hand pointed the way to the top floor for Special Occasion Wear. She pecked Gerald on the cheek and nuzzled her face into his neck as they stepped out of the glass lift.

"Two weeks and we'll be Mr and Mrs Crawford." She spun around to face him. "I can still hardly believe it. We could have gone our whole lives and never even met if you hadn't come in for that gold tie!"

Gerald glanced up to see the security camera angled towards them. He smiled and kissed her lips. The tie was no accident. He'd seen Sophie open up the shop and something about her elfin face had mesmerised him. However, she liked to believe it was fate and Gerald was happy to leave her with the distorted memory.

Sophie strode over to a collection of sparsely hung velvet dresses on heavy mahogany hangers.

"Whoa," she said, "have you seen the prices? Even in the sale!"

Gerald hung his arm around Sophie's shoulders. "And why not? It isn't every day you get married." He pointed to a cream trouser suit with wide trousers and a fitted jacket. "How about that? Very sophisticated."

Together they took a step closer.

"Very two thousand pounds." She rubbed the lapel between two fingers to get a feel for the fabric. "Good quality, certainly. The flowers are huge though, quite a statement. Gerald," she said, nestling into his side again, "I still think I'd be better in Style House, finding something a bit more me."

Gerald smirked and felt compelled to remind Sophie that she owned a Gent's Outfitters. She should love great tailoring and pretty fabrics. And yet that was one of the things he admired; her ability to be who she wanted to be and that person was herself: Sophie Higginson, thirty-two years young, vibrant, sexy, compliant. She didn't buy expensive clothes for the sake of it and didn't want a huge wedding, rather a more intimate affair. Gerald had conceded on that one. He'd told her he'd have liked nothing more than to show her off to the world, prove to all the people who'd criticised him for the break-up of his previous relationships that they were fools to doubt him. As he'd relented on the guest list, he was sure he could persuade her into this cream suit.

He squeezed her shoulders. "You'll look enviously slim and sophisticated, just a little classier for the occasion." He held the suit against her slight frame. "Much as I adore you in those miniskirts and thick tights," he added quickly. The suit would draw attention discreetly to her bulbous breasts. It was their wedding. It wouldn't harm his invitees to see the more elegant side of his young bride.

Sophie gave Gerald a playful dig in the ribs.

"Suits are great on men your age, Gerald." She ruffled his hair.

"You always look smart and classically cool," she added quickly, "but I'm not ready for this kind of stuff."

"Right." Gerald smoothed his hair back into place. "So I'm going to be the one who stands out at our wedding then, am I?"

"Hey!" she said, standing still for a rare moment. "You'll look like Gerald and I'll look like Sophie." She did a pirouette before linking her arm through his and leading him back towards the lift with an exaggerated sweep of her other arm. "As long as you're there," she said, adding in a lower voice, "and the press aren't, it will be the perfect day. Whatever we wear."

Gerald pulled his arm from her as she pressed the button for the lift. Was he the only one taking this wedding seriously? It was to be a civil wedding. Sophie didn't believe in God, so that was helpful, and it was Sophie who'd found the venue: a converted bandstand in the beautiful gardens of some manor house outside Leeds. Gerald might have booked somewhere more central, Harrogate town centre perhaps, where he might have persuaded friends who hadn't quite made the guest list to line the route where the bride and groom would pass in their horse and cart. That way he and Sophie could wave, show them they were in their thoughts, that they would have been invited had the venue been bigger. He supposed lots of people would be disappointed. But that was weddings for you.

Sophie clearly wasn't in the mood for buying the flowery suit today but it was pointless looking anywhere else. This was what she should wear. He slipped his hands around her waist and turned her to him.

"Can we skip the shopping?" he asked. "Forget the coffee?" Sophie beamed. "We'll get some champagne instead and take it back to your place." Sophie pulled from the embrace, plunged her hand into his and they stepped together into the lift. Gerald stuffed the clasp of hands into the front pocket of his new jeans. "The thought of you in that suit has made me a little frisky," he said, smoothing the top of his hair with his free hand.

SEVENTEEN

CARLY PRESSED THE BUTTON AGAIN. It never usually took so long for the lift to arrive. The illuminated number told her they were hanging around Floor Three: her floor. The queue of people behind her peeled away and she followed them towards the slow lift in the corner.

"The fools! It's the oldest trick in the book," Carly heard. "But security won't be the only ones, we'll get it in the neck too." It was Tim speaking, the willowy physiotherapist who manipulated her mother's joints and pressed on her atrophying muscles. "But how can we check every new doctor who shows his face?" He pressed the button for the third floor. Carly stepped forward but checked herself and took a pace back instead.

"We'll be kitted out with bulletproof vests soon." It was Christina who spoke, the Ward Manager, 'Matron' to all but herself.

Tim lowered his head to be nearer to the height of the three colleagues who flanked him. "I don't see why she can't be photographed," he said quietly. "So what if her picture's on the cover of some trashy magazine? I think she should get paid for the privilege and have the money transferred to the NHS." He reached into the lift and pressed the button to hold open the doors for other travellers. Carly quickly stepped aside and turned her back. She'd take the next one.

When she finally stepped out on to her mother's floor she was met by the security guard who often stood at the entrance to Tori's room. "Sorry for the inconvenience," he said. "Extra security on today, checking people in and out of the lifts."

"Because of yesterday?"

The guard frowned. "Not our finest hour."

Carly wandered slowly along the corridor to the entrance to Ward Three B where a guard she didn't recognise was checking identification. "Thank you," she said with sincerity. Once inside, she squeezed the antiseptic wash from its dispenser onto both hands and cleaned them thoroughly. The nurses' station was around the corner. She could hear Tim's voice. She cleaned her hands again.

"Tim's right. It costs an arm and a leg, 'scuse the pun, to keep her here all this time and no matter how well she recovers, she'll be behind bars anyway. Then we pay for that too."

Carly exhaled and leant heavily against the wall. She checked her watch: 6.25pm.

"No I haven't. I've never phoned." It was clearly Christina speaking, with her slow drawl, several tones lower than the other female colleagues. "I've never answered a call or texted, even at traffic lights," she said. "And you shouldn't either. Phones kill."

"60mph in the middle lane of the motorway is pretty incomprehensible." Was that Anna? Carly peered around the corner, but shot back.

"What was she thinking?" she heard Anna say.

"Well, she wasn't thinking was she, that's the trouble. People drive like they're the only ones who matter and sometimes they get caught out."

Carly exhaled. She stepped around the corner to see Christina gather up her papers. "She's got it coming to her," she said, "and if we don't want this kind of mess in here every week, they're going to have to throw the book at her."

Carly covered her ears and marched past, choosing not to notice Anna's smile in her direction.

The third security guard, tub-shaped and with the faintest whiff of blonde hair on his head and an ample crop on his chin, stood at Tori's door.

"Hey!" he said. Carly felt his eyes settle on her sunken shoulders and her shoulder bag which trailed on the floor, hanging on the tips of her fingers by the long strap. "Hot topic," he continued, inclining his ear towards the rest of the ward. "It'll pass, always does."

Carly greeted her mother with forced enthusiasm, taking her seat on the orange chair at the top end of the bed as she always did. She stared at her mother's hands thrown together on top of the sheet, the grid of lines exposed, which Tori so detested. Her maroon-polished fingernails sparkled defiantly. Jo must have visited. Carly didn't attempt to wake her. She couldn't summon the strength to speak, to be strong. She couldn't even bring herself to pick up Tori's finger tapping hands, lest they were still. She'd wanted to ask if she knew about someone called 'Etta' and to talk about their trip to Australia. She wouldn't need to tell her the details, solely the fact that Nicky was getting married would stimulate her mother into consciousness, surely?

She knew what people were saying, of course she did. She read the papers like everybody else. She leapfrogged photographers in her parents' garden and switched on the radio to find phone-in debates handing out prison sentences like interest-free credit cards. She knew how many of her mum's friends visited and how many of her own never got in touch. But the medical staff had taken her aback. They cared for all sorts, surely. Was Tori Williams so shocking?

She looked down. Her tears dropped one by one onto her mother's hands. "For God's sake!" she said to herself. "Please wake up Mum!" She sniffed and gurgled and warbled as the tears poured down. "I need you, Mum," she spluttered. "I need my mum." Now she grabbed Tori's hands, squeezed them, perhaps too hard, released them quickly and jumped up. "We're trapped," she said, kicking the casters under the bed. "This nightmare is only going to get worse. Reporters digging dirt about Grandma and Gerald, for God's sake, passers-by spitting at Dad, his pupils disrespecting him. And now this," she said, "a photograph in your hospital bed. It's even too naff for daytime telly. And that's not enough," she wiped her cheeks with the back of her hand, "no, because after all this crap, there's the court case to come and then pris—"

There was a knock on the door. Carly shot round to see it open up a touch.

"OK in here, pet?" Anna said. "These walls are paper thin—"

"Oh Mum!" Carly's hands rushed to her mouth. "I'm so sorry, I shouldn't have said—" she fled past Anna, into the barrel chest of the security guard, muttered an apology, ran past the nurses' station without so much as a glance at the staff and pushed past the waiting crowd and into the lift, where she threw herself into the corner and sank to her bottom.

– – –

This time the marshmallow walls were lead and Tori was bouncing from one side to the other. "Let me out!" she called. "I'm trapped."

She landed back in the past, this time over twenty-five years ago, on Friday 12th June, 1987. Her father has been rushed to hospital. He'd collapsed at work and the last time Tori had said goodbye to him was two weeks before.

"Concentrate Tori!" she said to herself, thumping her steering wheel with the side of her fist. A horn sounded. "A red light? Have I just driven through...?" She had no recollection of any other cars on the road. She didn't know how she managed to get to A&E. He couldn't die, she wouldn't let him die. He was only fifty-nine.

Tori couldn't believe what she was seeing. The same nurses who visited her in her marshmallow tunnel, who zoomed in and out of focus, and peered, always peering earnestly, never merely looking, were tending to her father in the operating theatre. They'd heard her. One pointed, another took a photo.

"You can't save him!" she called.

A surgeon asked for a scalpel. But a phone flew through the air instead, twisting and turning as it went, glinting in the operating team's enormous spotlight directed at her father's face. A student cranked up and down the bed as if he were a child playing with the mechanism. He looked at her and spat, so close it landed on her face.

"Focus!" Tori screamed.

A surgeon asked for a swab, a male nurse showed off his football prowess, from toe to heel, to 'on the 'ead sir' and the surgeon let the swab rebound off his forehead to lodge itself perfectly over the wound. An electronic 'Amazing Grace' was too loud. How could anyone ring him? Her father was dying!

"You're disrespecting him!" She wept. "No!" she tried again. "Look after him. I need him. Don't let him die!"

— — —

The door crashed open.

"Mum, Mum are you OK?" Carly rushed to her bedside and then back to the door. She flung it open and yelled to Anna to come. Please.

Don't let him go!

"She's distressed," Carly said. "Her head's twitching and her fingers are bending and flexing and—"

Anna swooped over to the top of the bed. "Right, we're on!"

She beckoned Carly even closer to her mother on the other side, to within inches of Tori's grimacing face. "Tori!" Anna shouted so loud next to Tori's ear it made Carly jump. "I'm your nurse. I'm Anna. You're in hospital!" she shouted. "You're going to fight, pet." Carly wanted Anna to stop, surely it would hurt? Tori grunted, her head for the first time in weeks not merely moving now but thrashing from side to side. "Carly's here. We want you back. Don't let us down!"

"Come on Mum. We miss you. Speak, please speak!"

Anna twisted a hunk of flesh on Tori's triceps. Tori flinched, both eyes still screwed tight. Her lips moved. Carly jumped back, her hands covering her mouth.

"Mum!" she squealed. "What are you saying?" Carly shook her mother's arms. "Is it, 'Go!' Mum? Please?"

Anna twisted some more skin, this time on the back of Tori's hand. Still Tori's head swung from side to side, her left eye opening and closing. This time it was audible.

"No. No, let him go!"

"Let who go, Mum?"

"Need him. No, let go. No, let go."

Anna and Carly looked at each other. They stumbled over the words together. "We won't let you go," they said.

— — —

On fast rewind, Tori's dream ran backwards. Her father's life had ended minutes before any operating table. There was no 'Amazing Grace', no mobile phone. They'd tried the defibrillator of course, mouth to mouth resuscitation at the scene where her father had collapsed but by the time Tori had reached the hospital, her father was pronounced dead.

— — —

Carly squeezed her mother's hand as hard as she could bear.

"We're not letting you go anywhere, Mum," she said. "We want you here, with us." Tori's right eye opened as wide as her left. As clearly as if she had a coffee in one hand, the phone in the other, she said,

"Not me, love, your Granddad. He was too young to die."

EIGHTEEN

THE USUAL PUBLIC CAR PARK for the hospital was full. Etta's heart pumped harder as she negotiated the one-way system and the innumerable arrows pointing to car parking spaces which didn't exist. She cursed herself and the rain that fell. Somebody is testing me, she thought, and I don't blame them. Every time she visited the hospital she swore it would be the last. When she'd taken on this part-time university course she'd vowed that her home life and her friendships wouldn't suffer. But now, as she sat alone in the car once again, she'd forsaken her monthly date with friends for the first time in its five year history, and she'd defied her partner who'd pleaded with her not to go to the hospital.

She threw her bag over her shoulder, thrust her key fob in the direction of the car and ran towards one of several hospital entrances. If I'm going to follow these hare-brained schemes, she thought, holding a jacket over her head with one hand and her bag to her side with the other, I need to plan better.

A swamp of voices caused Etta to slow her step. The noise guided her to the correct entrance. A crowd six deep blocked her sight of it. 'Tori the Texting Killer,' a banner said in letters each a foot high. There was a photo of a smashed car below. One word: 'PRISON' was written in red, diagonally across the picture. 'Texting Kills Babies,' another read. 'Text in Cars?' she saw, 'Behind Bars.'

Beyond the banners, the area looked like a cross between a technology convention and a trading floor. Digital cameras, long lenses and back-breaking cameras with Global TV inscribed along the side, were held in the air or rested on shoulders. Booms were stuffed like cotton wool through every perceivable crevice. Etta could make out certain words: 'admit', 'hanged', 'guilt' and 'no mercy'.

The police were going to speak to Tori Williams in hospital today, the Global newspaper had stated. Tori could speak now, was compos mentis, they'd said.

Etta shifted her position. The pillar on which she was perched numbed her bottom. She blew into her cold hands. Her hair couldn't hold any more rain and the water had crept inside her collar, making her shiver. She tugged her sleeves over her fingers. Had she seen enough?

She scanned the mass of protestors and journalists. There was some movement but nothing structured. Was she going to wait all day for nothing in particular? Did the air really feel more charged than usual?

Away from the crowd, the car park was full but people were scarce. Etta saw an elderly couple, bent into a 'C' shape, leaning on each other for support as they trudged in the direction of the smaller hospital entrance. A tall man strode towards the main door. With a laptop bag hung over one shoulder and his hands full of flowers and grapes, he shook his head intermittently to flick his sodden hair from his eyes. At the edge of the swarm he halted, turned on his heel and headed towards a different door.

Another man was standing still, his hands wedged into the pockets of an overly large, black puffa jacket, more at home up a mountain than covering his grey flannel suit which trailed in the puddles at his feet. He looked around him, made as if to step forward, stopped and exhaled again. He pulled a dark fleece hat down over his ginger hair, the ends curling up around the bottom edges. '12 o'clock,' Etta mouthed as he pulled the edge of his sleeve back to reveal a large, waterproof watch. He turned 180 degrees and looked in the opposite direction but quickly spun back, fixing his eyes now on the hub of the throng.

Etta breathed into the clasp of her freezing hands. "Go on Doug," she whispered, "don't let them beat you!"

— — —

He studied the familiar white vans with coloured logos and metal spaghetti sprouting from their roofs, the crouching men with camera lenses the length of his forearm and the overly thin men and women with an incongruous mix of notebooks or tablets in their hands. He'd contemplated trying to hail a sympathetic hospital employee to get him through. He was merely visiting his sick wife in hospital. It was a basic human right to be able to do that without having to answer to these idiots.

The incessant questioning started innocuously enough.

"Mr Williams, how is your wife?" It was Steve, with his narrow jeans and pointy shoes which made his stunted legs look even more weedy. Still, he'd clearly moved from behind the rosemary bush. Maybe he'd have a night off, too. "Will you be bringing your wife out with you, sir?" Since when had this Steve cared enough to refer to Tori as Doug's wife? Usually it was, 'The Texting Killer', 'Murderer' or worse of all, just plain, 'Tori'. As the weeks passed, the over-familiarisation aggravated Doug as much as the crime thriller terminology.

"Mrs Williams won't be leaving hospital today," Doug said. An arm blocked his path. The arm of this relative stranger, who had no regard whatsoever for Tori's wellbeing, had dared to halt him in his progression to see her. This was the kind of insolence Doug dealt with every day at school. "Excuse me?" he said with full headteacher aplomb. "Out of my way, please."

"Can she speak fluently, Mr Williams?" The voice was like dolly mixtures, Steve's smile like bananas. "Will she be explaining her actions?"

It's like playing with children, Doug thought. He thinks he's fooling me.

"The texting, Mr Williams?"

"One thing of which I'm certain is that she will not be speaking with you." Doug strode forward, leading with his ribcage to force Steve's outstretched arm from his path. "What right have you to speak to my wife?"

"Ha ha!" Steve's laugh was so viciously false; Doug was one punch away from silencing it. He sprinted around the side of the swarm of journalists and protestors to land in front of Doug and block his final steps to the main entrance. "What will Tori be saying to the police, Mr Williams?"

"Why doesn't her mother visit, Mr Williams?" a small man with a thick moustache asked. "Mr Williams, why doesn't Ruby go to her daughter's bedside?" another added.

Doug stopped, looked around. "How—?"

Words flew from all directions:

"What's your daughter doing in Australia?"

"Did Tori often text while she was driving?"

"Is your daughter coming back from Australia, Mr Williams—?"

"Where's Ruby today?"

"—Or is she estranged, too?" Steve's eyes were fixed, determined not to release Doug from his gaze. Doug looked over at the tangle of heads behind Steve, then back to him.

"How did you...?" he whispered, slowly shaking his head.

"What other offences has she committed?" the man with the moustache asked.

"Speeding, Mr Williams?" Doug looked scathingly at the extended eyelashes of a reporter from Global TV. "Previous speeding offences?" she repeated. "Come on, we've all had them."

"She's never been convicted of speeding." He regretted the words even before they landed.

"Never been caught then?" Steve concluded.

NINETEEN

DOUG KISSED TORI'S HAND. She was serene today, simply sleeping. He had to talk to her. He wanted to slap her to wake her up. He took her hand in his and studied the back of it, the veins so distinct. He could pinch the skin, like the nurses had done. He gathered as much as possible in between his thumb and forefinger and held it there. He looked at her closed eyes, listened to her breathing, so loud she was practically snoring. Carly had heard her mother speak, even the staff he'd never even met had heard her speak. He looked at his fingers holding the skin. He tried to twist the knob of flesh clockwise but his grasp slipped.

Instead he paced over to Tori's drip and punched the wall to the side of the Fresubin. Now his other knuckle was bleeding. He breathed out. "Stop it!" he said, under his breath. "Stop this right now."

He forced a smile as Georgia and a new assistant bundled into the room. "That's a nasty cut to your eye," Georgia said, as she tucked and smoothed, pulled and folded Tori's bed linen. "Are we allowed to ask how you did it?"

"Best not," Doug said nodding in Tori's direction.

"Well it's weeping and needs dressing." Georgia crossed her arms over her ample bosom, boasting her pumped biceps. He wouldn't bet on himself winning an arm-wrestle. "Find one of us at the nurses' station before you leave."

Doug gazed at the photos on the wall and walked over to them: Tori as a child on the beach in Northumberland, the characteristic wild curls matted with sand and ice cream; a cluster of wedding photos, in each Tori had her silver speckled shoes in her hand - she never bought shoes that fitted - and several photos of Carly and Nicky at significant moments in their childhood. "Chalk and cheese," he said out loud. "And when did adults replace our children?" Nicky was in her familiar pose, flanked by young men and women on mountain bikes with Coniston Old Man behind them. She had her whole life ahead of her and was tasting it at speed. Who could argue with that? There was another photo of Nicky, tanned and smiling wildly with Kyle linked through her arm. He missed his daughter and her *joie de vivre*.

Doug looked closer at a photo of Carly and eased it from the wall. She was with James, her first love, the boy she'd met five, was it six years ago? He would replace it. James had gone. Carly said she got tired of trying to explain.

"I heard you, you know."

Doug spun around.

"What you been doing now?"

"Tori!" He flung himself on to the bed.

"Woah," she said, "you'll get blood on me."

With his arms tight around her waist, Doug threw back his head and laughed. Both her eyes were open and he was able to haul her into a seated position. She gave a lopsided smile; looked as though she was kicking back, having a relaxing day off.

"So are you going to tell me who hit you?" Tori asked suddenly, her hand reaching up to touch Doug's face, her fingers tip-toeing over his cheeks until they rested on the graze next to the cut around his eye. Doug pulled away, taking her hand in his to remove it from the sore patch. "And why would someone hit you?"

He shook his head happily. "You wouldn't believe how good it is to hear your voice."

"Astasia-abasia."

Doug grinned. "Meaning?"

"Being treated as a child." Her eyes lingered on Doug's but then she tutted and said it meant she'd had enough of it. She couldn't even walk to the bathroom. "Can you take me?" she asked. "I want to look in the mirror."

Doug stopped himself screaming 'No!', his hands flying instead to her scalp to smooth down her hair. "You know you have a catheter?"

"I don't need the loo."

"I'll have to unhook a few bits and pieces." He knew how to disassemble all the tubes and other paraphernalia; he'd often helped detach Tori before the staff turned her. But Tori couldn't walk. He looked around him. He was sure he should ask the staff but he was worried they'd say no. And then Tori might close her eyes and be gone again so soon.

"Back in a tick," he said, and raced out of the door to retrieve a walking frame from the nurses' bay, laughing at the irony of telling Tori not to move, as he left.

– – –

He looked at his wife; surveying her like the contents of a self-assembly unit - all the components were there, but which one first?

"OK, Tori, I'm in charge here." He pulled the sheet away from her legs, took her arms and placed both around his neck. The left gripped tight, the right slipped down over his arm. "Use your left hand to hold your right around my neck, Tori."

"Old people use Zimmer frames," she said.

Doug smiled and pushed it away. "We're going to swing your legs over the side of the bed."

Even though Tori was visibly lighter than when she'd first arrived in hospital six weeks ago, the effort of assisting her into a standing position and her weight hanging around his neck was enough to make him pant. The pair stood nose to nose for a moment, Tori's toes skirting the floor. He assessed the short distance between them and the bathroom door.

"I go backwards, you forwards," he said. Tori's bent right foot shadowed Doug's left like a new skating partnership. He laughed out loud. "Oh this is beautiful. Now your left leg." He placed his right purposefully behind him. "Three or four more of these," he said, his voice speeding up with excitement. "OK, take your time, we've got loads of it," Doug said.

Tori didn't move. "Nothing's happening," she said into his ear, her left hand still gripping her right around his neck. Doug inched Tori back to the bed and lowered her into a sitting position. They would make it to the bathroom. That was the objective. It didn't matter how she did it.

He pulled her up from the bed for a second time, peeled her hands from his neck and placed them on the frame he'd slid in front of her. She shook her head, with little control, but it was progress.

"I'm in charge," he reminded her. This was the moment he'd waited for but it was terrifying, too. She could fall at any moment.

Tori managed a crooked smile. She pushed the frame with her best functioning arm and took a light step with her right foot.

Doug picked up her left and placed it a stride in front, the right following as if on ballet pointes.

"Right, then left," he coaxed, as much to keep his mind away from what Tori would see in the mirror, as any need for instruction. They continued this staccato progress, Doug forced to ignore the tears slipping down his face as both hands were so inexplicably involved in her advancement towards the bathroom. Should he have stalled her, blamed it on the need for a nurse to be around? Should he have pulled the afro comb through her hair first, and, once he'd worked out what went where, applied some make-up? Carly would be cross. She was in the habit of putting white muck on her mother's face when she visited. She was in tune with her mother's feminine needs, said that making her look as human as possible was damage limitation. Never mind that she looked vaguely more alive than a shop mannequin with the blue eye shadow on top of skin which hadn't seen the sun for six weeks.

"Right, now left," Doug said automatically.

"Yes Doug, thank you. It's only my feet which aren't working, my brain is perfectly fine."

"Of course," Doug said, disguising his slight flinch with an aborted sneeze. "You're walking, Torr!" Tears trickled again. "And you're talking. We'll have you home in no time now."

"How long have I been here?" Tori asked, standing still as she did every time she needed to speak, a blatant reminder that the multi-tasking wife of earlier in life may take some time to return.

"Oh, a good couple of weeks," Doug said. "Keep walking, nearly there." He pushed the bathroom door open with his bottom. "No more questions until we're inside," his hands ached where he held Tori under her armpits, "or I might be fighting you for that bed."

A couple more of Tori's lumbering steps and they would be in front of the mirror. But they'd need to inch 90 degrees around so that Tori could see the face that Doug had already started to see as her own.

"Love," he held her still before the turn, "none of us look our best when we're poorly."

"We don't," she said.

"Drugs, saline, liquid food, not great for the complexion, nor is getting no fresh air."

Tori laughed. "Please don't worry. I'm sure it's nothing which can't be sorted with a few slicks of lippie and coats of mascara."

"Right," Doug said. "Absolutely."

He rotated Tori the final few degrees, quickly manoeuvring himself next to her so that they could face the mirror together. At first she was silent, staring vacantly in the direction of the mirror. Then she screwed up her face a little and said that she couldn't see a darned thing without her glasses.

"Of course," Doug said, almost letting her fall in his hurry to take them out of his pocket. The sooner she looked, the sooner it was over. Doug lined up the frame with her face but the shape of her head must have changed because the arms wouldn't reach her ears and the bridge fell into one eye socket. Instead he held them in front of her eyes.

She screamed. One bold cry. And then she screwed her eyes shut and pressed her face into Doug's shoulder. "Good god," she mumbled. "What happened?"

TWENTY

TORI HEARD A DIFFERENT VOICE. She opened her eyes a touch.

"Cold, yes, bitter, actually."

"Would you take a seat, please." Now it was Georgia who was speaking. "Out of the way, if you wouldn't mind."

"Sorry, yes, yes, of course," the woman replied.

Tori turned her head slowly in the direction of the woman's voice, familiar, somehow - a faint Yorkshire accent, disjointed words pushed out in a clutter. Was it someone doing their job or someone who didn't want to be there? Tori's eyelids hovered midway between open and closed, enough to see an elderly lady sitting with a straight back on an orange chair closer to Tori's feet than her face. She had a woollen hat pulled down over her ears.

"Oh," Georgia said. "It's Mrs Crawford, I beg your pardon. Lovely to see you here."

"Please, call me Ruby."

"Welcome Ruby and well done you."

Slowly, silently, Tori opened her eyes a little wider and blinked hard to try to regain some focus. She saw the bedding wrapped tightly around her. How long had she been asleep? She glanced up at the television, figures filled the screen as if trudging through deep water. The numbers on the digital clock on the table to her right were vibrating. She stared until they stood still.

And there she was: her mother. She stood up quickly, wedging herself between the orange chair and the bed frame, her hands loosely twisted together, hanging down awkwardly over dark cotton trousers. Tori waited for somebody to speak. Instead Georgia strode to the other side of the bed and placed a warm hand on Tori's forehead.

"Tell you what, sweetheart, I'll come back later, leave you two in peace."

The door closed and Ruby sat herself down once again only to spring back up as if she'd been scalded. She picked up the front legs of the chair and dragged it along to the head of the bed. She sat down gratefully.

"I don't like to stand," she said suddenly. "I had a hip replacement planned but it's on the back-burner until you're up and at 'em again." She smiled, leaned further in towards Tori and placed her hands in different positions around her face as if crafting a sculpture. "Let me look at you." She went to kiss her daughter on the forehead but stopped an inch before. She clutched her face instead, looked behind her, back to the front and from side to side. "Can you see my face Tori?" She edged so close their noses almost touched.

Tori could see the redness resting on Ruby's cheeks. Were those tears she saw, blurring her eyes? Her white hair was as neat as ever in its chin length bob where it peeped out from under the scalloped edge of the hat which Ruby had no doubt knitted herself. Her lips were wobbling. She never used to shake.

"Well, what can I tell you?" Ruby said, with the clipped brightness she paraded in times of heightened stress. She sat bolt upright, her ankles crossed together slightly behind her. She told Tori about the get-well wishes her friends had sent; how she was lucky, most of her friends had the wisdom, which doesn't necessarily come with age, to be able to sympathise with Tori's situation. "But we don't need to talk about that now," she said. "Carly's coping well, you'd be proud. She's so young to be dealing with you being so poorly."

Ruby stopped talking. She took off her hat, fanned her face and bowed her head, her fingers fidgeting with each other. "I'm talking too much." She picked up a newspaper from the bed and tossed it into her shopping bag.

Tori couldn't remember her mother ever sitting in that chair. Did she come when she was asleep? Perhaps she helped with feeding, and yet it was Doug who always spoke of banana milkshake. What time was it? She was looking forward to scrambled egg for lunch, the toasted soldiers a milestone for her dormant digestive system. Had her mother massaged her shoulders even though it was Jo she remembered playing with her feet?

Ruby took hold of Tori's hand and positioned herself in her eye line. "Are you awake Tori? Can you hear me love?" Tori looked back at the clock. What time had Ruby arrived? "It's confusing because your eyes are open, you see."

"What time is it?" Tori asked.

"Oh, darling, it's—" Ruby fumbled with her sleeve to reveal her own watch. It was 11.30. "Nearly lunch time. You're having scrambled—"

"—eggs." Tori looked at Ruby. Searching. "Have you been here before Mum? I don't remember." Her mother's mouth opened then closed again with only a gasp of air to show for the process. "Could you prop me up?"

Ruby took Tori under both arms and moved her awkwardly into a seated position. "You look more like the real you when you sit up," she said, stroking her hair. "This no washing your hair business has stood you in good stead."

"I'm glad you came, Mum."

Ruby cleared her throat. "Me too darling." She stopped stroking. "Shall I brush it?" she asked. Tori shook her head. Ruby stood up and gestured to a large shoe box which had been tipped onto its side to form a makeshift bookshelf on the windowsill. "I could read to you."

Tori said she'd like that but she couldn't make out the titles from where she was lying. She looked away from the books, wrinkled her nose. It was the most peculiar sensation. She sniffed. It was the pungent smell around her. She sniffed again. She knew the whiff. It was her mother. Too much coffee. Tori chuckled. The first thing she'd smelt since she'd been in hospital was Ruby's stale breath.

"What is it?" Ruby asked. "What's funny?"

Tori laughed again. "My sense of smell is coming back, Mum. Have you got some perfume or nail varnish or anything I can sniff?" Ruby dropped back down onto the edge of the bed and tipped the contents of her bag into the middle, spreading them into a fan shape to give the best overview of the items. She handed Tori an apple but the smell was weak. She tried a sachet of hand cream that had come free with a magazine. Tori could smell little more than the chemical process but liked the feeling of its waxy soapiness when Ruby smoothed it onto the back of her hand. Had she always known touch or was this new, too? Ruby suggested Tori keep the rest of the cream for later. A book! Tori had always loved the smell of them and the paperback in her mother's bag was well-thumbed and the pages yellowed. She pressed it open over her nose; couldn't let go. It was rented cottages on holiday, her tiny study where she'd first set up Party Planners. It was teaching jobs, late nights waiting for Nicky to get home, reading the classics aloud to the girls.

And it was the mobile library with her sister.

Tori gave the book back to her mother and only then did she notice the cover: *The Time Machine* by H. G. Wells.

"It was Lottie's," Ruby said unnecessarily, taking the book from Tori. "She never finished it." She stood up and smoothed her hands down her trousers. "Long time ago." She strode over to the bookshelf. Tori noticed she was limping.

She brought the whole box back to the bed and sat herself down next to it, removed each one by one, considered their titles and returned them without comment. She'd let Tori choose - not that she and Tori would reach the end of any novel before she left hospital, Ruby was quick to assure, but there would be plenty of time to continue once she was safely back at home. Ruby was going to be Tori's main carer while Doug was out at work.

"I'm going to look after you, Tori," she said. "I'll come every day. Look, I still have your spares." She held up a rusty key which might have opened her garden gate years ago, before the lock had seized, and a Yale key which might have fitted the door they had when the children were little but Tori was pretty sure that wasn't the key for the reclaimed oak door they had now. She tutted. A few weeks away from home and even the most basic of details were blurry. "Never got rid of them," Ruby said, almost to herself, "just put them on a different ring."

Tori sat back from the box of books and rested against her pillow. "I wish you'd sat with me, back then," she said, "read a few pages to me, perhaps."

Ruby stopped shuffling the books around, arranging them in height order. "I know."

"When I couldn't see anything, couldn't touch or smell, it might have helped me, you know, come back to life, even if I can't remember much about anybody being here now."

"I know," Ruby said again.

"You never came, did you?"

Ruby picked up the box of books and placed it carefully on the floor. She smoothed the sheet where it had been and let her eyes settle on the spot.

"When your child dies, you die," she said.

"But I was alive," Tori said, her voice the loudest she'd heard it since she'd woken in this bed. "I was still here, in an agonising twilight zone and you could have helped me come back to life."

Ruby nodded. "Yes," she said. "I know that but I was scared." She took Tori's hand in hers but Tori tugged it away. Her mother's lips were pulled together in so tight a circle that all the lines on her face seemed to follow - if she let go, air and noise would explode from her. Tori looked at the clock, barely ten minutes had passed.

"I'd like to have a sleep, if you wouldn't mind."

Ruby blinked hard a few times. She opened her mouth to speak but gathered herself instead and set about her nervous ritual of uncreasing her trousers with her hands.

"You'd like me to go," she said eventually. Tori pressed her cheek into her pillow. "Yes, of course," Ruby said. "I'll be back tomorrow."

She walked two steps towards the exit and, focused on the stark linoleum, she asked if Tori really needed her to leave.

"I could just sit with you so you have company."

Tori exhaled loudly which was Ruby's cue to rush back to her bedside.

"Talk to me, Tori!" But the only word Tori could find was, 'selfish' so she chose not to say anything at all.

"It's so hot in here," she said, "shall I buy you a fan, one of those hand-held ones, hmm?"

Tori smiled. "I'm not so hot."

"I can certainly bring you some fruit, your skin's very dry, and there's a fridge in the day room. Did you know?" Ruby would bring her some milk, a whole pint of fresh, cold milk, none of this warm sterilised stuff the hospital provided. "In a glass, Tori, as you like it."

Tori shook her head. There could be a whole dairy farm out there. She had no idea what was beyond her room. Besides, she hadn't drunk milk since she was a teenager and thought the nurses would take a dim view of glasses being brought into hospital.

"I'm so very tired," she said.

Ruby bent over and kissed Tori on the forehead. "I'll come tomorrow," she whispered. "And the next day, too."

TWENTY-ONE

ETTA PROPPED HERSELF against the wall at the shallow end of the newly refurbished pool. "Is twenty lengths enough?" she asked. "My heart isn't in it today."

"I thought you'd never ask." Sara threw her ear on to one shoulder to let out the water.

Sara was gazing at her and it made Etta even more conscious of her pale, blotchy skin and her collarbones protruding so far Andy could balance a pint on them, he'd said. She picked up her heel with one hand, forced it into her bony bottom to stretch out the thigh, and smiled to placate a couple of swimmers irritated by Etta and Sara's obstruction to a completed length.

This was the first time they'd swum together in the two months since Etta had begun her meteorology course. They used to pride themselves on this weekly early bird catch up, managing whole sentences with each stroke by dint of their upturned faces.

"Et, you have to eat more," Sara said.

With her hands firmly attached to the wall behind her, Etta was cycling through the water, staring at the lane ahead.

"Et, did you hear me?"

On this, the first full day off Etta had granted herself since the beginning of the course, she wished she was in bed. Usually, on the single day every week when she wasn't at the building society, university or hospital, chapters on isobars and cyclones, gulf streams and satellites poured through her headphones while she mopped, swept, tidied, washed, prepared, decorated and pruned her house, family and garden.

Today, Sara had persuaded her to swim, just for half an hour.

Etta stopped cycling, let go of the wall and placed both feet on the bottom of the pool. "I'm sorry, I'm miles away," she said. "Tori's front page again. I haven't had a chance to find out what's happened."

"It will be something and nothing."

"I'm going to go to the hospital tomorrow, to check everything's OK." Etta looked at Sara. "I've always been skinny."

Sara shook her head. She lowered her shoulders towards the water, pinched her nose and submerged her face. When she came back to the surface she said,

"I heard they're hopeful Tori will leave hospital before Christmas. And that will be good for everyone, the end of the line."

"Oh no!" Now Etta was much more animated. "This is just the start of it. The staff know very little of what Tori will be able to do. The final outcome will be as much about Tori's personality as how well her body has knitted back together. There's a good chance her sight will return to a certain extent but nobody has any hope of her recovering perfect vision. Physio could strengthen muscles if Tori commits to it but mobility in her joints can't really be tested until she's stood on her own feet for a length of time—"

"Breathe, Etta," Sara said dimly.

"—you know, her speech is particularly promising but nobody

will predict whether she'll speak as eloquently as before. Medical experts want to get her back to her own environment and her husband's support as soon as they possibly can—"

"Woah!" Sara pulled Etta up short by placing her hands on her shoulders. "Etta, stop! I meant for *you*, will that be the end of the line for you?"

Etta lowered herself back into the water and shivered as she stood up again. She took hold of the wall behind her and brought her knees to her chest.

"I'll give the M62 a go, just as soon as Tori's left hospital, a new beginning for both of us."

"I guess that's progress," Sara muttered. "It's no wonder you're tired." She pointed to Etta's knees as they skimmed the surface of the water. "You're all bone." She pushed herself away from the side. "We should really swim while we're here."

— — —

Etta sat down in the café that hung in the mezzanine level between the large and the small pool and placed a saucer over Sara's coffee. This place reminded her of a portable classroom with the counter at one end displaying rows of sandwiches and sticky buns like a primary school maths demonstration and the plastic-topped tables replacing the rows of desks with the same precision.

Sara bound up the iron steps, her blonde hair grabbed into a ponytail, full of the waves she hadn't had time to straighten away. One hand clutched at her forehead, the other held her phone to her ear. She looked up from her mobile, squinted at her watch and sat herself down opposite, smiling to register her thanks for the coffee.

"Etta," she said without any pretence of an introduction to the subject. "You see a link between Tori and Nikhita don't you?" She laid her hand lightly on Etta's shoulder. "I get it but I'd hoped you'd put it behind you."

Etta played with a twenty-pence coin in her lap. The café had been forgotten in the overhaul of the sports centre, even the change was dirty. "Yes I see a link, of course I do," she said. She gestured to Sara's vibrating phone but Sara shook her head.

"That chapter's closed, Etta."

The phone stopped ringing only to restart, a staccato shuffle over the tabletop. Etta picked it up and handed it to Sara. "Should you…?" Sara took it calmly from her and placed it in her bag.

"The chapter's closed," she said again.

Etta leaned in. "It should have been me in prison."

"No it shouldn't," Sara said, her lips tightening. "You committed no crime."

"Was deemed to have committed no crime," Etta corrected, and leaned back.

Sara stood up, her coffee untouched. "Nothing," she said, bundling her purse and phone into her floppy bag, "that happened to Tori Williams would change the decision that was made two years ago." She apologised for needing to leave, she had to be at her desk by 9.30.

Etta took Sara's hand and guided her back down. She thanked her. She was asking a lot of their friendship. She would always be grateful for her help through this difficult period in her life.

Sara shrugged her shoulders. "That's what friends do," she said, reluctantly balancing on the edge of her seat.

"But?"

"I can tell you still haven't told Andy."

Etta shrugged her shoulders, her eyes firmly fixed on a crumb on the table.

"Et, the stress is killing you." She picked up her forearm and let it flop back down on the table. "I can see it happening before my eyes."

"I should have told Andy, you're right—"

"Hallelujah!" Sara said, clapping a hand against her forehead.

"—but I didn't."

"Do it now!"

Etta shook her head and Sara stood up to leave again. Etta stood up, too.

"Please try to understand." She reached out to her friend who crossed her arms. "I've thought about it at lot, it's all I ever think about. But I can't get beyond why I should tell him so long afterwards."

"That's what partners do," Sara said quietly.

"Why should he have to shoulder the burden? He can't make it right."

Sara hoisted her bag back onto her shoulder and glanced at her watch. "People in relationships don't keep secrets of this magnitude from each other."

"That doesn't mean it's the right thing to do though, does it?" Etta said, pursing her lips. This secret was a dead weight, a penance. "I think it might be selfish," she said, "not fair on Andy."

Sara opened her mouth to speak but shook her head instead, mumbling that she had to leave. But she didn't move away, simply grunted.

"I'll tell you what's not fair." She let her bag fall from her shoulder, her hands on her hips. "Making me keep a secret from your partner, that's not fair."

"I feel dread—"

Sara put her finger to her lips. "Stop it, Etta," she said, "no more excuses. I can't be part of this." She picked up her bag again, stared at her friend. "You have to tell him, otherwise I will."

TWENTY-TWO

"**WPC DENBY.**" Doug cleared his throat. Everything he'd rehearsed sounded ridiculous now. It would have been easier if the officer had taken him through to an interview room, or even a cell, anything other than these hard chairs, side by side in the waiting room with the mustard coloured carpet, a poor attempt to disguise the vomit stains from a good proportion of the station's visitors, Doug assumed. Still, at least the waiting room was empty.

"WPC Denby," he repeated.

"Mr Williams," she said, allowing an elongated pause before saying, "how can I help?"

They exchanged pleasantries. Doug filled in a few gaps in WPC Denby's knowledge of Tori's continuing recovery, and acknowledged her good wishes for further advancement.

"I've seen enough of this kind of thing to know that the difference between survival and otherwise is little more than luck," she said, "but that after that, a patient's personality and their attitude are big factors in their quality of life."

"Right," Doug said, trying to shake the image of his wife really coming into her own whilst being beaten up in prison.

"I realise this is a little unorthodox," he said.

"It generally is when people ask for a favour without an appointment. Please continue."

The words flowed out in a rush. The content of the letter, how he and Carly believed that the letter writer had to be called Etta, and that Etta must want to help or she wouldn't have written the letter in the first place.

"That's generally how it works." WPC Denby stood up and ambled over to the flimsy water station in the corner. She returned with two plastic cups, steadied them both on the floor, lifted her chair and replaced it opposite Doug. She gestured to the cups and Doug handed one to her, leaving his own on the carpet.

"So, Mr Williams," she said, once she'd settled herself with one incongruously large foot up on the chair, wedged against an inner thigh, "let's see if I understand this correctly? Somebody with a name we think might be, 'Etta', hard to tell with her script and Lord, we ask you why this potentially 'Etta' person didn't email, it would have been so much simpler for us all—" She smiled at Doug, lifted her eyes up to the grey ceiling and allowed them to linger before focusing on him again.

"This Etta person—" She raised a hand to show that Doug was not invited to speak, "—writes a letter but leaves no contact details. I have to ask, with an ardent attempt to avoid patronising you, did you check for an address on the back of the envelope?"

Doug looked at WPC Denby with her thick make-up and orange splattered collar where it had missed, and shook his head. "I mean, yes," he said. "No sender address."

"No sender address," she repeated, her hands clasping the foot still pressed into her thigh, "that would make me wonder if the writer of the letter wanted any further contact with you at all."

Doug stood up but WPC Denby motioned him to sit back down, her cue to finally drop the foot so that her knee no longer tipped into Doug's personal space. She stretched out her legs to the other side instead, crossing them at the ankles for good measure.

"I would ask myself the same question," Doug said. "In fact, I continually ask myself the same, except that this Etta person said that she would call me because it would be better to speak in person. You don't offer to call someone if you don't want any contact with them, do you?"

WPC Denby stood up and crossed her arms. "In that case, Mr Williams, I suggest you wait for the lovely Etta to call."

"Obviously, but—"

"But?"

"But it's too late—"

WPC Denby held up her hands to stop him talking. "Mr Williams, let's speed things up here," she said. "Tell me you are not seriously expecting me to give you the contact details for somebody who has chosen not to have their details recorded, who has chosen not to be contactable by telephone by strangers, who did not leave a return address and may," she rolled her eyes, "or may not be involved in an investigation?"

Doug looked down at his hands resting awkwardly on his lap. WPC Denby announced that they were both busy people and suggested they end the chat there.

"No!" Doug looked up sharply. "I mean, that's not what I'm asking. I just wondered—" Oh God, he sounded stupid, "—if you did happen to know who I'm talking about, I mean, it isn't ridiculous that you might know her, she certainly knows a lot about the incident, if you did know her, perhaps you could—"

"Could what exactly?"

"—put in a good word for me?" he said, his tiny voice an

accurate representation of the humiliating embarrassment he felt.

WPC Denby laughed, an enormous, single guffaw which she chose to throw in the direction of the colleague behind the counter who confirmed the shared amusement with his own fixed smile and shake of the head.

Then she stopped smiling and moved swiftly over to the exit. "Mr Williams," she beckoned him over with a great swoop of her arm, "thank you for giving me the story of the week. Now, please leave the building so that I can get on with some police work." She flung open the door.

Doug allowed himself a moment before standing up.

"Mr Williams," she said, still flapping an arm in the air. "You're a headteacher, aren't you?"

He nodded.

"Lord, help the next generation," she said, shaking her head.

Doug reached the exit and looked at her. He did his utmost to instil civility and respect in his pupils and to strive that no young person under his care should ever be made to feel stupid.

He smiled but apologised as he caught WPC Denby's little toe with the edge of his shoe as he hurried past her without a goodbye.

TWENTY-THREE

THE BANNERS BILLOWED then sprang back, taut again - billow, taut, billow, taut. Etta had already read them. 'Liar!' they shouted out, 'Killer!', 'Sack the Judge!' And the one she repeated over and over: 'Etta Dubcek pay for your crime!' Etta dropped the rolling pin on the floor with a bang, her floury hands jumping to her ears.

"It's too late now," she shouted. "Don't you see? I repent."

"What's too late, Mama?" Johan asked, strolling into the kitchen with the strap of his school bag wound around one leg, his scruffy trainers packed with mud. "What have you pent?"

Etta flung her hands back down to her sides and spun around to face her son. "I ... it's complicated."

Johan stopped, surveyed his mother. "Why did you put your hands on your ears and why is there flour on the floor?"

"I'm such a dreamer aren't I, Johan?" Etta drew him into a hug. "Did you thank Tom's mummy for the lift?"

Johan stepped away, stood on the back of each trainer to remove them and kicked them into the corner of the kitchen. "You weren't dreaming Mama," he said, "you were speaking."

Etta reached out for his hand before he could leave the room and picked up his abandoned school bag from the floor. "I had a bad thought, Johan, but it's gone away now." She sat down on the two person battered sofa, a hand-me-down from Andy's mother who'd suggested on more than one occasion that a re-covering of the balding brown cord would give it a superb spruce up.

"Come and read to me Johan!" She reached into his school bag for his reading book. "Nearly too heavy for this," she said, as he shuffled around on her lap to get comfortable. "I'm not going to think about that bad thought anymore."

He started reading. He was clearly too tired, would have preferred to have been outside playing football with the older boys who lived next door. But Etta didn't want to let him go, needed to hold him, hug him fulsomely.

When Andy entered the room with Adriana at his side, Etta's chin had sunk to her son's shoulder. He was still reading in a staccato fashion. Hastily she wiped the film of water from her eyes as Andy approached.

"We're just having a moment, aren't we Johan?"

Johan placed his arms clumsily around his mother's neck and kissed her on her cheek. "Done my reading." He jumped down from her lap and asked her if he could, please, go and play football.

Andy patted Adriana on the bottom, told her that she should make use of the last few minutes before tea, and sat himself down on the arm of the sofa.

"I heard you," Andy said.

Etta gulped. "It was a funny turn, nothing more. I admit I'm a bit stressed." She moved closer to him. "No kiss?" She strained her neck to reach him. But he stood up, walked over to the work surface, picked up the rolling pin, placed it on the side and asked where the dustpan and brush were these days.

Etta sighed and joined Andy. She leaned against the work surface and threaded her arms around his waist. "Please, just be patient."

But Andy wrenched her hands from him. "You're covered in flour." He strode over to the large window, which covered much of the back wall, and stared at the small, walled garden, his eyes dancing over the clumps of forgotten dandelions. "It's Tori Williams," his focus was still outside, "ever since her, your dreams have come back and what if you 'eff' and 'blind' in your daydreams as well as your nightmares?" Etta walked slowly over to the window to join him, resting her hand hesitantly on his back. "There's nothing sexy about swearing in front of the children," he said.

They watched in silence as Johan and Adriana tussled with each other on the neglected grass until Andy shrugged Etta's hand from him and said that everything had been getting better.

"Remember the course, Etta? This stupid meteorology thing, where we put our lives on hold so you realise your dream."

Etta gasped so Andy quickly qualified, "It's a dream I support because it has a purpose and is an investment. But—"

"But?" Etta whispered.

"This obsession with this woman has taken over and we're going backwards." He shook his head. "I'm at a total loss as to why you can't get over the first accident. Have you forgotten that's what it was," he said, "an accident?" Etta looked away but Andy followed her eyes.

"Etta?"

"Yes of course." She managed a smile more suitable to a confrontation with a customer. "People still play a role in accidents though."

"A role?" he leaned a little too heavily against the inadequate single glass pane. "Your role was 'blameless'. Surely?"

"I don't know how you can be blameless if you nearly killed someone," she blurted out.

Andy shook his head, smacked the palm of his hand against his forehead. "You didn't choose to do it." He enunciated each word with unnecessary emphasis.

"You can't understand." Her voice was barely a whisper. "You weren't there."

"So, your therapy is to spend time stalking your new role model, Tori Williams, a woman who killed people because she couldn't put down her phone?"

Etta nodded. "A stupid, reckless moment," she said. "She's not a killer."

"Not stupid, Etta, fatal. She was complicit, you weren't. Surely you can see that? You were involved in an accident. She caused a crash. They're two entirely different things."

"Entirely different, yes." She squinted at the clock. "I have to get the pie in," she said. "Adriana's request." His mouth fell open and then snapped shut. "Bought pastry, obviously, incompetent mother that I am..."

Andy took hold of her wrist to stop her walking away. She knew this look of scrutiny, his effort to decipher in the merest twitch of the face of the woman whose expressions he knew so well, what he could possibly do to make this all go away. Etta wrestled herself free. If he really wanted to know, he'd ask.

He followed her over to the work surface and shouted over the top of the clatter of pans falling out of the cupboard.

"Stop all contact with this criminal, this killer, and get on with the course! That's what will change your life, not some social outcast."

Finally, the pans stopped spinning but next there was a great sound of smashing glass from the green house. They rushed back to the window. Adriana was crying, Johan hugged her.

"Nobody's looking after them," Andy said, inclining his face up towards the ceiling to enlist the help from God. He turned, poised to stride out of the room, but Etta touched his forearm. She'd sort out the children. She'd study properly and wouldn't utter a single obscenity in dream or reality. She kissed his cheek. "Let's leave this here."

But Andy said no and that it wasn't enough. Once the first, 'no' had drifted from his lips he repeated it, more forcefully every time, as if each round gave him more conviction. "No," he said, shaking his head. "No more Tori Williams. This is the deal—"

"—a deal?"

Andy nodded, said that Etta had to stop visiting the hospital, hanging around drinking tea, or whatever she did with that woman's mother. "And stop lying to me that you're at university when you're not."

Etta gulped. "Yes," she whispered. "I'll try."

Andy looked at her, "You'll try?" But before she could answer Adriana burst into the house screaming and flinging herself into Etta's arms because she'd cut herself on a splinter of glass. Etta bustled her over to the sink and held her finger under the tap. It was a tiny cut. Andy followed her. "Is that it?" he hissed into her ear. "You'll try?"

"What's the deal?" Etta said.

"The deal," Andy said, attempting to scoop up some of the excess flour on the worktop but deciding instead to shove it onto the floor. "There is no deal," he said.

TWENTY-FOUR

DOUG SLAMMED THE DOOR to his tired Volvo, which, like him, needed a full service and a thorough clean. He marched towards the side entrance to school. Through the gloom of a recent sunrise with a smattering of rain, he could see Steve loitering at the main entrance across the staff car park, making no effort to hide. He wouldn't make it easy for him. Steve appeared to know the rules and would be long gone before there was any sign of even the most conscientious of his students. But his constant presence unnerved the staff and the invasion of his own personal space unnerved Doug, too.

Doug stood still, a few paces from the door, considered a new tack.

"Morning Steve!" he called. "Over here." He whistled the theme tune to Dad's Army as Steve approached, cautiously at first, wary of booby traps, but fairly skipping towards him now.

"So," Doug announced, his briefcase on the ground between his legs and his hands on his hips. "I will ask you this once and only this once. Is there a specific reason why you spend your entire working week – not to mention the weekend – shadowing me and my family like some perpetual Scooby Doo meets Groundhog Day episode?"

"No need to be flippant, Mr Williams," Steve said, with that ridiculous stick-on grin which Doug would like permission to rip from his face.

"You know," Doug said, as Steve withdrew the hand Doug hadn't shaken, sliding it into his pocket, "I could understand at the beginning. This was an enormous human-interest story. But you all got your wish: Tori Williams is Public Enemy Number One—"

"That wasn't my wish—"

"—people everywhere, regardless of whether they've used a phone while driving," Doug said, "are feeling particularly pious because they've never killed anyone. And bytheway," he added quickly, pointing to Steve's hand in his pocket, "feel free to record this, I have no secrets."

Steve removed his hand and said, "Thanks very much, mate, very kind," as he hopped from foot to foot in the October damp cold. "But I have to correct you. I don't feel any more or less pious as a result of your wife's behaviour because I've never come close to killing anyone."

What was that look he had? Doug had always assumed it was an air of smugness but occasionally the smile dropped and Steve's eyes lost their shine.

"Has it ever occurred to you that if you spoke to my wife you might find that she didn't need you to make her hate herself? Tori has an enormous sense of right and wrong," he said, "and I fear the day she is well enough to be told what happened." Doug picked up his briefcase and put it down again. He pulled down his shirtsleeves. Finally, he'd managed to put his point across and it felt cathartic.

Steve crossed his arms. "No," he said, slowly, "I haven't considered it and I'd be interested in hearing about that."

"Then perhaps," Doug said, faltering a little, "you might turn your head from the Global's sensationalism to the humanity in all this mess."

"Absolutely," Steve said, "that's exactly why I'm here." He'd finally stopped smiling and the novel grace and reasonableness were just as unnerving as the Cheshire Cat routine. "But just so we're being upfront," he said, retrieving his phone from his pocket, flipping it over in his hands a few times and holding it at arm's length to show that it was indeed recording, "it's what *she did*, it's not *what happened*. You mean, when you 'tell her what *she* did.'"

Doug shook his head. "Pity your loved ones if you are ever in my situation." He turned on his heel, chuntering to himself as he walked swiftly back to the side entrance. He ignored the sound of Steve's feet pacing behind him until he felt a hand on his shoulder.

"I have some understanding," Steve said.

Doug pondered whether to request that Steve just piss off now but he was replaying in his mind what had already been recorded and wondering if he'd been careless. Finally, he put his briefcase on the ground, looked at his watch, turned to Steve and said that staff would be arriving soon.

"Just tell me what you want from me, make it easier for both of us."

"Sure." Steve tightened the band in his ponytail and wove a couple of wayward strands of hair behind his ear. "I want the first interview when Tori leaves hospital."

Doug threw back his head and affected a peal of laughter. "You?" He laughed more spontaneously now. "You wouldn't be my first choice." He crossed his arms in front of his chest. "Come on, pitch it to me!"

Steve crossed his arms, too, the pair facing each other a foot apart, Doug looming over the diminutive reporter.

"You're a little naïve," Steve said.

"How so, clever clogs?"

Steve pulled his arms even tighter across his chest and said that he was a good writer, Doug might be better to stick with the devil he knew.

But Doug was confused. "You're a photographer, aren't you?"

"More of an investigative journalist," he said. "Freelance, with a special interest in this case."

Doug couldn't bring himself to ask about the 'special interest' but when he finally managed a "How so?" Steve's guard was ratcheted back up to full.

"Not so fast," he said. "You give me the interview and I'll tell you all you need to know."

Doug shook his head. "Your turn to be naïve because you need an interview with my wife so much more than I need to know about your sordid little motives."

"Someone will get an interview with your wife," Steve said, hands firmly wedged on his hips. "The Global, for instance."

"Never."

"Don't blame you. The dross they print about a woman who made a mistake!"

"It shouldn't be allowed."

"A very foolish mistake," Steve said.

Doug shook his head, muttered that he wasn't going to fall for that one and made his way back to the entrance where he keyed in his pass code behind a cupped hand.

"Fool," he heard Steve say from behind him. Doug pushed open the door and felt the cold of an empty school an hour before central heating kicked in. He left his briefcase on the floor and raced back out of the door, grabbing Steve's shoulder to stop his slow pace. Steve dropped his phone into which he'd been recording.

"Mr Williams!" He bent down to pick up the phone, his smile from earlier returned to his face. "You're back!"

"Investigative journalist you say?"

Steve nodded.

"Could you find me someone in return for an interview with my wife?" he asked. "Someone helpful to her plight?"

"I expect I could."

— — —

Steve pulled open his car door. By the time he'd climbed inside, he'd already taken his phone from his pocket and, muttering, "Stealing sweets from babies," clicked on Twitter. He scrolled straight to #TextingTori and flicked through the latest tweets.

"Thank you very much." He skimmed through the trending list, a grin on his face. "Like I said: fool."

TWENTY-FIVE

TORI WOKE TO THE SMELL of sausages. She lay for a few moments, savouring the idea of a casserole, luxuriating in the extra dimension her renewed sense of smell had given her. She could hear clearly and see a manageable representation of life. She couldn't really taste what she was offered but she had her memory and her imagination, she could pretend the hospital meals tasted like the restaurant version if she chose.

But her favourite sense, she'd decided, was touch. Did she appreciate how much she'd relied upon it before it was taken away? The sheets pressing gently on her stomach, a hair in her eye, crumbs from Carly's biscuit caught in her bed. She'd even rejoiced in the first shots of pain from the injections and tubes, because to be able to feel her environment was to 'be'. She learnt the depth of the scars on her face through her fingers. The flaky dry skin on her hands felt twenty years older than the last time she'd moisturised them but who cared? Her fingers had lamented the condition of her hair and confirmed the softening of the skin on her lips following the reintroduction of proper food.

But most of all, touch meant closeness. Currently it meant her mother holding her hand.

"Fancy you being here again!" Tori said, but she recoiled at her acerbic tone and quickly added, "That's nice."

"You've been asleep," Ruby said softly. "It's 5pm but they've saved you some tea." She smoothed Tori's hair as she'd done when she was a child. "I'll fetch it, stretch my legs."

"No," Tori said. "Please stay."

Ruby smiled. "Of course," she said, "of course I'll stay." She switched off the television which loomed from a pair of brackets in the top corner of the room. Everybody switched off the television when Tori woke up. She'd have quite liked to watch the news, caught up on what she'd missed since she'd become a hermit.

Ruby looked across the four walls, admiring the collage of memorabilia, which now stretched over half of a second wall as well as the area around the door. She looked at Tori, then back again. "Can you see this?" she asked. Tori shook her head.

Tori leaned on her mother as they stood and pointed to moments in her life extending the whole distance from the baby in her christening gown, 'face like a bulldog', Ruby admitted for the first time, to last summer.

They moved to Tori's first ice-skating session. Ruby pointed out Lottie gripping her little sister's arm to keep her upright for the photo.

"You were only five, you did very well." The two women looked at each other. Nothing came of Tori's ice-skating. It was Lottie who won the medals.

"Look at all that hair," Tori said, tapping a photo of herself in baggy green uniform, sporting thick, wild bunches, one higher than the other. "Eight years old. Just before the bobble hat."

Ruby swallowed. "Yes, you never did say who gave you the idea."

Tori looked at her mother then back to the photos. "It was my idea," she said. "I didn't know it was a sign of mourning and still practised in some religions. Did you know it's called a 'Tonsure'?"

Ruby shook her head.

"I was quite disappointed when Mr Eagle gave it a name in RS. Bloody cold head though, how long did I keep it up?"

"A good year or so," Ruby said. "Did you always shave it yourself?"

"Yes."

Ruby grimaced. "We didn't talk much then did we?" Tori's gaze was fixed on the wall ahead. "We could talk about it now?" The question lingered. "We have lots of time."

Tori looked at her mother and back to the collage of photos, her finger hovering over a photo of Lottie holding up her O-level certificate.

"It was my way of dealing with it," she said. The head shaving was this eight-year-old's effort to make sure she wasn't forgotten under the deluge of grief that accompanied her sister's death. It worked for her. People noticed her. "Even seemingly ignoring it, skirting miles around the fact that my mane of long, dark hair had been replaced with baldness, was a way of showing they'd noticed. For the child of grieving parents, it was," Tori said, "very helpful."

"I was hurting too badly. I didn't see it."

"I know," Tori said. Her bald head appeared on the day after Lottie's funeral and her bunches were consigned to the part of her life when she'd had a sister. It was natural to her. "I found it easy to see the new me staring back from the mirror. My life had changed. I'd changed."

Ruby looked at Tori. "Childhood isn't supposed to be so sad," she said. "I let you down."

"You did your best."

Tori had been standing too long, felt her weight pressing down on her mother's shoulder. She turned back to the wall, leaned a hand against it for support and pointed with the other to a photo of Ben Nevis. She could only see edges and mounds in the picture of her and Doug at the top but it was enough to give her a grateful smile. It was Doug who'd introduced her to the mountains and in the twenty years thereafter, there hadn't been a month without an ascent of some sort. They were fiercely proud of being the founding members of their climbing club.

"None of us are perfect parents," she said, as much to break the silence. "Not even me," and gave a bleat of a laugh. But Ruby let out a stifled, 'no we're not,' instead of a wry chuckle and said,

"Can you see what that is?"

Tori peered in closer. "Two up, two down," she said, "first house with Doug."

"You can remember it! That's astonishing."

Tori beamed. "Of course Mum, I remember it all. Every detail. Everything until I came here."

Her mother jolted, upsetting Tori's balance. "You remember?"

"I think so."

"That's you, us, me, everything," she asked, "but not the accident itself?"

"Not the crash I caused when I was on my phone," Tori said quietly. "If that's what you mean."

Ruby's hand rushed to her mouth. "I was told not to talk about it."

Tori asked her mother to help her back to bed. She got so tired, she could only stand for minutes at a time and even then, only with support. When she was seated again, propped up, she said slowly,

"I know I texted. I see a phone every time I close my eyes." Ruby moved from the edge of the bed and back towards the door. "What else is going on? Is there a problem with insurance?" she asked. "Won't they pay?"

Ruby shook her head. "No problem with insurance."

"I've got points on my licence, is that it?" But before Ruby could answer, Tori grimaced. It was more than points, she'd lost her licence, that was it. "Well, from the state of my face," she said, trying to catch her mother's eyes as they flitted from side to side, always a flash before Tori could grab them, "I probably deserved it."

Ruby's gaze rested on the bed covers. "It isn't that," she said. "I'm not supposed to tell you."

Tori beckoned Ruby over to a spot on the bed next to her. "Mum, you're scaring me now."

Ruby didn't move, her hands covering her face. "Love, I know the pain of losing a child and a husband."

"I know you do."

"I know what it's like to lose people more dear to you than anything in the whole world."

"Yes Mum, better than most."

Ruby cleared her throat and walked back to the bedside. She sat down next to Tori, crossed and uncrossed her legs, stared at her hands folded in her lap.

"Mum?"

"When you sent that text," she lifted her eyes to Tori's, stared into them, "you didn't just injure yourself." She inhaled then exhaled, grasped Tori's hands, her gaze still fixed on her daughter's. "You killed a couple: a man and a woman. They were married - very young."

Tori's mouth fell open. She gulped, pulled her hands from her mother's. Ruby's lips parted to speak but closed again before voicing any words.

"Say something, Tori," she said eventually.

"Red," Tori said. "Their car was red."

"You remember?"

Tori nodded. It all made sense. She'd killed people. That's why people didn't visit. "That's why Nicky hates me," she said.

Ruby picked at an imaginary mark on the corner of Tori's pillow. "Nicky found the media attention particularly difficult and has moved to Australia with Kyle," she said. "We're all going to the wedding in December. It's something to look forward to."

"Nicky's getting married?" Tori didn't know Kyle, nor that Nicky had a boyfriend. Her mother dipped her head. "Please, no more surprises," Tori whispered.

Ruby stared at her. She stood up, her whole body rising and falling before sitting back down again, this time not on the chair but next to Tori on the edge of her bed. She puffed out her cheeks, shook her head.

"Mum?"

Ruby said that what she was about to tell her was the last of it, that there was nothing else Tori didn't know. She laid her arm awkwardly around her shoulders.

"You're going to tell me there were more people," Tori said. She pulled away from her mother, stared at her lips, tried to anticipate the words before they were spoken. Finally, Ruby whispered,

"Another family, yes."

"Please," Tori said, her head shaking from side to side. When Ruby didn't answer she grabbed her hands, tears dripping down her face and said that she had to tell her, she had to know.

"It was their baby," Ruby said.

TWENTY-SIX

TORI SAT ON THE EDGE of the bed dressed in a pair of linen trousers which were too big, even with the drawstring at full tightness, and a lilac t-shirt which broadcast the disintegration of her breasts. She didn't really care. It was Doug who'd apologised; he hadn't known what clothes to bring in for her. Anna was a little curt when she reminded Doug that there was a frost outside.

He guided Tori's foot to the floor then focused on the loops of her laces, pulling them in opposite directions. This was the first time Tori had worn shoes for two months. Doug had bought a *sensible* pair, to wear only until she got her stability back, he'd promised. They were a size smaller, Tori never knew that feet lost weight too.

"Don't cry, pet, you'll set me off," Anna urged. "We'll miss you, you know that."

How could anybody miss her? She was a killer. While her every need had been tended to in hospital, a married couple had been buried. If she hadn't been driving along the M62 that night, if she hadn't lifted her phone to text her husband about something which was all under control anyway, they would still be alive. And then there was the baby. Ruby had never got over losing her sixteen-year-old daughter. How would the baby's parents ever come to terms with the fact that somebody else's selfish stupidity meant that their child would never grow up? Tori gulped and found herself retching. Anna grabbed the cardboard hat used for vomit and thrust it under Tori's chin.

"All right, love?" Ruby said. "You doing too much?"

Anna stroked Tori's hair. The bowl only caught tears. "Stay strong, pet."

Doug shook his head, pulled up Tori's sock. "You have a good cry, Torr," he said, raising his head to glare at Ruby. "You see?"

Ruby held his stare. "And let them tell her?" she snapped. "Better us than them."

"You had no right," Doug said, slamming Tori's second foot back down to the floor just as soon as the laces were tight. "All these years—"

"That's enough!" Ruby said, her finger jumping to her lips.

Tori signalled to Anna that she could remove the bowl as she attempted to smear away the tears with the back of her good hand.

"Please," she whispered. "I can't cope with you two falling out."

Doug cleared his throat and got to his feet. Tori was right, a united front was needed. "The parasites will be waiting." He threw an arm out towards the window to emphasise the terrifying outside.

– – –

"Texting Tori is a killer!" the protestors chanted. 'Killers behind bars!' demanded their banners. But a few of the placards were lowered in silence as the horde saw Doug wheel fifty-one-year old Tori Williams out through the hospital doors, looking like she'd been around for eight decades. Her forehead was the only area of white skin untouched by the scars that shaped her face, and with one eye now slightly higher than the other she looked at the journalists and protestors as if permanently asking a question.

The hospital's press officer had briefed Doug in the art of not answering. With his eye firmly fixed on the concrete a metre ahead of him, Doug steered Tori's wheelchair through the crowd in the direction of the relative sanctuary of Jo's car. The hundred metres of car park stretched out ahead of them like the distance between England and France. He and Tori would wait with Jo and Amelie until Ruby and Carly had pulled off the decoy in the neighbouring ambulance, guiding the gaggle of journalists to the rehabilitation centre and supposed place of convalescence for Tori over the next few weeks. Leaking Tori's fictitious whereabouts to the press had given Doug a great dollop of pleasure. The centre was thirty miles from where Tori was really headed.

Tori heard kind words being spat in her direction.

"...glad to be out?"

"...have her home?"

"...pleased with recovery?"

"Where's your other daughter Tori?" she heard one journalist shout. "Has she fallen out with you?" Tori concentrated on the path in front of her, as they'd practised.

"Will you be getting a new phone?"

"Are you going back to work?"

"Is it true Party People have sacked you?"

"Don't be ridiculous, it's my own business," Tori spluttered, louder than intended.

"How do you plead, Tori?"

"Guilty!" she said. What had they expected her to say?

— — —

"Tori!" she heard Doug say sharply in her ear. "Keep to the plan. Jeez!"

The security officers struggled to keep the weight of the crowd from encroaching on Tori's chair.

"Back off!" she heard them growl continuously. "Away!" More police appeared and joined forces with the swaying chain of arms offering thin protection against the mob.

"Lord get me through this," Tori heard Doug moan to himself.

"How do you feel about your actions, Tori?" someone shouted. "Horrendous!"

This time it was the press officer's turn for reproof. He moved to the second part of the plan, sooner than anticipated.

"I have a statement," he shouted. "Space, please." Some people shuffled a few inches backwards. "Give me room to breathe." Tori felt herself being pushed faster now towards the allotted car. "It's your choice," she heard the press officer boom out behind her. "Do you want to hear this statement or not?" The circle of journalists re-orientated themselves to fix on the press officer's words. As planned, Doug managed to move forward without too much commotion, forging a path through the crowd of hostile spectators who anticipated the speech with great excitement.

"Innocent until proven guilty," they heard behind them. "Needs time to recuperate," and, "Will answer to this country's judicial system." Tori's wheelchair continued forward, the police officers silent now, motionless with their backs to the crowd, their arms splayed out against their allocation of the front row. Tori wasn't supposed to look but couldn't help but catch the eye of one of them. She smiled to show her gratitude. The police officer gave a slight nod in response. A small woman behind him peered over the police officer's arm and jabbed a finger in Tori's direction.

"Laughing now, are ye, ye bitch? You'll be laughing on t'other side of your face once this country gets their 'ands on ye."

Tori gasped. "Don't!" she heard Doug hiss as he gripped her shoulder.

As the lacklustre statement reached its small crescendo, Doug rushed Tori the last steps to Jo's car. They smoothed shut the back door a couple of seconds before those of the ambulance crashed loudly together. Meanwhile, Ruby and Carly had launched themselves into the non-emergency ambulance with as much commotion as the seventy-eight-year old and her granddaughter could muster. The ambulance slid away from the car park as designed; its role in the deception begun.

With his hood pulled up around his face, Doug sat perfectly still in the passenger seat at the front of Jo's specially selected Ford Focus. Only his eyes moved. He used the rear-view mirror to look through the blackened windows as the journalists left the area on motorbikes and in cars.

"I feel sorry for the folk in the rehabilitation centre," Jo said, "I wouldn't relish that lot on my doorstep!"

"They're not there yet," Doug said gravely, "who knows how long this will give us. Days, hours, perhaps only minutes, it's anyone's guess."

"It depends whether we tricked them all, I suppose," Jo said, tentatively starting the ignition as the sound of engines revving out of the car park eventually dwindled. Amelie, holding Tori's shaking hand in the back, turned towards the rear windscreen.

"Oh God," she jerked her head back to the front, "someone's watching us!"

Doug pushed Amelie out of his eye line and saw a small woman with long, chestnut brown hair, smiling in their direction. Her hands were stuffed into her deep pockets and there was no sign of a phone or camera.

"I think she might be OK," Doug said, letting out his breath. "I've seen her before. She stepped in when I had my tête-à-tête with the journalist, calmed things down a bit."

"Maybe she's our guardian angel," Tori croaked.

"Well," said Doug, "I haven't been charged for it have I?"

After a few minutes, Jo was able to increase her speed up the A61 towards Ripon and some of the tight air around them seeped away.

"OK chick?" she called behind her.

Tori couldn't answer. The trees were disappearing too fast, the sky morphing into the Yorkshire Dales behind as they got closer to Deepbeck. The world Tori once saw clearly had merged into a slurry of greys and greens before her best functioning eye.

"Need to get used to it, got to get used to it," she murmured. Amelie squeezed her hand tighter. The radio insisted on ballads; slow, rhythmical heartache squealing from the speakers in the front. Tori shook her head and shook it again,

"No red. Please, no red metal today. No red—" Her hands rushed to the silver acorn around her neck, a birthday present from Doug given to her only moments before. Amelie whispered in her ear,

"Why don't you close your eyes for a minute? We're nearly there."

Tori shook her head. "No! I must see it. Only way to survive, confront it." She put her hands to her ears and moaned as if in her sleep. "But that sound: the engine, the tunes, the wind—"

Amelie leant forward and tapped Jo on the shoulder, "Could we slow down a bit?"

"No," Doug snapped back. "I'm sorry, Tori," he strained his neck to see her frightened face in the rear-view mirror. "They could have already worked it out. We have to keep our advantage."

Tori wasn't listening. "I know that sound," she said. "I remember the engine, like it was in the wrong gear. And no sirens, I thought I was OK because there was no siren."

"You remember the ambulance ride?" Doug asked. "But you were barely alive!"

"I just recall how it felt," Tori said. She screwed up her eyes, delving further into the detail. "Everyone was attentive. Voices asked if I could hear them and told me not to move."

"I guess you didn't know why you were going to hospital," Amelie said. Tori looked back out of the window. Life was certainly darker since she'd been apprised of the facts.

Tori gasped as Jo turned the car left into Harewell Lane. The grass was overgrown and there was a car missing on her long drive but nonetheless, this was unmistakably home. The rosemary was doing as well as ever but she would have to get her clippers on the privet hedge. She looked at her right arm, squashed into her side at a 90-degree angle as it always was these days. The privet would be a job for next summer.

Doug hurriedly extracted the wheelchair from the boot and unfolded it in only twelve seconds as he'd practised. Jo and Amelie manoeuvred Tori out of the car and lowered her into the chair. Her landing was a little too rushed and as Tori winced at the pain in her hip she wished her hand was capable of rubbing the area.

A woman scurried past without a word and shot towards the back of her house.

"Hi Mary!" Doug called to the receding bottom of his neighbour and friend of twelve years. He closed the boot and placed his hands on the grips of the wheelchair as if he'd been pushing his wife all his life.

"It's not her," they heard Mary explain to her husband, once she was safely around the corner and in the sanctuary of her own garden. "It's what she's done I have a problem with."

"Not a great welcome party," Tori suggested managing an attempt at an uneven smile for her husband who'd bent down to quickly kiss her cheek. "Never did much care for balloons and banners. All that helium," she said, "can't possibly be good for the environment."

Doug looked at Tori and for the first time since they'd left the ward, he smiled. "Good to have you back."

Tori wanted to enter through the front of their 1930's detached family home. Doug had painstakingly renovated the heavy door last year, taking a toothbrush to the encrusted grime in the stained glass panel. She noticed that he'd fitted the old school bell above.

"Please Doug?" she squeezed his hand. But he shook his head. He had every inch of the journey worked out and would not allow sentiment to alter his plan. Instead, he wheeled Tori over the crunchy gravel to the back of the house, Tori clutching the sides of the chair as best she could as it lurched from side to side, while Jo and Amelie carried the bags.

He felt for the key to the patio door but faltered before taking it from his inside pocket. The sound of a car engine cutting out abruptly, the clunk of a door and the chilling sound of hurried footsteps up to the front of his house, were apparent to all.

TWENTY-SEVEN

ETTA SANK INTO THE SOFA and pulled Adriana up from the floor of the dining area where she'd been introducing a family of Sylvanian mice to Mr Dog who was inclined to sell the lucky mice some fruit Catherine Wheel lollies from the Sylvanian sweet cart, if they remembered to say please.

"Let's have a snuggle, you," she said, nuzzling her face into the gap at the back of Adriana's long brown hair where the school plaits had been. Adriana bounced on her lap, humming.

"One man went to mow, went to mow—" Etta sang.

"—A meadow!" Adriana continued with a clap of her hands and veritable jumping up and down on Etta's insubstantial thighs.

With a nod to the tune, Etta sang, "That's right Adriana, and oh what was he wi-ith?"

"His dog!"

"Two men went to mow, went to mow a meadow—"

"Two men, one man and his dog," Adriana completed at the top of her voice, her face upturned to the ceiling as she shouted, "went to mow a meadow."

Another flash, just inside her eye line. Work wouldn't ring her at home. Her rules. Same for everyone. She'd turned her phone to silent, deliberately left it on the worktop at the kitchen end of the room, but couldn't pretend that its jumping across the surface wasn't distracting. She'd listened to an article on the radio as she'd driven to pick up the children from school earlier. Young mothers were spending so much time on their phones that their children were growing up 'stimulatory impaired'. She'd walked to the school gate with a not insignificant amount of relief as she'd considered the stories she and the children had read together and continued to do so. But when her phone had beeped a hundred yards from the car and Johan and Adriana, with their hands squeezed into hers on both sides, had simultaneously dropped them, and come to an immediate halt so that she was able to take the phone from her pocket, she'd retrieved it, noted the Twitter notifications and returned it to her pocket feeling a little chastened.

Etta and Adriana sang together, interrupted by sporadic squeals of laughter as Etta tickled her daughter under her arms. Once started Etta was compelled to continue, reaching the never seen before heights of thirty-four men and the dog, until Johan entered the room and presented her with an excuse to halt proceedings with a sigh and an exclamation of how fabulous Adriana's counting was.

"We did sums today, Mama, and Mr Percy says if I carry on at this rate I'll be doing the hundreds next week."

"You don't know what that means!" Johan said, jumping onto the sofa, squeezing in next to his mother who greeted him with a little dig in the ribs just as Adriana jumped from her lap, pressed both hands onto her hips and told her brother that she'd known what hundreds were for *forever* and it meant she could do counting.

Etta left the pair to continue their discussion and wandered over to the kettle instead, allowing herself a nonchalant glance at the screen while she made herself a cup of tea. Every beep had come from Twitter. She was being harassed by notifications and by one man in particular: @investcribb. The tweets were OK, nothing too personal or provocative, and surprisingly interesting. She might have expected his tweets to have a financial leaning and he'd not included any detail in his profile. But instead he spoke of little other than #Toristext. The text: *rather than pillory one person, shouldn't we vow not to #textwhilstdriving ourselves*, was what drove her to follow him originally. Last night he'd tweeted: *have to ask, why #text is seen as a worse crime than #speeding*. She saw his point. But phew! That had caused a reaction in the Twittersphere. It had got #textwhilstdriving trending again, not to mention #twowrongsdontmakearight and #killerstoprison. Might Tori not go to prison? And had somebody leaked to the press that Tori might not go to prison? WPC Denby wasn't so unprofessional as to mention it to her. Mind you, WPC Denby wasn't Etta's biggest fan; it was fairly unimaginable that they'd share any cosy secrets. Perhaps it was the length of time the story had stayed in the public's vision which encouraged strong opinions on Tori's fate. It seemed to Etta that every time Tori Williams so much as learnt to grimace or cough the whole crash was pumped into life again.

Etta took the milk bottle from the fridge and tutted as she slopped too much into the mug. She fished out the teabag. What was wrong with her? She always removed the bag before adding the milk.

Was the hysteria driven by the police? It would be in their interests to keep the story going. In less than three months since the original #textingwhilstdriving incident, mobile phone crime had dropped by a consummate 18% across the country. Although Etta had raised an eyebrow when she read the stat. She knew all too well the difference between act and detection.

"Enough!" Etta shouted over the top of the children, suddenly realising how much their voices were raised. She retrieved the reduced price iced lollies from the freezer with great aplomb and an 'ahem' to make sure she'd regained their full attention. As they bound towards her, the brrr and flash of the phone next to her made her jump. This time it was a direct message taunting her. She peered at the screen: six direct messages. She placed it face down on the counter. She wouldn't read the messages now. @investcribb needed to get a life.

Etta bent down, holding an ice lolly in each hand. Adriana grabbed hers and planted a loud smack of a kiss on Etta's cheek. Johan took his with a little more decorum, wrinkling his nose and allowing himself a giggle at the idea that they would have ice lollies when they weren't on holiday and after they'd had pudding for tea.

"On special offer, Johan," Etta said, "just this once," and winked at him.

Etta helped Adriana detach her wrapper as she hopped from one foot to the other. "My Mama is very smiley, today," she said, as she propelled herself with a procession of twirls across the room and back again with exquisite timing to take the lolly from her mother.

Etta checked herself, replaced the smile which Adriana's observation had removed, and gulped.

"I've had a great day today," she said. "I heard a funny story, shall I tell you it?"

The children jumped onto the tall chairs around the table. Etta sat herself down opposite with her cup of tea in one hand and plates to push beneath their chins to grab the drips of melting lollies in the other.

"Sometimes the little guy wins and I love it when that happens."

She introduced the main characters. There was the lady in hospital. She'd made a stupid mistake but sometimes stupid mistakes have a bad effect on other people and everyone gets cross.

"Is that why she was in hospital, Mama?" Johan asked.

"No!" Etta exclaimed. "Well, yes, the mistake meant she was in hospital because she wasn't concentrating when she was driving. It's bad not to concentrate when we drive."

Johan said with a careworn tone, which Etta realised he'd learnt from her, that they already knew that. He shifted right and left on the chair. "Who were the bad guys, Mama?" The friction of his school trousers against the polished seat made a parping sound causing Adriana to wail with laughter.

Etta raised her eyebrows. "The bad guys were the photographers, the people who take photos," she qualified for her daughter.

"Why are they bad?" Adriana asked.

"You take photos!" Johan said.

Etta smiled a little wearily. "OK," she said, "lots of people, photographers, people who write for newspapers and normal people who live normal lives take photos and that's OK. But some people take photographs of people they don't know. And these people don't want their photographs taken. Flippin' paps," she added, under her breath.

"And they're the bad people in this story?" Johan asked. It was Etta's turn to swivel a little on her chair. She held out her hands for the sticky lolly sticks, took them over to the bin, paused before deciding against turning the phone screen side up and returned with a wet cloth to clean their hands and ice lolly smiles.

"For the purpose of this story, the lady in hospital was the good guy."

"Even though she made the mistake?"

"That's the point of a mistake, Johan," Etta said a little sharply, before saying more softly. "She didn't mean to do what she did."

At the sound of the familiar click of the front door opening, Adriana jumped from her seat and ran to greet Andy as he entered the room with an all-engulfing hug, arms and legs flailing around him. Johan sprinted over, kissed Andy on his stomach and ran back to ask Etta what happened next.

"Well," Etta said, leaning in a little closer. "Remember the lady who made the mistake? She tricked all the nasty people taking photographs into thinking she was in an ambulance going to one place but really—"

"News time for the offspring is it?" Andy said, as he approached the two of them at the table. He kissed Etta on the cheek a little brusquely and sat himself down on the arm next to her. "What happened to *Squash and a Squeeze*?" he asked, but before Etta could answer he reached over to Johan, ruffled his hair, said that he'd heard they'd had ice lollies and would he be a superstar and fetch his dad one, and then it would be time for bed.

Johan groaned. "I never get to hear the end of a story," he said. "I just want to know if the lady who made the mistake got away from the nasty photographers."

"Photographers aren't nasty, as your mum knows," Andy said, an unwavering stare directed at Etta. "They're just doing their job."

TWENTY-EIGHT

TORI LOWERED HERSELF DOWN to the quarry-tiled floor in the hallway, positioning herself opposite the open door into the living room, and unfolded the umpteenth newspaper she'd scoured since she'd been home. She'd spent a lot of time sitting on the floor over the past twenty-four hours, midway between her two destinations. She wasn't using that wheelchair for a moment longer than she had to. She grimaced as she spread the paper over her lap. Since when had Doug read The Global?

Perhaps it was because her new glasses had been fitted with lenses the depth of milk bottle bases but nonetheless, the sight of Doug's face in the newspapers was distressing. She was startled at what a difference to good skin and a thick head of hair eight weeks of restricted sleep and vitamins could make. She'd expected she'd look grim, unrecognisable even; she'd been in a high-impact collision after all. But she hadn't been prepared for Doug's appearance.

As she stared at the black and white face of her husband looking uncharacteristically cross, she searched the vast bookshelves of her brain to find a better word to describe her *disappointment*. 'Chagrin' seemed too light and pretty; 'disenchantment' was too detached and 'inadequate' seemed to miss the point that there was certainly enough of the blackness, her homecoming had been large, momentous, definitely, but the reality had also been woefully far from her expectations.

She was glad her mother had prepared her for the strength of feeling outside the sanctuary of the hospital. She thought of the ten or so reporters and their pathetic attempts to hide in her garden. It was ironic that now that she had finally been granted some natural light in her immediate environment, the press forced her to keep her curtains drawn.

When she'd lain in her hospital bed opposite a collection of photos, cards and messages which she appreciated but could not see, Tori had pictured the huge sepia photo above the fireplace which stared proudly at her now. It was the four of them, all casually intertwined with arms linked through others or tossed around shoulders. It was only six months ago, at the beginning of the summer when they'd taken a rare family holiday together, walking in the Swiss Alps.

She looked over to the stairs, at the patterned carpet which extended up and over the whole of the top level. The worn patches no longer irked - preferable as this flooring was to the hospital's cold, linoleum. One day she'd like to run up and down them again. She'd made some progress, had trudged up the flight of stairs, supported by Doug as she'd insisted, her good leg dragging the other. The prize was a night in her own bed with its wooden headboard, not a railing in sight, and a mattress which surrendered to her body like water. She'd looked forward to that moment and for the first ten minutes, she'd been able to forget her aching, twingeing body.

'Desolate,' that was the word.

She'd have a cup of tea. How she'd longed to make herself a cup of tea when she was in hospital and now she had her own kettle. Could she manage? She didn't want to ask for Doug's help.

His levity and excitement at having Tori back with him only served to deepen the despair. As a child, 'disgrace' was the harshest indictment of all. She had been naughty, of course, atrocious sometimes, but the memory of the ten-year-old told in hushed tones by shaking lips that she'd *disgraced* herself and her family, still tightened her lungs. Forty years on, Tori had destroyed life and brought nothing but disgrace and shame to herself and all who loved her. She felt sick when she thought of the grieving families and of the lives she'd ended. She felt bludgeoning guilt knowing it had all been avoidable. But most of all she felt despair; despair for Doug.

Because he had to live with her.

"Hello you, shove up." He sat down next to her, their backs straight against the wall, legs stretched forward like children. She leaned against his shoulder, asked what it was like for him when it all happened.

Doug smiled, tapped her thigh. "You don't need to know," he said.

"Will you tell me?" she asked, snuggling up closer. "I missed two months of the world's wheels turning. I need a handle on what's going on."

Doug said that they'd sent a lot of letters at first which he'd kept in bin bags. "One day I'd had enough of moving them around the utility room, all that hate and anger bagged up in our house, so I had a bonfire."

"Any excuse for a fire," Tori said, and they laughed.

Doug lifted her head slightly so that he could stretch his arm around her shoulder. "The good news is that we haven't had any for a while."

"Emails?" Tori asked.

"Nope," he said. "I changed all our addresses. None of them bear any resemblance to any part of our names."

Tori shrugged. Nobody was asking for her email address at the moment. "What about phone calls?" she asked.

"Ex-directory." Doug squeezed her shoulder. He asked her why she was so interested, she was better off not knowing, wasn't she?

"I think I'd have liked to have read them," Tori said, "you know, forewarned is forearmed."

Doug breathed out, removed his arm from her shoulders. "Here goes," he muttered. "Most people felt you should be held up as an example to ensure nobody else ever behaved as badly again," he said, mechanically. "And that could only mean one thing: prison. There," he cleared his throat. "That's it."

"All from strangers?" Tori asked.

Doug got to his feet and held out a hand to her.

She shook her head. "Of course they weren't," she said. "Even Nicky's disgusted with me. Australia, for goodness sake!"

"We'll Skype," Doug said. "Then we'll be able to communicate properly." He linked his arm through Tori's and dragged her to her feet, saying that the wedding would smooth things over. Tori leaned her head on his shoulder. She thought her relationship with her estranged youngest daughter might need more than a little 'smoothing over'.

The great school bell chimed at the other end of the hall, causing such a reaction that Doug struggled to keep her upright.

"Please," she gripped Doug's sleeve, "no visitors."

"It'll be Ruby." Doug lowered Tori back down to the floor.

Tori couldn't face her mother today with her mask of cheeriness and the clipped way she and Doug communicated, both attempting to disguise the puzzling animosity between them.

She concentrated on the hushed tones through the splinter of a gap in the doorway and realised the other voice was also male. A journalist? But the press didn't ring the doorbell; they just sat in her front garden waiting to pounce.

She let out a long breath when she heard the door slam shut and watched only Doug rush towards her.

"Who was it?"

Doug grabbed her strong hand and hoisted her up to standing. "The worst of the journalists," he said. "By the way, do you know anyone called Etta?

"I can barely remember my own name, Doug, you'll have to give me a moment."

"I think your mum knows her," he said, guiding Tori into the living room, "not that she's letting on." He steadied her as she lowered herself down to the Chesterfield. "Take all the time you need," he said, "but if you can think of any connection to this Etta, it could be life-changing."

Tori looked at Doug and shrugged her shoulders. She encouraged her feet in the direction of the sputtering fire. She couldn't imagine her mother having a secret. She reached towards the coffee table but it was too low for her these days. Doug had laid out a bowl of pistachios and another of crisps. He called to her from the kitchen that he was bringing Shiraz.

He handed her the soupcon of wine she requested and she tried to thank him when he placed the pistachios on her lap but her voice wobbled and she found tears dribbling onto her cheeks. Doug sat down next to her, placed the glass back down on the table and hugged her so tightly that she was forced to pull away; all her bones still ached from weeks of inactivity. Instead Doug took her face in his hands and they sobbed together, their noses touching. Eventually Doug laughed, wiped his face with the palms of his hands and dabbed clumsily at Tori's cheeks with his sleeve. He handed her the sip of wine.

"Drink with me," he said, "sometimes a little fuzziness just makes this hell hole of a situation easier to cope with. And you know what," he said, drinking his wine in one gulp and banging his glass back down on the table, "relax and you might find yourself remembering this Etta person."

Tori sipped the splash he'd poured her and this time he filled her glass to a slick over halfway. She leaned forward to lift the glass from the table, cursing her rigid back. She reached her fingertips to it but only enough to send it crashing to the floor, glancing off the table leg.

"It doesn't matter!" Doug jumped to his feet, "Doesn't matter at all." He rushed out of the room and returned with the dustpan and brush, a floor cloth and a replacement glass.

"Doug," Tori whispered, as she stared into the mosaic of glass pieces in the pool of dark red wine seeping into the red carpet. "I—"

He ran to her, kneeled at her feet only inches away from the puddle, his hands resting on her lap. "Yes?"

She stared at him, back down to the spillage which had finally stopped creeping, and into his eyes again. She let out a gasp as her mouth fell open. "I know her," she said. "Etta. I know Etta."

"Yes!" Doug squeezed her thighs but apologised when she winced and he rubbed them instead. "More, Tori. What do you know?"

"Her name is Henrietta and she was with me in the Jeep." She took his hands in hers. "She was with me that day."

"You remember that?" Doug said. "That's impossible!"

"Through a dream - a nightmare. A recurrent nightmare. I just remember her voice," Tori said, her own voice wandering as she nudged further back into her dreams.

Doug grasped her shoulders. "Keep going!"

"She was talking, always talking. She held my hand, I wanted to thank her but the words wouldn't come out."

"Oh jeez!" He squeezed her shoulders so tightly she lifted them from him. "So she was your passenger?" He sat himself down next to her, lifting his feet onto the low table so that they wouldn't sit in the spillage.

Tori shook her head, shivered as if she'd just returned from a trance. "I don't think she could have been because we know I was on my way home from a client meeting in Manchester. I'm sure we'd know if I'd put another person's life in danger."

"Yes of course."

"I can only assume she tried to help after the crash." Tori pressed a toe into the damp carpet. "Now," she said, "I'm sorry I'm incapable of clearing up the wine but I'm more than happy to have another go at drinking my first glass since the summer."

Doug looked at the puddle as if it was nothing more than a drop and said, "Anything else, Tori, anything?"

"Why is she so important?" She gestured to Doug to remind him of the replacement tipple. "Just a smidge," she said, concerned about the effect of alcohol on a body still clattering with pills.

He poured the wine, handed it to her, made sure it was firmly in her grasp and asked if there was anything else.

"Nothing."

"Think again, Tori, this is so important, crucial to the case."

"What's she done?" Tori asked, shaking her head. The best she could manage were freeze-frame snippets of memory. "I really don't think I'm much use to you on this one."

He jumped up, ran through the damp carpet in his black socks without seeming to notice and out into the hall to return with a letter. "Listen to this!" He threw himself back onto the settee, unusually out of breath from only a few steps.

It took me weeks to be able to see the scene more clearly in my own mind, but I am more and more certain that I saw somebody driving erratically. This person was jumping lanes and driving too close to the cars in front. But it wasn't Tori. This person was in a red car.

Doug held the letter to his lips and kissed it. "Thank you, Etta," he said aloud. He took Tori's face in his hands and kissed her on the lips. "And thank you my beautiful, most wonderful wife. You have saved us!"

Tori took a sip of wine. "You'll have to explain it better than that."

"You've shown us she's kosher!" Doug said. "She's not one of these nutters who writes to us as part of some dodgy insurance claim. You've corroborated that." He punched a fist into the air and filled his own glass again. "We'll find her, whatever it takes, and she'll save our lives!" They chinked glasses.

"Hallelujah!" Doug said.

Tori took a mouthful of wine. She couldn't bear to quash his enthusiasm.

TWENTY-NINE

TORI SQUINTED THROUGH THE GAP between the living room curtains and the wooden window frame of the bay window. She saw her mother's bubble car trickle down the road, turn into her drive and park - presumably all in second gear. She hadn't entirely come to terms with Ruby's absence in hospital and wondered if she ever would, even though she was some way to understanding it now. But the sight of her so feeble as she forged her way through the line of cameras, and the knowledge that there were still times in her life when only her mother would do, meant that Tori threw her good arm around her when she opened the door.

"I'm so sorry," Ruby said in place of a greeting. She escorted Tori to the settee in the living room, instructed her to sit patiently and wait for her cup of tea. It was a two sugars day.

"Has she given any idea why they brought the wedding forward?" Ruby called from the kitchen.

"I can guess," Tori muttered.

"It's easy to jump to conclusions though," her mother said quickly, placing the two mugs on the coffee table and gasping at the sight of a red stain on the carpet the size of a small bath. "Tell me that's not blood, Tori?" Tori rolled her eyes and said that she didn't make a habit of killing and Ruby scowled, stirring the teas frantically.

"We both know what young love's like. They'd be impatient. Or maybe the registry office had a problem with the original date?"

"No, Mum."

Ruby stirred, and Tori placed her hand over hers to make her stop.

"Nobody would delay their wedding day if they could avoid it but they might bring it forward," Ruby said.

"I'd delay it," Tori said. "Carly would. You would, if it meant your mother and your family could be there."

Ruby placed Tori's mug in her hand and suggested she gave her shoulders a massage, standing behind her before she could protest. Tori shifted in her seat. She was always stiff either through the exertion of trying to make her body move faster than it should do, or because of the knots in which she frequently held herself. She could hold her right hand flat, for example, but only if she twisted her shoulder 90 degrees to the side. She'd ditched the wheelchair weeks ago and she could walk tall - like a soldier, the physio suggested, like a supermodel, she preferred - but only if she used her tiptoes on the right. She shuffled into a better position on the settee and stretched the left side of her neck, her right ear gratifyingly only inches away from her right shoulder these days.

The truth was, Nicky didn't want her there. She'd panicked when she'd heard that she'd left hospital. "She'd have thought the original date would be safe," Tori said, "that I'd be a fixture on the ward or already in a prison cell. Or dead."

Ruby flinched, pressing harder on the knot just in front of Tori's now bony trapezius area. "Maybe it wasn't as calculated as that," she said. "Nicky is very young after all."

— — —

What else could Ruby say? It was incomprehensible that Tori had missed out on her daughter's wedding. She'd always had excellent relationships with her children. Ruby admired the way she maintained individual rapports with each: more cautious with Carly - she had always been more fragile, more needy - and more of a friend to Nicky whilst retaining her respect.

"Once upon a time," Tori said eventually, "Nicky would have confided in me and I'd have told her I thought twenty-one was a bit young to be getting married."

Ruby could find no words of sympathy, nothing to contradict the truth her daughter was speaking. She was glad she was standing behind her and could avoid her battered eyes. She massaged one, then the other, of Tori's shoulders silently. She was cross with her granddaughter and wished she'd known what she'd been planning. But she grudgingly acknowledged that her own reaction to Tori's predicament hadn't been entirely orthodox, nor desirable. Was she really in a position to criticise?

Ruby smoothed her fingers down both sides of Tori's neck. She took a deep breath. "Give her time, love," she said. "One day she'll explain. We've, well—" She pushed harder, causing Tori's shoulder to weave in and out as if struggling to free itself from her touch.

"I'm listening Mum."

"I was going to say that we've all found different ways of coping with what happened."

Tori looked down at her slippers and when the pause extended beyond comfort, she said, "Yes, of course."

They could pass hours like this, Ruby caring for her daughter. The last time she'd looked after any dependants was when Tori's children were young and she was still a teacher. Granted, Tori had recovered well enough to pull on a pair of slacks herself now and could even lift the hopeless right arm high enough to pull on a large-necked pullover. She could make a cup of tea - when she remembered to put the teabag in the cup - stack the dishwasher or polish her most treasured possession: the mahogany dining table. But the effort was exhausting. Ruby visited every day. Tori needed her and she was happy to do it. But the massage, the lifting and the carrying all sapped her of her energy too. At seventy-eight years old, Ruby was worn out. Her postponed hip replacement had never seemed more urgent.

"Do you think I've lost her forever Mum?" Tori asked. She turned her head to look at her. "I do speak to her you know but we may as well be talking to cardboard cut-outs. She tells me she's fine, very happy, in fact. She doesn't ask me how I am. When I ask her about the wedding, she pretends the line's bad or they haven't finalised the date yet."

Ruby placed both hands either side of Tori's face and turned her head back to the front so that she could focus on a particular ten pence sized knot in her neck. "Sooner or later she'll realise her whole family missed her special day and she'll want to make amends."

Tori tutted and circled her left shoulder backwards, nowadays she could also manage a quarter turn with the right. Ruby waited until the circling had stopped then moved her focus back to her shoulders. The right still hung so much lower than the left. If she could tease it back into position, Tori might not look so vulnerable. She would leave her with some exercises.

"Perhaps she'll surprise you and come back for the trial," Ruby said. Tori shot back that she didn't think the trial would be top of Nicky's priority list.

After a day spent with Tori, Ruby felt as though her heart had been pulled from her, remodelled like putty, and replaced. Tori's mind would spin from items for the shopping list, to bankruptcy, to her worries about any of the few people who remained in her life, in the time it took Ruby to comb her knotted hair. She had never known emotion pour out in such a slurry. Her mind was a cement mixer, constantly churning until the contents had no choice but to spill out.

And this depth of feeling, this exposed emotion was infectious. Over the past few weeks Ruby had found an honesty in herself which had been repressed since childhood and there was something refreshing about picking through difficult issues and knowing there was no place, and no need, to hide.

Besides, even if Ruby had preferred to run away, there was no exit from the house because the committee of vultures on the drive outside were even more stressful than Tori was.

She had a new relationship with her daughter. It was painful and draining but she was enjoying getting to know her all over again. She would admit it to nobody, but for her at least, the accident had its upside. Tori appeared to have forgotten that her relationship with her mother had been, at best, strained before the accident.

"I wish I could turn the clocks back," Ruby said suddenly. "I wish I'd gone into the room."

Tori touched her mother's hand where it rested on her shoulder. She cleared her throat. "It wasn't just about Lottie, was it Mum?"

"I was angry with myself when Lottie died. I still am, always will be."

"It wasn't your fault."

"I let my sixteen-year-old daughter get herself into a situation where the only thing that could possibly save her life was a stomach pump. That's my fault," Ruby said. Tori squeezed her hand. "And then there was your dad. When he died, I wasn't angry at myself, I was furious with the world, with other forces, God, whatever it is. I'm still cross about that now."

"Oh Mum," Tori lifted Ruby's hands from her shoulders and beckoned her round to her side of the settee. She coaxed her to sit down and hugged her trembling torso. "They wouldn't want you to be feeling like this. Anger is no good for anyone."

Ruby said anger was easier. She couldn't cry anymore.

Tori hugged her again before pushing her gently away so they could see each other's faces. "And then there was Gerald," she said. "You really can't be cross with yourself about him, he's devoted his life to duping helpless women!"

Eventually, Ruby smiled. "Poor Sophie, she could be my granddaughter."

Tori giggled. "I hope he has some stamina left."

She described to Ruby the dreams she'd had in hospital; that all were grounded in truth and most were far too disturbing to recall but those with Gerald at the centre had been light relief. Ruby felt a pink hue crawl from her neck, up over her ears and across her forehead when Tori described the dream in which Gerald had spoken at length about his marvellous sex life with her mother.

"Oh yes," Tori said, "he puffed out his chest and said that you had it so much better with him than you did with Dad. Even though he would hate to speak ill of the dead."

Now Ruby was laughing. The pair laughed so hard, barely a sound came out.

"Lucky Sophie," Tori spluttered. "All that experience."

Ruby pretended to spit on her hand and painstakingly wind a mock stray hair around an ear before repeating the procedure on the other side. "Remind you of anyone?" she said. Their laughter was painful. They hugged their stomachs. Gerald was always touching his hair; the more attractive the woman, the more he spat.

Tori said she hadn't laughed like this since last summer. It was the best physio she'd had.

As the laughter subsided she wiped her eyes and stretched the dormant muscles around her mouth. After a pause, she said, "It's fine Mum. I get it. It felt like everyone left you one by one and you thought I was going to do the same."

Ruby sat up straight and cleared her throat. She wanted to tell her, needed to tell her, but Tori was reeling from the wedding of her estranged daughter and had just laughed in a way Ruby thought she might never see again.

"You're right," she said. "I couldn't bear to lose you as well."

"But this time it was my fault?" Tori asked.

"Yes."

"I agree."

"That's settled then," Ruby said, lifting herself up from the settee.

— — —

Tori heard the crockery clatter into the sink and water pour into the kettle. She hoisted herself up to standing, moved towards the kitchen and hovered at the top of the stone steps, in the doorway between the kitchen and the dining room. Her mother stood at the sink under the grimy, diamond-leaded window, her eyes fixed on the water pouring into the washing-up bowl. Even from the side, Tori could see that her face had the grey hue that tiredness brings, a grid of deep lines between her brown eyes and temples. Her mouth was quivering as it had recently started to do.

"You were too cross to sit with me?" she asked. "Because it was my fault?"

Ruby nodded. "Yes."

"You stood outside even though I might have died?" Tori shook her head. "It doesn't make sense."

Ruby wiped her forehead with the back of her hand and left a smear of bubbles in their place. She washed the teapot in the bubbly water - including the spout - swilled it with tap water and dried the inside with a teacloth. Then she placed it back down on the tray, searched around the kitchen, found a teaspoon and a milk bottle to wash and plunged them into the bowl.

"Mum?"

Ruby pressed a rip of paint-caked paper to the wall and watched it spring back again.

"Mum!"

"I was worried," Ruby said. "We hadn't been getting on."

"Getting on?" Tori shook her head. "Don't people put disagreements behind them when loved ones are on their death bed?"

"Yes, yes, Tori, they do." She scrubbed the outside of the milk bottle with a worn brush and repeated the process with fresh water. "But it was different for me."

How could it have been different? Even with all the sadness Ruby had endured this was still her daughter on a precipice between life and death, in a place few people understood, a place where everybody would want their mum. Ruby's hands were lost under the bubbles now. She studied every corner of the kitchen but there was nothing else to wash.

"I shouldn't have believed Gerald," she said, "but you know how convincing he can be."

"I don't know what Gerald has to do with me," Tori mumbled, sliding down the door frame to sit on the floor.

"After Gerald and I broke up, you and I weren't communicating very well," Ruby said. "I was scared of sitting in that room holding your hand and not finding the right words. What if my presence or maybe the tone of my voice had the opposite effect of making you want to wake up?"

"I guess I'd have willed myself to wake up to tell you that you were a silly sausage." Tori forced a smile. But Ruby wasn't laughing. In fact, she wasn't doing anything. Her hands remained stagnant in the washing-up water and she refused to raise her eyes from the sink. She simply turned to Tori and said,

"It had gone beyond that."

Tori stared at her mother. She felt a cramping in her stomach. She breathed out, her cheeks filled and emptied of air. Just how bad was the communication?

Finally, Ruby lifted her hands from the bowl of dirty water. She shook off the excess bubbles and dried the rest on her apron which she removed and folded over the radiator to dry. She walked right past Tori into the dining room, cleared her throat and dragged two of the leather, rollback chairs from behind the dining table. They sat opposite each other, a foot apart. Tori could see a tremor in her chin. She respected her mother's efforts to be honest about something so clearly difficult but nothing she was saying made any sense.

"Just tell me it all," she whispered. "How bad can it be?"

Ruby tried to take Tori's hand but she folded her arms. "I don't want this to change what we have now," she said.

Tori simply shook her head. "How long had it been going on?"

"Tell me that nothing that happened in the past can be bigger than what we have now," Ruby pleaded. "We've learnt from our experiences, haven't we? We know people make mistakes?"

"Mum!" Tori said. "Just. Answer. Me." Her clipped speech the only way to stop herself shouting.

"Yes, of course," Ruby said, her eyes flitting from Tori's, to the kitchen, through the doorway and back again. "You and I—" she started, only to stop abruptly. She coughed, walked over to the far wall and leaned against the Welsh dresser. In a voice which barely carried, she said,

"We'd hardly spoken for three years."

Tori stared at Ruby. Three years? How could their relationship have deteriorated to such a level? She still didn't understand.

"What could have been so bad?"

Ruby rushed back towards Tori. "I believed Gerald over you," she said. "I believed you'd manipulated circumstances to split us up." Again she reached out for Tori's hands only for her to snatch them away.

"And you never questioned?" she said. "For three years you thought that was the truth?"

Ruby shook her head. "He played with my mind when I was at my weakest."

Tori pressed her temples. The pain in her head from the early days was back. She needed some space, couldn't listen to her mother anymore. She heaved herself up from the chair and walked out of the dining room towards the stairs. She had to lie down, close her eyes, make the conversation go away. The pain in her head was stabbing now, shooting nausea into the pit of her stomach with every pulse. With each step through the hall her legs trembled and the pain sent walls of white light to the front of her eyes. She would sit here for a few minutes, close her eyes against the worst of the pain and hope that she could find some answers. She clutched her head in her hands.

What about everybody else? Why didn't Doug cajole her into seeing sense? Did he even try? He clearly had a role in the big post-coma cover-up, too. What about Nicky and Carly? Did they miss seeing their grandmother? Perhaps they didn't know. Carly and Ruby always seemed so close now.

Tori squeezed her palms into the sockets of her eyes. What a mess! She should have left history alone, enjoyed the fortuitous memory loss. Her mother's love was undisputed now. She'd put her life on hold for Tori. She closed her eyes again, saw Ruby on the swing seat delighting in the children. She remembered Ruby screaming, "No!" when the doctor told her Dad had died and she could only imagine her at Lottie's bedside when she passed away.

She thought about her coming to the hospital every day just to sit outside the door.

Tori had let the rift fester, too. She glanced up at the hall clock: twenty minutes had passed while the pair had sat on either side of a wall again.

— — —

Ruby had moved her chair further into the middle of the room and was staring ahead, tangling her fingers in the long string of glass beads around her neck, her eyes half closed. She jumped when Tori whispered her name and turned quickly to face her.

"You came into the ward," Tori said, her back pressed against the heavy door. "What made you change your mind?"

"When I knew you weren't going to leave us, that's when I knew I could come in."

"And?"

Ruby stood up. She didn't approach Tori but held her hands out to her instead. Tori pressed deeper into the door. "And?" she asked again.

"And because I had a conversation with someone."

"Someone?" Tori said. "Jesus, Mum, enough of the riddles—"

"Etta Dubcek."

"The one at the accident?"

Ruby nodded. "A young woman, more sense than years."

"The one Doug's looking for?"

Ruby dragged her chair back to the table. She suggested she make tea, twizzled the beads through her fingers. "That would be nice, now we're both a bit calmer," she said, and moved towards the kitchen.

"No!" Tori snatched the beads from her mother's hands and threw them onto the table where they exploded into thousands of tiny reflective pieces. "I don't want tea. I don't want secrets. Just tell me how this Etta girl can persuade you to visit me and yet the sight of me clinging on to life isn't enough?"

Silently Ruby bent down to the floor and picked up the largest fragments of glass.

"Mum!"

"OK!" Ruby held up both hands. "OK." She dusted the glass from two chairs. When Tori was convinced that Ruby wouldn't speak until they were seated, she reluctantly dropped down onto one of them.

"Etta guessed," Ruby said. "She knew it was about more than Lottie. She told me that she hadn't spoken to her own mother for seventeen years and that now she'd left it too long to make up. But—" She reached forward to touch Tori's hand but Tori busied herself with the shards of glass, sweeping them into a pile at the edge of the table. Ruby returned her hands to her lap. "I ask you not to tell Doug I know her."

"Suits me," Tori whispered. "But why wouldn't you tell him? The poor man's been driven to distraction by this Etta person."

"I wanted to protect her," Ruby said. "She's a frail little thing."

Tori looked at Ruby. Was that it? She felt guilty enough about the shattered beads, wasn't keen to challenge her again, but it didn't ring true. Ruby's relationship wasn't perfect with Doug but nonetheless, his marriage to Ruby's daughter would stand for more than Etta's petite stature, surely? She cleared her throat.

"Mum?"

Ruby shook her head. "Please stop, you'll cut yourself." She jumped up to fetch the dustpan and brush but as she walked past the back of Tori's chair, she grabbed her hand.

"Be honest!"

Ruby lifted up her foot. She'd stood in a piece of glass.

"Mum?"

"I suspected that you wouldn't want Doug to get in touch with Etta either."

THIRTY

TORI PLACED EIGHT CARROTS, three parsnips, an onion, a piece of ginger, a good handful of coriander, 25 grams of butter, a litre of stock, a grater, a peeler and a large, stained saucepan on the work surface.

She smoothed her hands down the pinstripes of her apron and hobbled through the hall into the living room to retrieve the A4 magnifying sheet which Carly had bought for her. She would confirm the ingredients using her mother's battered Good Housekeeping bible, even if she'd never looked up the recipe on any of the previous occasions she'd prepared her family's favourite carrot and coriander soup.

When Doug returned from work an hour later, he found Tori seated on the kitchen tiles, her body wilted against the cupboards, a saucepan upended on her bent knee.

"No! Tori?"

Her eyes snapped open. "I can't find the cookery books," she wailed. "Can't cook, Doug. Not even soup."

"Sssh," Doug sat down next to his wife and took her into his arms. He told her that he'd moved the books. They'd both been using the iPads more before she went into hospital so he'd had a clear-out and made space for the vegetable peelings and the plastic bottles in the cupboard behind her.

"I can't peel anything, fingers, won't hold—"

"I can do the carrots."

"And I tried to chop the onion but it rolled away."

"Why don't I slice and you stir?"

"Because you can't do everything, Doug, that's why." Tori tried to thump the cupboard door but succeeded only in a dusting movement. "You go to work. I cook. That's how it should be now," she sobbed. "I'm no use to anybody!"

"But I don't mind doing it, Torr, really I don't."

The couple sat on the cold kitchen floor like puppets thrown together, swaying, soothing and moaning. Doug smoothed Tori's hair. Tori pulled away, plumped up her curls.

"Right." He picked her up from under her arms, "We're going out to dinner."

"No!" Tori was shivering. "Don't make me Doug, please. I can't go out to eat. I'm not ready yet."

He held her face in his hands. He might have protested, forced her progress but he looked in her eyes and said, "Looks like it's a Takeaway Night."

— — —

Doug cleared away the foil cartons, took Tori's glass of sparkling water from her and set it down on the coffee table which he slid further into the centre of the room. He joined Tori on the loveseat, said how 'cosy' it was.

"I yearned for the day you'd be out of hospital and we'd sit here together."

Tori reached out her good hand to turn out the lamp as soon as Doug's lips touched hers. Two stones lighter than the last time they'd made love, now it was the scars on her face and the atrophied muscles, as well as the pieces they'd cut out of her arms and legs, which made her seek darkness.

She tried to focus on Doug's enjoyment as there was scant chance of her own. It was difficult now that she no longer had full control over her lips and jaw: a disconsolate Miss Piggy, she thought to herself, impersonating a goldfish. Her lack of condition quickened her breath giving the illusion of more pleasure than she really felt. Still, it was a small gesture when Doug had given up so much for her. Never mind that the discomfort in her lungs made her worry about pneumonia, Doug deserved her unfaltering attention and if she could inadvertently persuade him of this, then so be it. Thankfully his climax was reached before a thud against the bay window made them jump apart.

"Third egg this week," he said, jolting from the seat. He put his trousers back on and threw Tori her over-sized jeans and jumper. "I thought the eggs had stopped." He knelt at her feet. "I hate the vulnerability, can't be naked in my own house any more."

"I just hope it isn't anyone we know," Tori said, waiting for Doug to help her fasten her jeans. "I think it will carry on until I'm in prison."

He picked up her jumper and pulled at the sleeves to turn them the right way out. "Hey," he soothed. "Don't speak like that. With Etta's evidence, the whole red car debacle, I don't see how you possibly could go to prison."

"Right," she said.

She lifted her left arm to shoulder height as a request for Doug to manoeuvre the pullover first over the better functioning arm and then over the right, which was stuck at the elbow. It was so painful that the caring, careful procedure Doug operated reminded her of the wire loop game at the fairground where, touch the metal with the ring in your hand and you enjoyed an electric shock.

"You can stop worrying, Tori. We're together now and I'm not going to let anything, anything," he repeated, "part us."

Tori lifted a hand to her forehead. It was perspiring. She had no control over her temperature these days. She pulled the collar further up her neck because she was cold enough to shiver. Doug shook his head.

"You wouldn't survive two minutes in prison," he said, with an attempt at humour, even if neither of them laughed.

Tori picked at a tassel on the cushion Doug had placed behind her back. "It isn't proving easy to track down this Etta woman, though."

"Granted your mum is still pretending she doesn't know her," Doug said, "bloody ridiculous. If she's going to lie, she needs to practise." But if he couldn't make any sense out of her, then he had one more trick up his sleeve. He walked over to the settee on the other side of the room, located the remote control and only when he'd ambled back to Tori and started a determined search for stray cushions, did he say,

"The trick is very much a last resort as it carries a price tag with it."

"Perhaps it's not worth it then," Tori said.

Doug stared at Tori but his face soon folded into a smile. He pointed at her. "Digging are we? Want me to say again that I'd do anything for you?" Doug switched on the television, snuggling in beside her. "You already know that!"

"I'd love to watch a film tonight," Tori said, her eyes wandering back to the tassle, "with hot chocolate." She asked Doug if he would make it. "It would take me till bed time to negotiate the screw top lid, and the one handed kettle filling, and pouring, not to mention the transportation of the two cups back into the room, which," she said, "I know I need to practise but I have an awful headache so tonight isn't the best night."

Doug planted a quick kiss on her forehead, said, "It's a bit late for a headache," and marched off to the kitchen with a spring in his step as if he'd just lost his virginity.

Tori rubbed her eyes. That was some exertion by today's standards. She got so tired these days and if she didn't spend her day in and out of a cat nap, the pain in her head grew so strong she could be sick. She tugged Doug's pullover from the gap between the seat and the cushion and draped it over her. She would shut her eyes for a moment, just for a moment, and when Doug returned with the hot chocolate, she would raise it.

— — —

Etta sipped her favourite Sauvignon Blanc but it tasted strong, over-fermented even. Andy didn't seem to think so, he'd poured the remains of the bottle into his own glass and she was still on her first one. She shuffled her bottom towards the back of the sagging sofa and tried to focus on the programme, rather than the constantly alerting phone at her feet. She should be doing none of any of this but working on her assignment. Instead, she'd agreed to have a night off, cuddle up on the sofa, like a normal couple. She stared at the presenters in the hope that their enthusiasm for other people's houses would wear off on her but home improvement programmes were never her thing at the best of times. They forced her to look at her own house and her eyes could never get past the children's toys littered across their tiny living room, which she should really have tidied away before she sat down.

Etta picked up her phone from the painted boards at her feet.

She wondered if it might be the cold air squealing through the gaps making her phone jump about, rather than a new message, but the light was flashing as well.

"Sorry Andy, 'silent' isn't really silent, is it?" She picked it up and scrolled through a long list of Twitter notifications. All from the same person, of course. Andy unhooked his arm from around Etta's shoulder and moved a few inches away.

She looked at him, his face resolutely forward. She'd quickly respond, finish the conversation and then switch the phone off completely.

"We could watch a film. I can't remember the last time we watched one together." She gave Andy's shoulder a nudge but he simply crossed his legs away from her, and kept his eyes doggedly fixed on four people wallpapering a room.

"Andy? How do you fancy—"

"Sounds great," he muttered, "not that I can possibly understand why you might want to spend any time with me."

She tossed her phone face down on the floor and moved across the space towards him but he pointed the remote at the television and said, "Don't force yourself," before increasing the sound.

– – –

Etta stood in front of the kettle, thought of her mother's words in her ear: *a watched kettle never boils*, with her distinct Slovakian accent but nonetheless, perfect English sentence construction. How did she know so many idioms and proverbs in her second language? She was a dedicated academic, if nothing else.

Funny that she should think about this now - probably because standing still, waiting for hot water, was not something Etta the adult, working and studying mother ever did. She sidled back into the living room, grabbed her phone, and sprinted back to the kettle. With the mugs aligned, teabags in the cups, milk bottle next to them, there was no harm in her ticking off these notifications. She and Andy weren't even in the same room.

It was his direct messages which got under her skin. Seven of them in this latest batch. She wasn't a kid. She wasn't stupid enough to accept his constant invitations to meet a fellow like-minded spirit. Even if it was undisputedly refreshing to be in contact with someone who felt similarly to her.

In the time it took her to pour the water over the teabags, her screen had already filled again. She looked at the list and felt the pressure: the ball rolling down her windpipe, the need to respond, the etiquette, her voice to be heard on #Toristext, this incredibly important topic. Perhaps she should hide the notifications? The tweets would still be there when she looked, but she could answer them on her terms. She lifted the teabags from the mugs, tossed them into the sink. This could be her pledge to Andy: eventually she'd come off social media altogether. He was right, she didn't have time for it and no, it didn't make her happy. Photos of Sara and the others meeting up without her certainly didn't make her feel any better about herself. She poured in the milk and smiled at the sudden surge of empowerment. She'd get through this current crisis in her life, finish the story with Tori without Andy knowing, finish her own story, then she'd return to full sociability. More fresh air, less screen! She'd begin tonight. She'd change the alert options, should have done it ages ago.

She took the two cups of tea into the living room, choosing to ignore the lack of acknowledgement from Andy when she placed the mug at his feet. Instead she'd fetch biscuits, even arrange them on a plate, do it properly and then tell him her resolve. Who was he kidding? He loved a Saturday night in drinking tea and eating biscuits! *A way to a man's heart is through his stomach*, she could hear her mother saying, her head nodding sagely as she imparted the wisdom.

She paused on her latest journey to the kitchen only briefly to shout, 'Sleep right now!" up the stairs to the giggling children. Chocolate biscuits were always the best option. The open packet fell out of her hand as she took it from the cupboard above the kettle, dropping biscuit pieces and crumbs all over the work surface as it ricocheted off her phone. She wiped it hastily clean, eager to check that the flimsy screen hadn't cracked. She froze. @ettadub *You need to meet me.* It wasn't even a private message, just there, a tweet, blatant for all to see. @investcribb had gone public. He was goading her, his name reaching out, grabbing her, holding her by the throat. How could she have been so stupid? Investment? He'd never mentioned money!

Her finger moved slowly to his profile picture. As soon as she'd enlarged it, she shrank it back down again. He'd added a description. She hardly dared to look. '@investcribb: ex-police, investigative journalist,' it said, 'All views my own.'

She rammed her feet into her wellies, grabbed Andy's mac and as she yanked open the door and heard him shouting, "Where the fuck are you going now?" She said that she'd be two minutes, no need to worry, and ran towards the park. This man, this @invest journalist Stephen flippin' Cribbins, whom Ruby had said was, 'quite devious really, the way he hounded Doug and Tori and was never far from their house', was working it out.

He was on to her.

— — —

Doug walked back into the room with the two mugs of hot chocolate and a box of After Eights squeezed under his arm. Tori wrinkled her nose. He was fattening her up.

"Doctor's orders."

"Unlikely," she said, "even with a hospital diet of vitamin spiked milkshakes, I'm still on the 'overweight' arc on the chart."

Doug shook his head, "You're beautiful, I know that much."

Tori looked at her husband with that determined smile and his unending loyalty and tenderness. The sight of his tired face with the grey bags and the eyes which had shrunk but still sparkled and his thinning hair which had lost its spring, caused her bones to ache even more.

She patted the space next to her. "Come and sit back down next to me."

He smiled, pushed the table back over towards them, put down the mugs and leaned in to kiss her before jumping onto the loveseat next to her.

"Right," he said, scrolling through the options, "humour, horror…?"

"If I went to prison," Tori said, her eyes on the television screen as if she could see as far as the blurbs about the films, "it wouldn't be forever, I would come out again, you know."

"Ha! Not alive I don't think." Doug squeezed her thigh. "A night for the best thriller ever made?"

Tori laughed. "We should have shares in it." She leaned forward and picked up her mug from the coffee table, replaced it and picked it up again. Because she could. Life had improved considerably since the physio had insisted she spend most of her waking hours working on the flexibility in her back. She took an After Eight as well, shaking it from its wrapper.

"It'll be a while before we're playing the After Eight game," she said.

"Some of us have never been very good at that." Doug held his gaze on the screen as The Shining loaded. "You've made enormous progress already and that's down to your graft and dedication." He tilted his head to land a peck on the lips. "The nurses said it would be."

Tori snuggled into him. How could they possibly be parted again? Her world had concertinaed and Doug, always at the helm, was an even greater soul mate than he'd ever been. A tear landed on her cheek. She hadn't expected it and wiped it quickly away.

This was cruel of her. She had to be honest. "How about if I went to a women's prison?"

"Aren't you missing the point?"

"Some are very relaxed, Doug, with women able to go home at weekends."

"Sorted," Doug said. "Just every single week without you."

"If I'm not considered a future threat to society but must simply – and I agree with this – pay for what I've done, I might have a very good case for going to one of those."

Doug switched off the television and faced Tori. "What's all this talk of prisons? Do you know something I don't?" Tori shook her head and he squeezed her hand. "I'll get straight back on the case tomorrow. Perhaps we could both have a go at extracting some contact details from Ruby. We could pin her down, one on each side." He smiled, his vulnerable grin, and Tori felt unkind not reacting to it.

"I can't help thinking prison might work for me, Doug," she said, her hand cupped under his chin to encourage his face back towards hers. She had an enormous lump of guilt perched in the conscience part of her brain - she spread her fingers over the top of her head to illustrate as if she knew where that would be - and suggested to Doug that prison might ease it.

"You can't begin to imagine how good that would feel."

Doug swivelled himself around so they were now facing each

other in the loveseat, like a tiny rowing boat. "You don't need prison for that," he said sharply. "Carly, me, Jo and Amelie, even Ruby in her complicated way, we willed you back to health so we could be together again." He stared at her. She could see his eyes glazing. She couldn't bear it if he cried. "We could help you," he said. "We could get you counselling. You could do some voluntary work, for Pete's sake. You don't have to throw yourself at the mercy of prison inmates."

When Tori shook her head, he tried again.

"Anything but prison, Tori!" He shifted his bottom. He'd been sitting on the remote control. "If not for you, won't you do it for me? Let us see what this Etta person knows," he said. "Then you can decide whether you feel it's right for us to encourage her to go to the police with this."

Still Tori said nothing, until a small, "I can't."

Doug shook his head, got up from the loveseat and paced over to the settee instead. He sat on the edge, his head in his hands. "As long as you're still happy when you've been beaten to a pulp."

Tori levered herself up and took painstaking steps over to the other side of the room. "I don't know what you want me to say," she whispered, sitting herself down next to Doug but this time leaving a sizeable gap between them. "Of course I'm not happy about my options but perhaps the only way I can gain closure is through punishment and you tell me where I can get punishment if not through prison."

"I don't know: God? An apology to the families? Something, anything, just not prison if you can do anything to avoid it."

Tori laughed, a hollow, weak laugh and said that people didn't want her apologies or her prayers. They wanted her dead. "As this country doesn't hang people any more, the best they can hope for is that I go to prison."

"I don't care what they want."

"If I go to prison," Tori said, "eventually they might forgive me and then I might be able to forgive myself."

Doug looked at her, shook his head and said calmly and deliberately that if prison was going to have such a positive effect on her future then yes, she should push for it.

"In fact," he said, "why don't you pretend you were driving that red car? That should do it." He picked up the empty mugs and the barely opened box of After Eights and said that he'd gone off The Shining tonight and could do with an early night.

They ascended the stairs in silence. Doug with his arm around Tori's waist. She conceded that he would need to help her drag her jeans over her ankles. He loosened the tie-belt of her sensible pyjamas so that they'd now fit a water butt and loaded her brush with toothpaste so that she could clean her teeth herself. Then he helped her climb into bed. Finally, he spoke, suggesting they continue the conversation when they'd both had some sleep.

Tori looked at him over the top of the duvet and said, "I sent a text while I was driving, Doug. My car went into the back of another car and people died. I'm sorry, but I don't want Etta to help me cheat."

THIRTY-ONE

TORI PEERED THROUGH THE GAP in the curtains and searched the road for parked cars. Today they were sparse in number. A red Beetle was parked opposite but didn't that belong to Mary's daughter? She could ask her but Mary wasn't too keen on chatting at the moment. The grass to the front was almost as it used to be, obviously a little flattened and muddied by the weeks of heavy boots tramping across, not to mention the litter detailing what the parasites had eaten for their lunch, but otherwise, a semblance of normality had returned.

She looked at her watch, remembered she couldn't read the time without her comedy glasses or the magnifying sheet and wandered back into the kitchen to use the clock instead. 8am. Perhaps they were kicking off later these days. She shuddered. Maybe they'd studied her family hard enough to know that Doug religiously left for work at 8.30 on Thursday mornings, his only late start of the week.

She pressed her nose to the glass, focused on the rosemary bush. Was that a human form behind it? She shuffled across the living room to the loveseat where she'd left the binoculars. Of course it was. In the mad world into which she'd been catapulted, it was good to know that some things were constant, such as Steve leaning against the rosemary bush, flattening it with his back, watching the road on which very little was happening.

"Tragic," she muttered to herself.

"Right, curtain twitcher." Doug walked over to her at the window, a piece of buttered toast in his mouth. "Need to be in a little earlier today, catch up on lost time," he said with a roll of the eyes. He gave her a peck on the cheek and reminded her that Ruby would be here before nine o'clock, so why didn't she sit down and have a few minutes on her own with a book and the magnifying sheet before their personal, ageing occupational therapist put her through her paces? "Go on," he said, "trot trot." Tori looked at him. Did she scrunch her nose at his unusual choice of expression? She could never be sure these days whether what her brain told her to do and what her muscles actually did, were very well connected. Doug simply shrugged his shoulders and said that she really shouldn't be on her feet for too long.

She followed him out of the room and he gave her another fleeting kiss before the front door slammed shut behind him. Tori began the slow walk down the hall to the kitchen. She straightened the photo in its red-glossed frame on the wall of Carly and Nicky battling over a Christmas cracker, a Mother's Day present of a decade ago, and hesitated. Then she marched as fast as she was able back to the window. She was in time to see Doug shake Steve's hand before scuttling across the drive and into the car.

THIRTY-TWO

TORI SAT DOWN on the cast iron bench on the patio and wrapped herself in the fleecy camping blanket. The teapot sat on the circular mosaic tiled table, with its odd missing squares. Nicky had toiled over it for months for her Art A-level. And now she lived on the other side of the world and Tori didn't know whether to hug it or smash it up. Her mug of tea cocooned in her hands, she tutted. This was the closest she came to leaving the house without assistance but clearly privacy wasn't part of the bargain. A cursory glance through her binoculars was enough to suggest a camera lens poking at her from the Leylandii at the end of her garden.

"Right." She stuck a hand straight up in the air. She waved; a favourite band, brilliant concert kind of wave, shouting, "Coo-ey!" and, "Over here!" The Leylandii gave an extra quiver. She lowered the binoculars. "Come and have a cup of tea," she shouted, her hands cupped around her mouth. "You must be freezing."

Nothing.

"Don't pretend you didn't hear me," Tori muttered to herself. "The garden isn't that long."

She prised herself from the bench, helped by the way the sun had tightened the seat so that it now sloped down towards the stone chippings, which were wearing a little thin. She planted one foot in front of the other. This was not a moment to fall over. She stopped dead centre of the grass, good hand on her hip.

"It is you scurrying about in the undergrowth. Hello Steve," she said, although technically she couldn't see who it was without her binoculars to hand. "Tea's getting cold and if you don't join me and my friend for a cuppa, I'll call the police. You are, in fact," she shouted, already turned back towards the house, "trespassing."

Jo was washing-up at the kitchen window. Tori smiled, wagged a finger and gestured that she should come outside instead. Jo opened the patio door, blew into her hands, and said that she'd finish these few bits. "Gosh," she said, "you have a visitor." She dashed back inside.

"Steve Cribbins." He held out his hand and offered a rubbery smile. "Great to meet you properly."

"Greetings," Tori said, and busied herself with pouring tea into the mug originally assigned to Jo. "I hope you like tea," she said, "keeps me going." He took it gratefully.

"This is my garden, my land," she said. "The rosemary bush, where you spend most of your time, Jesus, don't you have a life?—"

"Don't—" he said, raising a finger in the air.

"—is my rosemary bush. I planted it with a stem given to me by my mother." Her hand found its way onto her hip. "Every time you trample on my property and spy on my family going about their everyday business, it irks me that little bit more." She held her thumb and forefinger apart to denote the small but significant amount. "So no, I can't say I am particularly pleased to have finally made your acquaintance but I am interested in what you find quite so compelling about me."

There was a tapping on the patio door where Jo stood with her arms outstretched, mouthing, 'OK?' Tori gave her a thumbs up.

"Great tea." The smile returned to Steve's face as he replaced the mug on the table. "It's because I find you quite entertaining," he said, ramming his hands into the pockets of his tatty green parka. "And I'll admit, I feel a teensy bit sorry for you." He repeated Tori's gesture with the finger and thumb and she pressed her lips into a smile rather than grabbing his fingers and twisting them into a knot.

"I wouldn't if I were you," she said. She was aware that Jo still stood at the window and beckoned her to come out. "At least I'm not spending the winter sitting in hedges. Who'd want to be the paparazzi?" She crossed her good arm across her chest. "I hope they pay you well even if you're not required to have an ounce of responsibility for the lives you crush."

Steve took a step closer to Tori so she placed her mug on the bench to prevent any attempt to sit next to her.

"I'm not actually a photographer," he said, "if you're asking. I'm a journalist, sort of an investigative journalist."

She smiled. "Well, Sort Of Investigative Journalist, it's still cold in that hedge, I'll bet."

He shrugged his shoulders. "And no, I don't get well paid."

Jo placed an extra cup as well as a jug of fresh milk on the table, peered into the pot and scurried off again with it in hand, calling, "Let me know if you need a minder," behind her.

"Time to go I think." Tori thrust out her hand for Steve to shake. "Let's continue our discussion another day," she said. "Although it would be nice to do it like grown-ups. The hide and seek game has grown a little thin." She winked but held back a grimace - since when had she started winking?

"Of course," Steve said, winking back. "Mr Williams knows the rules." He thanked Tori for the tea and sauntered off.

"What's that all about?" Jo asked, squeezing Tori's shoulders.

Tori smiled at her friend. "Beats me."

With the fresh tea poured, Jo spread the fleece over them both on the bench and they drank in appreciative quiet, their legs snug, fresh air on their cheeks. Tori slopped the last of her tea over the pot-bound geraniums and passed Jo the drawstring bag.

"Looks important," Jo said, as she took the large brown envelope from it as requested and revealed a wedge of papers. The first sheet was a heavier page, cream, with a rough surface. She noticed the address at the top and squeezed Tori's hand. She skimmed the letter, uttering abstract words such as, 'prompt', 'usher', 'November', 'Thursday'.

"29th!" Her eyes widened. "That's in two weeks!"

"Well," Tori said, "we knew it was coming."

Jo read out more of the details: the procedure for the day, that Tori would have the help of an usher to direct her to the correct courtroom and that, as this was a driving offence, she must organise alternative transport home as a precaution.

"Transport to prison being provided," Tori said.

Jo took her friend's hand again, holding on to it this time. "Nobody mentions prison here."

Tori looked at her. "Don't they?"

Jo read the letter again. "It merely says the hearing will take place at 1pm in the magistrates' court in Leeds. There's lots of further information attached—"

"Crown court," Tori corrected.

Jo returned to the letter, tracing her finger under the address. "No, definitely the magistrates' court," she said, "and no mention of the Crown court."

Tori took the letter from Jo, placed it on her lap and adjusted her magnifying sheet in an attempt to bring the words into focus. She tossed it aside and picked up her binoculars instead.

"Tiny font," Jo said, pointing to the significant line.

"Oh, I remember." Tori handed the document back to her. "Magistrates' first and from there the case will be referred to the Crown court."

"Right," Jo said. "Surprising that the procedure isn't detailed in the letter when there's so much other information," she mumbled, as she skimmed through the pages of supplementary notes. "Right down to where you can get yourself a water. Shall I take this away and read it for you?"

Tori's attention had moved to her foot, grinding the chippings below. She shook her head. She'd prefer to keep it with her.

"Well, this is all you need to know for now and this is clear: November 29th, court four, charge," Jo swallowed, "the charge against you is, Driving Without Due Care and Attention."

Tori stopped the grinding. "What did you say?"

"Here," Jo pointed to the bold type in the middle of the page. "There it is, nice and big," she said, rubbing Tori's back. "Driving Without Due Care and Attention."

"No mention of Death by Dangerous Driving?"

Jo shook her head. "No, there's no mention of that."

Tori's heart slammed into her ribcage. She took the letter back from Jo and held it at arm's length. Jo held the magnifying sheet inches from Tori's nose.

"That's it?" she said. "That's it? No Death by Dangerous Driving?"

"That's right."

"I've been charged with Driving Without Due Care and Attention?"

"Yes!" Jo said. "But what does that mean?"

"It means—" Tori's hand rushed to her mouth, the sheet of paper falling to the ground, "—it means that they can't send me to prison."

THIRTY-THREE

ETTA LOOKED AROUND at the myriad of heads in the grand auditorium. The hair was mostly glossy and coiffured or combed into a high ponytail for the girls or low for the boys. Few of her fellow students used an A4 hard-backed notebook as she did, an ink pen when she could find the time to buy the cartridges or a liquid gel roller pen otherwise. Instead, they inserted whatever notes they were taking straight into a variety of electronic devices which Etta couldn't afford. She didn't want them, didn't feel she needed them but hoped she didn't look a fool.

Her notes were, at best, erratic. Phrases would begin well but inappropriate and nonsensical half sentences would quickly become interspersed. The warm, stuffy lecture halls were the problem. Her head would sink down towards the tiny, hinged desk hanging from the back of the seat in front. Generally, she'd catch herself before her head met with the hard surface but a couple of times, she had been woken by the bang.

Today the lecture was on humidity. Her eyes were bright and alert; the only sign of fatigue she'd let slip was the yawn stifled behind her hand.

"Dew point temperature is the point at which the air becomes...?

"Saturated," a voice answered from the front.

"Saturated, thank you young man," Dr Harper said.

Etta had to concentrate in Dr Harper's lectures. He was one of the few who called out particular questions to specific people and he picked on her, it seemed, more often than most.

"We get high relative humidity when the temperature is close to the dew point. Everybody agreed? Let's move on to pressure." He scanned the audience for a response to his rhetorical question.

Etta's eyes wandered away from the lectern down to the phone in her lap. She would do exactly what she'd done every day this week: ignore him. He could mention her, saturate her TweetDeck with #Toristext, send her all the direct messages he liked, she would not meet up with this @investcribb. It was a battle of wills and he wasn't to know that hers had been punctured and sliced by his persistence. No, her silence would beat him in the end.

She exhaled. The next vibration was simply for a missed call from Andy. She thought better of responding. She'd missed enough lectures. She could do without being thrown out of this one. Students may titter about Dr Harper's eccentric traditionalism, but few dared to flaunt his rule against taking calls in the lecture hall.

"Taking this to its end point, low pressure would therefore be associated with which...? Yes, you there, with the excessive bobble on your hat." Dr Harper pointed to a small girl sitting in the far corner of the room. "Someone tell me what she said," Dr Harper bellowed.

"Well, she said 'fair' but it's 'stormy', isn't it sir?" answered the stocky youth to Etta's right. Etta stared at him. Thank goodness he'd stepped in. She hadn't a clue what they were talking about.

'Get to school. Important,' a message flashed: Andy.

"Flip!" Etta said a little too loudly, causing Dr Harper to look away from the presentation and directly at her. "Sorry, sorry," she mumbled as she bustled her belongings into her bag and pushed past her neighbours in search of the nearest exit. Dr Harper turned back towards the large screen with great affectation.

— — —

"Incident? What sort of incident?" Etta called into her phone as she hurried to her car.

"A brush with the press," the school secretary replied with all the nonchalance she could muster when a seven-year-old child in the school's care had taken on a Fleet Street photographer. "We tried to call you earlier, Miss Dubcek. Johan was quite wound up, very agitated. You can get here for an 11am meeting I assume?"

When Etta arrived, Andy was sitting in the headteacher's office on an undersized chair with a cup of tea and a biscuit, his arm loosely laid around his son's neck. As Etta flung open the door, he appraised his partner from head to toe and back again, rather as if she were an unexpected house guest, than the mother of their son.

Etta rushed over to Johan and cuddled him from the other side so that his head barely showed through the arch made by his parents.

"Mama!" he squealed, ducking out from under her arm. "Can I go now? I'm missing football."

"You OK?" she asked, examining all areas of his face, her eyes flitting from corner to corner.

"Yeah." He shrugged his shoulders. He looked so small in this room with all these adults. "Nothing happened. The man made me cross because he was taking your photo. I know you don't like it when the flipping paparazzi take people's photos when they don't want them to."

Etta smiled at the headteacher. "Direct quote," she said, with a certain degree of pride.

Johan was dismissed. The headteacher reprimanded his parents for Johan's comments which were deeply regrettable and put in jeopardy the safety of every single child in the school, not just their own. The pair were ushered out of the office after signing the incident book and on the understanding that the school was in consultation with the police on this matter, as they would be whenever children and photography were involved.

Andy grabbed Etta by the wrist, dragged her towards him. "We are going for a coffee."

— — —

Andy sat opposite Etta, on the other side of the square table, chewing his lip. They never had a chance to have a coffee together, just the two of them, not that Andy was in any mood to chat. Etta used to come in here with the children as a special treat after school when Johan was in reception. They hadn't been for months. She had no time any more, nor money.

It hadn't changed. The walls were lime green with a layer of grime resting on top. Great swirls of orange and yellow flowed from one end of the room to another, mocking her as they mimicked her life, the aimless rolling from one situation to another, the tsunami taking control away from her.

She focused on the coffee: bitter and strong. She peered at Andy over the top of the tall white cup and gave a 'mmm' sound as if she was trying out for a role in a commercial. Andy looked away.

She studied the clientele to check for lingering journalists. There were three mothers she didn't know at the table in the corner, each with at least one baby or a toddler at their side. An older couple sat next to them, engrossed in a couple of newspapers laid flat on their table. She strained her neck to examine the text.

Andy was staring at her. "Don't you give a damn, Etta?"

"Oh!" Etta blinked to regain focus. "Sorry, I was concentrating on the coffee. It's the best in Rochdale."

"I don't care about the coffee."

Etta placed her hand on his. "Are they sure it was a journalist though?" she said. "This is a seven-year-old boy. He could have mistaken a parent with an SLR camera for a journalist."

Andy snatched his hand from hers and placed it around his identical white mug. "Why would a parent with an SLR be furtively taking a photo of you as you dropped off your son at school?" he asked.

"Why would a newspaper photographer be taking a photo of me as I dropped off my son at school?" Etta said quickly.

Andy stared at Etta. "You tell me!"

Etta opened her mouth then closed it again. She gulped her coffee instead, grimaced and caught the eye of the waitress whom she asked for more milk.

"I thought you said it was the best coffee in Rochdale," Andy muttered.

Etta shook her head and said in a low whisper that people were watching them. Andy leaned in closer to her and said that he didn't care about other people, he cared about his family. "Well?" he asked, pulling away so that the waitress could place the milk on the table. "I'm listening."

Etta shrugged her shoulders. "I don't know. Do you think it's something to do with Tori Williams?"

Andy raised his arms in the air. "Congratulations Detective Inspector Dubcek," he said. "She got there in the end."

Etta tutted. "I may have visited the hospital a few times but other than that," she said, "I can't see what I've done wrong. Why are you so cross?"

Suddenly Andy threw back his head and laughed, a great loud, rippling chuckle. "Oh, Etta," he said, "if you could try living with you at the moment."

Etta froze. "Why do you say that?"

Andy stirred his coffee.

"Andy?"

He crossed his arms. "Forget the nightmares and I know you're not the only person to be obsessed with their phone," he said, in a voice more akin to his, "but all this secrecy is doing my head in." There had to be something more about her contact with Tori Williams, something she wasn't telling him because it didn't add up. "Maybe," he said, "maybe you don't need to tell me if it's so bad that you can't bring yourself to discuss it with your own partner—"

Etta tried to respond but Andy held up his hands.

"—All I know is," he said, "that it has to stop. I will not let you put our children in danger. These clandestine meetings with her mother, the letters you write - oh yes," he added, looking Etta in the eye, "I've read some of the many rejects in the recycling - it's an obsession, Etta, and something about your obsession is interesting to the press."

Etta circled the toe of her boot in the matted nests of dust accumulated around the table legs. "I'm not sure—"

"Unless you want our lives talked about in the same way they speak of the Williams family, it has to stop now."

"It isn't that easy to cut all ties," Etta said. "It reminds me—"

"I don't care any more." Andy pressed his lips together, head shaking from side to side. "Our children are involved."

"I have to work through my own demons, Andy. Just bear with—"

Andy thumped the table. He stood up and tugged his coat from the back of the chair. He leaned into Etta, spoke too loudly into her ear.

"Fuck your demons," he said. "No more contact with any of them. This is our children we're talking about."

THIRTY-FOUR

TORI LOOKED BACK over her shoulder into court four. The single tier bench for the reporters was already empty. She'd watched the glut of national and local press scribbling notes or staring at her as they'd weighed up and confirmed their judgements. So tightly packed together, they'd also spilled into the spectator area where Jo and Amelie had established an awkward group in the middle of a hostile audience. Next to them were Doug, sitting bolt upright throughout, and Carly who looked so much older than her twenty-four years in her cheap suit, with her curls tied back and bags under her eyes. Ruby was next to her, periodically massaging her shoulders or proffering a handkerchief. Tori shook her head; Carly should never have been in this position. Next to Ruby was a pretty girl with long brown hair in bunches to whom Ruby had also spoken occasionally and who'd offered Tori fleeting smiles of encouragement. Tori had chosen to look at them just enough to soak up their encouragement but not to dissolve into tears; the only way she could maintain her focus and her nerve.

She had expected the court to be more majestic. It could have been a hotel conference room if not for the enormous coat of arms with its lizards watching her from all angles and reminding her to 'Seize The Day', which she thought might be quite tricky from behind a closed cell door. The group of three magistrates who'd deliberated over the letters and references which would determine her life's course from this day forward, sat high up on a stage at the front of the court behind a continuous desk draped with a deep-green velour cloth. There was the stern-faced woman in her seventies whose gaze rarely left Tori's face, an overly large man sporting a toupée which kinked awkwardly and a woman of Carly's age, rarely looking up from the pile of papers sitting ominously in front of her. They set about the task as if they were overseeing a piano exam: giving no clue to their view of the performance; moving jerkily to the next question and writing only a few words after each offering. Doug had told Tori to smile a little when she spoke, ingratiate herself, but she couldn't meet any of their eyes in case she saw disgust. Only when the chief magistrate reminded her that now was her opportunity to say something in her defence and she'd answered, "It's all there, in my letter," did she turn to face them directly, loosen her high neck collar and say, "I'm so ashamed."

Doug pulled Tori and Carly into him and hugged them. "It's over," he said. "Time to go home."

"Yes Dad," Carly said, swaying slightly on her 10cm heels, stolen from Nicky's wardrobe – well, she wouldn't be needing them – as she detached herself from his embrace. "It's fantastic," she said brightly, and without letting her smile drop. "We can do this, Mum!"

Jayne, their assigned court usher, asked if they were ready. It intrigued Tori that the three magistrates sat at the top of the court in their worn, casual suits, yet the ushers, the gofers as Jayne had affectionately described herself, shrouded in their enormous black capes had all the effects of a Principal at Hogwarts.

"I'm ready," Tori said.

"Wait!" Carly studied her mother and teased a few wayward locks into her high bun. She blotted a tissue over her damp face and thrust another into her hand. Doug coughed. This was the last time any of the Williams family would have to face the media and he'd like to get it over with as quickly as possible, please. Carly took a step back, appraised her mother, grimaced fleetingly and took another tissue to her face. She blotted her own as well, and tightened the thin band around her ponytail unnecessarily.

"The shirt doesn't match, does it?" Tori asked.

"It's fine," Doug said.

Tori had planned to wear an old work suit but they were all at least two sizes too big. She couldn't face shopping and the sideways glances of the shop assistants as they studied her scarring and considered her reputation, so she'd bought a pair of trousers online and for the rest she'd had to make do. The result was that the grey, floppy linen trousers were mismatched with the high-necked lace shirt Doug had encouraged her to wear with them. He'd visited the magistrates' court twice before Tori's trial and, besides studying the body language of those who had - and those who hadn't - found favour with the magistrates, he'd examined their dress code.

"You look great," Doug answered, holding his arm in a triangle. "Perfect." Tori linked hers through the space. "We're going."

Jayne led them to the main doors without a word. She'd explained the court procedure to the three of them with such gentleness this morning that they could have been with a nurse again. She'd plied Tori with tissues and given such frequent reassurances of their strong family unit and its consequent ability to cope with the trial, that they had started to believe in them.

Waiting at the door to replace Jayne was Tori's lawyer, Sebastian Thackeray, an eminently well-qualified man who undoubtedly had Tori's interests at heart, even if he hadn't always understood them. He spoke plainly and had been known on several occasions to tell Tori to, 'Shut the fuck up,' but in court today he was charming. So adept was he at acting for his client, when he'd explained to the magistrates that she was of previous good character and in fact, a highly principled woman, (notwithstanding, of course, this single error of judgement) he'd positively glowed with adoration, his eyes sparkling as if it was love at first sight.

"Right," Mr Thackeray said, standing a foot in front of Tori and breathing garlic fumes into her face. "Remember what we spoke about. No eye contact. Do not answer any questions. Speak only from your script. Thank the audience and then we will escort you to your car."

"Yes," Tori said. "Thank you."

"One more thing," he gripped the handles of the ten foot high, oak-panelled double doors, each with only a peephole to allow any sight of the outside world, "be prepared for the racket when I open these."

A mixture of the glare of the mid-afternoon, winter sun and the bellow of the crowd in the public square nearly forced Tori back behind the door. She teetered at the top of the three court steps while she tried to find her focus. Doug pulled her arm even tighter through the link with his. Sebastian Thackeray stood at her right side, saying only, "Waait, waaait" as if she would soon be allowed to open her Christmas presents. Carly was forced to stand behind. Tori wished she was closer.

Her brown eyes flitted from a cluster of banners, to a variety of flashing cameras, to a bank of heads jerking and straining. The sight of so many people falling out of the sides of the courtyard was enough to suck the air out of Tori's body. Her muscles were useless. She might faint. She breathed in. She had to speak, wanted to speak, but the words were stuck; a vice squeezed her throat. She pulled her arm from Doug's, put her hands to her neck and felt her clammy skin. She exhaled.

The noise petered out. But the quietness of the crowd was every bit as stifling as the shouting had been. She felt Doug's hand on hers.

"We could go."

Tori looked at his face next to hers and back at the crowd. She shook her head. "It's my one chance, Doug."

"Hello. I am Tori Williams," she announced. "I am standing before you today knowing that I am lucky to be alive." She looked down at the shakily written notes screwed into a ball in her grasp. "I am happy with my-my sentence," she stuttered, "and I know that it could have been harsher."

"You should be in prison!" shouted a stocky man in the front row. He was only two feet away. She raised her hand to acknowledge him and couldn't help take in the swarm of faces around: the man with a shaven head a foot away, his arms so fiercely crossed it made his biceps look twice the size; the group of children in maroon coloured school uniform who stood still, their phones poised for photographs. There was a woman rocking a pram, three men in dark suits with their backs to Tori.

Did she really warrant so many policemen?

She lingered for a moment on the banner held by a child on her father's shoulders which Carly begrudgingly read for her.

"What if it was your child?" she said, loud enough only for her mother to hear.

Tori swallowed, straightened her back and lifted her head.

"I'm aware that if I'd been charged with Dangerous Driving, I would have gone to prison and I would have been in my mid-fifties before I got out," she started again.

"Irrelevant," she heard Doug say.

"If I'd ever been guilty of an offence in the past," Tori regarded the spittle which landed on her lace-up black boots, "my sentence would have been more severe." People threw their hands into the air. The collective sound of tutting and gasping resonated, even over the flap of the St George's flag and a cold winter wind.

"Stick to your notes for Christ's sake!" Doug said, much louder this time. "They don't see it like us."

"Two thousand pound fine?" she heard from the back of the crowd. "It's an insult."

"Disgusting criminal!"

Tori gestured in the direction of the latest voice. "Yes sir, in a way I am a criminal," she said. "I sent a text whilst driving and I ploughed into the back of the Mondeo. Regardless of how badly Mr Reynolds was driving, he may not have killed himself and his wife and the baby in the next car if I had not also rammed his."

Doug tugged at Tori's arm, his head bowed. "You got a death wish?"

She pulled her arm away, uncurled her notes again. Over the mass of heads, arms and faces moving with increased animation, over towards the right hand side, ten or so people away, and with a ring of space around her, was a woman in a black dress. Her coat was bunched under one arm and her blonde hair splayed out underneath a dark cap. She held a young child's hand. Their stillness unnerved Tori as much as the anger thrown in her direction. She returned to her notes.

"I am in a state of disbelief and total shame," Tori read, through clenched jaws, her cheeks pink and blotchy, "and will never forgive myself for my moment of madness. I am the lucky one because I get the chance to try."

"No one feels sorry for you! You're a killer!" the shaven-headed man said, his arms still crossed. "You got away with murder."

"Back!" the police officer roared. The crowd had inched forward and were within an arm's length of Tori's face. Mr Thackeray stretched his right arm out across Tori to encourage his client to move back towards the court exit. Much more and he would order her back into the relative safety of the court. He was a bulky man and Tori had to stretch to see over the top of his pinstriped sleeve.

She handed the scrunched up paper to Carly, tugged her blouse down to below her waist and stared forward. A tall man, his shoulders a good few inches higher than everybody else's, angled his head in her direction. She squinted, she couldn't make out his face but saw his college blazer and the unnecessary sunglasses.

"It's Gerald," Carly whispered in her ear. He raised his hand to wave. What was he doing here?

"You know," her voice was bullish, louder now, more like her own. "I could have been charged with Dangerous Driving but I wasn't. I didn't commit a crime through malice, it was a moment of stupidity. And I hadn't been speeding and I didn't mean to kill anybody. Before I drove my car that day, I was a normal person doing an everyday job—"

"Your crime killed people, lady. Destroyed their families."

Tori held up her hand, registering a tall, blonde-haired man of about sixty who pointed his finger directly at her. "Yes of course," she said, "I will always live with the fact I destroyed other people's families."

"And your own family!" added the lady next to him, gesticulating to the audience around her. "I pity them."

Doug stared at the woman and Carly squeezed Mr Thackeray

out of her way so she could link her arm through her mother's.

"I can't turn the clocks back although I would do anything to be able to do so," Tori continued. "But if people can learn from my lesson—"

"Think you can fuckin' teach us something do you now love?" the shaven headed man shouted. "How can you come here and tell us what *we* can learn about right and wrong?" The crowd screeched words of agreement. A single person clapped and was joined by a few others until it seemed that over half the people had joined in the applause, only breaking from the clapping to curve a hand around their mouths to project some choice obscenities of their own in Tori's direction.

Tori shook her head, and shivered.

"No, no not at all," she said in a voice too quiet for anybody other than her family or Mr Thackeray to hear. "If I can make good my mistake—" she managed a little louder.

"Will you stop the fuckin' preaching!"

"Do NOT respond," Mr Thackeray hissed.

"I've had enough of this," the same man said, spitting now as he spoke. "I've heard enough you murdering bitch." He waved his fist in the air. "Fuckin' nutter you are." He screwed his finger into his temple to demonstrate, turned to the crowd behind him and raised both arms into the air in apparent disbelief. "Thinks she's a fuckin' saint now." The crowd roared their agreement, so loud that when Doug spoke right next to her, Tori couldn't hear.

"We're leaving," Doug tried again, but Tori stayed where she was, staring after the man as he pushed himself back through the crowd. She took in the frenzy he'd whipped up. Instead of shouting now, people were baying. She was a gladiator who'd reached the end of the line; the audience had enjoyed the anticipation of the fight but now they wanted to take control.

"I told you not to move from the script," Mr Thackeray said. "You have put us all in a dangerous situation."

Tori felt Doug's hand on the small of her back. "Now!" he said. "We're going."

But before she could decide whether to persevere in spite of both her husband and lawyer's protestations, over the top of the commotion she heard a different kind of voice.

"Let her say her piece." The man was to her left, within a second row of journalists, a microphone in one hand and an identity card around his neck. He was different from the flock of journalists who pressed against her front door. He wasn't wearing the jeans and requisite white t-shirt, hair secured in a ponytail, nor was he staring at Tori in their audacious manner without so much as a flicker of distraction or momentary glance away on realisation that their eyes had locked. With his crisp white shirt and gold tie, he was smarter, more relaxed. Human, maybe.

"Mrs Williams, you were saying that if people could learn from your mistake…"

"Yes," she said, "perhaps something good could come from this." Before she could elaborate, reporters' questions flew at her from all directions.

"Can you tell us about your disabilities, Mrs Williams?"

"Why were you having chicken for tea?"

"Was it usual for you to text instructions to your husband?"

"Doesn't your husband cook, Mrs Williams?"

"One at a time please," Mr Thackeray barked. "You're lucky Mrs Williams has chosen to speak."

"How will you manage without a driving licence for three years?" a voice asked from the left.

She turned in its direction, took in the grin of the woman who towered over the swarm of people around her and said that a driving licence would be of no use to her. "I'll never see well enough to drive," she said. Doug jabbed an elbow into her ribcage.

"How do you feel about being made a test case Tori?" the same woman asked.

"I'd have preferred a prison sentence so that I could show my repentance," she said, "work to gain atonement."

"This is media suicide," Mr Thackeray whispered, directly into Tori's ear.

"I'm just telling the truth," she said. "People should be more honest."

More questions pinged at her like bees escaping a hive: so many stings they were indistinguishable from each other. Tori looked from reporter to protestor. Only when the reporter in the gold tie spoke, his hand stuck in the air as if in class, did Tori allow herself to ask him to repeat the question.

"In view of the fact you weren't given a custodial sentence," he asked, "what are you going to do now?"

"I'm going to move forward," she said. "I could visit companies and schools and talk about the risks of reckless driving, how one moment of madness can lead to a lifetime of sadness."

"It's not about what you want love," a voice called out. It was the man with the small child on his shoulders. "It's about right and wrong and if you kill a baby you should be banged up."

Tori felt Carly pressing against her side. Her suit jacket was thin and she could feel her shivering.

"Right, that's it," she heard Carly say under her breath. She pushed past Tori's elbow to stand a step in front of her parents.

"Have you never lived?" she shouted. "Have you never made a mistake?"

"Carly, restrain yourself!" Her father flung his arm across her stomach in an attempt to move her back away from the crowd, but she stood firm and pushed his arm away.

"It was a moment of madness," she said. "That's why my mother was found guilty of Driving Without Due Care and Attention, because she made one stupid mistake."

Tori yelped, taking in the look of incredulity on the faces of the crowd.

"She didn't mean to kill anybody." Carly's voice cracked but she carried on. "Even the police don't think she was driving that badly, otherwise she'd have been in the Crown court for 'Dangerous Driving' and she wasn't." A gasp spread across the audience.

"Stop right there!" Mr Thackeray said.

"That's what the press should be writing. That's why anybody who understands anything about the law knows my mother shouldn't have gone to prison. They should write that, too."

It was the reporter again, the respectful one. He thrust the microphone towards Carly's midriff.

"Toby Hanson, Yorkshire Vale Radio. Miss Williams," he said. She turned in his direction. "I think our listeners are concerned for the bereaved families. How do they gain closure?" Carly stared at the reporter. Tori tensed. She knew Carly had become practised at fielding provocative questions at the hospital and even outside her own home. She was used to her pupils firing insults, slighting her family, goading her. But the plump journalist, with his alluring Irish accent, had asked a reasonable question and Tori knew this had thrown her daughter.

Mr Thackeray looked at Carly and then at Toby Hanson and said in his best, gravelly voice that Ms Williams did not need to answer his questions. Her mother has been good enough to share her thoughts with him and he was sure that everyone had enough to be going on with. He turned to look at each of the family in turn to seek their agreement.

Carly shook her head. She raised her hand, serving to dampen the rumble of the crowd a little, and turned back to the reporter. "It's a valid question, Mr Hanson," she said. "But I don't think it's one for our family to answer. I think it's a question for the country's judicial system."

"Quite," he replied, running his fingers through his thinning, blonde hair, spread in all directions over his head to cover as much scalp as possible. "But you must have a view. Shouldn't the punishment help the victim even if it's at the expense of the perpetrator?" When Carly faltered, he added that the victims and their families didn't get to pick up their lives if they didn't see that justice had been done, which was met with a huge roar of appreciation from the crowd.

Carly's face was pink, her top lip wet with sweat. "My mother will punish herself," she said. "She can't do any more than that."

"That isn't enough for the victims," another reporter suggested.

Carly was forced to shout: "She's a good woman, a decent person."

"Your sister doesn't think so, does she Carly?" a woman's voice interjected.

"Stop!" Tori nudged Carly to the side and stood on the step next to her, hooked her arm through her daughter's. "Please, stop," she shouted, her bottom lip quivering. "Direct your questions to me and me only!"

"No!" Doug snapped. He, too, moved to the step below so that the three of them were standing in a line; Carly flanked by her parents. "My wife has answered all the questions put to her in a court of law," he said. "She has been dealt the largest punishment ever awarded for a momentary lapse of concentration." He stared directly at the most vocal area of the crowd and said that if they had a problem with that, he'd suggest they speak to the Crown

Prosecution Service. "Now, my wife will not be speaking to you again and this has nothing to do with either of our daughters." He turned his back. "Come on," he said to his family, jostling them back to the court building, forcefully this time.

"My partner was killed in a road traffic accident," Tori heard from behind her. The voice was loud but calm. She stopped walking. "My daughter and I are on our own." Tori pulled her shoulder away from Doug's grasp and turned in the direction of the lady with the cap, holding the child's hand. She'd moved closer to the court steps.

"Putting Mrs Williams behind bars won't do anything to help anybody. She'll serve her own sentence wherever she is." The whole family turned to face the lady, leaving only Mr Thackeray who sighed crossly and stared at his patent black shoes. The mother didn't appear to be talking to anyone in particular, rather to the air around her and certainly not to the journalist who'd sprinted over and was now holding the microphone under her bottom lip. "It won't bring the deceased back," she said. "Another family will be parted from their loved one."

People were standing at a respectful distance from her, quiet now, listening. Now that she had people's full attention, she barely needed to shout. "What we have to do is try to forgive," she said. "We have to be civilised." Nobody spoke. The journalists scribbled and filmed. "There's too much anger, too much hatred. If we play this game, we're all losers in the end." Tori met her gaze. "That's all I have to say."

The mother turned her daughter away from the court. The crowd parted, allowing the pair a route through. The journalists reclaimed their positions, rushing mobile phones to their ears, tapping out messages on phones, hurriedly now speaking to camera. The protestors' banners still billowed but fewer words accompanied them. The father removed his child from his shoulders. The blonde man and his wife argued.

A noise swelled in the crowd again as the heavy door behind Tori creaked open. She saw Mr and Mrs Pickering emerge from the court exit with their daughter gripped in her father's arms, dressed in a pink taffeta fairy dress, clasping a magic wand. They were hustled into position and the audience fell silent again.

"Mr and Mrs Pickering have prepared a short statement which Mr Pickering will read to you," their lawyer said in stilted tones. "They will not be taking questions."

Mr Pickering kissed his daughter on her forehead, handed her silently over to his small wife, breathed out and extracted a piece of paper from the inside pocket of his suit. Tori and her family sank back towards the wall. The journalists double-checked that their equipment was working.

"For accidents to happen," Mr Pickering began in a broad Yorkshire accent, "numerous errors have to occur. Tori Williams was texting when she was driving and Peter Reynolds had been driving irresponsibly. Both of these people are to blame for the death of our son, Joshua." He glanced up from his paper, his hand signalling in Tori's direction.

"We will never see Josh again. We will never be able to cuddle him or watch him grow. He will never play with his sister, Amy. He will never ride a bike." He looked over at Tori more now as he spoke: a series of quick glances. "It doesn't matter how long a driving ban Mrs Williams was given, my son will never ever drive a car." His wife stared forward, vaguely lifting and lowering her daughter's long hair with her fingers.

"This charge, this whole case has been too lenient and has only increased our grief. It is this country's duty to make sure that no other family ever has to endure a similar tragedy but Mrs Williams' sentence will prove no deterrent to other selfish drivers." The throng was silent, the only noise the clicking of cameras and the whirr of electricity. Mr Pickering folded the paper into four, his fingers shaking. "We will not rest until we have done everything in our power to make Mrs Williams pay for the death of our son. We owe it to ourselves, to Amy, but also to society to sue Tori Williams through the civil court. Thank you," he said, and loosened his tie. "Now, we'd be grateful if you'd leave us to grieve in private."

"No questions," their lawyer said as he and two police officers shielded the family through the crowds towards their waiting car.

"Can you confirm you'll sue?" a journalist called.

"How bad is your loss?" But the couple kept their focus ahead, as if the questions hadn't been asked.

The screams and shouts of the crowd which had been suppressed, burst from them now like air from a punctured balloon. Fingers jabbed in Tori's direction. People pushed those in front of them so that they could get closer, spilling onto the court steps despite the best efforts of the police.

"Back inside the building," an officer said, his face stern and inches away from Tori's. He herded the family back inside the court to a waiting area. "Don't even attempt to leave yet."

— — —

"Well," Mr Thackeray wiped his forehead with a handkerchief, "now we wait to see if you did any irrevocable damage." He stuck out his hand and shook Tori's firmly, lingering on the handshake uncharacteristically. "You'll find time is a great healer," he said, "for all parties." Then he reverted to his more normal businesslike manner and said that his office would be in touch regarding costs.

Mr Thackeray left through the main exit. Tori leaned against the wall before sliding down to the floor. Doug sank down next to her and Carly did the same on the other side.

"OK Carly?" Tori asked carefully. "It's been a hard day for all of us." She put her arm around her shoulders. "Come on love." She shuffled closer. "It's over."

"It's not over," Carly spluttered. She lifted her head and tears fell down her cheeks. "They're going to sue. Nobody told me they might sue. This thing will run and run."

Tori needed Doug for help but he was staring straight ahead, not offering any response.

"We're fighters in this family," she said. "We'll cope." She heaved herself up into a standing position and leaned against the wall for support. She reminded them that she'd escaped prison as they'd wanted her to do. They were all together, as they'd hoped. Tori heard Carly moaning into her hands, incoherent sounds. Doug didn't flinch. His long stare unnerved her. She tilted her head towards him. "We need to get out of here," she whispered. Still he stared forward. "Everything will feel better at home."

The tears had stopped but Carly's head was wedged in her hands. "We're right back at the beginning," she said. "Waiting."

Doug had closed his eyes. Tori saw a different usher making her way towards them. "Up, you two, get up!" she said in a low voice. "Please don't let them see you like this."

More people were milling around now, more briefcases, more tattoos, more family groups with two or more generations. The usher sidled up to Tori and suggested that they should be leaving, that the crowds had gone from outside, that her mother had her car waiting for them and that she was sure everybody would feel better once they'd vacated the scene.

"Besides," she added, scanning the immediate area, "this space is open to the public. Anybody could come in here." She tipped her head towards the steady traffic of people behind her, contemplated the two sitting on the floor and asked Tori if she should fetch a security officer to help or did she think they needed medical assistance?

Tori shook her head and watched the usher walk away. She felt a tap on her shoulder and swung around.

"Tori, I know this is a bad time but may I—"

"Leave us alone!" she shouted. A look of horror spread across the face of the tiny lady with the beautiful hair who'd sat next to her mother. "It's Etta isn't it?" Tori asked, more softly now. Etta nodded. "I'm sorry, Etta, I am grateful to you but now is not a good time."

THIRTY-FIVE

TORI HAD IRONED the white linen tablecloth herself. It certainly bore some crinkles but nothing so bold as a crease. "Not bad," she said. "Small steps."

Ironing was difficult. She'd quickly mastered left handed control of the appliance but holding the item to be ironed in place with the forearm of her injured arm was quite a challenge. Shirts were impossible. Tori farmed them out to a colleague of Doug's for £20 a basket. She wished she could iron them herself. She wished she could be the one to fund the £20.

With the linen cloth heaped in the centre, Tori attempted the challenge of spreading the eight-by-six feet of material in a regular manner over the dining table. As she pulled with her working fingers, the steadying forearm released too much or too little of the linen until inevitably, the whole cloth slipped on to the floor on the opposite side. She started again. This time she used a few mats to hold the material on the table while she teased each edge over the four sides.

"Acceptable." She stepped back to admire the relatively smooth cloth stretching towards the velvety leather chairs in deepest claret, which had cost Tori any sniff of profit from Party Planners in its first year. For the first breakfast of their new life, the couple once again had a cloth on their table.

Tori had woken early to greet her shopping delivery. She loaded the croissants into a basket and placed the organic muslin over the top. She arranged each of the six assorted jars of jam, honey and marmalade around the centre of the table. Slicing a loaf of bread was time consuming so she settled for a couple of pieces, cut three quarters of the way to the base and peeling engagingly from the crusty white loaf. Since the shock of her high cholesterol reading shortly before leaving hospital, Tori no longer ate butter, even on special occasions, but she'd ordered some for Doug so that he could perform his unsavoury ritual of dipping the buttered croissant into his coffee. With the coarse ground blend waiting in the cafetière, she filled the kettle as she always did these days, using a jug to carry the water from the sink. While it boiled, she piled the strawberries and ready-chopped chunks of melon into the awaiting glass bowl.

"Good," she said. "Fruit juice is all we need and then I'll wake him." Tori looked at the enormous round clock with its bold, black numbers. She should hurry. They would only have half an hour for breakfast before Doug had to leave for work. She wished he could take a day off, that they could spend the time together, try to work things out. But Doug was already struggling to keep his job, it would be better not to ask for compassionate leave to comfort a wife for whom few people had any sympathy.

She hesitated when she passed his empty wine glass on the floor in the hallway. Doug had drunk too much by the end of the evening and wasn't in the mood for talking, or listening, to Tori's, 'We will get through this,' and 'You broke down, it's bound to happen, nobody saw.' He had gone to bed and Tori had been left to do all the clearing up that was within her capabilities. Later she lay in bed, tears slipping from her eyes, unsure whether she was upset by the threat of another court case or the dissatisfaction with the closure of this one.

She navigated the stairs back down into the hall and heard the papers arrive through the letterbox with a series of thumps. She picked them up, one by one, and dumped them in the utility room.

As she poured the hot water into the cafetière, she heard Doug pace towards the front door. "Special breakfast today," she called to him. "New era."

He kissed his wife on the cheek. "The papers should be here," he said, "shouldn't they?"

Tori fixed her eyes on the microwave counting down the seconds to warm milk. Doug repeated his path to the front door and then passed Tori on the way back again, en route to the utility room. She called that she thought it would be nice if they sat down and had breakfast together, without any distractions.

Doug dropped the pile of papers onto the dining table without comment.

"You always tell me not to read those things," she tried again.

He moved the stack around the table, pushing the food and the condiments to one side to make room.

"Look at this!" He tugged a tabloid from the middle of the pile, the protruding word 'Scot-free' the only hint he needed. "'3-0 to the Texting Killer: Mrs Williams walked away from court yesterday afternoon with a fine and a driving ban.' I hardly dare look but I have to," he said as Tori placed the coffee on the table and moved the pretty muslin topped jars close to where she'd originally placed them, before sitting down.

"I wish you hadn't spoken, Tori. You've alienated people even more."

Tori poured hot milk into two mugs. "California Roast," she said. "We like this one."

"This editorial," Doug continued. "'Mrs Williams has made a mockery of the law. Because it states that the use of a mobile phone in the car alone does not constitute the need for a prison sentence, Ms Williams was tried for 'Driving Without Due Care And Attention'. I ask what is careless about texting your husband to remind him to put his tea in the oven? Texting is a fully conscious act. When she picked up that phone, Ms Williams was completely aware that she was driving dangerously and thus should have been tried for just that. Dangerous Driving, is, I remind you, punishable with a prison sentence. Careless driving is not...' blah blah." Doug skimmed the remaining text.

"We knew they'd write this," Tori said quietly.

"'Why isn't Mrs Williams behind bars?'" Doug read out again, finally taking his place at the table. "'How many people need to die before a case of this kind is tried in a Crown court, in front of a judge and jury?'"

Doug lifted his head from the paper and noticed for the first time the spread she had laid out in front of him. "Thank you," he said, and touched her hand. "You've made a huge effort."

Tori's eyes were red from lack of sleep, her matted hair piled on top of her head because she hadn't yet had time for a shower. "It wasn't any trouble."

"You've got to learn to play the game, Tori. Keep quiet," Doug said. "Don't give them anything, because they will hang you with it."

"They're trained to get you to speak."

"The reporters, perhaps, but the protestors aren't. You don't know who you're dealing with when you talk to one of them."

"Decent folk probably," Tori said, taking a spoonful of strawberries. "People who care."

"Yeah, well people who care do reckless things like throw eggs at your window and worse." He gathered a few papers into a pile, put them on the floor beside him and reached for a croissant. "They're warm," he said, forcing a smile and clutching one in his hands.

Tori looked at Doug properly for the first time that morning. His eyes were small and moist, a little bloodshot. She could make out the faint freckles on his nose and the horizontal line on his chin which marked the start of its protrusion. She could see him better than a few days ago. Every week that went by Tori felt her condition was improving.

Doug looked away and shook his head. "It's stressful, Tori," he heaped a lump of butter onto one half of his croissant, "and it's going to get worse before it gets better."

"You're sure they'll sue aren't you?"

"Of course they will," Doug said. He dunked the remaining piece of croissant into his lukewarm coffee and wandered out of the dining room, pastry flakes dropping to the floor. "What have they got to lose?"

Tori heaved herself up and followed Doug into the living room. "Or to gain," she said. "What's a sum of money when you've lost a child?"

Doug looked at Tori, then back through the small gap in the curtains.

"Yep, knew it, Steve's back, behind the rosemary." He waved at him and let the curtain fall back. "And the leeches will be outside school. The kids will love it." Doug shook his head. "Oh Tori," he said, "why didn't you just say you were sorry, like you intended? We could have got you into the car as quickly as possible."

"We shouldn't have to be prisoners of our thoughts," she said.

"Otherwise I may as well be back in that coma."

"I have to face the mobs at school."

"I don't want to make life difficult for you Doug."

"I know you don't Tori," he said, retrieving his puffa jacket from the settee. "But you do."

Tori moved a step closer and thread her good arm around Doug's waist in an attempted hug but he removed her hand and said that he couldn't possibly be late for work. He fastened his briefcase. "I'm weary, Tori. You've had less than two months of it. I've had double that." He glanced at his watch, shook his head. "Do you even know what you're trying to achieve? Do you think you can change the views of a nation?"

"Maybe if they understand that I'm a normal person—"

"You're expecting the press to do a U-turn and claim that Tori the Texting Killer is really quite sweet?" he asked. "Have you read that shit?" He charged back into the dining room, Tori following as fast as she was able. He picked the newspapers up from the floor, pushed Tori's plate to the side and piled them in its place. "Have a read, so you know what you're up against," he said. He jabbed at a headline: "'Williams Pleading for Prison!'" he read. "One of the more accurate—"

"So what do you suggest I do? Give up?"

"I suggest you keep quiet." Doug picked up another of the papers and traced his finger under the headline: "Look at this: 'Texting Killer Not Court for Offence.' Oh ha ha, yes, very clever."

"That's quite good actually," Tori said. Doug looked at her with disapproval before snatching open the paper.

"'Texting Killer says driving ban won't touch her,'" he read. "'Mrs Williams mocked the leniency of her punishment.' That's great." He smacked his forehead. "Talk about a tabloid gift."

Tori took her seat back at the table but refused to look where

Doug was pointing.

"How about this?" He waved his hand in the direction of the paper. "'Texting Killer blames death on Mr Reynolds, deceased.'"

"But that's not fair! I didn't say that."

"Tori, that's my point." Doug crouched down to be at her eye level. "It doesn't matter what you say or how you say it, the press, and most of this nation, have got your card marked and the only way to avoid the worst of it is to keep your trap shut." Doug smacked a peck against her forehead and reminded Tori that they only had one income now and he had to get to work. They had the court costs to pay and they hadn't even started on the civil case yet.

"If we've got a roof over our heads after this lot we'll have got off lightly," he said, marching into the hall. "Meanwhile, all I ask is that you help me keep my job."

Tori shuffled to the bay window and watched through the gap as Doug strode past the reporters, his head aloft. He could barely prise open the car door with the weight of the journalists pressing on it. Only his acceleration could shake them from the windows of his car where they clung like flies to a Venus flytrap.

She dropped the curtain to fill the gap. Whatever she thought, whatever she did, she was trapped. She couldn't stray far from the house without physical - and often emotional - support. She couldn't speak as she saw fit, for fear of inciting further vitriol from the press and outraged protestors and all its repercussions for Doug's job. She slumped down to the floor. Was this it now? Days filled with untruths spread over her dining table. Three quarters of a family, a smattering of friends and unemployment her only solace for the future? She was Tori Williams: unemployable, un-invite-able.

But the trouble with sitting back and waiting for something to happen was that it might not. And for Tori, the idea of spending the rest of her life restricted by the walls of her house and the needs of everybody else was as daunting as lying in hospital, wondering if she was ever going to be able to speak again.

She packed the uneaten pastries back into their muslin bag. She brought a tray from the kitchen so that she could pile it up with unbreakables and carry it on her hip. She switched on the radio. She was not going to be miserable. She had enjoyed setting the table and Doug would appreciate the gesture when he thought about it later.

"Tori Williams exchanges a moment of madness for a lifetime of sadness," the radio said. Tori stopped clearing the table and turned to face the speaker.

"The best way to explain it is, 'Knock for Knock,'" a well-spoken voice said. "It's when exact proportions of blame cannot be attributed to an incident. It's really an insurance term. Both sides pay for their own losses because they recognise that it isn't always possible to assign exact proportions of blame. Similarly, if the inquest wasn't able to provide the Crown Prosecution Service with the extent to which the texting, as opposed to the other driver's recklessness, was to blame for the accident, any charge of Dangerous Driving would be difficult."

Tori turned up the volume.

"But surely the texting is a crime in itself, regardless of whether or not the other driver was at fault? Shouldn't Mrs Williams be judged solely on the fact she used her mobile phone whilst driving at 60 mph along the M62 motorway?" Tori recognised the voice of the presenter asking the questions. She could picture him in his gold tie and crisp white shirt. She sat back down.

"I would suggest that the texting is *exactly* what she has been judged on. There were no witness reports of any aggressive or irresponsible driving up to this point. Mrs Williams has no previous history of motoring offences and she pleaded guilty at the first opportunity when interviewed by police. They will have considered all this when deciding the charge. That's what a 'single lapse of concentration' is. For her to have been charged with Dangerous Driving she would have to have shown *gross negligence*. The Crown Prosecution Service obviously felt that they had no conclusive evidence of this being the case and would not have been able to prove it in the Crown court."

Tori breathed out slowly. Who was this man defending her on Yorkshire Vale Radio? How did he manage to explain things so clearly when her attempts only attracted outrage? Perhaps she'd finish off the coffee after all.

"So the fact that she allegedly killed three people counts for nothing?" the presenter asked. She told herself to be strong. He was being deliberately dogged. He understood both sides very well yesterday.

"I bring you back to my original point," the expert said. "Did Ms Williams kill three people? We don't know. The evidence is inconclusive. Witness reports attest that the other driver was driving badly. It has been well argued that he was driving more dangerously, for a longer period of time, than Mrs Williams."

Tori imagined Toby Hanson in his radio studio. His face in a constant half smile, enjoying the debate. This was the kind of discussion she'd yearned for. But whenever she spoke of anything to do with the accident or the court proceedings, her friends and family clammed up as if their acknowledgement alone would bring the scene back to life in front of them.

"But surely that's not what we're talking about, because Mrs Williams drove into the back of the driver who was driving badly so she has to be punished for this, regardless?" Toby asked.

"This is when it becomes very difficult for the families of the loved ones because the law can't be allowed to judge guilt solely on the consequences of the action."

"Why not?" Toby asked. "I expect the families of the deceased would think that fair."

"And the prison service would be heaving with those people caught on the wrong side of luck as opposed to the wrong side of the law."

Toby clicked his tongue, thinking, radio-style. "Help me here," he said, "people go to prison for killing people don't they?"

"Of course."

"So we have many examples of perpetrators paying for the consequences of their crime. A murderer goes to prison because he or she killed somebody, not because the action was 'dangerous'?"

"The murderer goes to prison for both those reasons. And Mrs Williams is equally being punished for her crime. People say she got off lightly but that depends on how you view the penal system. Should people who are no threat to society, and who show utmost remorse for their crimes, be sent to prison?"

"Ah," Toby said. "Prison isn't merely about the community's safety though is it? It's about upholding our society's moral code and providing a deterrent."

"Exactly," Tori said. "That's what I tried to explain." She took a croissant back out of the bag. One wouldn't hurt but she'd eat it without jam, save herself the sugar and the effort of single handed spreading.

"That's correct. However, I'm not sure how society would gain from putting Tori in prison. It would cost the taxpayer a good quarter of a million to keep Mrs Williams in prison for five years." Tori gasped: even more money than she'd thought. "Within a month she'd be forgotten which would negate her use as a deterrent. If this lady uses her time as she's been suggesting, to educate people and to persuade everyone to switch off their phone in the car, then the benefit to society could be a hundred-fold greater."

"Yes!" Tori slammed her hands down on the table. "I can do that!"

"And that folks," Toby's voice cut back in, "is our phone-in for the hour. A Moment of Madness for a Lifetime of Sadness: should Tori Williams, often referred to as Tori the Texting Killer, have received a custodial sentence for her involvement in the death of a husband and wife and a little baby boy?"

Tori dialled Jo's number using the ten pence size buttons on the oversized retro phone that Carly had presented her with a few days ago. She smiled to herself. It was a favourite question of protestors and journalists alike: 'Have you been doing any texting lately?' Yet the prospect of making out the mobile phone keys, not to mention summoning the manual dexterity to use them, was a dream she'd abandoned weeks ago.

"Jo!" Tori said, excitement in her voice for the first time in months. "Come for brunch, you and Amelie! It's my turn, well overdue."

She launched into re-setting the table. She banished all newspapers to the recycling box, laid three sets of cutlery, retrieved the condiments and assessed the quantity of pastries. Did they sell croissants at the post office?

She sat down to put on her coat, as the occupational therapist had advised, located her grandfather's folding walking stick from the cupboard in the hall, complete with its curling brass badges celebrating walks he'd conquered, and remembered where she'd left the house keys on only the third time of retracing her steps. She leaned heavily on her stick with the door successfully closed behind her. Alone on her front step for the first time in over three months, she closed her eyes and smelt the air as if she'd stepped off the plane for a two week holiday.

"And off we go," she said to herself, shuffling past the baffled journalists, with her head held as high as her bent back would allow. Their damp silence didn't last long. Tori had only just turned left at the bottom of her drive before the crowd had trotted into position, a swarm in front and behind, carrying her towards the towpath as if she were Queen Ant.

'The benefit to society could be a hundred-fold greater,' Tori repeated in her head to blot out the noise. She needed to remember that.

"Are you enjoying your independence?"

"Do you have plans now you've dissolved your business?"

She had to concentrate to stay upright over the frozen lumps and mounds formed by hooves and bicycle wheels. There was only one connecting field and a short stretch along the main road through Deepbeck to come. Tori used to do this route with bags of parcels over both shoulders, pushing Nicky in a buggy, even holding Carly's hand, and still arrive at the post office within ten minutes.

"Nice family house, must be quiet—"

"Do you miss—?"

She halted. The crowd of six or seven people stepped on each other's heels and butted elbows as they, too, came to an unexpected stop.

"Do I miss my daughter? My innocence? My old life?" She moved closer to the owner of the voice. It was a dumpy, grey haired lady, with brandy snap curls through which Tori was tempted to push a finger. She didn't have a microphone, boom or camera, not even a phone or a notepad. Tori thought she knew everyone who walked the paths through her village.

"Yes, if only I could turn the clocks back. No, I will never forgive myself. Of course I miss my daughter and oh God, yes, oh yes, I am sorry." She coughed. The playing field was a few yards further. She moved forward again. "Now bugger off and enjoy the rest of your day trip!" she called after the older lady who was quickly retracing her steps.

Tori only needed a few more pauses to catch her breath and shake the heaviness from her legs and by the time the post office was in view, her breathing was as affected by the excitement as the exertion. Her last stop was a brief sit down at the bus stop. It was a long seat, with room for a good three or four more, but instead of the worn oak bench which had served Deepbeck for a few decades, now it was a cold, steel slab which cut into her bottom at the stern edges. Only one journalist sat down on the bench, and indeed, a gracious foot away from her.

"Hello Steve," she said, "your friends all gone?" She gestured across the road to the cluster of reporters as they strode one by one into the Barley Mow. "I'd catch them up," she said. "Their lives are much more interesting than mine."

She pressed down on her good hand to push herself up to standing, but her weight was too much and twice she fell back down to where she'd started. She was obliged to take Steve's arm when it was offered and he escorted Tori the last few steps to the post office with neither of them uttering a word.

Tori didn't know why she wore her watch as she couldn't make out the hands but the new post office worker told her it was 10.15am when she arrived.

"Thirty minutes. No matter," she said to herself. "I'll do it in twenty-nine tomorrow." The postman smiled somewhat conservatively. There were no croissants today but he suggested a sliced loaf which Tori bought because she didn't like to offend, her face reddening as the queue behind her watched her wrestle it into her bag and struggle to hoist it back onto her shoulder.

The post office had been updated while she'd been away. Tori was pleased to see that the rickety stand containing flower-strewn cards for mother-in-laws, had been replaced with an entire wall of every possible variant of greetings card. Brilliant! She'd send a card. It took her a few minutes to decide on the design. It was tricky choosing between, 'To a perfect couple,' and, 'My dearest daughter and her delightful fiancée,' when she couldn't even remember her new son-in-law's name, but she plumped for, 'Thinking of you on your special day,' because it had been true. She shook her head. She would rescue this relationship, right here, in the post office, with the first words she'd attempted to write since sporting a deformed hand and an arm which wouldn't straighten at the elbow.

— — —

She laughed as she put the key into the door when she arrived home. She didn't even hear the questions thrown at her by the familiar troupe of reporters. She'd transported herself into her village and back again. She would get quicker. She would walk further. She felt alive and perhaps more importantly, was almost happy that she was.

This independent foray into the outside world was the opening of stage curtains onto a different set. It wasn't simply the freshness of the cold air numbing her fingers, nor the achievement of walking that small distance with half a leg that had wasted away and an eye which could barely see the pavement in front of her, but it was the taste of being Tori again. Granted this was the new model with a modification, the one with the evidence that she was a sinner imprinted on her brain as well as her body. But for a few minutes today, Tori had been able to live with the post-August version of herself and this was a breakthrough worth smiling about.

She successfully removed her coat. But instead of filling up the kettle for her friends' imminent arrival, she returned to the front door. She opened it wide and posed for a moment while the photographers searched for her worst angle.

"You know, people," she said, when the cameras had been lowered, "I think we've all sinned at some point in our life, haven't we?" She smiled graciously and closed the door again.

THIRTY-SIX

JO DIDN'T DRIVE TORI HOME from her weekly hydro-therapy session, but parked the car opposite Charltons instead.

"My treat." She linked arms with Tori to help her over the road and into the teashop. Tori clutched Jo's arm even tighter as they approached the doorway with its huge brass frame, highly polished without a hint of a smudge. Jo patted her hand and said that the first time would be the hardest.

"It isn't so much entering the restaurant," Tori whispered, "more that, I'm-not-a-photographer-I'm-a-journalist-Steve Cribbins is here." She flicked a finger to show him leaning against the restaurant wall, one foot resting against it. He was a pace away from the main door, smoking an e-cigarette and staring straight at the pair of them. Jo told Tori to hold her head up high. When they were close enough for him to hear, she said,

"Tori only gives interviews to people over five foot eight with a decent haircut."

He looked her straight in the eye and with his white teeth bared said, "Tori will soon realise that she doesn't have much choice."

The front-of-house gentleman in his top hat and tails spotted the lady with a walking stick and waved her to the front of the queue. Tori thought she saw him falter when his eyes landed on her face but with kind professionalism, he guided the pair to a table by the window.

"Thank you," Tori said, chuckling as she took an exaggerated sip of her rose petal tea. "I wasn't sure I'd ever exchange the hospital canteen for a chic café in Harrogate, just a few weeks ago." She looked at her friend over the top of her china cup. She wanted to tell her what she'd been thinking while she was circling her ankles in the hydro pool.

"I'm going to become Victoria," she said, her eyes trained on Jo, who put half of her scone, covered with a good inch of butter and jam, back down on her plate.

"Sorry?"

"Tori is the killer persona—"

"Oh please, Torr! Don't talk like that."

"—and there are other bits of my past I don't like."

"Goodness! We all have those," Jo said.

But she had it all worked out. She would be 'Tori' in the press and Tori the criminal-who-got-away-with-it. Jo flinched at the words but Tori held up her hand to prevent her from speaking.

"To everybody else, everybody I care about," she emphasised by pulling her glasses further down her nose, "I will be Victoria, as a mark of my new life." She sunk her top teeth into her bottom lip and said that it started today.

Jo squeezed her friend's hand. "What sort of new life?" she asked.

"I'm not the Tori I used to be. I smashed it all up and I can't stick it back together again."

"You're still you," Jo said softly.

Tori shook her head. Since August she'd been stripped bare with a spotlight shining on her horrible bits. Tori Williams had nowhere to hide. "So the press and the protesters and those who still want me banged up for life, they can have their Tori Williams."

"The rest of us, we get Victoria: the real version," Jo said.

Tori beamed, raised her good hand in the air as if swearing an oath, "As of today, I am Victoria Williams."

Jo pushed a curl away from Tori's eyes. "OK," she leaned against her wicker-backed chair. "Change your life. I get that. But I don't think you're the kind of person who could draw a line under who she is or what she's been."

Tori shook her head. She had no intention of being someone who denied her past. She would be honest, admit her guilt, deal with it and move on.

"Right," Jo said, relaxing a little. "So this Victoria Williams person, she puts the dreadful event of last August behind her?"

"Yes, that's what I want. Life's travelling at a pace without me. I'm sick of sitting around, waiting."

Jo finally ate a piece of her scone and mopped the crumbs from around her mouth. She understood what Tori was saying, but would it work? She was in no doubt that Tori would manage but what about the practicalities for those close to her?

"I don't think people will remember, nor want to call you Victoria. Because you're Tori. That's who you are. We'll have to get to know you all over again."

"I think people will get used to it, like a new hairstyle," Tori said, piling her curls on top of her head for dramatic effect and letting them fall back down again. "It's a positive thing. I'm drawing a line in the sand." She chased the crumbs from her cake around the plate with the prongs of the dessert fork in her one functioning hand. She declined when Jo offered to help and mopped up the crumbs with a finger instead.

"OK," Jo held up both hands in a gesture of submission. "Victoria Williams, you are a survivor. And if it will help you to manage life's rocky path, I will endeavour to call you *Victoria*," she said, adding appropriate weight for the first time she'd used Tori's new identity. "Victoriah," she tried. "Victoriaaar," was another version she didn't like. "Victor?" She lingered on 'Vic'. "Can I call you Vic? Everyone else could call you Victoriaaar."

"Sounds a bit like a pub," Tori said.

— — —

Jo insisted on paying, even though the two friends had always shared the bill in the past. "Vic, Vic, Victoria, Vic," she sang, as she took the money from her purse.

The table was cleared and the gangly waitress was leaving the table but Jo peered past her. Victoria craned her neck to see who'd caught her attention.

"You have got to be joking!" There in tight jeans and a college scarf, sporting an enormous pair of black sunglasses and a round woollen hat pulled down over his forehead, was her sixty-eight-year old stepfather.

"Pretty girl with him," Jo said. Before Victoria could respond, Gerald had bustled the woman forward so that she was standing at their table.

"It is Tori!" She shuffled to the other side so that she could see Victoria's face. "You look very well." Victoria smiled stiffly and shook her hand.

"My dear Tori," she heard.

"Gerald," she answered, dropping the girl's hand. "I'm called Victoria now."

Gerald stepped around the table and linked his arm through

his companion's. "Victoria, then," he said, raising his eyebrows. He turned to Jo, took her hand and kissed it. Had they met before?

"Family parties, oh, ages ago," she said, and turned to smile at the girl on his arm. "May I have the pleasure…?"

"This is my wife, Sophie," Gerald explained, looking pointedly at the date on his watch. "I think you could still call us newlyweds."

"We got married on the 6th of October," the new wife said.

Victoria couldn't take her eyes off Sophie. Her hair was white blonde, peaking like uncooked meringue on top of her head, with a few splinters teased into fine feathers to cling to her forehead. Smartly dressed in a tailored black suit, clasped together with a row of metal clips under her bountiful breasts, the outfit would be more at home in Victoria's wardrobe but this Sophie looked barely older than Carly or Nicky.

"6th October?" Victoria said. "That was the day I left hospital."

Gerald and Sophie looked at each other. "When we visited you there, and we came often, we spoke about having another party to celebrate, one that you'd be able to attend, Tori," Gerald said quickly.

Victoria shook her head. She didn't like parties any more. She looked down at her feet in the comfortable loafers she'd exchanged for her heels.

"Victoria," she said. "It's Victoria."

Jo sprang from her seat, her arm shooting around Victoria's shoulders. "I'm sure that would be lovely," she said. "Shall we leave the newly-weds to it?"

Victoria smiled, leaning on the table to help lever herself up. "One question, Gerald," she said, "why so quick with the wedding?"

Gerald directed a toothy smile at Sophie, dragged her in to his waist. "For love, I suppose."

"You didn't think a test run might be a good idea?" Victoria asked. "You know, check this one out a bit first?"

"Victoria," Jo said, nodding towards the exit, "shall we—?"

Gerald shot a quick glance at Sophie who was standing stock-still, eyes wide. He said that when it was love, people knew it, particularly at his age.

Victoria looked at Gerald with his grey hair hidden by black dye, his jeans pulled up a touch too high. "I'd just hate you to make another mistake," she said, "ruin someone else's life."

"Hey!" Sophie said, detaching herself from Gerald's side and pointing a finger at Victoria's face. "Your dad's been unlucky, that's all."

"Stepdad, Sophie."

Gerald patted Sophie's hand. "It's all right," he said, "Tori found my relationship with her mother difficult, didn't you Tori? Very understandable, I might add, what with your dad and—"

"It's Victoria," she corrected. "You didn't treat my mum well. That's my problem with it."

"Right," Jo said. "It's been lovely." She grabbed Victoria's coat from the back of her chair and helped her to guide her arm through a sleeve.

"I'd have let the dust settle," Victoria said, "I wouldn't want you to end in a fourth quickie divorce—"

"Control yourself Tori! You're not so perfect yourself," Gerald snapped, his arm outstretched as if in mid aria. He checked his audience, his gaze lingering a touch too long on an elderly couple, where the female dipped her head to show her solidarity and her partner sat bolt upright, lips pursed.

Victoria waited for Gerald's eyes to return to her and then she said, quite calmly, that she'd made a stupid mistake but at least she hadn't lied and cheated her way through every relationship.

"You have no idea what goes on in my life," Gerald said. Now as he considered the room there were many more diners enjoying the shenanigans and some conversations had petered out. Others blatantly turned their heads to face Gerald and his group. "People let me down all the ruddy time," he said, saliva bubbling from his lips.

Victoria shook her head. She offered Sophie her hand to shake goodbye. "Perhaps you'll be the one to see him through." Sophie looked at Victoria, her hand unconsciously floating up to meet Victoria's, her mouth now fallen open. "History's against you, that's all," Victoria said. "Surely you have to question his staying power?"

"Ruddy hell!" Gerald pulled Sophie in closer, his face trapped in a familiar, outraged yet defiantly ebullient, expression. "Sophie knows I've chosen badly in the past," he said. "And she knows our love will outstrip this life." He manoeuvred Sophie back into the direction from which they'd come. "To think I defended you!" he said, en route to his table.

Jo placed Victoria's bag over her shoulder for her and held out her arm to escort her to the exit. "This new Victoria might take a bit of getting used to," she said. But before she could continue she put her finger to her lips and pointed to the table where Gerald and Sophie were sitting.

"Fourth divorce?" they both heard in the distance. "Three wives already?"

"She's evil," Gerald said in a theatrical, bitter whisper. "Ignore her."

"Three wives isn't what you told me, Gerald. Two wives is what you told me."

THIRTY-SEVEN

DOUG MANHANDLED HIS BRIEFCASE under an arm, swung his football kit over one shoulder and clenched the laces of his boots between his teeth. His kit hadn't moved from the backseat of his car since the end of last season but whatever happened between now and 7.30pm, he was determined he'd be on that pitch for the first whistle of Deepbeck's over-40's match.

He breathed out as he turned his key in the front door. He'd got so used to the questions that followed him into his home, he still couldn't believe they were no longer there. He turned half circle and stared back at the rosemary bush. No Dr Martens sticking out of the back, or hand pressed into the grass for support after a long day of sitting. He took a pace to the side. Nothing. He dropped his bag, kit and boots to the ground, paced over to the bush and walked full circle around it.

"Mr Williams," he heard.

He exhaled loudly. "Mr Cribbins," he said, and tutted as Steve walked towards him from the side of the house. "Change of scenery was it?" he asked, ready, again, to unlock the door.

Steve leaned against it, his arms crossed. He said that they had a deal and wondered if Doug had forgotten? He was here to remind him because a deal was, after all, a deal. "I kept my side of the bargain."

Doug glanced at the bay window, one of the first few days when Victoria had dared to open the curtains. "Come with me," he barked, and marched across the driveway to the path at the side of his house from where Steve had come.

"You didn't need to go to quite so much trouble to keep me out," Steve said, pointing to the pair of padlocks and the refurbished bolt Doug had spent most of his Sunday trying to bring back to life. The smile was so bold on Steve's face today that Doug curled his fists into balls at his side.

"Do you have any idea how much a scoop like this is worth?" Steve asked, and Doug shook his head, saying that it was of no interest to him. "A hundred grand." Steve scuffed his toe in the gravel, dispersing the neat covering. "Minimum." Doug's mouth had dropped open so he snapped it shut in an attempt to halt Steve's glee. "I could pretty much name a price," he said. "Who isn't going to pay big for the first article on Tori Williams?"

Steve was talking about Doug's steep introduction to journalism, how it was surely better to be with the devil he knew, at which Doug raised an eyebrow, and that the price earned itself another nought in the case of Tori Williams because she was the only one who could tell her story. "Gold dust." Doug shook his head, muttered that it was an obscene amount of money, but it didn't halt Steve's flow. "I have to admit, we banked ourselves another few grand when Tori waxed on about wanting to go to prison. God love her," he said. But when he noticed that Doug had given up trying to interrupt and was instead emitting a low growl, he said, "Hey mate," his hand on his shoulder, "we'd go fifty-fifty."

Doug stared at Steve, shook his fingers from him, and covered his face with his hands. When he emerged, he straightened his back, held his head up high and said,

"Listen, 'mate'," his eyes narrowing, "there will be no article," and turned to walk away. He had to resort to counting in his head to blot out Steve saying that there would indeed be an article, there had to be because he'd given him Etta Dubcek's details and he hadn't put his life on hold for a promise not to be upheld.

It was only when he heard, "Of course, there's always the alternative," that Doug muttered, "God give me strength," and walked back around the side of the house. Steve was leaning against the gate, his legs crossed at the ankles, popping a piece of chewing gum into his mouth.

"You're developing into a classy journalist I see: deals, alternatives and no pretence of scruples."

Steve simply chewed his gum with his mouth slightly open. Doug stood his ground for a while, hands stuffed in his pockets, one patent shoe rubbing against the other. He blew out of the side of his mouth, shook his head and edged over to him. The two men stood together with their backs against his gate.

"Twenty grand," Steve said. "Give me twenty grand and I walk away."

"Twenty thousand pounds?" Doug kept his back straight, his voice formal. "I don't have twenty thousand pounds."

Steve continued to chew.

"Vic- Tori, will never forgive me if I do a deal with you for the first interview," he said. "Can you understand that?"

Steve nodded, "Yes, I can."

"That's progress," Doug mumbled. "Then perhaps you could show some compassion for a man in a catch-22 situation with two court cases to pay for which are likely to cripple him financially?"

Steve took out his chewing gum, snapped a leaf from the laurel lining the path and wound it around the gum. He dropped it into the wheelie bin at the corner of the house.

"I'm a reasonable man," he said, once he'd returned to his position against the gate. He asked if Doug knew how much of his life he'd spent researching the story he'd promised him, or what it was really like to earn a living. "You in your posh house with your fast car and your headteacher's wage."

Doug couldn't help but smile. "Yes, I know what it's like to earn a living," he said. "I also know what it's like to have a career in jeopardy."

"So you'll understand why there are only two options: an interview with Tori or the money. I think you'll find I'm being quite fair," Steve said. "The article would propel my career to a different stratosphere of journalism. Twenty grand would simply pay the bills."

"I haven't got it."

"Then sell something!" Steve gestured to the modest amount of land around Doug's house.

Doug shook his head. "I really haven't got it."

He held his hand out for Steve to shake. "See yourself out, Mr Cribbins." He raced to the front door, heaved his work and kit bags up off the ground and finally put the key in the lock.

"Just so you know," Steve said, as he pushed past, "I have four other mouths to feed at home and they don't have a mother."

THIRTY-EIGHT

VICTORIA ANSWERED THE fourth call of the morning sitting on the cushioned seat in the bay window of the living room. She waved at Jake and Ella, in their red school uniform, topped off today with woollen hats with long flaps and tassles. They held one each of Denise's hands, their legs skipping to keep up with her. Victoria smiled. She used to walk that fast, too. Jake waved back before his mother was able to shake his attention away.

This time Victoria let the caller speak, responding with the odd affirmation and, 'I s'pose so,' to the well-rehearsed speech she'd heard several times that day and every day this week.

"Yes," she said, "I certainly can see how an article of this type would be useful to readers, to everyone really, anyone who can drive." She also thanked the woman for her kind words about her speech at court. She had meant it, absolutely, when she said that she wanted to make a difference, to speak out and encourage people not to make the same mistakes again. "But I imagined doing that in a safer environment, such as in a school."

"Aim high!" the reporter said. "Debut with me at The Global

and you've instantly hooked yourself an enormous audience. Our readers are very princip—"

"Oh, utter codswallop!" Victoria switched off the phone, shaking her head and rolling her eyes as if the reporter was next to her.

She shuffled through to the kitchen. At least the incessant phone calls gave her something to do while the nation chattered about her. She opened the fridge door to reveal an empty egg box, a pint of milk and a couple of out of date yoghurts. She closed it again and went off in search of her coat.

She reached the post office in sixteen minutes, almost twice as fast as when she'd first re-walked the route a month ago. She braced herself before she entered as had become her ritual. The postmaster never had much to say to her but there were members of the public she knew of old who would deign to pass the time of day if the queue were long enough, which had to be classed as progress.

She tugged at her cuffs, pulled out a feather peeking through the quilting. She wasn't sure she wanted polite conversation with people who palpably found any sort of relationship with her difficult. She was different now. Her view of life was clearer: if love was conditional, was it worth having? If a friendship was so vulnerable to breakage, was it worth investment? Victoria had her two real friends in Jo and Amelie. Perhaps she was the lucky one. Who else was in the position to trust their friends to such a degree?

She thanked the lady with the tight purple curls for helping her to load the pastries, ham and salad into her bag. Victoria didn't recognise her. Did she know who she was?

– – –

"Morning Steve!" she said, shambling past him, as he leaned

against the lamppost at the end of her drive, blowing into his hands. "Not coming any closer today?" she called behind her. "I hope we haven't offended you." She put the key in the door but dropped her bag from her shoulder and delved inside.

"Steve!" She beckoned him up to the doorstep. It was much quicker for him to walk to her than the other way around. She handed him an iced bun. "And I might bring you a hot cup of tea if you try particularly hard to be nice to me. You must be freezing."

"I'm always nice," he said. He took a fulsome bite of the iced bun, thanked her although his mouth was full, and said that she was also a lot nicer than people made out. She shivered, turned back to the door.

"As that's probably a form of back-handed compliment, I'll make you that cup of tea anyway. And incidentally," she said, standing in front of her open door now, "it doesn't matter how nice you are to me or how much time you spend at my property freezing your nuts off, if you're after an article like everyone else, you'll be disappointed."

– – –

Even though Victoria's daily challenge of walking to the post office took much less time these days, it still wore her out. She couldn't muster the energy to type nor to climb up the stairs to the study, so she laid out her wire-bound notebook and selection of pencils on the dining room table and settled herself down to write.

'This story is about a very un-interesting person who did a terrible thing,' she began. "Hardly enticing," she muttered through the end of the pencil she was chewing. 'Someone who wants to make amends.' Too worthy, she thought. She removed a few splinters from her mouth. 'Someone who made the biggest mistake of her life'. She cringed and put down her pencil.

She needed a second cup of tea. While the kettle boiled she found some thick white sliced bread and squirted it with salad cream to spare the frustration of trying to spread low-fat margarine evenly over the bread as it spun around under her knife. The ham slices could be manoeuvred out of the packet but she'd do without tomato. Ruby would slice one up for her tomorrow. With the watercress and bean sprouts successfully scattered over the bottom layer of the sandwich, she considered the shrink-wrapped cucumber she'd spotted in the door of the fridge earlier. She'd never much cared for it anyway. She placed the two slices of bread together, added the sour cream and chive crisps and took the sandwich she'd yearned for in hospital to the table.

She had to persevere. She owed it to herself and to her family. If she didn't write this book, somebody else would write the other version of her story. And she may as well have stayed in hospital.

Specks of snow were falling. She thought of Steve, surely he wasn't still loitering outside? Perhaps she should invite him in, let him sit in front of the fire. It bordered on cruelty knowing he might be out in the cold. She shook her head. He was a free man.

Victoria started again. 'This is the tale of an ordinary person whose life changed forever when she drove into the back of another car.' It was useless. She was infamous; the public knew what she'd done. She needed her autobiography to add something else. 'Life is about consequences,' she tried. 'What we do today, affects our tomorrow. I know that. I have always known that. But on Friday 17 August, in a moment of madness, I forgot. That's when I killed three people and families were destroyed. When I drove into the back of the Mondeo, all our lives were changed.'

— — —

"No-one will care," Doug announced, as he walked into the living room having reluctantly read the first few pages, after he'd had some food and a shower. It had been a hell of a day. Victoria folded herself into the settee but her troublesome left leg popped out immediately. She could do little with it other than hold it straight.

"Nobody will give a monkey's what happened to you," Doug reiterated.

Victoria felt ridiculous. Her once white towelling dressing gown smelt damp. She spread it over as much of her outstretched leg as possible. She was always so cold now her life was run at a fraction of its former frantic pace.

"Great."

"It's too pitiful, Vic and not grand enough." Doug kicked his work bag out of the way and joined her on the settee. He turned towards her, a reassuring hand on her thigh.

"You aren't the victim," he said. "The reader won't be interested in your life but in your mind and how you were able to do such a thing."

But that was the question Victoria couldn't answer.

"Could we talk about this some other time?" Doug asked. "Give you a chance to do some planning?"

"I've been thinking about it for weeks," she lied.

"Maybe you need to think about it some more."

Victoria pulled herself up from the settee, snatched the few pages from Doug, stumbled into the utility room and threw all her aspirations into the brimming recycling box.

"There you go. Rubbish," she said on her way back. "Just like everything else to do with my life."

"Good." Doug patted the place next to him.

"Good?" She stood opposite him. Her left arm squeezing her right tight into her torso, taxing her latent balancing skills.

Doug sighed. "I don't want you to write a book."

"That's obvious."

He picked up the remote control and lifted his feet one by one onto the coffee table. "I'm glad we're clear on that."

Victoria took the control from his hand, sat herself at the far end of the settee. She needed a focus, a challenge. "This is my life we're talking about and I'm only fifty-one," she said. What did Doug propose she do instead? "What if I live till I'm a hundred?"

Doug raised his hands, told Victoria to calm down.

"Calm down?" she said. "Calm down! If my heart beats any slower, I think I'll pass out."

"Leave the dust to settle. The parasites, *most* of the parasites," he qualified, "have only just left our garden." He lifted his second beer of the evening from the coffee table and upended it gratefully into his mouth. "Recuperate, Vic," he said. "Look after yourself. It's perfectly clear that the world outside is not going to do you any favours."

Everybody told Victoria to look after herself but she was mightily sick of convalescence. Everybody needed a sense of purpose, a reason to get dressed in the morning. Currently her life was so inconsequential, she could manage the whole week without knowing what days had passed.

"You'd be happy would you, for me to sit and wait for the world to go by without me?"

"Happy? Who says I'm happy about any of this?" He agitated his half-empty beer bottle in her direction. "You have your new name now. Be that new identity, ignore that woman who caused an accident, and when everyone has gone quiet, we can find you a new career."

"Meanwhile we wait. Meanwhile everyone else gets to talk about me and I'm prevented from speaking." Victoria attempted to tighten her dressing gown with one hand but let it hang loose. She picked up the collection of pencils she'd pushed aside for dinner, and made her way to the recycling bin to retrieve the original pages. Neatly pressed together, she returned to the settee with them.

"I will write this book."

Doug prised the papers from her hand and dropped them onto the floor next to him. "I haven't expended so much nervous energy over the past few months, keeping the press out of our lives and keeping us off the front page, to watch you invite them all in again."

Victoria peeled herself off the settee. She wasn't able to bend down far enough to pick up the papers but managed a swift kick so that they rearranged themselves like stepping stones on the carpet.

Doug shook his head. "I never had any aspirations to be on the front page of a newspaper and the reality of it is every bit as bad as I'd imagined. Don't you feel that, too?"

"I guess—"

"You guess?"

"Sometimes there's a bit of a buzz."

Doug stared at Victoria, rubbing his temples with his fingers until finally closing his eyes and snatching the last swig of beer with them firmly squeezed shut. The bottle empty, he opened his eyes with a jolt, rocked onto his feet and left the room. Victoria followed him, resorting to hands and feet to crawl upstairs because it was quicker than walking. She would not be outdone by Doug because he could take the steps two at a time. Before she'd reached the top step, the bathroom door slammed shut. Locked. Victoria didn't even know the lock was still working. She sank down to the floor and leaned against the door. She would wait.

"I know you're out there," Doug said.

"Even when I'm so light on my feet," Victoria mumbled.

She heard the clank of the heavy porcelain lid to the cistern, which had to be removed periodically for the ballcock to be depressed when the tank failed to fill. Finally, the water rushed into the toilet and she heard Doug say that everything was falling apart, as he washed his hands. He snatched open the door and Victoria fell into the bathroom. Once he'd manhandled her back into a sitting position, this time leaning against the wooden panelled side of the bath, he muttered an apology. He put down the cracked toilet seat, the original Thomas Crapper which had felt a luxurious indulgence at the time, until the dots of woodworm had joined forces and created a labyrinth of hairline cracks - the internet laughing at them: they'd bought a fake. He sat on top, arms and feet both crossed.

"I'm listening," Victoria said.

"Forget about the *buzz*." His index fingers wiggled to further ridicule her choice of word. "I will not have the Williams' family life story sitting on someone's book shelf, delved into at the end of the day with a glass of wine and a bowl of pistachios." He stretched his arms out wide to add some theatre. "With passages recited to loving partners in a mixture of wonderment and contempt. I don't want to be in somebody's downstairs cloakroom," he said, "shit firing into the john, the soundtrack to our sex life."

"I'd like it to be helpful, not salacious—"

"My turn to speak!" His hands shot into the air, the toilet lid cracking a little further beneath him. He jumped up, dragged Victoria to standing. He gripped her shoulders, looked down into her eyes, teeth biting into his bottom lip.

"For once," he said, "I'm saying no."

THIRTY-NINE

VICTORIA ARRIVED AT the bus stop with ten minutes to spare and was grateful for the time to compose herself. Doug didn't think she was ready to take the bus into Harrogate on her own. He had her best interests at heart, he assured her, and she believed him. She just couldn't allow herself to give in. Not that the act of boarding the bus and paying for the return ticket didn't unnerve her. Discerning the steps, climbing through a narrow entrance and taking money from a purse were some of her most difficult challenges and she worried both that an impatient queue would form behind her and that nobody would be there to help. Currently there were two teenagers waiting with her at the stop. The smaller one, a scrawny boy with long, uncombed hair smiled at her.

Surely they read the newspapers?

The double-decker emerged from around the corner. She could do this. The first time would be the hardest. However, as she negotiated the steps into the bus, a steadying hand cupped itself around her elbow and the boy with the straggly hair asked her if she'd like help with her purse when she struggled to open the zip.

"Thank you," she said, "you don't know how much I appreciate that."

Once in Harrogate Victoria felt like the new girl at secondary school: she could feel the buzz and the purpose of the people who walked so much more quickly around her but she had to take a few moments to orientate herself to the immense volume of the place. Buildings melded into one through her distorted view. Paths looked so much longer than they used to and the roads much busier. She studied the first of three she'd have to deal with in order to reach the library. The double lane carriageway brought a rush of vehicles past her feet. What if they forgot to stop at the pedestrian crossing? She pulled the sleeves of her angora jumper down over her hands. She'd plumped for gloves and a once-rejected, itchy alpaca hat knitted by Ruby, because they'd be easier than a coat. The wind raced between the fibres. She fleetingly considered checking out the sales for an emergency coat but remembered that she didn't do that kind of thing anymore.

She took a deep breath and waited, watching. The first batch of pedestrians crossed while she counted the pips as the green man flickered: twenty-four. She let the lights change from red to green and back to red one more time, just to be sure. Yes, twenty-four beeps, definitely.

"Tori?" she heard, as a blurred form lurched at her from the winter mist. The figure touched her shoulder. "It is you! Margaret Marriott-Parker here. How are you?" Victoria took in her features as her face leaned into hers: a sharp nose and bronzed skin, her hair piled into a chignon pulling her cheeks into a facelift. This woman had given her ten thousand pounds' worth of business last year. "You're on the mend I see, that's good," she said. "Working?"

"Hello, Margaret." Victoria whisked off her hat and stashed it in her pocket, pasted a smile instead of a scowl. "Business isn't great, thank you for asking, but I'm looking at other avenues. How's the retail sector?"

"Busy, busy," Mrs Marriott-Parker said through her own frozen smile, and spoke of next year's Christmas party which they were already planning, a culmination of lots of new ideas, every member of staff understanding their importance to the food industry. "Such a shame you can't be involved," she said, sashaying in her three inch, pencil thin heels in time with the gusts of wind, which had blown Victoria's hair into an airport sock, flowing obstinately into her ex-client's face.

"I've lots of new ideas myself." Victoria snatched at her flailing hair. "I'm thinking outside the box."

"You'll be writing a book, I should imagine," Mrs Marriott-Parker replied, examining a scuff on the tip of her patent black shoe, "after all you've experienced." She pointed across the road. "Green light," she said. "I'll let you get going."

"I'll call you." Victoria's heart raced as she placed one foot purposefully in front of the other, carefully and deliberately but moving faster than she'd have chosen. She heard Mrs Marriott-Parker call some pleasantry but she didn't look back. Safely on the other side, she leaned against the Jubilee Memorial while she caught her breath and looked up at Queen Victoria who was definitely smiling.

"What was I thinking? 'I'll call you,'" she mimicked, "'looking at other avenues.'" This was the type of banal conversation she used to have. She returned her hat to her head and set off again, her step quicker this time as she strode out of her comfort zone. She stood on the kerb of the second road she needed to cross, no traffic lights but cars queuing to join the main road. Dare she walk between stationary cars? A driver beckoned her through. She had no choice.

She held her head high. She didn't want it. She didn't want that career or those acquaintances who only gave her a thought if they felt she might be useful. But she did need a focus. Distraction was what carried her through the day. And it was inordinately difficult to keep busy with little means of independence, a business smashed to pieces, fewer visitors than a hermit in the Hebrides and the reputation of a pit bull terrier. She still believed she'd have been better off in prison. At least there she'd have been given something to do while she attempted to assuage her guilt.

Positive Mental Attitude! She would not be beaten today. This trip was a step in the right direction. "PMA," she whispered. Nicky! It was Nicky whose voice she'd heard in her ear, in the early days in the hospital bed, soft but hurried, "PMA Mum, you're PMA Elite, you can do this."

She barely noticed the crossing of the third road, quickly bisected the small garden, managing a wave to the rumpled gentleman on a bench who waved his brown bottle of beer in response, and fairly marched up the eight stone steps to reach the library entrance. She pulled open the heavy wooden door rather than pressing the button for automatic opening, and scuttled over to an empty booth as if she visited the library all the time.

Damn WiFi code! Why couldn't it all be set up for them? Technology was supposed to make everything so much easier and yet it would have been quicker to hobble over to a shelf and choose a directory than wait for this PC to get going. She made her way over to the Enquiries Desk and joined a queue of four others, their faces obscured by screens. If she hadn't been the only person without a phone, would they have chatted to each other? Quietly, obviously.

"Next please, when you're ready," the assistant said, neat sideburns rising and falling as he spoke.

"It's the WiFi code," she said, before reaching the desk. "I'm sorry to be such a dimwit. I'm sure you have signs everywhere telling us what it is." She wafted her good arm around to demonstrate the potential for signs in this glamorously refurbished Victorian décor.

When the man simply stared in response, she apologised again, "My brain's not what it was," she said, "I was in an accident, brain injury, and nothing's quite as obvious as it was before."

He stared, unflinching.

"Is it written down somewhere?" She was thankful for the excuse to rifle through the moulded plastic display of leaflets, which were a little too large for their allotted slots and curling at the edges.

"You're that Tori Williams, aren't you?" he said, eventually. He pushed his chair backwards, the castors squealing. "I knew I recognised you. Don't know how you dare show your face." He flounced into the distance, leaving Victoria to apologise for the lack of staff to the queue which had formed behind her.

— — —

Victoria turned off the bridleway and into Harewell Lane.

"Someone's lost the spring in their step."

"Steve. What a lovely surprise." She brushed past him. "You know it's not been a great day when I'm almost comforted to see you," she said into the air behind her.

He ran round to face her. "That's a compliment, right?" His face lit up, pretending it really was.

Victoria smiled. It wasn't a coma she'd thrown herself into last August, but a rabbit hole. She was the 21st century Alice in Wonderland and all these strange, obnoxious, irritatingly animated beings who propelled themselves into her life, with all their opinions and preconceptions, were pretend Wonderland inhabitants. She wondered when she'd wake up.

"Take my arm," he said. "You're wrung out."

Victoria waited a moment, considered his bent elbow, his, do-it-for-me-pout.

"My day wasn't all bad," she said, allowing herself to be pulled in the direction of her home. "I've made progress. I don't ever want people to make the same mistake I did."

"Good luck with that." Steve tossed his grey ponytail over his back. It was very thin at the ends, a bit of a rat's tail. Victoria wanted to grab it all in one hand and lop the end off.

"I'm taking the first steps to doing what I promised," she said.

"Any money in it?"

Victoria pulled them both to an abrupt stop. "I'm not looking to make any money." She shook her head. "Never." She squeezed her arm even tighter through his. "You can put that in whatever article you're writing. And really—" she surged forward again, "—shouldn't you be getting on with it?"

Was it wrong to feel a smidgeon of satisfaction that, for once, it was Steve made to feel uncomfortable?

"People are queuing up to speak to me," she said. "The reason your friends—"

"—they're not my friends."

"—colleagues," Victoria corrected, with a roll of her eyes. "The reason your colleagues have left my garden is because they've gone to their desks, two finger typing, pages flying from the printer, heads slapped as they revel in beating their colleagues to the first official, unauthorised biography of Tori the Texting Killer."

"Very poetic," Steve said. They reached the front door and he hurriedly unravelled himself from Victoria. "But I hope you're wrong. That wouldn't be very fair at all."

"Everyone else gets to broadcast what they think," Victoria muttered, "and yet I have no voice." She let her bag slide down to the ground. "Anyway," she brightened, Steve wasn't the only one who could plaster an emotion over his face, "today I've sent a personal email to every secondary school within a fifty mile radius. I'm going to change lives."

"You have impressive spirit," Steve said, "I'll say that for you."

Victoria delivered a playful tap to his shoulder. "That's very nice of you to say so." She smiled. It was more genuine now. "I want to plant the suggestion into malleable teenage brains that once they start driving, they should put their phones in the boot. One day that suggestion might become the norm."

Victoria looked at Steve, and, still waiting for a response, said, "Once upon a time, people didn't wear seatbelts."

He stuffed his hands into the pockets of his parka. "That would be an amazing achievement."

"Thank you, Steve." She cocked her head to the side. "That's the nicest thing anyone's said to me today - this week in fact - Carly," she said, "you know Carly, my daughter, of course you do, you know all of my family—"

"—apart from Nicky." Victoria couldn't help but acknowledge his quick wit with a hasty smile, before explaining that Carly had scoffed at the idea, claimed that it was totally untenable: phones were embedded in their culture.

"The thing is, Steve—" she offered her bag to him and asked if he wouldn't mind retrieving her keys, it was so much easier with two hands, "—all the people who change the world are ridiculed at the beginning."

"Ain't that the truth," he said, nervously rummaging through her belongings. He suggested he unlock the door for her. It was much easier for him.

"I never thought I'd say this about someone," Victoria said, "but you're much more agreeable when you don't smile so much."

The door swung open. "I do what I have to do."

She tilted her head and waited a moment, opened the door wide and invited Steve to have a cup of tea with her. She led the way into the hall beckoning him to follow. "I can tell you some more about my plan."

FORTY

DOUG TUGGED AND SNATCHED, pulled and tore the thickest part of the rosemary bush from the ground as Victoria watched from the window. He started the car without knowing where he was going but half an hour later, found himself in Skipton.

Carly held the door open for him without a word. He kissed her on the cheek, then strode past her and into the belly of the converted flat which smelt of melted cheese.

"I'm at my wits' end, Carly, really I am." He threw his jacket over the coat stand. "My wife writes some tabloid tat and you and I are the ones on the front page."

"Photographic evidence of us losing it." Carly ushered him towards the table in the dining area of her poky, open-plan flat. She suggested he take a seat.

"I coped with her being in hospital," he said, shaking his head, "even the build-up to the court case. But this!" He tugged the newspaper from his bag and slapped it against his forehead. "I'm so sorry you were drawn into it."

Carly took the paper from her father. He didn't answer when she asked him if he'd like a drink, simply sat himself down on the chair she'd pulled out for him. She put the newspaper on top of the stash of twenty others which sat on the table next to the untouched pizza, and took a seat next to her father.

"I bought every last copy of the Global from the newsagents near school." She gestured to the pile. "Once I'd seen a copy open on my desk."

"I'll give you the money," Doug said, but Carly shook her head.

"Some year tens had kindly highlighted the salient bits in the article: their teacher's mother lost her virginity at sixteen; the drugs; right breast smaller than the other. You know how it is, all the information you really want your fifteen-year-old pupils to get their hands on."

Doug looked at his daughter and declined the bottle of beer she pulled from the fridge. She seemed so young again. Her mother had no right to put her through all this.

"There were pages pasted up everywhere," she said. "At least some people had the decency to pull them down but they'll be back, the whole article will flash up on whiteboards tomorrow."

"Another fine working day to look forward to," Doug muttered. "I'll lose my job through something like this. I was respected, the school was doing well, top of the league tables for miles, you know that."

"People will see through all that's happening though, won't they?"

Doug dabbed his perspiring face with a tissue. "I worked hard for that job."

"I know."

"It was a big promotion leaving such a tiny school for something four times the size. People doubted me, I proved them wrong."

Carly swallowed the remnants of her tumbler of Chardonnay and lifted the box of wine from the floor onto the table to pour herself another. "Your reputation will bring you through this."

Doug wasn't so sure. People's lasting memory would be of that photo of him and his daughter sitting in desperation on the cold floor of the court building. The headteacher of a secondary school didn't get away with being the laughing stock of the community for long. Parents would vote with their feet. How many assemblies had he done on the building blocks of a reputation, only to be destroyed in an instant by unacceptable behaviour? Even if there was some sympathy for him, parents wouldn't take the risk with their children.

"Numbers will be down, you'll see. When the pupils leave, I will, too. Simple." He took the beer Carly had placed on the table. "And as I try to impress upon your mother, her chances of ever finding new work when she's the nation's most popular hate figure, are about as high as a mayfly living until tomorrow. Meanwhile, jobs for deposed headteachers are scarce."

Finally, Doug opened the beer just as Carly's childhood Swiss cuckoo clock called out that it was 10pm.

"Ten o'clock news," she said.

"I don't know if I can watch it."

Carly sat herself down on the brown velour settee and picked up the remote control. She patted the space next to her. "We have to know what everyone's talking about; have to stay a step ahead of the students." She plumped up a cushion. "You have no choice, Dad."

He sat down next to her.

The newsreader with her cream, satin blouse and leopard-print glasses introduced the report as, 'Tori Williams' frank letter to the Global newspaper.' A voice-over recited whole paragraphs verbatim of Victoria's full page article, as the screen filled with photographs.

"Where on earth did they get those?" Carly asked.

'First drunk at fifteen,' the voice over said. 'I took dope, preferably in cakes, for the first couple of years at college. Nothing stronger, ever. Boyfriends: many. Extra-marital affairs: none. One night stands: two.'

Doug turned his face into the settee. "This is it," he said. "I am officially in hell."

'Bust size is a 36C on the left but has sunk on the right to an A as the surgeons had to remove shards of plastic from the dashboard which had ripped into the fat. I could have had reconstructive surgery but with my being in a coma, there were other priorities.'

"I can't watch any more." He moved into the kitchen area where he could still hear every word.

'My weight has dropped from twelve stone eight, to ten stone three since the accident. Even copious amounts of vanilla milkshake via a tube couldn't keep me in the manner to which I'd been accustomed. However, I'd also like to say that I'd never known stress of this magnitude and with my weight loss has come a stomach ulcer.'

"No one cares, Tori Williams," Doug said as he shuffled back into the room, hovering at the edge of the settee.

Gerald, dressed in top hat and tails, was pictured in a swarm of enormous cameras. His arm was tight around Sophie's waist, who was equally smart in a cream suit emblazoned with daisies the size of dinner plates, but she wore a grimace as broad as Gerald's smile. Then came Doug and Carly's schools, the post office and Doug's football club. The front of his house was where the footage lingered the longest. After a couple of weeks of relative solitude - Steve Cribbins the obvious bloody exception - the trusted pack of hungry reporters had recorded Doug storming out an hour ago, in plenty of time for its airing on all major channels.

He sped over to the television. "That woman there," he said, his finger touching the screen. "Christ, it is! They've even filmed Etta Dubcek."

'I have a loving family who are supportive in their own way,' the narrative continued. 'Some find it hard to cope but of course they do, we never prepared them for this.'

"Mum!" Carly squealed at the screen, "Give them a bullet, why don't you?"

'I feel dreadful for all my family and for the friends who have stuck by me. They don't deserve this interference in their lives.'

"I can't watch Dad," Carly said to her father, not moving from her seat but placing her hands over her eyes.

'I find the deterioration in my sight difficult and I feel for those who've never seen what I was able to see for fifty years. Only having one working arm exacerbates the problem. But I will work to overcome my disabilities because giving in to them can't change what I've done.'

The film rested on Victoria on the steps of the magistrates' court. The words she'd spoken on that day replaced with a voice-over which said: 'So, please, I ask you to butt out. Now you know everything there is to know about me. Nobody else drove that car that day, nobody else picked up their phone. My loving husband, Doug, my devoted daughter Carly and my faithful mother, Ruby, leave them alone now, please.'

"Finish now," Doug pleaded with the screen. But the camera moved to the Pickering family where they'd stood outside the court and spoken of their loss. The film focused on their daughter in her fairy outfit. 'Don't text,' the voice-over said, 'Don't phone while you're in the car. Don't take chances with other people's lives and don't take chances with your own.'

The film paused on the shot of the Pickering family before slipping back to the studio. The newsreader stared into the autocue and read the final paragraph without any backdrop.

"'And to the families of those people I killed, I am truly, deeply sorry. I will never forgive myself and don't ask you to do so either. However, I ask you to understand that I will spend the rest of my life trying to make up for my moment of madness.'"

The newsreader allowed a flicker of absolute quiet and a slow, resigned blink into the camera before she introduced, "The rest of today's news."

"Well done Victoria, even we didn't see that coming." Doug paced back to the settee. "I wonder what she's got in store for us tomorrow? Post-disability sex - how to do it the Doug and Tori way."

"Dad!"

"How to build a career through decades of graft only to beat it and thrash it until it ultimately buckles. How to fall in love, build a fortress of trust, only for one of you to tear it all up and show it piece by piece to the world." He jumped up from the settee, walked the length of Carly's flat and back again.

Carly gestured to Doug to sit back down again but he continued pacing. "Do you know why she did it?" she asked.

"Books, I suspect. She's paranoid. Thinks everyone's writing stories about her." He screwed his hands into fists, let out a moan. "But she always gets it wrong, Carly, every pen-pusher in the land, professional or amateur will have been inspired to fire up the PC after this article."

Carly shook her head. "It isn't like her. She's normally so wise."

"She's given them twenty different story lines." Finally Doug took a seat. "She's done the hard work for them."

Carly chewed at the skin around her nail and when she took out her thumb, she picked at the jagged edge. Doug gently pulled her hands apart. Her thumb was bleeding. He offered her a used tissue from the bottom of his pocket, which she took without protest.

"But it *is* like her," he said, the warmth pulled from his voice. He walked over to the table, picked up the newspapers and torn-out pages which had fallen onto the floor and stacked them one by one into a uniform pile. A few torn-out pages floated back down to the carpet. He bent down to gather them up but changed his mind, picked up the papers he'd stacked and flung them onto the floor. The contents splayed out, covering much of the dining area.

"She's totally different now."

FORTY-ONE

DOUG LEFT HIS DAUGHTER'S HOUSE at ten o'clock the next morning. He couldn't remember a time when he'd ever missed assembly without good reason but he couldn't bring himself to stand on stage in front of pupils today. He'd compose himself in the car and was thankful for the extra half an hour of travel time Carly's flat had given him.

He hadn't rung Victoria last night. Carly had done it. He couldn't speak to her; couldn't think of anything constructive to say. She was doing her utmost to ruin their marriage. Why should he help her do it?

Halfway to school Doug switched off the 'happy music' Carly had forced upon him. She was right, he had to know what people were saying if he was to have a chance of fielding the abuse of his pupils, so he tuned into Yorkshire Vale Radio. 'Broadcasting nationally,' it sang. He slammed on the brakes, narrowly avoiding the path of an oncoming cyclist. He could have been sick.

– – –

Etta sprinted to the far corner of the library, took her seat at a round table with a cluster of four computers and rammed her headphones into the port. "Come on, come on," she muttered, drumming her fingers on the table, the circle on screen turning inexorably slowly as Yorkshire Vale Radio searched for WiFi.

"Yes," she squealed, "of course I do," when a command box asked if she wanted to listen. She apologised for speaking out loud, even though there was no one in her vicinity.

"A mistake is a mistake, whatever the consequences," she heard Tori Williams saying on peak time radio. "Even though I regret what I did and will do so for ever, I'm not sure who it helps if I don't at least attempt to move on. Toby, isn't it better to do something meaningful with my life rather than let another one go wasted?"

"But has the article moved you on, Tori, or has it merely re-fuelled the public's interest in you?"

"A bit of both?" Etta said, and covered her mouth, looked around.

"Short term perhaps. But people wanted information and I gave it to them. So, now I hope we can be left alone."

"I have to ask you, Tori, there is a feeling amongst some people that you actually en-joy this publicity," Toby emphasised his point by stretching out every verb with his distinctly Irish accent. "That you are in fact cour-ting the press, that you are to some extent, re-velling in your new-found notoriety."

"I struggle with my new life," Tori said.

The presenter left a sizeable gap. Etta couldn't be sure if it was for emphasis or because he couldn't think what else to say.

"I'm sorry about that, truly I am," he said. "And yet, there is some sympathy for this approach, Tori. We're getting texts this morning which support you speaking out."

"Are you?"

"We are indeed. Rachel from Gloucester says that you've voiced your regret and your sorrow many times now and that we should find it in our hearts to forgive you."

"Thank you, Rachel," Tori said.

"Caroline from Towcester finds your honesty 'refreshing' and Phil from Durham says that everybody makes mistakes but only the strong apologise."

"Caroline and Phil, I appreciate that."

"Terry from Gloucester tells us he woke up this morning and apologised to his wife for the affair he'd had six years ago. We can talk to Terry now. Hi Terry," the presenter said, his voice a couple of tones higher. "What did you want to say to Ms Williams?"

Etta leaned back, breathing out. There were no death threats, no dubious males coming forward to announce that they were one of Victoria's one-night-stands. Nobody offering cut-price boob jobs. She could bear to listen.

"Today is the beginning of the rest of my life and it feels great," Etta heard Terry say. "And it was hearing Tori's letter that made me think I could do it. Being honest about who you are and what you've done is better for everyone."

"Gosh," Tori said.

And there were others.

"When the damage is done, isn't it better to attempt to rebuild with something better?"

"Let's leave her to do something positive with the rest of her life."

"We can't bring 'em back," someone suggested.

Of course there were also angry texts and callers, but Tori fielded them as if she were a diplomatic ambassador.

"I completely understand your point," she said.

"There are no right or wrong answers."

"We all have to make the best of the life we've been given."

When a man spoke in gruff, clipped tones, Etta straightened her back.

"I can't believe what I'm hearing. I've never rung a chat show before but I'm so angry today."

"Tell us why, Geoff," Toby goaded.

"Nobody gave you that phone love, you chose to make that mistake," he said. "You can sit there with all your fancy language and your new age therapy but the deaths you caused were unnecessary. Only you picked up the phone and texted your fella."

There was a pause. "Absolutely," Tori said eventually. "I am entirely to blame for using that phone."

"You have to live with that!"

"Yes, that's something I'm trying to do," she said, calmly. "But if we as a society cannot own up to our mistakes and in turn forgive our neighbours for them, surely we are operating only the most basic of animal-like existence?"

"What makes us human beings love, is that we have rules and we have prisons."

"Thank you Geoff, we appreciate your call," Toby said.

— — —

Etta ran through the entrance to the School of Earth and Environment. Ms Moxley, her tutor, had suggested she come to her office half an hour before the seminar for an 'informal chat'. She had already lost ten minutes.

As she sped through the union building, she saw Tori's face emanating from every television screen and every front page. She and Andy had watched the national news in silence together last night until Andy had jumped up, shouting, "What the?" and hurried over to the television to point to Etta on the screen. She'd told him that the photograph could only have been taken during the 'incident' which was still being investigated by the school. But it did nothing to calm him. He left the room with arms thrashing, expletives whispered in an unsuccessful attempt to keep them from the children, asking when Etta was going to sort out this mess. Etta had rushed into the kitchen to busy herself with sandwich making for the four packed lunches required every day and she'd been as close as she'd ever been to breaking her silence with @investcribb. Of course it was him taking photos at the school. Who else cared about Etta Dubcek?

"Henrietta Dubcek, you are a case," Ms Moxley said, not unkindly, as she pulled out a chair at the table for her, choosing to stand behind her own. "I got you a coffee," she said. "I expect it will be cold by now."

Etta thanked her and apologised for being late. She knew why Ms Moxley wanted to see her again, and attempted to explain that she was going through a bit of a difficult period but that she wouldn't miss another deadline.

"It isn't the first time, Etta, that's what worries me," her tutor said, leaning over the back of her chair, "and it worries the rest of the department. I haven't even seen this month's study. I thought that tropical storms in the Pacific would be right up your street."

Etta did little better than to bluster a naïve explanation as to why she'd chosen this to be the one assignment she didn't tackle, knowing students were allowed to miss one in the first year.

"In exceptional circumstances," Ms Moxley responded. "And we don't expect it this early on. Look," she said, pulling out her chair and finally sitting herself down. She leaned into Etta, her hands flat on the table, fingers spread out exposing neat fingernails and a thin wedding band. "I don't like to see anybody fail. You could leave our university with a decent BSc in Meteorology—"

"Thank you," Etta said. She breathed out loudly.

"—but not like this." Ms Moxley sat back, extended the distance between her and Etta. "As your tutor, I advise you to scratch this year. Try again next year."

Etta's hands rushed to her face. "No! Don't make me do that, please!" She stood up. "This is my lifetime ambition."

Ms Moxley asked Etta to sit down. She knew about her role in the accident involving Tori Williams and had great respect for the way she'd clearly handled herself and the situation. She recognised that the experience hadn't ended there.

"I even saw you on TV last night," she said. "I have young children too and I can't begin to imagine how you're managing your family life and your other job on top of all this, let alone your studies."

"I'm OK," Etta said softly. She was not going to cry.

"Take the rest of the year off. Come back next year."

Etta looked down at the coffee she wasn't drinking and blinked hard to erase the water in the rims of her eyes. How had she got herself into this situation? With the click of a button, Ms Moxley could put her back where she'd been last year: the part-time manager of a building society with no prospect of ever doing anything else. Except next time, there would be no money for the first year's fees.

"I can't restart," Etta said.

"It takes a lot to get over something of this kind."

"You have to let me try!"

"Especially when it's surrounded by so much publicity," Ms Moxley said. "We won't forget about the incident when you re-apply."

"Two," Etta said, almost under her breath.

"Sorry?"

Etta brought her eyes up from the table so that their faces were finally level. "There were two incidents." She shook her head. "I can't tell anyone."

Ms Moxley lifted her fingers from the table, cradled them over her nose.

"Take some time off," she said. "With our blessing."

"No!" Etta's face drained of colour. "My partner would be devastated."

"I'm sorry, really I am."

"I'll sort this out," Etta said, with no regard to the tears now running down her face. "One more chance," she said, "please!"

— — —

Etta sprinted out of the university building over the lawn scattered with people smoking, the rain pummelling her shoulders as if in punishment. She ran down the paved walkway past students hurrying in the other direction and took the first turning she could find, into a cobbled street running between the backs of tall town houses, long since converted into offices. She stood against a yellow plastic skip and slowed her breathing, wafting her hand in front of her face - which did nothing to blot out the smell - before snatching her phone from her bag.

"Sara?" she said, "oh thank God."

"What's up?" she asked. "You're panting. Have you done it? Have you told him?"

Etta cleared her throat.

"Etta?"

"We're trying to get along better. If we don't mention Tori Williams, we communicate OK."

Sara's voice was quiet. Etta barely heard her say that she really wasn't interested in speaking to her until she'd done the right thing by Andy.

"I've compromised," Etta said. "I don't even see Ruby anymore."

"And me? Have you done the right thing by me, your friend of forever?"

"You're my best friend, Sara."

"The next conversation we have will be when you tell me that Andy knows."

"Andy isn't sure he wants to know, as long as I—"

The line went dead. Etta stared at her phone. Just like that. Sara had put the phone down. It was absurd. Ridiculous. She dialled her number again, three times. But Sara didn't pick up.

Etta wandered back up to the university, to a seminar with Ms Moxley on wind farms for which she hadn't prepared, one in which she'd be joined by only a handful of students who would each be spouting from copious notes taken during their research. Would it be better to arrive late or not at all? Would Ms Moxley understand that she'd needed a moment or would she see it as yet another snub of the course, a step further back into the water when Ms Moxley had only minutes earlier thrown her another lifeline?

She reversed her route back towards town, to the café with its pink cups and the silver wrapped biscuits.

She dug into her bag for the right pen. Black ink, as her mother had taught her. She slid out her notebook, tore a sheet carefully from the back and began to write a letter.

FORTY-TWO

VICTORIA HAD MADE AN EFFORT. She'd re-touched the make-up she'd worn for her visit to the radio station and her scars were certainly less angry-looking under a layer of tinted moisturiser. Now she was wearing the jeans she'd bought in celebration on her way home from the show, two sizes smaller than she'd ever bought in the past. Even more gratifying was that the shop assistants had been prepared to serve *Tori Williams*. They told her they'd all stopped what they were doing - and they included some customers in this - to listen to Tori speak on the radio this morning. They thought she was very brave.

She'd set the table, complete with cloth and posh cutlery, over-coming the usual challenges this presented with less huffing and puffing than usual.

"Are you enjoying the salmon, Doug?" She pushed the jug of iced water over towards him. "We haven't had fish for a while, I don't know why, there's always a deal on and even I can douse it with milk and bay leaves, pack some foil around it and chuck it in the oven."

Doug slowly, carefully, returned his cutlery to the table. "I've lost my appetite."

"Let's have a spot of wine!"

"Let's not," he said.

Victoria cleared her throat, finished her tumbler of water and disappeared into the kitchen. She returned with a beer which she poured into a glass and placed in front of Doug.

"Was it really terrible at school?"

"Terrible?" He swigged most of the beer and wiped his mouth with the back of his hand. "Let's see. It started with warbling ringtones, all out of sync, they didn't even bother to choose the same version of 'Centerfold', and by lunchtime, I was hiding in the staff toilets."

"Oh, Doug."

"A preventative measure so that I didn't ram my phone down the nearest throat at the next rendition of, 'My blood runs cold, my memory has just been *bloody* sold.' So yes, pretty 'terrible'. Thanks for asking."

"Didn't get any better?"

Doug finished his beer, and laughed: a single note. "I squared up to a few in the corridor, if that's what you mean. Said I was disappointed they were still listening to their parents' music." He belched behind a fist. "I mean, can't they find some lyrics from their own era for a bloke whose wife's lost the plot?"

Victoria took the plates into the kitchen, wedged one, then the other, against her stomach to scrape the food into the bin with as much of a clatter as possible. She filled the washing-up bowl with soapy water and threw in the cooking utensils.

Doug stood like a bouncer in the doorway, arm stretched up against the frame.

"Well, don't you think you've lost the plot?"

Victoria pursed her lips.

"It's not normal to goad the press, invite them all into your garden. I assume Steve has his mates back?"

"They're not his mates." Victoria plunged the plates into the sink, crashing them against a pan. It was difficult to wash crockery with one working hand. The best she could do was lean the dirty item against the side of the bowl and try to get some traction that way.

"I don't know how you can be normal when you're trapped between two lives," she said.

Eventually Doug made it into the kitchen, took a stool from the breakfast bar and sat himself down next to her. She scrubbed a plate until her wrist hurt and Doug took it from her and placed it on the rack to dry.

"You know this can't continue. Right?" His voice was softer now, but the hidden topic still pressed down on her shoulders.

"And you know you're not perfect. *Right?*" She stopped washing, stared at her fingers in the bowl, few suds covering them, misshapen and fat with excess fluid. "In fact, it could be argued that your cosy deal with Steve played a significant role in my article."

"Cosy deal?"

"It's the most ridiculous thing, so out of character for you to scheme behind my back."

Doug pushed the stool to the side and placed his hand around Victoria's waist to cajole her away from the sink. "We need to talk," he said, but she flung out her hip and dislodged him.

"You knew how important it was to me that the trial was fair." Finally, she faced him, brandishing a stained wooden spoon. "You knew I'd have preferred to go to prison and serve my sentence rather than have you ask witnesses to put a bit of gloss on their story—"

"That wasn't what I was asking—"

"I saw you!"

He shook his head.

"Twice! Once behind the rosemary bush and another time when you parked up, then spent twenty minutes around the side of the house in hushed consultation with Steve who you pretend to hate."

She flounced past him, sending the stool cascading along the stone floor behind her. He followed her into the living room where she sat herself on one end of the settee, legs stretched out to ensure there was no room for him.

"I expressly asked you not to pursue contact with this Etta girl and you did," she said, as soon as he entered. "So you have no right to be angry with me."

Doug crouched in front of her. "You've jumped to conclusions. I did it for the right reasons."

"As did I. I truly believed it would benefit—"

"You weren't thinking straight and I'd never have forgiven myself if you were six months into a prison sentence and suddenly woke up and realised that."

"I've never been more sure of anything in my life."

"But Vic, I didn't use the contact I had." Doug tried to take her hands in his. It took him three attempts to grab them as they flapped around. "The letter came from the court so I didn't need to go to Etta." He squeezed her hands. "In the end the court made its own mind up and that's what you wanted – you didn't need to cheat."

"But you cheated, didn't you?" Victoria shook her hands from his. "You betrayed my trust." She twisted away from him, her head wedged tight, as if looking at something behind her.

"We both have a case to answer," Doug said softly.

Victoria shifted even further into the back of the settee, her gaze held tight against the wall. Her eyes pricked with tears but she would not be made to feel guilty. She was trying to make a better life for both of them.

Doug groaned and left the room. When he finally returned with the bottle of red wine he'd earlier refused squeezed under his arm, and clutching a few bags of crisps, the first already opened, Victoria reluctantly moved to the end of the settee to make space for him.

"Bloody starving," he said. But before he could set down the bottle, mid-crunching of a mouthful of cheese and onion crisps, he stopped. He stared at the bag, an own-label version from the variety pack he used to reject in favour of Tyrrells.

A smile crept over his face. "I get it." He let the packets of crisps fall onto the table and put the wine down without noticing its tilt as it teetered half on the table and half on a mat. He smacked his forehead. "It's going to pay off our debts! Not only to Steve but all the court costs, maybe the rent on the sad old Party Planners office, do you think? Jeez, maybe even the civil case, too?" He knelt at Victoria's feet. "How much did Steve get you?"

Victoria swallowed, ran her fingers through Doug's hair. "I do recognise that you're always the one to stop our fights," she said, "and I love you for it."

"Vic?

"Steve? I think he did OK." She moved the bottle of wine so that it stood flat.

"How much?"

"We're certainly not in debt to him anymore."

Doug fell down to his haunches, cleared his throat. "The amount, Victoria?"

She bit the inside of her cheek, so hard it bled. "I couldn't," she said, shaking her head. The salty gloop oozed into the rest of her mouth. "It's blood money, isn't it?"

FORTY-THREE

VICTORIA SAT HERSELF DOWN at the kitchen table and smoothed the twelve page form with her hand. The paper was too thick, the three concertina sections re-folded most uncooperatively. She knew the coat of arms embossed at the top. Mr Thackeray - free of charge - had warned her to expect the letter, she reminded herself.

It was nearly two months since Victoria walked out of the magistrates' court. Occasionally she'd dared to imagine that the Pickering family might have had a change of heart, perhaps a wobble over the finances needed to bring the charge to court, or even decided that any verdict was futile. But their child was dead. Nothing had changed for them. They had no reason not to take Victoria to court once again.

She felt different about this case. At her first trial she hadn't wanted the magistrates to address her in such a respectful manner and had wished the ushers hadn't been so understanding of her physical disabilities. She'd have been happy for the public at the back of the court to have heckled louder, rather than be told that they had one final chance before being escorted from the premises.

But now she'd started to shed the skin of Tori the Texting Killer and was beginning to forge a new life. Any further ruling wouldn't make her feel any worse than she did already, while suing her for thousands of pounds would punish Doug. He was the one with the capacity to work harder to pay it back. He had already committed to marking extra exam papers, something he thought he'd seen the back of twenty years ago.

It took Victoria four hours to fill out the civil court's 'Questionnaire'. The title implied a magazine-style quiz, with no right or wrong answers, only conclusions bearing compliments for every personality type. This 'questionnaire', however, was her single opportunity to show why she contested the claim that she alone had killed somebody else's child.

She clutched the completed form and proudly set the house alarm. Even though she couldn't read the digits on the keypad, she remembered the pattern of the code. Her brain cells were re-grouping.

"The sooner it gets there, the sooner it's over with."

She smiled at her neighbour, raised her hand and said "hello". Mary tilted her head in acknowledgment. She still didn't speak but on good days, positive days, Victoria wondered if she didn't know what to say, as when someone announces they have a terminal disease and people bow their heads rather than ask how long they have to live.

"Nice day, Mary," Victoria called out as she turned left out of her gate and passed Mary's garden wall.

"Aha," she said, not altogether discordantly.

She and Doug needed to seize the initiative Victoria decided, invite the neighbours around for drinks, supper even.

After Victoria had deposited the mail, she took a different path from the post office. Her heart beat harder. In the past month she'd only ever dared to turn right, reversing the direct route from her house. Victoria patted her pocket. The other letter was still there.

She sought out the bench in the park where she first sat when Carly was a baby and needed feeding. The river seemed to flow faster than it had back then; it was fuller somehow. She pulled her collar up higher, sank into the bench and felt the cold slap her cheeks. An area of decking jutted out over the riverbank on the other side. Nobody had wooden patios when Carly was born; they thought they'd rot. Otherwise, the setting was largely unchanged. The horse chestnut tree still stood proud, a parasol to the picnic tables below. Where would she be when its pink flowers returned?

She breathed in. The cold air tickled her throat. It was a miracle she was there to take it all in. She'd written to all the staff at the hospital to thank them and visited the ward occasionally when she returned to Outpatients for every variant of physiotherapy. But she'd never thanked Etta. If Etta hadn't been in the car behind her, would she have sat on this bench again?

Had Etta saved her twice? Was the driver of the car in front truly driving badly? Victoria had to believe it was true.

She took the flask of half-milk coffee from her bag and placed it between her knees. She squeezed tightly and praised herself for holding the flask upright while she successfully unscrewed the lid from the top. She set the cup down on the bench and poured herself a coffee. Only when she'd finished the first cup did she put it on one side to carefully unseal the envelope, take out Etta's letter and place it on her lap.

Dear Tori,

I hesitate to write as I certainly don't wish to cause offence and I'd understand if you didn't want anything to do with me. Our only connection is through the accident and I'm sure you're doing your best to put that behind you. I sincerely hope you are managing to cope with your injuries and that your life is easier than it was.

However, it did occur to me that you might think that I am not who I say I am. I know the tricks the media can play and I know protestors have hounded you. I thought I should therefore explain something about who I am and why I would like to make contact.

Etta was thirty-five years old with a young family. Her parents had refused to finance a degree course in meteorology when she'd left school, as opposed to the career in medicine on which they'd pinned their hopes. Etta had taken a job at the local building society out of spite where she remained for the next seventeen years. Now she was realising her dream but juggling the part-time degree with a part-time job and two young children was taking its toll.

There was a time when I was busy, Victoria thought wistfully. She looked up from the letter for a moment. She'd have another coffee before she continued. She looked over to the empty duck pond from which she'd hauled a drenched, pre-school Nicky too many times. Carly never fell in. She was much more likely to take her mother's hand than play 'tightrope walking' around the edge.

Victoria balanced the empty cup on one of the slats of the bench and smoothed the letter flat again.

She read that Etta lived in Rochdale and had been heading home from Leeds that day in August. She wondered if Etta was a particularly careful driver and that was how she'd avoided a similar fate to her own? If Etta had crashed into the back of her, would either of them have survived? Would Etta have been charged with Driving without Due Care and Attention? Perhaps she was using her phone too. Perhaps that was what she wanted to tell her.

You exude strength when you speak, even when you are expressing remorse. I know you will manage to rebuild your life, Victoria read. She smiled, it wasn't strength, it was necessity. *Rarely in my life have I been quite so impressed by an everyday citizen. If more people thought like you, were in touch with their feelings and honest about them, the world would be a better place.*

And I have as much to learn as anyone.

I was in a regrettable situation where I hid behind a lie that was created for me. I took the easy option and, two years on, I am little better at coping with it. I'm sure you can help me which is why I need to speak to you so badly. My friend says I'm looking for closure. I do know my life changed forever the day I pulled up short of driving into the back of your car. The crash and waiting with you re-opened an unfinished memory. I need your advice on how I can face it and then put it back where it belongs.

The one thing I can't do is ask forgiveness of the person I wronged.

Would you call me?

Best wishes

Etta (Henrietta Dubcek)

P.S. If I do not hear from you I will respect your privacy and wish you a peaceful, happier future.

P.P.S. Please hang up if my partner answers the phone.

— — —

Victoria reached home in sixteen minutes but it felt like she'd flown in five. She snatched the letter from her bag and unfolded it as quickly as her single hand would allow. This girl had saved her life and she hadn't even thanked her. She couldn't allow herself to have second thoughts.

The phone rang four times. Her hands were clammy, even though it was minus one outside. Her heart was beating so hard she could feel it in her throat. 'Please no answer machine,' she said to herself. 'Please, I can't bear it.'

"Hello, yes, I'm Etta Dubcek. Who's calling?"

"Hello Etta, I'm—"

Victoria heard Etta swallow. "Yes, hello Tori, I know your voice. Thank you, thank you so much for ringing."

"No, I—" Victoria's mind rushed backwards. A wind pulled, dragged her back into Jo's car as they fled from hospital, the trees, the blue of the sky and the terrifying speed. She was back in the hospital bed, talking to her mother, it hurt, it banged in her brain. People spoke all around her, she couldn't answer, Gerald and his girlfriend - his wife - kept talking, talking incessantly, confusion, why were they there?

"Tori?" Etta said. "This must be difficult, are you OK?"

And then there was the red, the red metal hurtled towards her, the phone spinning through the air, several hundred revolutions before it bounced noiselessly onto the carpet. A woman's voice, this voice, 'Rumpelstiltskin,' it said. 'I hope it isn't Rumpelstiltskin.'

Victoria threw down the phone and crashed to the floor, clutching her ears. "Stop! Stop!" she cried, her eyes screwed tight, her hands in fists. The call disconnected, the dial tone the only noise outside her own head. She forced her eyes open. But open or shut, the red metal was still there. 'You're breathing,' she heard from the end of a tunnel, 'Hang on in there.' This voice she heard, Etta's voice, was kind, soothing. She was the goodness in the accident, the reason she was alive. Victoria levered herself up from the floor. She dusted herself down and smoothed her hair.

"OK," she said to herself. I can do this." Her fingers hung over the keys ready to redial. But the red metal returned, whooshing from every corner of the room, from nowhere, to within inches of her forehead and then it would spin away. Is that how the red

Mondeo had been, fragments shooting through the sky? Victoria had no idea. Her most vivid memory of the accident was only of someone holding her hand and making her feel warm. Victoria looked at the keys again. Her hand trembled. This time it was her own house phone that taunted her. It was enormous, like a replica advertising a telephone shop.

"It's no good," she cried, her eyes pierced with frustration as well as sadness. "I can't go back there, not now."

FORTY-FOUR

VICTORIA TOOK IN THE WALLS of the tiny studio. A veritable posse of stars of the stage and screen had visited these offices in the past. There was even a yellowing photo of Princess Diana who'd opened the studios thirty years ago. Victoria wasn't the oldest person to have visited the radio station, but based on the evidence before her, she was certainly the most disfigured. Was she the most flattered to be asked?

"Hi Tori, welcome back, nice to have you on the show again."

"Thanks for inviting me Toby." Her heart was beating so loudly she could hear it in her headphones.

"Our pleasure. We've had a massive response since you last spoke."

"I seem to have that effect," she said.

"Your view of a world which thrives on forgiveness has stirred the imagination of our listeners." Toby adjusted his headphones. "People are interested in your anti-blame culture." He was as immaculate as ever in a pale pink shirt sporting tiny silver clocks for cufflinks. Feed off his calmness, she told herself, taking deep breaths.

"Lots of people agree with you."

"I'm heartened that I'm not alone."

"You certainly aren't! You've caused a veritable outpouring. So many people with un-reconciled regrets." Victoria smiled as Toby gestured to his computer screen. "I have this one here," he said, leaning closer to the yellow sponge covered microphone. "*My son broke two front teeth falling from the climbing frame at preschool*, writes Rowena Black, a mother of four from Sheffield. *I sued the preschool and won.*" Toby peered over the top of his computer screen at Victoria, his round gold glasses had dropped to the middle of his nose. "*I justified my claim to myself because I thought I might need to pay for extra dental treatment in the future. I had mixed feelings but assured myself that the staff had acted irresponsibly in not ensuring my son played safely and that the case would encourage them to put in better systems for the future.*"

"But," Toby's voice slowed for the punch line, "*the preschool hadn't insured themselves correctly and my payout caused them to close down. That was two years ago and they'd been closed ever since.*"

Victoria's lips parted to speak.

"Hang on," Toby said, raising his hand. "*But hearing Tori made me think. I realised that I felt hugely guilty and always would do if I didn't admit publicly that I'd made a mistake, that I was sorry and this is what I was going to do about it.*" Toby stopped reading.

"What did she do?" Victoria asked.

"You can ask her yourself! Hello Rowena, nice to have you on the show."

Rowena's voice was soft and measured. With a slight hint of a northern accent she explained how she drew out the remainder of the insurance payout from her savings and raised the extra through a bank loan. She met up with the original preschool leader and asked her to set up the group again. Initially the leader was reticent until Rowena described the posters she planned to put up on the village noticeboard.

"What did they say?" Toby coaxed.

Rowena laughed nervously. "Well, the posters said that I'd blamed the preschool for something beyond their control. I said that our children must be allowed to play, that accidents happen and when they do, our whole community shouldn't suffer as a result. I wrote that I wanted to make amends and asked that any parents interested in seeing a preschool in the village, come to a meeting in the church hall."

"And did they?" Victoria asked.

"Not only did they come," Rowena said, "not only are we opening up the preschool with all the original staff plus some money in the pot for new equipment next month, but, and this is the best bit," her voice speeded up, "we've also made a pact." Toby was smiling, he knew what was to come. "If there's an accident in preschool we have an agreement that suing is only to be used as a last resort."

Victoria raised her eyebrows. "Go on," she said into her microphone.

"I know what you're thinking: great idea, but it will fall apart the first time anyone trips over badly."

"Afraid so," Victoria said.

Rowena could hardly say the words fast enough. They'd all signed a contract. If there was any talk of legal action, the parents would make a group decision. Every parent or carer would cast a private vote on whether or not they thought suing the preschool was a justifiable action and sustainable by the community.

"If not, the aggrieved parent has to abide by the democratic decision."

"Wow!" Victoria said. Toby was grinning, holding his hand out to encourage her to continue. "That's brilliant," she said. "Of course it's not legally binding but I can tell you people won't challenge it. Nothing is worth losing the respect of those around you."

"I know," Rowena said, galloping through her words. "And there's an excitement in the village. We're talking about doing it for everything. We're not going to sign up to this compensation culture anymore. Nobody has to search for someone, or something, to blame as a means to justify their own actions."

"What do you mean by that?" Toby asked, with the characteristic elongated drawl he used for emphasis. "How can blaming someone else be justification?"

"We mean that by painting somebody else's behaviour black, our grey behaviour doesn't appear to be so bad."

"OK," Toby said. Victoria was used to the presenter feigning non-comprehension but if Rowena contradicted herself, he would swoop on her in an instant. "I see the logic but you're asking a great deal from people. Sometimes people need retribution."

"Financial retribution? We're challenging that. We want an environment where it's good to be honest about our own failings, where a heartfelt apology will suffice."

"Rowena, it's a wonderful idea, truly. But will people subscribe to it?" Victoria asked. "Take your own son's example. Regardless of whose fault it was, he did fall, he did harm his teeth. That could prove expensive."

"Yes," Rowena said, "his smile leaves something to be desired." She paused theatrically. "But the orthodontist friend of a dentist in the village is treating his teeth at cost price."

Toby couldn't find argument with this. He looked straight at Victoria and gave her two thumbs up. 'Wow,' she mouthed back.

"If there wasn't a practical alternative to compensation in times of real need, this system would fail. So we help each other out, that's what we do now," Rowena said. "We're not fighting to get the best deal for ourselves as individuals but pooling our friendship and resources." Toby attempted to thank Rowena for her call but she didn't want to go. "I urge people to try it. Really, you won't look back. I can't tell you how much this has meant to me. I am happier than I have been for ages."

"It sounds admirable," Toby said rubbing the side of his nose and looking at Victoria with the hint of a smile on the edge of his lips. "But I have to ask, is this system bordering on a cult, Rowena?"

"It's merely a group of people who are tired of being angry and are striving for a better existence."

"What if someone doesn't want to sign up?" Victoria asked.

"Then they don't. But people are interested because they recognise the benefits of stronger community."

"Hippies?" Toby said, chewing the side of his mouth.

"Maybe!" Rowena answered with a great peal of a laugh. "But you can't deny you're curious too, aren't you Toby? I think you'd set up camp where you lived if you could."

Toby chuckled. He said he'd let Rowena experiment with it first and asked if she'd return to the show in twelve months' time to let him know how the scheme had developed. He looked over at Victoria to encourage her to speak, but said instead, "I have to tell you, Rowena, Tori is crying."

Victoria shook her head, wiped her eyes. "It's an amazing story," she said. "Very exciting. But I do have one question if I may." Toby nodded. "How would your community deal with a situation where a child had been killed in an accident?"

For the briefest of moments Toby looked shocked. The producer behind the screen looked up, opening her eyes wide.

"Go on," Toby said to Victoria when Rowena didn't reply.

"It's a special case because nobody can do any favours - no cost-price surgery or replacement children. So what's to stop the bereaved family members from seeking a piece of the offender in return, so to speak, some money perhaps, or a stint in prison instead?" Victoria cringed at her own language.

"I'm not sure it is so, erm, different," Rowena said, tripping over her words as she formed her thoughts. "You focus on love and friendship for the people left behind. People who've lost someone need this more than ever, don't they?" Rowena was warming to her theme again. "That's what's been taken from their lives so we have to give that back. We shouldn't replace the missing love with anger."

"Rowena, we're putting you up for the Nobel Peace Prize," Toby cut in, raising his hand to ensure Victoria remained quiet. "It's been a great pleasure having you on the show and we'd love to have you back next year, if you'll come."

"Of course," Rowena said.

"Now," he was almost breathless with the speed he was speaking, "and now we must go to the news."

— — —

"Victoria Williams," Toby said, as soon as they'd gone off air, "you play it close to the line!" He laughed, opening his mouth wide, his thick lips too large for his small, round face. "That's what we like on our show."

Victoria shrugged her flexible shoulder. "Rowena said it so much better than I ever could."

Toby handed her a polystyrene cup of tea and told her that on the contrary, she was coping admirably, was a natural on radio and welcome on his show any time. He was enjoying the rare opportunity to focus on a good news story, for once.

"It's clear to me," he said, "that bitterness eats you up, however justified it might be. But some people can't cope with pain any other way. And the more anger they feel, the more compensation they seek."

Victoria agreed. And there were those who played the system. "A driver attempted to claim compensation from my insurance company for the effect the sight of the emergency vehicles at the accident had on her nervous system."

"You can imagine how awful that must have been though," Toby said.

"But the woman didn't see anything of the accident. She sat in the traffic jam, that's all. Then you get Etta, the girl who sat with me and you don't hear a whimper of complaint."

"That would certainly stay with you," Toby said, holding his hand in the air again and clutching at his headphones with the other.

He restarted the show with many more examples of how people had made changes to their lives since Victoria had first spoken on the radio. She couldn't quite fathom it. She'd merely wished to justify her own continued existence, and had felt somewhat of an oddity in doing so. But there was a whole courtroom of guilt out there, begging for appeasement. Some of the lies people had told were outrageous. She'd have expected them to feel remorse about cheating on those held dear to them and arguments which had been allowed to fester. She knew people dodged paying tax and cheated the benefit system, but she was particularly shocked to hear one woman say she'd paid £800 to a friend to take her driving test for her. This started a string of callers who'd bought an early sighting of their exam paper from the internet.

Victoria was enjoying herself. Toby treated her as 'Victoria', not Tori. He respected his callers and was interested in them. Only once did he curl his lip in disgust at a man who'd beaten a dog practically to death to hit back at a neighbour who'd parked in front of his drive once too often.

Of course there were many non-believers who called in to the show with various degrees of indignation.

Barry from Halifax thought that Tori sounded as though she had enough money. "Easy for you to say you wouldn't want compensation," he said. "You wouldn't need it."

Victoria mouthed, 'help!' and Toby answered quickly.

"Hi Barry, Toby here, can I ask, what do you do for a living?"

Barry was a plasterer. "I can look after me sen and me family but I wouldn't be able to pay if all me children's teeth were knocked out, even if it were cost price," he said with a rasping West Yorkshire accent.

Victoria leaned into the microphone. She'd only heard of Rowena's plan a few minutes earlier. She knew she liked the idea of it but her brain didn't react as quickly as it used to. "I suppose we have to hope that if communities work better together, somebody else would also help you out in this situation."

Barry chuckled loudly. "There 'aint no dentists doing things for free where I live, love."

Toby thanked Barry for his excellent call.

Phyllis introduced herself as 'very cross'. She was confident she spoke for many in finding this 'new age' camaraderie hard to stomach. "The legal system is there for a reason and every man, woman or child should have the right to be looked after if someone's done them wrong," she said without addressing her comments to either of the pair in the radio studio.

"We're not talking about people not being looked after," Victoria said, her voice wobbling, "we're talking about building a better place for everyone."

"Shame the people you killed won't ever get to see it," Phyllis shouted before Toby cut short the call. He shook his head and Victoria heard a jingle play in her headphones.

"Sorry, that one slipped through, Tori."

"It's OK," she said. "She's right."

FORTY-FIVE

VICTORIA PLANTED HERSELF by the window of the bus station café to wait the fifty minutes for the next direct service to Deepbeck. At least the tea was cheap. Surrounded by the opulence of Harrogate she was crushingly aware that she no longer earned any money. Today was another milestone. She'd taken the bus to the hospital without incident and without assistance from Ruby or Jo and hadn't told either of them about her physio appointment in case they tried to persuade her out of going alone.

She'd brought a wad of paper and a choice of pens with her as she thought she might attempt the journal Doug suggested she write. Writing it on business paper would make if feel more like a memoir and less of a diary. A diary was a pastime, she'd explained to Doug, which should be the exclusive domain of children and the unemployed. She was merely 'in between jobs'. If the writing went well today, she could miss the next bus and take the later one. She could make these kinds of choices when she was on her own.

It was her concession. Really, she'd have preferred to make another attempt at the book.

She sipped her tea from the plastic cup and contemplated the paved area in front of the shopping centre opposite, a mix of squares and rectangles. She'd seen fire-eaters and jugglers there in the past, people handing out fliers for a musical at the Royal Hall or a competition to win a car. Today, propped open, was a sandwich board where she could just make out the artist's impression of Harrogate's forthcoming temporary ice rink. Victoria wouldn't be trying it.

She hadn't seen a sandwich board for years. She thought about the poor people of her youth - vertically challenged old men, forced to walk up and down the high street, sporting the A-frame which advertised hot dogs, the cinema, a one-day-only sale in the already bustling department store around the corner. It was simple yet effective promotion but the men looked as though they carried the woes of the world on their shoulders. The only ones with any animation were those advertising newspapers who sang out the titles, propelling them from the depths of their ample stomachs, rendering the title of the newspaper entirely unrecognisable. It was a source of amusement to Victoria and her sister as they'd laugh their way through a list of fabricated alternative titles, ever more outlandish with every stifled giggle.

A smile crawled across her face. She could almost hear Lottie giggling at the prospect of what she had decided to do. She borrowed a roll of Sellotape from the young employee behind the counter. Next, with broad strokes on a piece of the paper intended for her memoir, she wrote:

PEOPLE IN GLASS HOUSES SHOULDN'T THROW STONES

On another she inserted a bold, black arrow. Above it she wrote:

IF YOU'VE EVER MADE A MISTAKE, SIGN HERE!

She headed over to the sandwich board and attached her notice to it, then heaved it with her good hand over her head and onto both shoulders. She hadn't carried any significant weight for months and the initial impact made her nauseous. She took a deep breath. With the remaining paper squeezed under her armpit, she shuffled across the area hardly bigger than a driveway, the weight on her bad leg causing it to sink into the ground on every step.

She managed a small smile in the direction of a lady with identical twins who sat side by side in a buggy playing with each other's fingers. The look of horror on the lady's face as she read the board and watched people gather around her, made Victoria feel pitiful. But she cleared her throat and pulled back her shoulders. She was committed now.

A gangly man of about Carly's age considered her invitation. His hair was peaked into a fifties quiff and he was wearing tight, faded jeans and red suede shoes, which were tipped with metal toe caps and protruded way too far beyond the cuffs of his trousers. He dropped his cigarette butt to the floor, stamped it out and strode over to the paper piled on the ground beneath Victoria's hastily drawn arrow. He wrote a couple of words, signed his name, then jerked his leather jacket down towards his waist and walked back towards the crowd.

A child, barely in double figures, looked up at her mother, who shrugged her shoulders. The girl made her way to the paper and inserted her name and a few words which Victoria couldn't discern from the distance. The child's mother caught Victoria's gaze and gave a discreet dip of the head.

There was a steady stream of people now marching, sidling or lolloping over to the pile. Some looked grave as they added their name and comments to the list, but many smiled as they left. One man shook Victoria's hand and told her she'd made a lot of sense on the radio the other day.

"Hello Tori!"

She knew the voice. She looked up to see him standing in line behind a small lady with bedraggled curls whose hand quivered when she wrote.

"Gerald," Victoria said. "You're in Harrogate."

He said he was visiting Sophie at work. It was easier to catch her there than at home. "Then I saw the commotion."

Victoria bid farewell to the lady whose hand had stopped shaking. She didn't look down to see what she'd written. She thought it rude, a bit like counting money when it had been handed over in a pile as a gift.

Gerald approached the stack of paper, took a slim, silver ink pen from the top pocket of his blazer and unscrewed the lid with unnecessary deliberation. He wrote his missive with an extravagant flourish of pen on paper.

"I leave you with that," he pronounced after inserting his last full stop with panache.

— — —

Four or five sheets of paper had been filled before two police officers wandered up to Victoria with a grin on their faces. They told her she had five minutes to wind up and by the way, did she realise that she could face a fine for unauthorised use of council property?

"Absolutely," she said, adding that it would have been worth it. She piled up the paper and pens as she listened patiently to the police officers explaining their apparent displeasure and why it was important that people bought a licence or gained permission for any public demonstration. Victoria was quick to state her full understanding that she would not be charged on this occasion but any subsequent digressions of this sort would be judged severely. She would comply totally with the law from now on.

But she had enjoyed herself and found herself saying, "And I daresay a few of the people who signed enjoyed the experience too."

It would be forty minutes before the next bus was due which meant she'd arrive home later than Doug. And then she'd have to explain where she'd been. She wished she had him alongside. Without experiencing it for himself, she understood why it was difficult to adjust. But he loved her, he would understand, if not totally, and if not today.

Was she behaving oddly? She found it difficult to judge. The consultant said that serotonin levels in a brain that had suffered trauma remained high for several months, often years, after the event and could cause irrational behaviour. Was serotonin making her more honest, more courageous? Was this possible? Or were the circumstances to blame for her being more overt and, she had to grudgingly admit, more aggressive since the accident? The obstacles hurled at her were challenging at the best of times. Sometimes she couldn't stop herself lashing out. Sometimes the frustration of living with a voice that people didn't want to hear, meant she had to search for a different means of expression.

Of course her emotions could simply be running sky high due to the fact that Christmas had been and gone and for the first time in Nicky's twenty-one years of life, she hadn't spent it at home.

— — — ˙

Before Victoria reached her front door, Doug nipped past her. "Going to football," he said and threw his kit bag into the back of the car. Victoria picked up the boot that had fallen out en route. Doug never zipped up his bag. She had given up suggesting he do so many years ago. He took the boot from her and tossed it onto the front passenger seat before climbing into the car. Victoria stood, her head bowed. She would talk to him tomorrow.

"You know, I would be the first to defend you if people were abusive," Doug said, his hand poised to close the door. He stared at the dashboard. "I would love you even if the entire world turned against you. But I don't see why I have to put up with this when you're doing it all to yourself." He yanked himself back out of the car and forced Victoria's downturned chin upwards with his finger so that she was compelled to look at him. "It's exhibitionism, Tori Williams," he said, emphasising the deliberate use of the name she'd banished through the snarl in his voice. She stepped back.

"And while we're on it, I don't care for hearing about it first via a triumphant Gerald."

"Gerald will never understand," Victoria said, "but I considered this carefully before I did it. People's reactions were largely positive."

Doug's eyes narrowed. Victoria felt obliged to look away. "What is this obsession with the public's reaction to you?" His voice was clipped. "Why, all of a sudden, is it important? You lived fifty years and they never offered an opinion. Now you're deliberately drawing attention to yourself, thinking this is all real."

"These are genuine people."

Doug threw his hands into the air. "They're laughing at you!"

Victoria shrugged her shoulders. "I don't think they are."

"This Toby," he said, "how long will it take him to drop you, do you think? How many pieces of paper will these people sign? When they're bored, Victoria, it will be worse than it ever was." He shook his head and got back into the car.

"We can talk later," Victoria whispered, "after football." She placed a hand clumsily on his shoulder but he shook it off. "Give the pub a miss," she said, crossing her arms, "and we'll talk about it then."

Doug jammed the key into the ignition and gripped the steering wheel with both hands. "You are not the woman I married," he said, his eyes fixed forward.

Victoria gasped.

"And you're making me into someone I do not want to be." He slammed the driver door and drove away too fast.

Victoria stood on the drive, stared after him. It was true. The woman he married had gone.

She looked at the pages stuffed into the top of her bag and for the first time, she felt foolish. She should put them in the recycling bin. Or burn them. That would be the end of it.

Not everybody had thought her a fool. If Doug had seen what people had written, he might not have been so cross. People had written on her sheets of paper. They'd seen the benefit too. They'd enjoyed the process and shaken her hand as they left. Of them all, only Gerald's words were hurtful. She'd made things extremely difficult for him and Sophie, he'd written. This was yet another of her mistakes and for that it was she who should apologise. Otherwise, there were no personal attacks or obscenities on any of the four or five sheets.

The remarks were short and often simple. The first was from the rocker with the red shoes. He merely wrote, 'I should have called.' The ten-year-old was sorry for being a scaredy-cat. Somebody wrote, 'I'm sorry I don't try harder,' and another said that she was sorry she'd lied about how much she spent. Victoria noted that, 'I shouldn't have claimed for more,' was written down in two separate places. 'I shouldn't have gossiped like that, I feel ashamed,' another wrote. 'A new start,' somebody else had written in tiny, immaculately formed writing, 'I'm going to sort it all out tonight.'

She pushed the papers deeper into her bag and walked slowly up the paved path to the house, pausing to pull out the odd dandelion growing between the cracks. She wouldn't shred the papers straightaway but she'd hide them. There was no point in upsetting Doug further.

There was a flicker of movement at Mary's front window. Victoria couldn't make out her expression but she raised her hand and Mary tilted her head in response. As she got closer, she saw the ventriloquist's smile which belonged only to Mary, her lips pressed firmly together, forcing the edges upwards. She'd been a good friend to Victoria over the twenty years they'd lived next door to each other. Victoria missed her.

Mary disappeared from view and Victoria hesitated for a moment, before striding up her neighbour's path as fast as her straight leg would allow. She didn't need to knock on the door before Mary opened it.

Victoria smiled instead of saying hello, a small, nervous smile. Mary fluffed up her loose silver curls before turning her ample body back towards the house and gesturing to Victoria to follow.

"Have a seat in the living room," she said, making her way to the kitchen. "You'll be needing a tea," she called behind her. "You're freezing."

Victoria sat in the olive wing armchair nearest the simmering coal fire while the kettle boiled. Her eyes and nose streamed with tears. She didn't want Mary to see her like this but she couldn't find a way to stop. Her shredded tissue was now useless and she had to resort to her sleeves to wipe her eyes, and the palm of her hand for her nose. When Mary reappeared sporting the frilly apron she'd worn every day since Victoria first met her, carrying the wooden tray she'd given her one Christmas, Victoria could only look at the floor and apologise.

"I shouldn't have come." She shook her head and blew wisps of sodden tissue into the carpet. Mary pushed a box of fresh ones onto her lap. "I've never cried like this, Mary, the whole time," she said, taking a fresh tissue. "It's such a mess. We're such a mess." She howled into her lap. Mary set the teacups on the table which doubled as a chessboard.

"Sssh." She offered Victoria her cup but set it back down on the table. "Two sugar day," she said, heaping the sugar in for her.

Victoria lifted her head, her eyes swollen and stinging, her hair matted around her face. "Thank you, Mary." She reached for her tea. Gulped. "It's good."

Mary smiled and took a sip of her own. She clattered the cup back onto the saucer. "Look at you love, you've no padding." She jumped to her feet and left the room without explanation. When she returned she was holding a plate of home-baked fruit loaf, thickly buttered, and a selection of her speciality Viennese whirls. "Go on," she said, setting both plates down in front of Victoria. Mary sat herself on the footstool in front of the fire while she placed two more pieces of coal on top. She looked at Victoria.

"I've, well," she looked back at the fire, "I've found it difficult."

FORTY-SIX

VICTORIA READ ONE of the large print books she'd recently discovered in the library. It was 11pm. Time for last orders in the Barley Mow. She lifted herself out of bed and slowly made her way back to the bathroom to clean her teeth.

At 11.40 Doug still wasn't home even though, for him, the pub was a five-minute walk away. Victoria felt sick. The last time she looked at the clock was 12.33. The sheet was cold beside her. When she woke three hours later, she inched her way out of bed and opened the door to the spare room. Doug was snoring. Victoria stood for a moment and sighed.

"Twenty-three years of marriage," she whispered. She let her dressing gown fall to the floor and inched towards the bed. She didn't want to turn on the light but found it almost impossible to balance with her shortened leg in the dark. She breathed out. She'd tackled harder things than this.

She lay on the bed with the narrow but cavernous gap between her and her husband, who was spread out on his stomach. She placed her hand on his hip and shuffled towards him.

"What did you say?" she asked.

"We need to talk," Doug said, muffled and slurred through lips pointing away from her. His body didn't move. His snoring resumed and as the hours passed, she managed to sleep despite its rhythm.

— — —

Victoria lugged herself into sitting position when she heard the squeal of the door to the spare room opening.

"Tea," Doug said, placing Victoria's on the bedside table next to her. He stretched over and kissed her quickly on her forehead, said that he had a few minutes and then would need to be going. She patted the bed next to her. But Doug didn't sit, instead he stood three feet away.

"Victoria, I think you need help." His voice was gravelly and monotone.

"What kind of help?"

"Counselling." His eyes were bloodshot, the seriousness of the conversation pulled at his face.

"Marriage counselling, Doug?"

"No, not marriage counselling. Although," he said carefully, "this is important for our relationship." Victoria exhaled, her heart thick and knotted again. "Trauma counselling," he said, stepping over to the bed where he perched on the furthest edge away from his wife. He looked down at the purple satin throw. He wouldn't meet her eyes but his voice was softer again. "I did a lot of thinking last night," he said. "You nearly died. You lost your job and your old life. Why wouldn't you try to create something new? I'm trying to understand this, Victoria, really I am."

"I know that, Doug," she said, leaning over to touch his hand. But he pulled away, shaking his head.

"The way you're dealing with it though, this new celebrity persona, it's never going to work. I want you to go to counselling, to find another way to deal with what happened." Doug reached into his pocket for a bunch of post-it notes which he put in a pile on the bed next to her. "I really must go." He kissed her, this time briefly on the lips. "Please, phone them," he said, before leaving the room.

If her tea hadn't still been warm in her hands, she might have doubted it ever happened. She sipped and looked down at the untidily written numbers. 'Jejune,' she thought. But his words weren't any easier to accept, nor the disarray of her life any tidier, once she'd grappled one of the words from her private store.

Would Doug ever be able to cope with the metamorphosis that had taken place after that day in August? Could he get used to Victoria because she really couldn't see how physically or emotionally she could ever go back to being Tori Williams.

Was she a decent human being?

She was alone. She had her great friends, of course, and her devoted mother and loyal daughter in Carly, but none of them had experienced anything remotely like this themselves. They could console and care for her. They felt her pain, her confusion, of that she was sure, but they could never *know* it like she did.

She needed somebody to empathise, an 'insider' to consider and then confirm, categorically, whether or not she was acting unreasonably, if she should handle things differently. She had snatches of real happiness now. She was convinced she'd felt the tension seep from the confessors when they'd signed her paper. It was a wonderful feeling to think that she was in some way responsible for encouraging people to address their own lives and make adjustments. That was why she'd enjoyed wearing the sandwich board, not some perverse pleasure at the prospect of her picture in the papers next day, looking like the Queen of Hearts.

But Victoria hadn't lived for fifty years without understanding that this wasn't all about her. Where was the joy in making strangers happy if her husband was miserable?

She pulled a skirt from the pile on the bedroom chair even though there was snow on the ground outside. It was quicker than struggling with trousers. She wrestled her feet into her slippers and felt her big toes slip through the holes in the ends. She pulled a large, pink jumper over her head and stopped briefly to glance in the mirror. She looked older than Ruby. As quickly as possible she stepped down the stairs and hesitated only momentarily before picking up the telephone from the telephone table.

"Hello?" It was a man's voice. "Yes, hi there, can I help?"

Victoria gasped. Should she ask for her? Should she risk their friendship before it had really begun?

But could she bear not to?

"Who is this?"

Quietly Victoria took the phone from her ear and used the elbow of her useless arm to switch off the receiver. She didn't move, simply stared at herself in the huge, rectangular mirror she tended to avoid these days. How had she looked to Etta in the car: asleep or distressed? Was she silent, or did she cry out in pain or panic? She wondered how Etta had got into her car. The police had shown her a picture; there was no space where the doors had been. She asked herself why Etta had stayed to help.

She put her hand on the receiver again and sighed. She looked at the scrunched up numbers for the counsellors which Doug had sourced for her, fuelled with alcohol, in the early hours of the morning. On each, there was a name and a number but if she was to go along with this, she'd have to do some research of her own.

She retraced her steps back upstairs and sat herself down on her orthopaedic approved chair at the computer in her study. It was a box room which, with the walnut pedestal desk handed down from her father taking up much of the floor, didn't really cater for an outstretched left leg.

When she searched for experts in her area, five pages of names appeared. Most meant nothing to her. 'Trauma Counsellor' wasn't really the stuff of everyday conversation. However, there was one organisation which appeared on every page and this was something she recognised: The Samaritans.

Victoria thought about her life experiences: her childhood loneliness and loss; the death of her father before she'd had a chance to prepare; a daughter, estranged, living on the other side of the world when she hadn't even seen her 22nd birthday. And of course, two people dealing with a catastrophe in very different ways. Her finger edged back on to the mouse. She clicked, 'Volunteer'.

Confidentiality and anonymity came up a lot, Victoria noticed, as she trailed through the documentation. That would please Doug.

By lunchtime, Victoria had printed off the application form and filled it out. She found the questions easy to answer, even if it took her longer than she'd have liked to record her responses. She was used to being honest these days, she no longer worried about what people wanted to hear. She wrote, 'reading and walking' where she'd have previously written, 'cycling and rock climbing'. And where it asked for her employment status she simply put: unemployable.

FORTY-SEVEN

JOHAN AND ADRIANA CONTINUED running around Etta's legs, taking it in turns to hide behind her, chasing each other with the old-fashioned feather duster they'd found in the over-full cupboard under the stairs.

"Johan, Adriana, quiet please, I need to speak to this lady," Etta said. "Ms Moxley, I'm so sorry, just a moment. Sssh, please, come on, out of here," she said to the children, a hand on both bottoms, pushing them out of the kitchen as she spoke.

"It's with a heavy heart that I'm calling," Ms Moxley said. Other colleagues had mentioned Etta's absence and lack of attention. "You sent in the wrong piece of work to Dr Harper."

Etta let out a gasp - she'd written the essay at four o'clock in the morning.

Her giggling children had slipped back into the room. "Please get out of here for the next five minutes," she begged. "I'm pleading with you."

"Etta?" she heard. "Do you understand the reason for this phone call?"

Etta opened her mouth to speak but couldn't manage any words.

"Some institutions are happy to take your money and fail you. We aren't. We'll refund the final term's fees," Ms Moxley said. "It's the right decision."

"No!" Etta's voice was barely audible. "I can't stop now—"

"It's the end of the road for this year, but not the end of your studies," Ms Moxley said. "Take care, Etta."

Etta waited for the click of the receiver, the end of the line, the full stop on what was supposed to be a new page.

But Ms Moxley spoke again. "Etta, can I offer you some advice?"

Etta nodded, her heart beating out of her chest again. She wanted to speak, needed to speak but still no words would leave her lips.

"Take some time out," she heard. "Re-focus on yourself and your family. Get your life back on track before you commit to this workload again."

"Yes," Etta managed eventually, lifting the receiver away from her ear, the grip wet where it was squeezed into her sweating palm.

"And Etta," Ms Moxley said. "Whatever's troubling you, sort it out. Achieve some sort of closure so that it doesn't get any bigger."

Then came the click and the line was dead.

Etta stared at the phone, let it drop to the ground. She slumped down to the floor. She let her head slide down to rest on the kitchen tiles and pulled her knees closer to her chest. She lay in the foetal position and closed her eyes.

— — —

Johan had answered the lady's questions. He'd known to ask for the ambulance once he'd dialled 999 as Mama had taught him. He'd told the lady his name and where he lived and that his mum was lying on the floor.

"Can you try to wake her? Can you do that for me, Johan?" the nice lady said. "You can shout as loud as you like."

He ran as fast as he could back into the kitchen with Adriana stuck to his school shirt at the back, copying every step he made. He stood next to his mother.

"Call out her name as quickly as you can please, Johan.'

"Mama?" he asked, his voice barely more than a whisper. "Mama!" he tried louder. And then from behind him came a screech of, "Maaama," from Adriana, so forceful it made him jump and nearly land on his mother. Adriana was kicking Etta now, her head tipped back, shouting to the ceiling as she kicked.

"Stop it, Adriana!" Johan said. Now he'd made her cry. He stepped over his mother's legs to give his sister a hug which is what Mama would have expected him to do.

"Johan?" He remembered the phone was still in his hand. "This is very important. An ambulance is coming. Now, your job is to tell me about your mum. Does she look like she's breathing? Is her chest moving, can you tell?" Johan nodded but forgot to speak. "You can put your hand on her chest to feel it go up and down."

And then Etta's eyes opened. She placed her hand flat on the floor to support her, rolled onto her side and said, "Goodness me, what's happening here?"

Johan stared, dropped the phone and fell to his knees. He clasped his arms around his Mama in a bear hug so tight, his arms almost lapped her. The lady asked him if that was his mum speaking.

"Hey!" she said, stroking his head and gasping a little as Adriana sat herself on the floor in front of her and snuggled into her stomach. "Mama got so tired all of a sudden."

"Johan!" he suddenly heard through the earpiece of the discarded phone. "Could you pass your mum the phone?"

_ _ _

The ambulance crew were still there when Andy arrived home. It had been no trouble, they'd assured. They were close by and it was standard practice to check these things out. They didn't think she'd fainted though, just got over exhausted. Was she doing too much? The older gentleman with the white hair and ginger beard had said that she needed to slow down, her health was more important than anything. If not to her, then to her children.

Would they know she'd slightly embellished her recounting of her physical reaction to the phone call? She'd stopped short of saying she'd been sick as that required evidence but it was true that she'd physically felt nauseous and in reality, could have been sick. She could also have fainted, perhaps.

What did she know? She'd had her dreams taken from her before, had them rubbed between her parents' hands until only crumbs remained, but she'd never previously taken the knife herself to slice them quite so definitely in two. What was it supposed to feel like?

Andy ran to Etta and took her into his arms. She looked awful, so pale, he couldn't begin to imagine what had happened. Was she in shock? And why would Social Services be in touch, 'simply a matter of procedure', according to the ambulance crew, 'nothing to worry about'?

As she tried her best to tell him the story, in between Johan's own precis of the events which were touched with a not insignificant dash of pride, and Adriana's reminder that it was she who had managed to shout loud enough to wake their Mama, she felt Andy's arms gradually relax from around her waist.

When she told him that the conversation with Ms Moxley was final; that there were no more chances, that was it, dream over,

Andy released his arms completely. He turned away, looked at his children and told them to get their shoes on, they were already two hours late for school. Dad would be taking them to school this morning and by the way, shouldn't Mama be at work?

FORTY-EIGHT

VICTORIA COULDN'T REMEMBER ever receiving such an enormous pile of post. She took the mail to the table. She'd open the letters more carefully over a cup of tea in the dining room.

There was a telephone bill and suggestion that she set up a direct debit as it would make it easier to pay. "How? Does it print money?" she asked aloud. Another company wanted to change her windows and sixteen charities thought she may be able to help.

There was a pile of twenty or more hand-written envelopes. She spread them out over the table and chose two with appealing handwriting. She liked that people still wrote letters. She smoothed first one then the other under her fingers.

Both asked for Tori's advice. They admired how she had coped with the weight of criticism and how she'd moved on from a seemingly desperate situation. The first wanted to know how she could do the same.

I stopped speaking to my brother over seven years ago, sixty-eight-year old Pamela wrote, *after he coerced my parents into changing their will to benefit his children. A few weeks ago I attended his funeral. There were so many people there who clearly loved him, I realised that my brother was about more than that single error of judgement and I wished I'd been big enough to see that.*

Pamela wanted to know how Tori would deal with a situation when however much she felt her repentance, it was too late for it to be heard. To this, however, Victoria had no answer. She put the letter to the bottom of the pile so that she could have a think about it.

The second letter was sent locally. It was from one of the signatories of Tori's list at the sandwich board. She stared at the handwriting in an attempt to recall which of the characters it was. She remembered the notation immediately, but not the author. 'A new start,' she'd written, 'I'm going to sort it all out tonight.' Katherine had offset £28,000 of her mortgage to feed her shopping habit. Aside from a rail of designer dresses and so many pairs of shoes she couldn't begin to remember them all, she had nothing to show for it. Her partner was oblivious even though he'd recently found himself a second job in an attempt to pay the mortgage off sooner and buy them some security.

After vowing to sort out this mess I went to my wardrobe and retrieved everything I'd bought in the past month. £785 worth still had tags on. I took it all back to the shops. I cancelled my pending internet purchases, my monthly subscription to the gym I never use and listed 34 pairs of shoes on eBay. Best of all, I applied for a night job stacking shelves in our local supermarket in addition to my day job as an Office Manager. I detest the shelf stacking so that's helping me to forgive myself. I haven't told my husband why I'm working so hard, which you might not approve of, but I will do when I've paid it all back. I have £26,690 to go.

Victoria grimaced. Katherine's debts were almost as bad as hers. Although she would appear to have greater potential for paying them back.

Tori, this is a happy story because I can live with myself again. Thank you, she wrote. *Until I stopped blaming my deprived upbringing, the pressures of my work and needs of my friends, I never would have been able to fix this thing.*

Victoria read the letters again and fizzled with the anticipation of responding. All of a sudden, as quickly as she'd lost it, she'd been given back some responsibility. She would have one more cup of tea before reading any more. Her replies would take her all day. It wasn't the answers she struggled with. Never had she thought so clearly about life and its many foibles, about what drove a wedge between people and indeed, often what made them happy, but typing with one hand was, at best, tedious.

She examined an envelope with the trademark 'Jupe' in the corner as she stood by the kettle waiting for it to boil again. She tutted as she performed her usual left handed trick to open the envelope. Why did these magazines insist on writing to her? If she wanted to take out a subscription she'd do so. She would not be bamboozled into it. The paper was bright white and of good quality.

"I'm definitely not subscribing if you're going to spend my payment on posh paper," she muttered.

I am writing to you personally as I have an exciting proposition for you. Victoria shook the paper in an attempt to straighten it. *We have been following your story closely here at the office. Although we obviously feel keenly for the families who weren't so lucky, no normal hearted person could fail to be touched by your side of the story, too.* Victoria gasped. She read more quickly.

My team and I are impressed with your passion and spirit and fascinated by your efforts to engage an unforgiving public. We would like to publish a double page feature on YOU, not on the accident, nor the court case but on the life you're clearly rebuilding and equally, on what makes you tick.

We would prefer to discuss our ideas and, of course, the fee in more detail with you but can confirm that we are suggesting a five figure sum for the two page feature.

I do hope this is of interest and look forward to your call on my direct line at your earliest convenience.

With very best wishes

Cresta Bloomenfeld.

Features Editor, Jupe.

A five figure sum! Victoria skimmed through the letter again. Surely that type of article couldn't harm? If the magazine really wanted to speak about the future, she could mention her talks to students, to be launched in her local secondary school in a few weeks. If she could successfully educate even ten per cent of the sixteen to eighteen year olds that there was never a good enough reason to text anybody from the car, her talks would have been worth it, the representative from the education authority had told her.

She told herself to stay calm, poured the hot water over the teabag. A five figure sum!

She could tell them about her upcoming 'informal interview' with the Samaritans. She was so excited about it, not to mention relieved not to have failed at the first hurdle when the voice with the gruff Scottish accent from the other end of the line had asked her to explain what she meant by 'unemployable'. He was sure Victoria understood, but it was important to clarify, that volunteering wasn't something people fell into when they'd exhausted all other avenues of work. Victoria was invited to attend eight training sessions. The first was set for Saturday.

Even her rehabilitation might prove to be an interesting subject. Amelie particularly marvelled at her methods of performing two-handed tasks with only one. The physios assured her that her recovery was nothing short of extraordinary and down in no small part to her hard work and positive attitude. Victoria hadn't felt as proud in years.

For once Victoria couldn't predict how Doug would react. Could he be persuaded that this was the piece of publicity to end it all, the one final sacrifice of their privacy in return for a bank account in the black? Perhaps, if that went well, she could come clean about Steve. But Doug was a man of principle and the mere mention of the word 'magazine' might propel him into a spin from which he'd never uncoil. She had to tackle this carefully.

She made her way back to the dining room with the fresh tea but decided against entering and walked instead to the phone in the hall. She hugged the receiver between her shoulder and her chin. She knew the number off by heart even though she'd only rung it twice before.

This time she would take a deep breath, she would stay in the present. She'd apologise for the previous effort to call but would Etta mind her asking a question? She sighed, pinched the top of her nose with her fingers.

Just dial!

How did Etta feel about being paid for articles relating to the accident, she'd ask her, that was all. Nobody else would understand the question like she did. Hers was the opinion she valued the most. It wasn't a slight on those she loved; often people went to strangers for advice.

And if Etta's partner answered? She wouldn't hang up. She'd explain that she meant Etta no harm but that she felt Etta could help her. She dialled the number, breathed out and waited for a response. But there was none. She tried again: no one home. Of course! Etta would be at work. Or at the university. Or even taking the children to the doctor's, the dentist's, or optician's appointment. How ridiculous that she'd expected her to be home at this time in the morning. Just because Victoria barely managed more than one task a day, didn't mean the wheels of everybody else's life turned quite so slowly.

FORTY-NINE

ETTA REALISED SHE WAS STARING; staring through the kitchen window and into the garden at the broken pane in the greenhouse. She imagined taking each piece of shattered glass and painstakingly fitting them all together, like the most intricate of jigsaws. Unlike a puzzle, regardless of her efforts, now that it was shattered it would never look the same again.

She didn't know how she'd got herself off the floor and onto the stool at the table. Had Andy helped? Did she make the cup of tea which stood on the table in front of her? She looked at the slug-like swirls of grey. Cold. She tapped her feet on the floor, looked at the clock: 11am. Three hours late for work and she'd given no explanation. That must have been them on the phone. She should have picked up. Twice they'd called, three times perhaps? What was wrong with her? Didn't she care about her job? She didn't seem to care about anything. Did she even mind that Andy was so upset? Did she feel it? She wanted to feel it but that wasn't the same thing.

Her children had been thrown into school late. She hadn't

combed Adriana's hair, let alone drawn her parting dead straight down the middle, before securing it into two plaits at the school's request. She would have nits by first break. She hadn't checked their uniform. Johan's trousers would be caked with mud from the boggy grass that made his football pitch in their garden.

She'd been thrown off the course.

Ms Moxley said she could start again, 'with their blessing'. Ms Moxley had no idea. Two years it would take to save up even just to take the first year again.

Besides, Ms Moxley may grant her blessing but she wasn't so sure about Andy.

She should go to work. One more cup of tea instead of the cold one, then she'd feel better. She dragged herself from the stool. She'd promised she'd call the doctor, get checked out. Tomorrow. She'd do it tomorrow. She felt so listless, didn't have the energy to call today.

Should she ring in sick? Was she ill? She hated it when people called in sick for no good reason, upsetting the balance for everyone. No, she must lead by example. A cup of tea! Then she'd gather herself, get back to work, move forward, move on from the course. Who'd have said she'd make a good weather presenter anyway? She was probably too old, too tired. Who did she think she was, believing she'd have the face to fit? Her fingers drifted to the pockmarks in her skin and fluttered over the blemishes. She shook away her hand in disgust. It was such a distracting habit, Sara always told her.

She was an irresponsible mother, a selfish wife and a disloyal friend. Talentless. She had nothing to show for her thirty-five years. Whatever gave her the right to think she'd have been able to understand her studies well enough to apply that knowledge in front of the camera?

She cast her mind to radio. It never stopped forecasting. Tori Williams managed to speak on the radio with no training. It was possible. She shook her head. She didn't need the course. All she'd have to show for it would be an ability to translate the weather forecast to her children; show off her knowledge of the difference in cloud shape and formation to interested passing ramblers.

She must let go of meteorology. And she must erase Tori Williams from her life, too. She was simply a person. What had Etta thought she could do for her - make the last two years go away? She'd advise her to apologise and that was one thing she would never be allowed to do. Ms Williams wasn't always right.

She wished she hadn't written that stupid letter to her.

The tea was too milky. She'd drink it anyway. She opened the back door and sat on the step. The air was gusty, blowing her hair into the tea. She lifted her face to the sky, breathed out, the rim of the step cutting into her bottom. Uncomfortable was better than feeling nothing.

Her phone buzzed: a text. Ms Moxley? Had she changed her mind, given her until the end of the year to prove herself? She jumped off the step and ran to the table where it buzzed again from inside her bag.

It was Andy: 'Work asking where u r?' the first text asked: 'Will call & tell them u in tomorrow,' was the second. No kisses. Etta stared at the phone: no other texts. Calls? Nothing. But Ms Moxley wouldn't ring her mobile; she'd used the landline this morning. Etta raced into the hall to the semi-circular table, her heart beating as she stared at the mostly redundant answerphone.

There were no messages. Ms Moxley hadn't rung, nor ever would again. She'd made the call to Etta early this morning to get it over with, then she'd have bought herself a coffee and by the second line of her lecture, she'd have forgotten Etta was ever a student there.

She wouldn't go to work. One day off wouldn't harm. She'd sort out some washing. Normally she'd attempt an essay, or visit the hospital in the early days, have a cup of tea with Ruby perhaps. Normally she'd be grateful for the extra time off. She wandered back into the kitchen, over to the heap of dark washing and stuffed it item by item into the machine. The door wouldn't shut. She took out two sets of Andy's overalls: still too full. She dragged the whole lot out again and left it sitting on the floor, back where she'd found it.

She was so tired. She'd go upstairs, rest her head for a few minutes and have a power nap, then things would feel better and she would call Andy.

FIFTY

"HELLO, MY NAME'S TOBY HANSON and welcome to Tori's Truth." Victoria flinched. She was starting to despise her old name. She looked around her. The studio seemed so much smaller than the other times she'd spoken on the radio. She was flanked by Barney with his matted afro, who was happily air drumming to the musical interludes, and Mike who was the most smartly dressed of all the contestants with his starched collars and brushed cotton trousers and a crease firmly ironed into the exact centre of each leg. Shelley sat next to him. She had bright pink lips pressed into a perpetual smile and cheekbones so high they buffered up to the sockets of her eyes.

"This is the game where we ask our panel of celebrities and some of you, *extraordinary* folk," Toby signalled to Mike in mock apology for the clearly scripted line, "to admit to their blunders, embarrassments and regrets, whilst their opponents wager whether they are telling the truth." There was a collective 'u-oh' from the participants in the studio. "We're going to give each of our guests the opportunity to tell two stories but one of them won't be true. The winner is the person who correctly distinguishes most Truths from Tale." Almost as an aside Toby added glibly, "But of course, you're all winners because you get absolution which is how the whole idea of Tori's Truth started." Victoria exhaled loudly and the producer scowled at her from behind her glass screen.

"So, why don't we have a word with our invited guests? Tori, how about you?" Toby smiled in Victoria's direction and offered his hand to signal her cue to speak. 'Difficult bit,' he mouthed to her.

"Yes, hello, I'm Tori Williams." Saying her old name herself, made her want to scream.

"Hi Tori, we all know you from the torrid time you've had in the press but may I ask, what on earth made you want to come on the show today?" Victoria breathed out again and looked quickly at the producer who flicked her wrist around at speed and narrowed her eyes to generate a response.

"I can't help feeling that there's a silver lining to the horrendous situation I was involved in." Victoria had practised this several times in front of the mirror but still the words caused her head to dip. "People are enjoying being honest, purging their souls, as you put it, and if we can have a bit of fun with that today, then why not?"

"Money, Toby, before you ask," the bedraggled comic interjected, smiling at Victoria. "That's how you got me here."

"And might I say, Barney Tyson, Yorkshire Vale Radio's chosen comedian of the year, how mighty fine you're looking today."

"It's my just got out of bed look," he said, with mock preening, "'cos I've just got out of bed." Victoria was too nervous to laugh. "Stand-up last night, you see, in Leeds, living the lifestyle," he said, his head sashaying from side to side.

The third guest, Mike, was the token *normal* person. It

tickled Victoria that she was clearly considered to be one of the professionals, even if it wouldn't have impressed Doug. She shook her head to get him out of her mind.

Shelley, the fourth contestant, starred in a locally filmed soap. Before the show she'd told Victoria that the quiz would be good research for her character but on air she said that she was intrigued to see how she would fare, would she be able to laugh about her misbehaviour publicly? "That'll be tough," she said.

Barney was first to go with his story of his first appearance at the Edinburgh festival when he was seventeen years old.

"There's me, in my silver jumpsuit, with these great flares flapping around my wedge heels," he said. "I'd taped the biggest cigar I could buy to my finger and I'd spent bloody ages—" Toby looked reproachfully at him, "—*ages*," he corrected, "ironing my hair into a nicely gelled quiff, reaching up ten centimetres from my forehead. I had this series of jokes based on Elvis's lyrics. He'd died you see, gone to heaven and come back as a *black man*." He laughed, a series of ripples through his whole body which caused Victoria to giggle and they both bounced in their seats like children.

But when Barney peered through the edge of the thinning, green velour stage curtain and saw the smoke, the expectation of the crowd and their 'pints of piss-coloured beer', he lost his nerve. He asked the compere, perfectly happy to add a few minutes under the spotlight to his own routine, to tell the audience that Barney's mother had died and he'd had to leave.

"It wasn't the fact that my mum didn't speak to me for three weeks following, nor that her first words to break the silence were that if she died in the next ten years I'd have hell to pay," - Victoria sniggered - "but I tell you, it was the sympathy of the crowd to my mourning that cut me up. I got a pile of letters of support. I was still at school. People would gather at the gates and watch me go in, their faces wracked with pity. It killed me but I never told anybody, even the compere never knew the truth."

The end of Barney's first story was met with a pre-recorded drum roll and 'Tori's Truth or Tori's Tale - you decide!'

Victoria and Shelley were convinced it was a Tale, nobody did stand-up at seventeen, right? Only Mike was correct in voting for Truth.

Even in the studio the laughter waned after its peak with Barney's story. The show was dependent on good raconteurs and Mike, although fiercely sure of his lines, couldn't have been described as that. He'd had to pass an audition to get this far, and been chosen from one hundred and forty-three applicants, which didn't bode well for the rest of the series. The show had to get better than this. Victoria needed it to be worth the discussion with Doug that would inevitably ensue.

— — —

It was Victoria's turn and she was finding it easier than expected to talk about Gerald.

"So after I'd seen the train tickets," she said, "I looked in his diary. This was 1999 and my stepfather was in his fifties. He hadn't signed up to mobile phones then and didn't use email." Victoria laughed. "It's easier to find evidence of people playing around nowadays," she said. "But I knew what was going on and the diary contradicted him and backed me up. Not that I'm proud of snooping around." She laughed again, nervously this time.

Barney wagged his finger and said loudly, "Shame on you Tori Williams," with a wide smile on his face.

"You'd be tempted to look in the diary once you had suspicions that your stepfather was playing around, wouldn't you?" Victoria seemed a little too earnest but there were a couple of nods of acquiescence from Barney and Shelley. Mike didn't even twitch.

"Shameful is that I told my mother."

"Oh my God! What happened?" Shelley asked, with a squeak in her voice.

"That's the first of your three questions team," Toby roared.

"My mother was disappointed in me and they split up." Everyone gasped except Toby who marvelled at how well the show was going.

"Was it your fault they split up?" Shelley asked. "Is that why you feel guilty?"

"I feel guilty for telling my mother, full stop."

"Don't you think she had a right to know?" Mike asked.

"Perhaps. But I don't think she wanted to know. It meant she couldn't pretend any more."

"Thanks guys, that's your three questions."

Toby asked for the first thoughts on Victoria's admission.

"Untruth," Barney said, when it was his turn. "I think she'd have felt guilty if she hadn't told her mother about her stepfather."

— — —

Victoria turned her key in the lock and could hear the phone ringing as she pushed open the door. She sat down on the hall chair before picking up. She knew better than to try to stand for too long after she'd walked home from the bus stop. It would be Ruby. She was the only person who ever called her on her landline these days. Even without a mobile, her few correspondents preferred to email.

"Tori!" Her stomach tightened as she heard the familiar West Country accent. "Gerald here."

"Hello Gerald, nice of you to call."

"I thought one of us needed to."

"Yes."

"You could have called yourself, perhaps. After we bumped into you in the café. I thought you might have rung to apologise."

Gosh! Gerald wasn't wasting any time on pleasantries. "Yes, I could have called, Gerald." Victoria sucked on her teeth. "It's difficult."

"Did you even read what I wrote at your silly soap box?"

"I gathered you weren't happy."

Gerald certainly wasn't happy. He had his own life and it was his right to live that life as he saw fit. Victoria agreed. She knew about that better than most.

"Why did you do that to me in the café?" Gerald asked, audibly spitting as he spoke. "To Sophie, why did you do that to Sophie?"

Victoria didn't need to ask what she'd done and she didn't want to get drawn into the conversation. After the initial euphoria of expressing what she'd wanted to say many times previously, she couldn't pretend that she didn't cringe when she thought about the conversation; when she thought about what she'd said to Sophie. Perhaps it was a little misdirected.

"Gerald, about your relationships, I was unkind."

"Unkind!"

"It isn't my business."

"No, it flaming well isn't. It was another in your incessant quests to ruin my happiness!" Gerald was shouting now. Victoria had to hold the phone from her ear.

"It's our history, Gerald. It's complicated."

"Yeah," he said, "isn't it!"

"You caused a lot of problems between me and my mum."

"I could say the same," he said.

Victoria breathed out, touched her brow. "I didn't break up your relationship, Gerald." She was sick of this. She was many things but she wasn't vindictive.

"I heard you on the radio."

"Ah," Victoria said.

Gerald wanted to know if Victoria thought it was funny to tell the audience that her stepfather was a philanderer in his youth and when Victoria said that nobody would know it was him and he said that people could easily track him down, she couldn't help smiling. This was vintage Gerald. "I can hear you chuckling," he said, louder. "It's a ruddy radio show, Tori, not some shrink's couch and a microphone."

Victoria shuffled in her seat. She said that the show shouldn't be taken too seriously and that there was a fair bit of humour in the stories. Besides, Gerald liked the odd dose of the limelight, didn't he? There was a long enough pause for Victoria to feel the need to check that Gerald was still there and he answered,

"Sophie, what about Sophie? She already hates you for bringing the press into our lives."

"Does she?" Victoria said.

"I've been unlucky in love and you can't accept that."

Victoria asked how Sophie was and when the line remained quiet, she said that she was sorry Sophie was having a bad time with the press.

"Just like you couldn't accept your mum loved another man after your dad," Gerald said.

Victoria asked Gerald if he thought his behaviour had any bearing on his luck and he said that he'd tried his hardest. No one was perfect.

Victoria was calm and deliberate; she'd spent years ruminating over this. Ruby was vulnerable, she was grieving and needed him. "So you take no responsibility for the break up with my mother even though you were unfaithful?" she asked.

"You should have kept your nose out then, Tori, and you should leave everything alone now," Gerald said.

Was he even listening to her questions? "Please, Gerald, call me Victoria."

"I say to you, Tori Williams," Gerald stressed, "that your mother knew what was going on and she accepted it."

Victoria looked at her feet and the mud she'd trailed in behind her. She noticed that she had two different footprints these days. "Yes, that's right," she said.

Gerald didn't speak. The silence spread around Victoria's hallway. She reached down and scraped at one of the muddy footprints with her nail. When she heard a cough, she moved the phone closer to her ear.

"You're saying that's right?" Gerald asked slowly.

"Yes, that's correct." Victoria waited again.

"That isn't what you said."

"Then you didn't listen to the whole programme."

The contenders had guessed wrong. Victoria's story was a 'Tori's Tale'. Her mother had found out about Doug's other life all by herself and lived with it for years. She was weak. When she got stronger, she got rid of him.

"So that was a lie on the radio."

"Not really Gerald. I did look in your diary and you were playing around. I didn't tell her what I knew because I didn't think she wanted to hear it. I regret that. I let her delude herself, waste her life and I've hated you ever since. There," she said, "I have been mean in the past and insensitive and for that I apologise," she paused. "But here, now, I'm being honest."

The silence drifted in swirls around Victoria's face. She'd summed up the past twenty years of emotion in one outpouring but she didn't feel any elation. She could hear Gerald's tongue tapping on the back of his teeth as it did when he concentrated.

"*Hate* was too strong Gerald, I shouldn't have said that."

It was a few moments before he spoke again. "I appreciate you explaining that," he said, pushing out an elongated sigh which Victoria wanted to believe was genuine. "It doesn't change what you said to Sophie, though," he said. "Now you have to tell her."

"No," Victoria rubbed one eye and stifled a yawn. The radio show had exhausted her. "You have to work that one out with her yourself."

FIFTY-ONE

ANDY TOSSED HIS BOOTS into the corner of the room, the steel cap of one marking the already tired looking skirting board. He threw his soaking, no-longer waterproofed trousers onto the floor by the washing machine and took a beer from the door of the fridge.

"Of course there's no note or text," he said out loud, having scanned the ground floor and even sprinted up to the bedroom on the off chance. "That would be too much to ask for." He removed the lid from the bottle with his teeth and pulled out his phone to check one last time, although there was really little point. There was a single text from his mother but at least it made him smile. Sometimes, not so very often, she showed her warmer side and he was so thankful to her for picking up the children and giving them their tea today. They were welcome to stay the night, she said, and she'd get them to school in the morning, would wash their uniform, no need to worry about that.

After ringing Etta and the call going straight through to answerphone once again, and barely managing to keep the phone in his hand rather than slamming it across the kitchen worktops, he thought he'd try Sara once more. She was also avoiding his calls. Maybe they'd eloped together. He cleared his throat. None of this was funny.

He almost missed it when Sara finally picked up the call. He'd decided after four rings that it was all a fucking waste of time, but he'd heard a rather surly, "Yes?" as his finger hovered over the disconnect button. He asked if she was OK and of course she said she was fine, in a voice which sounded as though she'd had three hours' sleep after a skinful and he was calling to chat in the middle of the night.

"I've checked all the hospitals for thirty miles," he said, "and the ambulance people were convinced it was a panic attack this morning. God!" he said, suddenly, "what if she's had another while she was driving and is yet to be picked up?"

When Sara answered wearily that she hadn't had an accident, Etta was safe and well, a stone landed in his stomach for a different reason.

"She texted me. If anyone asked, I was to let them know that she'd gone away for a few days."

Andy could have put the phone down but that was rude. He asked Sara again if she was all right. "You haven't had much contact with her lately," he said, "she hasn't upset you as well, has she?" And then Sara spoke in a tone he'd never heard before. He didn't think he'd ever heard her raise her voice.

"Yes, she's upset me, made our friendship pretty untenable, actually. So, if you think for one moment that I'm going to be involved in any shape or form in your relationship, you can butt out right now."

"Message received and understood," Andy said. Then Sara mumbled a sort of apology, that it wasn't Andy's fault and put down the phone.

Andy thought he was better off without conversations with women today.

And if his partner wasn't prepared to speak to him, and his children were being well cared for, then he'd do what he never, ever had the chance to do these days: he'd watch TV for a few hours, sink a load of beers and get himself off to bed as soon as he felt like it.

After three beers, beans on toast with so much butter he could still taste it on his teeth, and back-to-back quiz shows with contestants who didn't know their arse from their elbow, he was beginning to hate himself. Since when had he become such an uncaring bastard? Etta was ignoring him. He had no idea where she was. Who was he trying to kid that he didn't care? Was that a nervous breakdown this morning? Is that how it manifested itself? And he'd cared little more than to tell her she was late for work. He held his head in his hands. It was all so confusing.

It was wrong of him to go sniffing around, he knew that, but she'd forced it upon him. What he really needed was her phone but, of course, she'd have that. Even the SAS wouldn't be able to prise that from her. He began with the drawers in the kitchen. Any notes, random phone numbers, official letters. Debts? Oh God, what if they were in even more debt than he thought? He sprinted upstairs to the black concertina file in the corner of their bedroom, leafed through to the bank section, but found only a few statements from over a year ago. His eyes widened. Etta? What had she gone and done? Bought another house and gone to live there? He took a deep breath, sat down on the second-hand throne, draped in Etta's tights, in front of the laptop perched on the dressing table.

When the online statements matched his thinking to the penny, a strange whistle left his lips, like a dying rocket, he thought, strangely symbolic of the current state of his relationship as it fell out of a starry sky. He told himself to calm down. He sat still, stared at the screen, his finger hovering over the navigation button. He gulped. He had to do it.

In her absence, he thanked her for using the same password for everything.

"What the—?" he muttered as he scrolled down the notifications on Etta's Facebook timeline. "The woman's obsessed!" There were no stunning pictures of villas in the sun, thankfully, nor bicep curling males he'd never seen before. Nothing remotely suspicious. But there were lots of photos of the children, and he really wished she didn't sprinkle them quite so liberally over the internet.

The last time she'd posted was yesterday, he noted. 'Black day for me at Uni. I have to focus now or I will fail.' Andy sighed. He should have known that. He should have asked her about her day. She should have told him, rather than announcing it to a load of faces she hadn't seen since her school days.

What next? Instagram? Nothing. Tinder? He exhaled. No App. Twitter?

Andy leaned back, his hands behind his head, knees wedged under the dressing table, as the screen filled with notifications. There were pages and pages of unread ones and yet she only had eighty-six followers. Gingerly, he moved closer to the screen, scrolled down. One single follower's name appeared time after time: @investcribb. He looked for the messages tab: highlighted. It was no surprise to see screens and screens of unread messages but when he looked closer, they were all saying the same thing.

This @investcribb wanted to meet his partner.

FIFTY-TWO

ETTA LET HER CAR DOOR THUMP CLOSED. She looked up at the house. It was so much smaller than when she'd last seen it, dirtier too, the once white pebble-dash was distinctly grey. But little else had changed. The circular stained glass window she'd hated in her teenage years still faced the road defiantly. The poplar at the front of the drive was pruned and shaped, perhaps a little smaller? The car was different - a Ford Focus. Of course! Cars had changed since their red, no, maroon they were told they should call it, Triumph Acclaim of seventeen years ago.

Etta took in such a large gulp of the Preston air she felt a whack as it hit her lungs. What if they weren't in? She stood still, a pace before the three steps which led up to the double door. What if they didn't live here any more? She was so stupid, she hadn't even considered the possibility as she'd stuffed a pair of knickers and her toothbrush into her bag before setting off. She'd considered it many times before, of course, in the seventeen years she'd been sending them Christmas cards with no return address. She looked down at her shoes and pulled the two edges of her coat together.

It was cold, even for an English summer day, and yet she was sweating.

The only way to find out if they still lived here was to ring the bell.

The door opened a little stiffly. She couldn't see whose hand it was on the other side but once ajar, it was flung open to full range.

"Oci," Etta said. His hair was a little thinner. She'd remembered it as grey but plentiful. Now it was combed into little triangles and pulled towards his forehead. She couldn't help but smile.

"Etta!" Her father's broad face was brightened by a wide grin and his blue eyes stretched open like a child's. "My Etta's home," he said, his ever powerful arms outstretched, his head lolling from side to side. Etta flung herself into his embrace, wedging her head into his thick chest. She had thought it would be awkward. But it was Oci, just her Oci.

"Thank you," she said, "never have I needed your hug so much."

He ruffled her hair, pushed her away, appraised her face and pulled her back. "Magda," he called behind him. "Come here, quickly." He held Etta at arm's length.

"I know," she said, "I look so old."

"You look a little drawn."

Etta felt his grip tighten on her arms and she looked beyond his shoulder to see her mother walking towards them. The past seventeen years had sketched themselves on her mother's face. Her eyes had sunk into their sockets - so small, it was hard to tell if they were open. Etta wasn't sure what she saw. She wasn't smiling but nor was there anger or bitterness. Was there anything at all?

"Hello Mama," Etta said. But she didn't reply, merely bit her lip.

"Magda?" her father took his hands away from Etta's forearms and extended a hand out to his wife. "Etta's come to see us!"

Magda moved forward to a comfortable distance from Etta.

She walked so slowly. She used to flit around, jumping from room to room, shooting out orders, bustling up stray belongings and throwing them into the appropriate rooms. Glass frame, Ming vase? It didn't matter. If it wasn't in its rightful place, it would be thrown.

"Mama," Etta tried again. "Are you OK?" She lifted her arms cautiously, an offer of an embrace tentatively hanging in her fingertips, but Magda stood still with her arms locked at her side. Etta let her own arms drop back down to her waist. "It's been too long," she said. "I'm sorry."

"It certainly has," her mother said finally. Her voice was different, as if she was struggling to annunciate. She'd always spoken well, whether Slovakian or English, said good diction was the sign of a good upbringing. That was why Etta's parents had always spoken English with her. Under no circumstances would she be placed at a disadvantage by not having English spoken at home. It was a mistake. Etta could barely communicate with her grandparents when they were alive. She had regretted that.

"Is that it?" Etta said when she couldn't bear the silence any longer. "No questions?"

Madga didn't move, merely looked at the dirty pink rubber gloves still stretched over her fingers. "You're too thin," she said, and turned her back, snatching at the gloves. "Not looking after yourself."

Etta gasped, pressed a hand to her chest. "Your voice, Mama! What's going on?"

Etta's father put a hand on her shoulder. "We've got lots to talk about," he said. "Life's dealt a couple of blows but we're OK, aren't we Magda?"

Etta hid behind her hands. Shame rippled through her body.

Magda didn't answer Jozef but instead walked back the way

she'd come, along the oak panelled hallway, now painted peach, removing her gloves as she drifted away.

"I'm so happy you're here," Jozef said quickly. "Let's give Mama a moment then we'll all sit down together and have a chat." He guided his daughter into the living room and walked over to the glass cabinet where the spirits had always been stored.

"Drink with me?" Jozef flashed a bottle of Becherovka in her direction. "You are staying tonight?" Etta smiled. She'd like that. But she wondered if she could have a cup of tea instead?

— — —

Jozef lifted the tea cosy, gestured towards the lemon sponge slices and shrugged his shoulders. "I made them," he said, feigning offence before Etta could question it. "New man I am. I had to learn how to cook."

Etta gulped. She knew what had happened, that her mum had been ill and Etta hadn't even known. She had to ask and yet she couldn't bear to hear it.

"A stroke," Oci said. "Two years ago, so young really for something like that. Still," he lifted his tea to his lips, "you'd hardly know now, would you?"

Etta fumbled with the piece of cake in her fingers, crumbs falling on to the mottled red carpet. She reached down to the floor from her low chair, scooped up a few crumbs in her hands.

"It's, well, her speech," she said.

"No way of contacting you, you see."

"I was too wrapped up—"

"Plus your mother, well, after some time she didn't want me to even try, said she didn't want you to come back out of a sense of duty."

"She said that?" Etta sipped her tea, couldn't really taste it, looked around the lounge: so small, dark, oppressive.

"Didn't want to ruin your life," he said.

Her cup rattled in the saucer. "I should have—"

"Yes, I think so."

Etta lifted her cup but her hands were shaking so much she dropped it on the floor, tea settling in a pool around the stubby wooden legs of Jozef's paisley covered armchair. Etta jumped up.

"Oci! I'm so sorry!"

She grabbed a towel found hanging in the kitchen, dry as sandpaper, a faded orange. That would have to do. Her father was standing up when she returned. He took the towel from her and told her to sit down. He'd mop up the tea. It wouldn't be the first spillage - this carpet could tell a few stories. As he mopped at her feet, he spoke warmly but without meeting Etta's eyes.

"You know, there's nothing in a family which cannot be forgiven."

Etta gazed at her father as he simply inclined his head and smiled. This was the man who'd tried to stop her leaving when Mama had told him he should let her go. He'd kissed her on the cheek before she boarded the train to Rochdale with a rucksack on her back and a holdall in her hand, leaving for her new life as the lowest paid employee in the building society, and to live in a shared bedsit with someone she'd never met. He'd told her over and over on the short journey to the station that she didn't have to go; she could change her mind at any point. When she'd thrust her head from side to side in response, he'd become more agitated. This was a mistake. Her parents knew what was best for her. She had opportunities, mustn't squander them. When Etta had stared ahead without comment, Jozef had talked about Magda, how she'd given up the most to move from Slovakia to England, how she'd been highly educated, a respected pharmacologist in communist Slovakia, but had launched herself into housekeeping and motherhood when they'd moved. It was a mistake. She didn't want Etta to make the same mistake. Etta had brains and quite frankly, it was a travesty not to use them; a waste. A selfish waste.

But when he'd kissed her on the cheek he'd whispered that his door would always be open; that she would always be his daughter and that Mama would come round.

He'd kept his promise.

As she sat in the living room for the first time after too long, listening to Oci, she was sure of his love. She had a partner at home to whom she'd lied and who'd stuck by her, and two children whom she'd neglected recently. For the first time she understood those conversations with her parents. It wasn't that she thought they were right in trying to manipulate her, as she'd constantly accused, but when she'd told them that they'd done it out of hatred she was wrong. They'd done it out of love.

"And Mama," Etta said, "she's still cross?"

Jozef stood up and folded the towel into two. He suggested that now would be a good time for that Becherovka. Etta did drink spirits, didn't she?

She did drink spirits. Rarely, in fact, but today, right now, sitting in her parents' armchair having had her lifetime's ambitions slashed in the morning, an ambulance visit the home when she was entirely well after her grown up little boy had called 999, having learnt that her mother had suffered a stroke and with her father behaving like the Dalai Lama, she thought that this was a very good time to chink glasses.

"Na zdravie!" they toasted, making intense eye contact as her father had taught her, and they drank the golden liquid in one go. Jozef pulled his chair closer to Etta's and she collapsed back into hers.

"Your mum's been affected by the stroke," he said, and tapped the side of his head to point out the area to which he was referring. "Life's been more difficult for her. She doesn't have the patience, gets frustrated—"

"Perfectly understandable," Etta said.

"Well, you'll see for yourself, she's lost a little joie de vivre," he said, smiling hopefully, "I'm confident it will be back any day."

Etta leaned forward, her head bowed, "I'll help Mama. If she'll let me."

Jozef stood up, held out his arms to her. She stood up too, pressed her stomach against his, pushed her head so tight into his chest she could hear his heartbeat.

"I want to say sorry," Etta said. "That's the first thing."

Jozef spoke into the top of her head. "We're all sorry, Etta."

— — —

When Etta sank into her childhood bed at only 8pm that night, her body was exhausted with the pain and yet exhilaration of seeing her father again. Her limbs were heavy with the weight of seventeen years of inadequate and unresolved conscience. Lying in her bed knowing that there were no children to wake her was undeniably pleasant but she wouldn't be sleeping yet. Her mind was far too busy.

She switched on the purple angle lamp and took in the walls of her teenage room which had been left unaltered, like a museum piece, a study of a moment in a daughter's life: the wallpaper with its stripes of varying shades of purple and lime dotted with smudges of Blu-Tack after posters had served their purpose. The single shelf suspended on chrome brackets was purple, naturally, with her Lurlene McDaniel novels huddled together at one end, pushed aside by her album collection: The Verve, Cocteau Twins,

Ocean Colour Scene and not forgetting her ballad phase with David Gray and George Michael - they were all there. How could she have left all her music behind? Or did she tape it all before she left and play it on her Sony Walkman? She definitely took that with her. Was she so organised? How much notice had she given herself before she left for Rochdale? She couldn't remember. She should sell the records, she'd managed without them this long, it would make a good start to her saving pot to pay back her aborted meteorology course.

She'd got rid of the record player to make space for the item on the shelf below: her midi system; chrome, neat and sporting not one but two cassette holders so that she could tape from one to the other and that new-fangled pop-up lid on the top for the CDs which were to change the world, but not until she and her friends could afford them. When the midi system had been introduced they thought that was it: everything had been invented, no more musical evolution required. If only she could afford one. Hours of babysitting, two years' worth of presents and on her sixteenth birthday, the midi system was hers. She should sell that, too, people loved a bit of retro, together with the videos lined up on the window sill. The room was so clean, did her mother move the accoutrements of her daughter's life for dusting, only to set them back again?

Or did her father do all the cleaning now?

Etta heard a light tap on her door. She switched the light off, pulled the blankets up around her. "I'm awake," she said in a voice designed to imply she wasn't.

Magda walked into the room, slowly, as she did these days. Etta was glad she could only hear her, barely make out her unbalanced form. She hadn't got used to her new gait yet. She sat up reluctantly and switched the lamp back on.

"Does your husband know you're here?" Magda said.

"My partner," Etta said and ignored her mother's scowl at the correction. "He's called Andy." She patted her bed, "Sit down, Mama!"

Magda steadied herself with her hand as she sat down on the far end of the bed. Her bottom barely touching the eiderdown as she perched on the edge, both feet together on the floor, knees bent symmetrically, her hands in her lap. She looked as though she was waiting to graduate from finishing school.

Etta didn't tell Magda that she hadn't told Andy where she was going, nor that she had made no arrangements for the children after school. She shook her head to erase the discomfort. What had happened to her natural mothering instincts? Everyone made sure their children were safe. Thankfully Andy had been texting Etta, even if she hadn't been texting him. "He's a good man," Etta said. "He'll understand I needed to get away."

She also didn't tell Magda that she'd heard her return and fiddle around in the kitchen even though Oci had already made her Pirohy, her favourite childhood dish. Instead she'd implied that she was even more exhausted than she really was and taken herself off to bed. She had been going to apologise. She would apologise when they spoke but she'd hoped it would be tomorrow. Magda, her mother, the new Mama, was more terrifying than she remembered.

"Thank you for coming to see me," Etta said. Magda ran her hand over the top of the eiderdown to straighten it. Etta hadn't slept under blankets and a cover since she was a child. "It's nice you kept my room."

Her mother bowed her head. "I haven't the energy to change it."

Etta looked at her, plumper than she used to be, as a result of having to move so slowly no doubt, and the old woman she had become. Her parents were only sixty. Oci barely seemed to have changed but Mama looked like her grandmother did when she died at seventy-eight. The chestnut brown hair Magda had handed down to Etta was now silver grey and cut so short, Etta could see her scalp through it. Her skin lacked colour, did she go out enough? Her nose was fascinating. It seemed to fill so much more of her face than it did before. She chuckled.

"Yes?" her mother said.

Etta reminded her of their conversation about ageing. "Do you remember how you were horrified to learn that our ears and nose never stop growing and yet eyelashes never grow any longer than they are at birth?"

Magda shook her head.

"You said that once you turned forty you'd invest in false eyelashes, load them with copious quantities of mascara and always talk from behind your hand—" Etta stopped. Why was she talking about ageing when she'd lost a generation from her mother's life?

Finally, Magda faced Etta. "You think you'd stop caring what you look like when you have a stroke. Think you'll be grateful for your life."

"Yes."

"But you don't," her mother snapped, "I hate what I see every day."

This was the most Etta had heard Magda speak since she'd come home. The words were slow but entirely intelligible.

"You can hardly tell, Mama," Etta said. Her chin wobbled. She looked around for tissues. Magda handed her one from her pocket. "I could," Etta said, through a deluge of sniffs and tears which she couldn't wipe away fast enough, "Mama, I could have come back today and you, you know—"

"I might not have been here?"

"I'm so sorry."

Madga looked away, back down at her hands. "Why didn't you send me your address? I'll never understand that."

Etta bit her lip. "Did you ever try to find me?"

"You didn't want us to know where you lived," Magda said tersely. "That's what you told us when you didn't leave an address. That's what I understood."

Etta wanted to say that she was young, stupid, didn't comprehend the magnitude of the decision she'd made - all of which were true - but her mother was also right. Etta didn't want her to know where she lived. She couldn't pretend otherwise.

Magda stood up, seemingly untouched by Etta's tears or the conversation, nor to have noticed Etta's contrition. Gripping the door handle, her eyes firmly fixed on the lilac door frame, she said, "Oci said you wanted to help me. We'll make breakfast together tomorrow. I've bought a few items you used to like."

And before Etta could say that would be nice, Magda had closed the door behind her.

FIFTY-THREE

EVEN AFTER FIFTEEN MINUTES in the car, Victoria was still wheezing. "Thank you so much," she said to Mary. "What would I do without you?"

"You couldn't have got the bus in that state! What did they do to you in there?"

The Samaritans training had been gruelling. And this was only the first session. Victoria had been prepared for it to be emotionally draining. She'd imagined they'd be acting out scenarios and trying to empathise in upsetting situations, but she hadn't reckoned with how exhausting it would be, simply being in the company of a new group of people again.

"Bitten off more than you can chew love?" Mary asked as she opened the door to let her out of her car. "You should still be resting."

"I don't like resting."

Mary frowned. "You could leave it for a while." She linked her arm through Victoria's for support as they slowly made their way back up the drive. "Try again in a few months' time."

Victoria had no intention of quitting. She'd never done anything like this before. It was refreshing. "I'm definitely going back."

Mary rolled her eyes. She or Doug should bring her home in future. "I don't want to see you in this state again." She hugged Victoria at her door. "Sure you won't spend an hour at mine, at least until Doug gets home?"

"No thank you, Mary."

Victoria couldn't afford to take a step back or lose her confidence. Next Monday she would be standing in front of two hundred young people, persuading them not to do as she did. The message had to be hard-hitting, dramatic and memorable for it to work. Doug had warned her that every one of the students was likely to think of themselves as immortal, as the then Tori had also clearly done, he'd reminded her.

She was scheduled to visit two more schools in the area and next month she would be interviewed on Breakfast Television, promoting the Don't Be A Texting Killer Campaign. Doug couldn't possibly have a problem with that sort of profile. This was about the cause itself, spreading the anti-mobile-whilst-driving message even further, educating the most at-risk. Her own history wouldn't come into it.

She packed today's Weekender News and her magnifying sheet into the back pocket of her baggy black trousers and stuffed her glasses into her other pocket so that she could carry the glass of sparkling water in her left hand and make the journey up the stairs to the bath in one go. She put in two bath bombs and inhaled happily. It smelt of Jo's therapy room.

She uncurled, letting her head fall back for a few moments to let the tension and adrenalin seep out into the water. She was determined to have supper ready for Doug when he returned from football at eight. Perhaps she could forego her prescribed sleep?

She sat up and pushed her dripping hair back off her face. First she must read the editorial Amelie had messaged her about. She unfolded the newspaper and wrestled it over the soap rack which stretched from one edge of the bath to the other, being careful not to trail the broadsheet pages in the silver glitter and petal festooned water.

'Tori's Truth,' ran the headline, 'Fad or Forever?'

Before reading any further, Victoria scanned the text as usual for any reference to The Texting Killer, Off on a Technicality, Escaped a Prison Sentence or the Law is an Ass. The article appeared to be clean. Nonetheless, Victoria steeled herself.

The piece began with a brief description of Toby Hanson's local radio quiz show which was to be replicated on national radio. The idea had been bought by a major television channel, keeping the original title of Tori's Truth. Victoria lamented that her efforts to persuade them otherwise, with such titles as, Fact or Fabrication, Truth or Titivation and Fib or Fact had fallen on stony ground. It would make it impossible to hide the television venture from Doug.

The writer described the 'Tori's Truth' board game, which was to hit the shops next month and gave a glowing reference of the set of six self-help manuals which were to be launched simultaneously. Tori had been asked to write a foreword for the first in the series: How to Admit, Don't Blame, Forgive.

The Tori Phenomenon, the article said, *is sweeping the nation. It's more popular than Sudoku. We are purging our souls and with it comes a backlash against blame culture.*

OK so far, she thought.

Tori's Truth is one aspect of the Tori Williams' Phenomenon. Her outspoken views, her disdain for compensation culture, her pleas for honesty have caused a public unity, surge of emotion, and human empathy rivalled only by the death of Princess Diana. It is unprecedented in our history that a person of such public loathing should turn public opinion around so dramatically. People respect Tori's opinion. They admire her efforts to retrieve some good from the pain in which, she admits, she played a part.

Fascinatingly, although the coroner's report and the courts have all but exonerated her of the killing of the three other people caught up in the infamous road accident, Tori herself holds up her hands and says, 'I did it', or at least that, had she not been using her mobile phone whilst driving, the accident might not have happened, which, anywhere outside of a court of law, would be implicit of guilt.

Tori has proved to us that human beings can accept the truth. Indeed, they rather admire it. Whole communities are looking more deeply at themselves and at their reasons for disharmony. They are questioning why a difference of opinion should close the doors on a relationship, believing in the sanctity of allowing people to take ownership of a problem, rather like two school boys having a fight and a handshake later.

Victoria drummed her hands against the side of the bath.

Children and toddlers are playing again. A cracked tooth no longer means the closure of an institution but the help of a local expert. A broken arm doesn't signal the end of donkey rides on the beach but a couple of weeks in plaster and the instruction to hold on tighter next time. The child slipping on ice in the playground learns to blame bad luck, or the weather, and the school gets to keep its playground games. The thousands of pounds previously invested in insurance buys a lot more education.

I salute Tori Williams and all she is doing for our country. I for one, prefer it.

But, a word of caution.

"Here we go," Victoria said.

Can Tori's Truth prevail? Will this whole community approach to accidents and compensation endure or will it inevitably fail some people and initiate a slide back to the world of diminishing adventure borne from Compensation Culture? I say, let's appreciate what has happened here and fight to hold on to it. Who really wants to go back to the world where nobody is allowed to play unless somebody else can pay?

Victoria reached the end of the article and sat stock still, staring at the words. Was this Tori Williams really her? She shook her head. She wasn't responsible for all this. She was an ordinary person who simply thought people would be happier if they weren't out to get each other. She read the piece again, even though the bath water had cooled, and allowed herself a smile, a fist in the air.

But any joy was quickly tainted by the prospect of Doug's reaction. The larger the media bubble, the bigger the impact it would have when it burst, he frequently told her. His was the voice of reason. She knew that, but there was no harm in her elation, at least until he got home.

Re-energized, Victoria negotiated her way downstairs. She wanted to be sure their supper would be ready on time. Still distracted by the article, she almost tripped over Doug's kit bag sitting in the hall.

"It belongs in the porch, Doug," she said, without removing it.

She reached over to the blue porcelain pot with 'Tea' spread across the centre. Her hand hovered over the lid to be replaced. There was an envelope. 'Victoria,' was crossed out and, 'My Torr,' written instead in Doug's round, legible writing. Victoria's thoughts zoomed back to the kit bag in the hall, his football shirt revealed through the open zip. She thought of his football match tonight.

She left the letter exactly where he'd put it, squeezed between the tea and the biscuit pots. She poured the water over the teabag and moved over to the fridge for the milk, her feet wading through thick mud. She stirred two sugars into her tea, placed the mug on the dining room table and laid the envelope in front. She took her first sip. The tea scalded her tongue. She willed it to be a bill instead, even a letter of disgust from somebody who wouldn't rest until Tori Williams was locked up in jail.

She could read the writing on the envelope even without the magnifying sheet but she hesitated before taking out the paper and rose again to fetch the magnifier from the arm of the settee. She didn't want to miss a word and she didn't want to start reading.

She breathed deeply, her hand poised over the edges of the two page letter. She unfolded it slowly, hoping serenity would make the words easier to swallow.

Torr, my beloved.

I am taking myself away for a few days. I'm doing this for the sake of our marriage and because I need to clear the fog in my head.

Today I learnt of the book you are writing. It was your new friend, Steve, who told me. I think he genuinely thought I'd know. I'm disappointed you didn't tell me during the salmon in the bin evening. But no, a man who sat on my land and terrorised my family, who played a role in sending our daughter to the other side of the world, is the one to tell me about your big idea. And he was also keen to let me know that he enjoyed Tori's Truth. I refrained from asking him what the f**k Tori's Truth was.

I ask myself if you were going to tell me of the book before it was published but I know the answer.

I have failed you over the past few months. I have clipped your wings, tried desperately to persuade you to live your life how I think I would have done it, and offered no alternatives. I wish that I could learn to accept your new life but I can't. You see, I am also confused but I am sure of this: you are not a celebrity and we are not a centrespread couple. I have picked you up once from near death and I worry that next time it will be your spirit that will be shattered. When the readers get bored, the media will dig and dig until they find something else they can spin. And you will have nowhere to go. I can't sit by and watch this happen.

I urge you 'Victoria', please think about where this is leading. I wanted us to be together for the rest of our lives. But I cannot take the public with me too.

Your ever loving Doug.

Victoria stared at the paper. She turned it over, then back again. She raced back to the top: no address, no phone number. She didn't cry, couldn't.

Carly! She jumped out of her seat and rushed to the telephone, barely noticing that she fell on the way. The phone rang hollowly in Carly's house but she wasn't able to leave a message. She called Carly's mobile. No response.

— — —

Tears streamed down Jo's face as she ran up the hill to her friend's house. "Pull yourself together, for Christ's sake," she shouted at herself. "Be strong!" She waited on the doorstep for Victoria to answer the incongruously loud school bell. Today it seemed to take her longer than ever. She loosened her scarf and used the ends to daub the sweat from around her mouth. She never normally ran anywhere.

When she saw Victoria she stood still, unable to step inside and sighed so heavily it hurt her shoulders. "Vic, I'm sorry, so sorry."

"I know," Victoria said. "Come in so I can close the door." Jo stared again. Victoria stood aside to let her through.

"Tea?" Jo asked. "Two sugars?"

Victoria suggested a glass of wine instead and Jo followed her into the kitchen. "Doug and I barely started it the other night. My neighbour gave it to us." She took the bottle from the fridge. "At least she's forgiven me."

Victoria was propped against the fridge door she hadn't quite closed. Shaking.

"My husband's left me after twenty-three years." She raised the bottle. "This might help me cry."

Jo's stomach tightened as she took the bottle from Victoria and placed it on the worktop next to them. "Listen Vic," she said, hugging her friend, "who knows how you're supposed to react in this situation. Whatever you want, I'm here for you." Her cheeks were damp from her own tears. "I'm so sorry," she said, wiping them away. "You don't need this from me."

"No, I—"

"I really thought it was going to be better for you now." It was Victoria who rubbed Jo's back. Jo wiped her cheeks again. "Your mum's coming for a few days."

"Oh!" Victoria pulled away. "I don't know. Maybe I'd be better with some time on my own, to think."

Jo took Victoria's hands in hers. "We don't think you can fend for yourself all day, every day, quite yet."

"I'm not an invalid."

"Ruby will care for you in much the same way as she does already. She'll simply be sleeping in the spare room," she said. "Until Doug gets back."

Victoria slid her hands from Jo's and crossed her arms over her chest. "Will he come back?"

"Of course. You two are meant to be together."

"What if two people are meant to be together but the way they need to live their lives keeps them apart?"

Jo hadn't expected Victoria to be so lucid. "I guess both of them have to decide what's most important."

Victoria shuffled through to the lounge, Jo one step behind. Once they were on the settee and Jo had poured the wine, she listened to a deluge of questions she couldn't answer: how long do you think he'd been planning it? Do you really think it's space he needs or is it an excuse? Where would he go? Had Doug given any hint of his plans to Jo?

"No, certainly not," Jo said. "But why not ask him yourself? He must have his phone with him, wherever he is."

Victoria shook her head. "He said he needs space."

"You could tell him how you feel so he knows what he's dealing with."

"But I don't," Victoria said crossly, "I don't know how I feel." This time a tear escaped from her eyes. She cleared it quickly with a tissue. Only a few followed. "I daren't cry," Victoria said. "I don't know how I'll stop."

Keys rattled in the lock. Victoria jumped up but fell back down to the settee. "Ruby," she said.

Jo touched her knee. "I'll be back tomorrow." She rushed to the front door, much too quickly for Victoria.

"She's in shock, Mrs Crawford," Jo whispered, before any other greeting. "She hasn't really broken down yet."

"Perhaps I'm not that shocked," Victoria said from behind them. "Maybe I saw this coming but didn't want to admit it to myself."

Ruby's brow puckered. "Thanks so much for being here," she said to Jo, pulling her face straight again. "You're a great friend to my daughter and I love you for it."

Jo fumbled with her coat and scarf and said that it had certainly been a trying few months. "But she'd have done the same for me."

She hugged Victoria while Ruby made her way to the kitchen.

Victoria wouldn't let go. "I'm frightened." The words muffled in Jo's scarf. Jo stroked her hair.

"I'm scared it's a no-win situation." Victoria pulled away. "If I make the changes he wants me to make, I won't have a life any more."

Jo looked down at her feet. Eventually she said, "I'm sure there will be some compromises you can both make."

"I have to have a reason for my existence." She grabbed at her friend's hands. "I'm not the person he cared for in that hospital bed. And I can't go back to who I was before because I can't even remember who that person was."

FIFTY-FOUR

ANDY KNEW STEVE INSTANTLY. He was helped by the recently uploaded profile pic on Twitter, of course, no doubt his fifteenth take after combing his greying mane into that limp ponytail. He was lanky, scrawny, probably watched his weight. He might be better off getting down the gym, doing a few weights. Etta preferred a man with biceps. Andy pushed up the sleeves of his high-vis jacket. It wouldn't do any harm to expose the 'Et♥' tattooed on the underside of his wrist. Admittedly, it was created after a skinful but in amongst the regret and remorse and an investigation into getting it removed and the, 'You'd be much better off having it altered, mate, cheaper and more effective,' together with the affectionate squeeze of the shoulder and the, 'People go off people; shit happens,' he'd persuaded himself that one day it would come in useful.

Andy paced up to the bar, all highly polished cherry wood and brass pumps. Landlord Pete liked a pristine pub. He placed himself next to Steve who was sporting a tatty parka jacket. Should he hold out his hand, maintain the moral high ground? Instead, he beckoned Pete over with a, "Theakstons when you're ready, mate!" When Pete nodded in response, Andy cocked a thumb at Steve and said that he was paying. Steve sniggered, turned to Andy and stuck out a hand which Andy found himself shaking. It wasn't a genuine shake but nonetheless, even with Andy's tough guy routine, there was a little room for proper manners.

"Thanks for getting in touch, Andy." Steve's handshake was stronger than Andy expected. "Appreciate that."

Andy shrugged his shoulders. "Social media is for kids and I'd rather sort this out like an adult. So," he said, drumming his fingers on the bar, "let's open with why you are harassing my partner."

"*Was*—" Steve said, "—why I *was* harassing your partner."

Andy took a first, long gulp of his bitter and, after hastily spotting an appropriate beer mat to spare the bar, put the glass back down. "Not denying it then?"

When this Steve character simply smiled and ran a hand over the top of his hair, Andy cleared his throat. He caught Pete's eye. "We've got a right joker here."

"Him?" Pete shook a cloth in his direction. "Oh Steve's harmless enough, aren't you lad? Just a sunny fella." He pointed to the beer pots. "Another couple?"

Andy opened his mouth and closed it again. The contents of his stomach jumped up to his eyeballs and back down to his belly, the bile etching a reminder in his throat. "You know Pete, then?" he asked Steve. "You know my local?"

Steve waved an arm in the direction of the leather corner seat away from the cluster of people who'd recently joined them at the bar. "Shall we—?"

Andy was shifting from foot to foot. He made himself stop.

"These two are on me," Steve said, and set off for the far corner, leaving Andy to down his first pint in a matter of seconds and follow on, a step behind. Andy would have preferred to have waited, been firmly seated before he asked, but he found his hand on Steve's shoulder and as he turned him towards him, the words tipped out.

"You been here before?" he asked, "I mean, with my partner, Etta Dubcek?"

Steve shook his head so violently and with so much glee that it stretched his already smug smile up to his bloody emaciated cheek bones. He carried on in the direction he'd been going, reached the circular table and used his sleeve to wipe the beer he'd spilt. Both were seated as far from each other as was possible on a corner bench. With Andy determined not to ask another question until Steve had the civility to answer his most recent, Steve eventually blurted, "Do you even know your Mrs?"

"Do you?" Andy barked back.

Steve smiled that stupid grin, accompanied this time with a high-pitched cackle. "No, can't say I do know her personally. Cheers!"

"Cheers," Andy spat back.

"You really don't know, do you?" When Steve smiled, his eyes narrowing in equal proportion to the increasing width of the grin, Andy's hands fisted.

"Of course I know," he said. "Etta was involved in a traffic accident two years ago and the Tori Williams saga has brought back some unfortunate memories. But I really don't see what business—"

"Like I say," Steve swirled a finger through a puddle of alcohol, traced a heart. "You really don't know." He laughed this time and Andy had to hold his fists in his lap to prevent him lashing out and punching Steve on his silly little perfectly straight nose which had probably had some poncy work done on it.

"What's funny?" Andy said. "What's so fucking funny?"

Steve shrugged his shoulders. "You want to know what's so fucking funny? The unfairness, I guess." And for the first time the smile left his face. "The unfairness," he said, again, the word drifting off and losing itself in a mouthful of bitter.

As Steve drank, Andy noticed his hooded eyes, pink at the rims, and took in his fingers tapping softly on the table.

"Unjust might be a better word," Steve said, eventually, looking into the bottom of his empty glass. "We tell ourselves that fairness is for children," he said, "but I think we all struggle with the concept of injustice."

Andy thought of Etta, stuck in a moment, an incident enlarged by a troubled mind to ridiculous proportions. He shook his head, "Move on," he said. "Walk away from less than perfect situations." He dragged Steve's empty glass towards him and stood it next to his. "My turn to get them in," he said, a realisation suddenly dragging through this stomach. "You a lawyer?"

It was as though Andy had clapped his hands. Steve's head shot up, he stuck on the smile and announced that he was an investigative journalist.

"Fairly new in the job, if I'm honest, but finding it fascinating."

"You have got to be kidding," Andy said, his head shaking from side to side. "Not a fucking investigative journalist!"

Steve held up his hands. "I'm not kidding, but you're barking up the wrong tree." He pointed to the glasses. "Are you getting them in, or what?"

Andy waved in the hope Pete would bring over another couple of beers. He'd mutter something about his 'last slave' but he was a good egg. Andy felt Steve's gaze welded to him: part smug, part so very disappointed.

"The journalist role is where Etta comes in," Steve said, "and my work with the Williams' family gave me the connection. But it was coincidence. I"ll say to you one more time, Andy, ask your partner what really happened. You need to know."

"You tell me!" Andy shot back, suddenly more bullish. He wasn't used to this bullshit, where he worked, people came out with it. "You tell me about Etta's role in an unfortunate road accident where a girl was knocked off her bike. Tell me how my partner has suffered and berated herself for being in the wrong place at the wrong time—"

"She certainly was," Steve said.

"Tell me how you tell a woman that it wasn't her fault when she doesn't want to hear it, because I'm all fucking ears."

Steve scratched his head. "You get her to tell you the truth."

Andy thanked Pete for the beers, who asked him what his last slave died of and winked before sweeping up the empties. "I'll leave you to your sharing moment," he said.

"Shall I tell you the truth?" Andy's jaw was clenched. He refused to shout in here. "You are the one who ruins lives, meddling about in normal people's everyday, trying to make something out of nothing. Etta's falling apart right now as we sit here philosophising about it. She's squandered her lifetime ambition because of it and I tell you," he said, "it was an accident, and if you try to make out it was anything other than that." He banged his fist on the table. "Well that's libel."

Steve shook his head. The smile was back.

"Could you stop with the grinning—?"

Steve held up his hands. "I was called to the scene," he said. "In my old job. Traffic police. I took Etta's statement. I administered the roadside breath test."

"She hadn't been drinking," Andy whispered, his head bowed and shaking. Steve leaned back against the seat, arms crossed. "She was not," Andy said, more forcefully, "over the limit. She went for a drink at lunchtime to say goodbye to a treasured colleague on their last day in the job. But Etta did not," this time he emphasised the point by jabbing a finger on the table, "drink too much. Fuck, she'd be inside now."

Steve rolled his eyes.

"I was also called to the scene when my wife died." He lifted the glass to his mouth, took a swig and wiped the foam from his lips with the sleeve of his parka. "Before she'd been identified, of course. Then I was escorted away."

"Oh," Andy said softly. "I'm so sorry." What else could he say?

Steve's face was still, frozen as a mask, his eyes gazing beyond Andy's. "You know, at first I wanted to kill the driver. I wanted to kill everybody. I couldn't live without my wife." He squeezed a beer mat into a ball but it shot out of his hand. "I'll show you injustice," he said. "I'll show you what it feels like when nobody is punished for the death of your wife."

"Mate—"

"I'll show you the emptiness in my life, my children without their mother, my new job - I couldn't hack the police anymore." Now his head was lolling from side to side.

"What can I say?"

"I just needed somebody to say sorry," Steve said. "Just sorry."

This was why Steve had become an investigative journalist: to pay the bills and to find some of these people who'd walked free. "I wanted to get them in front of real justice, in front of the families they'd destroyed, so that they finally got it, too."

"I understand that."

"I trailed Tori and her family," Steve said, "all of the Williamses really, and yeah, when you hang around someone's house for hours on end, see them go about their daily business, pick up on their changing moods, well, then you see them as a person. And when you see them as family members, with people they love, trying to make a go of it," he said, "that makes it harder to hate."

Andy breathed out. "Not your typical paparazzo, then."

Steve held up his hands and when the pause had blunted the edges of the story a little, Andy raised Etta's role in Steve's sadness. He had to.

"Why did you move on to Etta, mate, and why now?"

Steve described how Doug had asked him to find her. "But he didn't want her details in the end and he was supposed to be paying me for them, so that pissed me off."

"That would piss anyone off," Andy said. The only thing to do in this situation, when the story was spinning and spilling from Steve's mouth, was to agree and sympathise. And Andy did, but in amongst the tragedy of this not so dislikeable bloke's life, he was struggling to shake the image of his Etta with a breathalyser in her mouth.

Steve picked up another beer mat and twisted it through his fingers. This time it span around the table. When it had finally withered to a stop, he said, "I'm not so proud of the next part, but grief and anger cause people to make strange choices. I went with Tori Williams' ridiculous ideas to make some money," he said. "I pushed her into that article in the paper. I knew it would make national news and didn't give a flying fuck what it would do to her already dire reputation."

"That would certainly make you a bit of cash."

He shrugged his shoulders. "All for my kids. But—"

"Yep?"

"Tori Williams, well it turned out she was all right," Steve said. "And you know, she did say sorry. She said sorry many times." He spoke of the book he was writing with her: a book about repentance and forgiveness. "Me!" he said, finally pausing long enough to take a drink. Even the way he drank his beer was calmer now. "Some days I'm still engulfed in all this grief," he said, "but others I want to shout from the flaming roof tops that I've seen the fucking light, my friend."

Andy savoured a mouthful of his pint. He'd expected some high energy tonight but this, Steve's story, this was a curve ball. He cleared his throat.

"I still don't understand where Etta fits in."

Steve scratched his head again, tightened the band on his ponytail. "When I started looking into Etta Dubcek, and when I realised that it was the same woman I'd seen waving at Tori's husband as he drove away from hospital, and the same woman who sat in court next to Ruby—" he paused to explain that Ruby was Tori's mother and Andy nodded: he'd heard of Ruby. "—and when I saw her squaring up to other journalists, including me—" he smiled "—then, right there, in a lightbulb moment, I only bloody recognised her from that incident. She'd taken the breath test, handed it back to me and it had fucking registered."

Andy banged his chest with a fist. "Christ!"

"It wasn't much," Steve said, "but it was there, bold as brass. She fainted and I caught her but that wasn't why I remembered her two years on." He poured the last of his beer down his throat and belched behind a fist. "No, I remembered her because my wife had died a month later, drunk driver, three times over the friggin' limit."

"Etta didn't kill anyone, mate—"

"—And yet I recalled being secretly pleased that when we'd got to the station, Etta's level had ducked under. This pretty little thing was safe, scot-free, *de nada*. I was pleased for her, can you believe it?"

Andy nodded but he couldn't speak.

"Because I liked her. Because she was devastated. Because I thought she didn't need prison and yeah," he said, "that was before my wife died. Then I wanted every bloody murdering bitch or bastard that had ever got behind a wheel with an ounce of alcohol in their body to go down for it, throw away the pissing lock and key."

Andy was struggling to concentrate. Steve was swaying and drinking and laughing one minute, losing himself the next: Tori Williams had single-handedly changed his mind back again; Tori Williams was an inspiration; Etta had guts to stand up for her on Twitter; writing this book with Tori was turning his life around so much more than the anger had ever done up to this point…

But Andy could only think of Etta, that when he'd asked her if she'd had a drink, she'd said no. And Andy had believed her because you had to believe the woman you loved.

FIFTY-FIVE

ETTA THRUST HER KIA into first gear, nudged up the small incline and switched off the engine. The peeling white garage door revealed the black it previously was. She would clear out the garage so they could at least get her car in there. The door needed some TLC, held together as it was with rust. Or should they change the garage altogether? They could turn it into a playroom for the children, move all of their toys out of the living room which could be more of an adult space, somewhere for her and Andy to have some quiet together. She flexed her hands on the steering wheel. "No regrets!" If her father had taught her anything, it was that being better in the future was the best, no, the only way to atone for the past. Now the new her, the unburdened, the brighter, newly dedicated daughter to Jozef and Magda Dubcek was going to show her partner some long overdue love and affection.

Andy's van wasn't on the drive. Of course not. It was Thursday. Johan and Adriana didn't have any of their activities on Thursdays. He'd have taken them somewhere special. This was the kind of devoted dad he was. It was fairly warm, certainly not cold enough for a coat. He'd have taken them to the park.

She'd find them. They'd have some family time together, the four of them, as it should be; not Andy looking after the children while she studied, not Andy looking after the children while she slipped out to the hospital, pretending it was the library. No more lies. Honesty was the basis of this relationship. She had some rebuilding to do but she was ready, bursting to do it.

The house had that emptiness it has on return from holiday; sterile somehow, but not because of the manic pre-holiday spruce or the dirty washing still confined in the suitcase for a few more minutes. No, it was sterile because nobody had breathed or spoken or laughed in the house for a few days.

It was irresponsible to have left without planning for the children, like an impetuous teenager running away with no money, not the employed wife and mother of two. But she hadn't been herself. In normal circumstances she'd never have thrown herself onto the floor to sleep because she couldn't think of what else to do. In the past she'd have made sure they were at school before she broke down, because that's what decent parents did: children first, personal crisis second. But she hadn't been herself. She'd been poorly, depressed perhaps. Mentally ill even? Mentally exhausted, certainly. Spent. Carrying the guilt of two years had taken its toll. But it was finished. She'd sit down with Andy tonight and tell him the whole story. She'd explain why she hadn't told him at the time. And then they'd start again: she and Andy, post-accident, post reunion with her parents. They'd visit them altogether as a family. The children could meet their grandparents. Andy could meet Mama and Oci. She wouldn't dwell on how she'd allowed the distance from them to happen.

Maybe, she thought, as she made her way over to the window to look out into the garden. The broken glass had been cleared and the grass had been mown. "Maybe," she said out loud, as she saw her reflection smiling back at her, "Maybe we should get married."

She took her phone from her bag. Nothing.

She'd foolishly mentioned Andy's lack of response to her texts and messages to her mother who was certain that Andy had given up on her - because no woman should ever leave her partner or children, even for a day. It had been difficult talking with Mama now that her glass seemed not half-empty, but two-thirds gone. She had to be patient. It was the after-effects of the stroke talking, not the real Mama.

She preferred to believe what Jozef suggested: Andy was giving Etta some space. When she'd first spoken to him from her parents' place, everything had been fine. He was cross. She'd explained it. Everything was fine.

She put the phone back in her bag. She'd surprise them all at the park. Oci had given her £50 to spend on the children. She'd suggest they all went out for a family pizza together instead. The children would finish playing, she'd slip her hand into Andy's and say she was sorry, then they'd go for pizza and they'd toast their new life.

Etta slicked some pink lip gloss over her lips and shook her hair out of its bun. She flung her head upside down, teased her fingers through the knots and threw herself back to upright. Ready to leave, she took in her reflection in the glass panel of the front door and gave her hair one last shake.

Well done, Andy, she thought as she opened the door. She hadn't had to manoeuvre herself around the garments hanging from the pegs. Now he was in charge, he remembered their coats.

She had to switch off the engine as soon as she'd started it up. It was Sara's voice coming through the speakers and she sounded odd, breathless even. She snatched the phone from its holder. Why did she even put it in there? She never used hands-free, would always stop the car if the phone so much as spluttered.

"Sara?" Etta began without a proper greeting, "What is it?"

Sara asked if she'd heard from Andy, and Etta began to explain that she was on her way to find him in the park with the children. Then she thought of the missing coats and the empty dishwasher, the emptiness and the quiet.

"He isn't at the park," Sara said, "but he's OK, don't worry," she added quickly, "they're fine, no accidents."

Etta breathed out, pinched the sides of her nose with her fingers and whispered into the phone,

"So, where are they then?"

"They're at his parents."

"You told him?"

"I'm coming over," Sara said.

FIFTY-SIX

VICTORIA HEAVED HERSELF out of bed. She let the shower drip over her despondently; it would never be replaced now. She dressed in the same outfit she'd worn for court all those weeks ago. She didn't bother with make-up, convincing herself that it was important that the pupils saw her at her worst, for maximum impact.

Ruby looked at her then looked away. "Hello darling," she said, "big day today. I've made some coffee, put out a bit of breakfast." She gestured towards the dining room. "Are you all prepared?" Victoria nodded.

Ruby carried the thermal cafetière of coffee and warmed milk on the silver plated tray that her mother had left to Victoria.

"It will be good to get the first one over with won't it?"

"I'm looking forward to it. It's nothing to be scared of," Victoria snapped. "I was a teacher after all."

"Of course! That's the spirit." Ruby winced as she sipped the coffee. Victoria stared at the assortment of rolls in the basket peeking out from under a tea towel, loosely tied to keep them warm. Two sorts of jam had been spooned onto saucers and two tiny silver spoons laid next to them. She hadn't noticed the artistically assembled pile of boxes right in front of her until now: a choice of six types of cereal in miniscule portions, the cereals she and Lottie used to crave as children to which they'd receive short-shrift about the expense and conspiracy of large companies. Lottie would have been thrilled to see them there today. Victoria would be too, in different circumstances.

"I did this for Doug," Victoria said.

"I thought it was a nice idea."

Victoria took a brown roll, scattered with poppy seeds, and held it up to her nose to take in its yeasty warmth. She picked at the crusty top. She wanted to eat the roll, wanted to show her mother her gratitude, but the dry lump she pulled from the top caught in her throat.

"We'll leave in twenty minutes then," Ruby said, pushing her coffee away.

"Yes, Mum, we agreed this last night."

"Right." Ruby needlessly picked up an empty plate to take it back into the kitchen.

Butter! Victoria would eat butter again, to help the bread slide down more easily. She reached for one of the curls of which there were far too many on another saucer in the middle of the table. She scraped it onto the side of her plate but it was no good. She couldn't eat bread this morning, nor cereal. She would survive on coffee; the caffeine would take her through.

She caught her reflection in the silver coffee pot and saw her sulking lips. Her eyes were smaller than gemstones with their permanent film of salty water. Her skin was grey and her hair matted. She scooped it up between her hands and looked again at her reflection. She'd pin it up with grips before they left. She grimaced. She'd look exactly as she had done in court but who'd have thought that today she'd feel even more tired and defeated than she'd felt on that day? Her hair fell back down to her shoulders. She tore her roll into two and placed a second lick of butter on her plate. She was tired of being so fractious. Doug had been gone for only a week but she didn't have time to be miserable. She had to focus on making decisions.

"Oh darling," Ruby called from the kitchen, a shake in her voice, "Gerald rang. He was fairly courteous, asked after you."

"Why?" Victoria poured herself more coffee. "Plotting something?"

Ruby returned with a pot of tea for herself. "Always." A smile touched her lips as she smoothed her hair behind her ears: Gerald style.

"Oh Mum!" Victoria reached out for her mother's hand. "I've been hideous. Can you forgive me?"

Ruby squeezed with her bony fingers. "If I can't be here for you at a time like this," her voice trailed away. "Eat your bread," she said, "and one of those fiendishly expensive boxes of cereal. And by the way—"

"Gerald's married for the zillionth time?"

Ruby flicked Victoria with her napkin. "Did you ever ring Etta?"

"I tried a couple of times."

"I think you should try again." Ruby reached into the fruit bowl for a kiwi. "You need to thank her."

— — —

As rehearsed, Victoria took her seat on the stage next to Ms Hawthorne, the Head of Sixth Form, who sat with her hands gently laid in her lap, raising her eyebrows periodically to certain sections of the audience. She was of similar age to Victoria but was of the groomed variety, with her shiny blonde hair tickling her shoulders in a relaxed bob. Victoria's hand drifted to a curl hanging from the pile on her head.

"OK?" Ms Hawthorne asked, without taking her eyes off the pupils. Victoria unclasped the buckle on her soft brown leather bag with the trembling fingers of her one functioning hand.

"Sort of," she said.

She took out her notes. She wished she could look over her presentation one more time. But she chided herself: the technician was in control. They'd both tested the equipment three times. The slides were ready. The big screen would work.

She looked from the stage into the hall at the collection of almost adult faces. What she hadn't told Ruby was that she'd never taken an assembly for anybody over the age of fourteen before. Many of these students could already drive. Some of them would already have the vote. These were no different from the pupils who made Doug's life unbearable. She took in the reproach on some of their faces, the revulsion as they focused on her scars and when she heard the sniggers as well as the uninterested chatter, she could imagine what Doug had been talking about. She hadn't been very sympathetic.

Her eyes trained on the audience, Ms Hawthorne leaned in closer. "Ready?" she whispered. Victoria cleared her throat. Ms Hawthorne stood up. She didn't speak but looked seemingly at each of the two hundred pupils in turn as her head scanned the hall and a quietness gradually wafted over.

"Thank you," she said. "Good gracious, I should think so, too."

She introduced Victoria as someone volunteering her time to come and talk today about saving lives. Fortunately, the applause was enthusiastic and practically drowned out the retro Nokia ringtone sounding from a handful of phones. Five or so pupils were dragged to the back of the hall by well-placed teachers. But before the students could be escorted away, Victoria called out,

"Could they stay? They probably need to hear this more than most—" she paused for effect, "—if they think it's so funny."

There was a muffled giggle of respect from near the front. Victoria recognised the boy. It was the teenager who'd helped her on to the bus the first time she'd ventured out alone. She raised her hand to acknowledge him and he clapped his together in a quiet applause.

Victoria had to concentrate. Her memory was at best unreliable and stressful situations forced inappropriate sentences from her lips. Multi-tasking was difficult so she must focus on showing the correct slides without panicking if she found herself out of sync. And she must obliterate from her consciousness the fact that two hundred young people appeared to be staring at an arm that stuck out at a 90-degree angle, something that she was so used to, she could almost forget - until, of course, people's stares reminded her.

Silence met the first screen as Victoria spoke of the story around the four pictures of her distorted car. She asked if anybody could tell her what kind of car it was. Most of the hands shot up. "A Jeep", they said. Of course they did. Sharpen up Victoria! Nobody would know that from the picture but they'd all heard it on the news.

After the first few photos of Victoria in hospital, inaudible comments sprinkled the silence. Ms Hawthorne looked sternly again at the assembled audience but with only partial effect this time. Victoria was worried that too much horror could de-sensitise the young people to the message so she raced through to the end of the presentation. She knew what she was doing. She was in control and it felt good.

She concluded with her final caption as planned: 'A Moment of Madness for a Lifetime of Sadness'. She'd heard it first on the phone-in following her speech on the court steps. Never had the phrase been more true than in the time since Doug had left.

Everyone was quiet. A few of the girls at the front dabbed their eyes. Some boys wiped more covertly. Victoria smiled. Ms Hawthorne thanked her and asked if the students had any questions. One hand crept up at the back of the room, barely surfacing above the row of heads in front. Victoria picked up her binoculars, it wouldn't hurt them to know her eye sight had suffered to such an extent. The girl had straightened, deep brown hair and was wearing far more make-up than Carly or Nicky would have dared to wear to school. A teacher handed her a microphone. Victoria couldn't believe how far technology had come since she last taught. The girl took it as if it were a pencil.

"My name's Natalie Jenkins and I'm in Y13," she said in a soft and educated northern accent. "I wanted to say thank you, Mrs Williams, I will never," she stressed, "use a phone when I'm driving." People chattered around her nervously. Many clapped. Some said, "Me neither."

"Can I ask you a question about another campaign you're running?" Natalie asked.

"Of course," Victoria said, a lump dropping from her throat into her stomach.

"It's the Anti-Blame Culture Campaign. We were debating this yesterday." Her neighbours nodded to corroborate. "There must be times when somebody quite clearly is at fault and then they have to pay, surely? And who decides which times these are?"

"Thank you, Natalie, and that's a great question," Victoria said, the back of her neck burning. She explained that Rowena Black was really the brains behind the campaign. It was her inspired talk on the radio that had influenced many communities around the country to rethink their attitude to compensation where it had the potential for adverse after-effects. And it was working. Every group, dependent on size and make-up, had its own unique system.

"I can't take credit here," Victoria said. "All I suggested was that forgiveness might better serve our communities. But for what it's worth, I think it's a wonderful gift to society. Don't you think people seem happier? Can you feel the buzz?" There were nods and grunts of agreement but Natalie put up her hand again and the microphone was passed back to her.

"We all agreed that it's a great idea but we stumbled when we debated this: when a gross error of judgement has been made, there are times when the person at the heart of it has to be shown that they cannot possibly make the same mistake again. Suing them is one way of doing this, we thought. How do these people learn and how do they pay for it if it isn't with something real like money or," she looked down, "a prison sentence?"

Victoria raised her head high and contemplated the crowd in front of her. "They learn because of their own conscience." She forced her voice to be strong. "They learn by knowing their life will never be the same again." She was ad-libbing. She hadn't liked going off script before she had the accident and she knew she was foolish to attempt it now. "Don't you think," she looked from one side of the room to the other, "that this is part of the bigger problem we face in society at the moment? We're used to instant answers to everything. We can't accept that sometimes instead of black and white, there's grey - that a rule will satisfy 90% of issues but if we try to dilute it to cover every eventuality, it could stop working altogether."

A hand ten places away from Natalie shot up into the air. "And in those 10% of cases people should be compensated, the perpetrators should be sued, or punished?"

"Yes, I should say so," Victoria said. "But I don't want to get hung up on the precise figures."

"So, do you think you should compensate the victims of your crash?"

This young man with his ragged, jet black hair and a nylon t-shirt dragged across his chest, wasn't like the people who'd demanded this kind of answer from Victoria in the early days. He seemed genuinely interested and to be enjoying the debate, as if he respected her opinion. So why did she feel so nauseous? Ms Hawthorne stepped in, her voice remonstrating even if her expression was cool. "That is an entirely different issue, Faiz. We are talking about how a community deals collectively with relatively minor issues."

"No, really, thank you Ms Hawthorne," Victoria said quickly, "I'm happy with this debate. Go on, Faiz, you think I should compensate the victims of the accident?"

"Yes. Even if the court doesn't know if they'd have died if the other man hadn't been driving badly, you said you shouldn't have been texting."

Nobody spoke.

"We can move on," Ms Hawthorne said, maintaining her stare straight ahead, imploring decorum amongst her impressionable cohorts. But Victoria shook her head. The student was merely speaking honestly. Isn't this what she found herself advocating time and time again?

"It's an excellent question, Faiz," she gestured to him. "I agree, when human life is involved, things get difficult. I wish with all my heart I could compensate the victims but what on earth could I offer that could change the past?" Faiz nodded. Others dipped their heads in support. "I think the best I can do is to ensure that this kind of accident never happens to another family again," she said. "Maybe the only way I can compensate the victims of the crash is by trying to make some small difference to our society in the future." She studied the sea of faces; most showing interest rather than anger. "Before Rowena Black came along, the idea of a simple accident had become the language of ancient dictionaries," she said. "Somebody had to be blamed for everything and we were living and breathing this at every level: in the household; in our schools; in our workplace."

A tall girl put up her hand to request the microphone and announced through her thin, beige coloured lips that her name was Brittany. Her trampolining club had been forced to close as it could no longer afford the insurance.

"What a shame," Victoria said.

Another pupil spoke of his village's collective decision to ask neighbours to pay a voluntary annual sum into its 'Compensation Collection'. The money was for distribution amongst people out of pocket in the case of an accident so that they didn't need to claim. "If any money remains at the end of three years, it's going to be spent on a village party." The boy raised his eyes skyward. "Everyone's banging on about insurance payments coming down and having a more harmonious community."

"Do you think it will work?" Victoria asked.

"Why wouldn't it?" he said.

The students continued to cite examples but because Victoria could only agree, it was too easy for her mind to wander back to the mess of her marriage. When the scenarios finally ran out, she was silent. She couldn't remember what she'd just said. Her face was sweating. People wanted her to continue.

"So, I say," she tried to compose herself. "So I say," she looked at the final screen of her presentation with the slogan: A Moment of Madness for a Lifetime of Sadness. She looked at the mass of expectant faces, so inexperienced yet so confident, so capable. "I say, don't try to make Rowena Black's ABC system embrace every single scenario," she boomed as much out of relief as conviction. "We are human beings, not computers, and we cannot legislate for every twist and turn in society. If we try to make this system clinical, it will fall down and we will slip back to the days when even our best friends could justify suing our ass…" there was a humming noise from the excited crowd and Ms Hawthorne raised her eyebrows as was her job, "…if there was a buck to be made." People clapped but Victoria raised her hand.

"Be open to the potential for a blameless accident." The words were flowing again and she hadn't felt this energised in months. "Avoid the need for revenge. Go out and be nice to each other!" There was more applause, the crowd were roaring as if it was some sort of rally. Whenever she'd spoken in the past the audience had been almost entirely hostile. This felt great. "Trust each other, help each other, be there for each other." She had to shout over the noise of the audience. The enthusiasm, the belief and conviction of the young people was infectious. "Admit. Don't Blame. Forgive!" she shouted. Natalie and her friends stood on their feet. More followed until the whole of the sixth form were standing.

"Well I never!" Ms Hawthorne said, clapping too. "We don't get this in Maths."

FIFTY-SEVEN

ETTA JUMPED ADRIANA DOWN from the tall chair with a simultaneous peck on the top of her head. Her reading was coming on beautifully. Johan presented Etta with a glass of orange juice, a touch too strong Etta suspected, but she'd have drunk it neat in view of the fact he'd prepared it for her today. He'd been cross during their last visit. He didn't want Mama and Dad to live apart. It wasn't how respectable parents behaved, he'd explained in a voice a little beyond his years. He set the drink down on the coaster on the kitchen table in front of Etta and handed her a Rich Tea biscuit which had softened in his warm hands.

"You're growing up so fast, Johan," Etta said, pulling him into a hug so that he was compelled to sit down next to her.

"Granddad helped me make a chisel from flint because we're doing about nearly thick man and they had the first tools," he said proudly.

"Brilliant," Etta said, "Neolithic man was very clever."

"'Nearly thick,' Mama, that's what Granddad said. Not as thick as stone age man but not as clever as homo sapiens. We're homo sapiens," he said with pride.

"Of course!" Etta smiled, hard and wide to stop herself asking Johan not to use words like 'thick' when it didn't refer to toast. "Lucky us."

Johan nodded and Adriana's head shot up from where she was lying on the floor, legs crossed in the air behind her, sticking people upside down on the fuzzy felt beach: handstands. She said that Granddad had made her a bakery for her Sylvanian families from actual wood because nobody needed to spend that amount of money, and Grandma had given her some real dough which she'd made into tiny plaits, baked and given to Adriana for the shop window. She jumped up to fetch it and as she dropped down to the floor again, this time cross-legged, Etta pretended that she hadn't noticed 'the surprise' earlier, half hidden under her coat when Grandma Miranda had dropped them off after school. 'Best to keep continuity,' Miranda had explained with her new-found ability to text. In truth, Etta was relieved that she didn't have to face any of the parents at school.

"It even has windows!" Etta exclaimed, ignoring the cement that had lodged itself in her stomach.

"Good job you got Mr Baker from Father Christmas," Johan said, shooting the knowing glance of a teenager rather than a seven-year-old at his mother.

Adriana nodded her head vigorously. "Grandma said they'd get me the rest of the squirrel family. Mr Baker's a grey squirrel," she added unnecessarily. She leaned forward performing an advanced lotus position with her legs still crossed so that she could peer into the roofless bakery. She busied herself with the painted box which had room for thirty-nine Sylvanian family creatures with a lean-to for their car.

Johan reached for his 'project paper' and Etta excused herself.

She would make a quick phone call. She picked up the landline but paused to check her mobile just in case. Only Sara. She'd called four times. And she'd texted: 'am checkin in'. Etta didn't deserve her.

Andy's mother was polite but curt. It wasn't appropriate for Etta to talk to Andy now. He was enjoying a well-deserved sit down in peace. It was too much doing a day's work and starting again when he got home. Etta cringed at the word, 'home'. Andy's home was with her.

"I do wish you two could sort this out like grown-ups," Miranda said, her voice squeaking at the edges. "If you were married—"

"Not all marriages survive, Miranda," Etta said pulling the phone a little further from her ear.

"Marriage gets you through the trials and tribulations," she said, "Not that I know what this 'trial' is about. Oh no. Because I'm only the grandmother. Nobody feels the need to tell me what's going on." Etta took a gulp of air. God forbid Miranda should find out. "Like I said to Andy, it remains your prerogative not to include me, but hear this, if you need somebody to clash your heads together I will be at the front of the queue."

Etta could picture Miranda rolling up the sleeves of her dark, woollen suit, preparing herself for the tough business of family after a day in court dealing with corporate fraud. She suspected that society benefited greatly from Miranda's choice to deal with large companies rather than parents and children.

"Actually, Miranda," Etta said, "talking this through in a grown-up manner was what I was hoping to speak to Andy about. I was wondering—"

"I'll pass on a message," Miranda cut in.

Etta breathed out, pressed her fist to her forehead. "I was hoping we could meet," she said. "Just the two of us," she added, hurriedly.

"I'll pass on the message," Miranda said again.

Etta turned off the phone without saying goodbye. She counted to ten. She wasn't going to cry. She smoothed a smile over her face and marched back into the kitchen to take up her place for the marriage of Mr Badger and Miss Skunk.

FIFTY-EIGHT

THE SAME GENTLEMAN who'd seated Victoria on her previous visit to Charltons glided up to her as nonchalantly as possible. Not easy when every single person waiting knew her distorted face from the newspaper.

"Your friend is waiting for you," he said, offering an arm for Victoria to hold and signalling to a round table by the window. There, Victoria saw the tiny frame of the woman who had been seated calmly at the back of the courtroom, who'd smiled periodically while her supportive evidence was read by the magistrates, who'd tried to speak to her after the trial. Etta waved, a cautious flutter of fingers. Victoria tried to raise a hand in reply but even her good arm was so heavy.

"Could I have a moment please?" She placed a hand on the wall to steady her. "Sorry, it's—"

"Take your time, Mrs Williams."

Please no red, she said to herself, Please no red metal. No big phones. She could feel her temperature rising, her face sweating. It's over, it's done, she repeated. She saw faces swinging towards her, their noses enlarged, their eyes too inquisitive.

"Are you all right, Mrs Williams?"

She heard a horn, words. She smelt rubber. She saw red, the whole windscreen was red. She heard a voice: her voice. 'What the hell—?'

"Can you hear me?"

Victoria looked around. She was lying on the floor. The front of house gentleman was to one side and Etta was holding her hand on the other. A man's face she didn't recognise floated above hers.

"We think you fainted," he said.

"But thank goodness for the plush carpets." Etta had a pleasant North West lilt to her voice. "You had a nice, soft landing."

— — —

Victoria fidgeted on her seat. She stared at Etta's waiflike face, highlighted by a stream of sunlight. She was a pretty little thing. It was extraordinary. She knew Etta's car hadn't entered the pile-up, that Etta had emerged with little more than a sore neck and painful feet, but somehow she'd expected some outward signal to people that Etta had also been there.

The sun was so warm through the bowed panes of glass that Victoria's forehead prickled with perspiration. She asked Etta if she fancied a walk instead.

"A short, slow walk," she qualified.

"Perfect," Etta said. "I can't really afford this place anyway."

Victoria smiled. There was one more thing. "Could you call me Victoria?" she asked. "Tori isn't really me. Only the press, and anyone I don't care for, calls me Tori now."

"I'd be honoured, Victoria," she said.

— — —

They stuttered down Edward Street. Victoria introduced Etta to the posh shops in tall stone buildings with their hotchpotch of windows, both feigning polite interest in them. Victoria bumbled along as fast as she was able in her comfy shoes but the uneven flagstones ached for her to tumble and since when had this hill been so steep? She'd brought her stick with her today, but was determined it would stay folded in her bag. They talked of how harrowing it must be for Etta to remember it all and how, yes, if Victoria was really asking, she had looked pretty gruesome.

"Apart from your hair," Etta said, "even with muck from the accident, it was hugely impressive," and she spiralled a finger to mimic the curls. "Listen to me, going on! Would you like—?" she hesitated, "would it be helpful to put your arm through mine? It must be difficult—"

Victoria popped her hand through the gap where Etta's hand now sat on her hip. "Thank you." She smiled to herself. Her injuries meant she walked closer to relative strangers than she ever used to walk to her friends.

Victoria led Etta past the Turkish Baths, pausing for a short history lesson and animated description of the smell of the water, then on past her favourite pub. Etta punctuated the conversation, when pushed, explaining why the clouds were dappled today and the winter sun so comfortably warm when it could force itself through.

Victoria suggested they find a bench on The Grove. "A large park," she explained, "where we'll be made to feel shamefully sedentary because everyone else will be playing football, or doing those purgatory training camp things." She wished she could go climbing again.

In the past Victoria would have made a beeline for the centre of the park but the first bench they came to on the periphery was the best she could manage. Since when had walking around the block taken forty minutes?

"Coffee?" Etta asked.

"And a bit of cake?"

After a wrestle over who was paying, Etta scurried over to the bandstand and Victoria sat down, her face tilted upwards, sun tickling her cheeks.

Carly couldn't last ten minutes in the park before 'gasping' for a take-out coffee and fairy cake. They'd sit and watch the ferocious activity and vow to buy an exercise DVD as soon as they got home. "An app, Mum," Carly would say latterly, "Need to get you into apps."

Nicky was perpetually moving and never sat down in daylight hours. She'd show such utter disdain at the suggestion of coffee that Victoria would also wonder what had possessed her to come up with the idea in the first place.

Etta handed over the coffee and placed two brown bags between them on the bench.

"Victoria sponge and lemon drizzle cake," she said. "You choose." Victoria suggested they both have half of each and Etta was quick to agree.

This didn't feel like a first meeting. Victoria hadn't prized it so much before the accident but these days, very well-meaning people skirted so far around the issue, they landed in a different conversation. She wanted to talk about Doug but stopped herself. It was a constant effort to keep him from nudging into her thoughts, making a mess in her brain. Etta would know. The Global had reported their 'somewhat inevitable separation'.

"I do have one question," Victoria said.

"Of course!"

"Mr Reynolds," she cleared her throat, "did you really see him driving the Mondeo badly before the accident?"

Etta covered her mouth with her hand so that she could answer without finishing her mouthful of cake. "You have my word," she said. "He was driving aggressively. He was tailgating."

"I think I saw it."

"But surely you can't remember anything?"

Victoria explained about the bursts of the red Mondeo which appeared before her eyes then sped away, telling her very little, except that she'd always be haunted by the flashbacks. "When I fainted earlier, I saw something new. I felt angry with someone. I couldn't believe what the person was doing and then the red image obliterated everything."

"That makes three of us," Etta said. "Somebody else reported the man driving badly but he later withdrew his statement." She leaned in towards Victoria. "That's good news, isn't it, that it wasn't necessarily you?"

"Is it? I still sent a text. I couldn't have been concentrating and those people still died. That's been my point all along," she said. "I'm guilty of selfishness."

Etta flicked her sleek ponytail back over her shoulder. "As am I," she said.

Victoria considered her for a moment, took in her wobbly smile and the subconscious picking of her cuticles, and asked if she could help with anything. "You said in your letter—"

"My partner's left me." Etta loosened her scarf. "He should have left me two years ago." She pulled the scarf from her neck so that it fell into her lap. "He found out I lied."

Victoria chose a single fondant petal from the top of the lemon cake and placed it on her tongue. "Must have been a big lie." When Etta didn't return her smile, Victoria cringed. "Perhaps all couples have some secrets from each other," she said, "some thoughts which are better not shared."

Etta blew into her hands and searched for her scarf. Victoria pointed to it where it had slipped from her lap to the ground.

"I knocked a girl off her bike," Etta said. "She was called, Nikhita."

"Aha," Victoria said, repressing even a flinch. "But she was OK?"

Etta nodded.

"That's good then." Victoria crossed her arms, stared forward into a flock of teens in long leggings and orange tabards, running at varying speed between traffic cones.

"I'd had a drink."

Victoria exhaled. "A drink?"

"One glass: a large glass with one small top-up. They breathalysed me but it didn't show."

Victoria's shoulders dropped. "Well, then it's irrelevant isn't it?"

"Guilty or not guilty, my judgement was impaired. And now I carry around the secret that the accident might not have happened if I hadn't gone to the brasserie at lunch time." She stuffed her hands into her pockets. Victoria said that she should borrow her gloves, her hands were too warm anyway, but Etta would need to help her pull them off.

She tentatively dragged the first mitten over Victoria's rigid right hand but felt her cold fingers and put it straight back on her again.

"I almost can't bear to tell you about the love and understanding I got from those closest to me, right through to people whose only connection was through a stupid article in the paper." She forced her hands between her thighs. "I got six points for goodness sake, for Driving Without Due Care and Attention, and everyone was giving me sympathy."

"Yes," Victoria said, shuffling round to catch Etta's face but her gaze was fixed forward, "that's quite a different experience from mine."

"While I was taken out for lunch more often than the Royals, Nikhita lay in hospital. I could have coped with deceiving everyone," she said, still staring across the path, "if only I hadn't told Andy I hadn't had a drink." A tear slipped down her face which she didn't wipe away.

Victoria stared at Etta, could feel her aching, see it in her dull eyes, but it was extraordinary, overwhelming. All she wanted to do was stand on the bench and shout it, tell the world that she was thankful, oh so grateful. Instead she sat bolt upright and told Etta to listen, really listen.

"If you'd been in prison, or perhaps serving a drink driving ban," she held up her hand to apologise when Etta flinched at the words that she also found hard to stomach, "you wouldn't have been driving the car behind mine."

Finally, they faced each other.

"And you wouldn't have been the person who was clear and focused," Victoria said, "who took charge, who wouldn't allow anybody to move me, who held me until the emergency services came—"

"How do you know about—?"

"My Mum," Victoria said. "That man might have taken charge and dragged me from the car."

"That gives me nightmares too."

Victoria shook her head. "Instead you were first at that scene. You cared for me. You spoke to me and you made the right decisions."

"Thank God," Etta said, and breathed out.

"Etta, without you and your actions, I don't know if I'd be alive today." Victoria leaned closer to her, their sides now squeezed together. "You need to embrace that."

"I can't," Etta whispered.

Victoria checked Etta's face. At least the tears had stopped.

"Nobody walks across this earth unblemished," she said. "It's how we deal with our mistakes which makes us who we are. Talk to him." She rubbed Etta's arm in a futile response to her shivering. "Say you're sorry."

FIFTY-NINE

VICTORIA LEANED AGAINST the passenger door of her mother's mud-splattered white Fiat. She lowered the hood of her fur-lined waterproof jacket, her go-to comfort for the end of a climb on a crisp winter Sunday, and tilted her face up to the sky to let the wind weave the last of the rain through her hair. These days she wore the coat to travel in the car to Cross Crags with her mother, for them to spend ten minutes away from teapots and treacle-crunch biscuits. It was all relative. The cold dribbling down her neck and the squally wind pummelling her cheeks were the closest she came to exhilaration these days. She tapped on the window.

"Rain's stopped," she mouthed.

The Fiat was parked half on the unmarked road and half on the woodland verge, at least, Victoria hoped it was the verge and not another boulder. Their walk was a quarter of a mile over the sheltered path through the trees to the edge of Cross Crags or 'Angry Rocks' as Nicky had called them from a tiny age. She closed her eyes. It didn't matter how forcefully someone removed themselves from your life, they left behind a colour in your memories which couldn't be wiped away.

Ruby rapped on the window and Victoria jumped away from the door. She was slightly baffled as to why her mother was extricating herself from the wrong side of the car.

"I couldn't get out," she said, "damn hip."

Victoria put her arm around her and they hobbled over the road together, not quite sure who was helping whom. The looming birch and beech trees gave them some shelter against the wind as they entered the wood, the intermittent sun squeezing through the leaves and splashing light onto the track. Victoria let her arm drop. It felt a good time to broach the letter which arrived that morning, an official looking thing which Victoria had expected to be from the courts.

"It's from the Pickerings' solicitor," Victoria said. "You know the civil case was likely to take place in the high court because of the high value of the claim?"

Ruby nodded.

"And you know my biggest fear was being called for mediation with those poor parents?"

"I know that," Ruby said.

"Well, look at this." She wrestled the envelope from her deep pocket.

Ruby ran her finger over it but handed it back and suggested they have a sit down to read it. They took a short detour from the path to a picnic table on the edge of a sloping adventure playground. The benches were damp and splattered with bird poo so Victoria suggested they sit on the swings instead. "Even swaying slightly might be good physio for your dodgy hip," she said, "and most of my limbs."

Victoria took the magnifying sheet from the drawstring bag

she wore crossed over her back these days and shook the letter to open it. She glossed over the civilities, the hopes for continuing recovery, the references and legal parenthesis. She cleared her throat and read:

"Although my clients will always hold you partly responsible for the death of their son, Josh, the ongoing legal procedure is painful and preventing them from coming to terms with their loss. They ask that you respect their wish to end the process and agree to settle this matter out of court."

Victoria lowered the letter and rubbed her eyes.

"And?" Ruby said.

"They want £27,450," she said, "half of what they'd expect to be awarded in court."

"Done deal."

"There's a proviso. Mum. I have to keep quiet and with immediate effect. My—" she picked up the letter and read from it again:

"—continued presence in the media is causing unnecessary additional stress at an extremely difficult time for their family."

She let go. The letter fluttered to the ground and came to rest in a muddy groove beneath Ruby's swing. Ruby picked it up and scanned it before heaving herself back onto the gnarly tree trunk of a seat.

"Victoria Williams you are off the hook," she said.

"I don't have £28,000."

"Use the proceeds from the book!"

Victoria's feet stepped two forward, two back, never leaving the ground. "I think you have a slightly unrealistic expectation of how much my book would net."

Ruby laughed. Victoria was the unrealistic one. "Have you any idea how many people will clamber to buy something you've jointly written?" She re-folded the letter and studied Victoria instead. "I'm so proud of you. It's you who's responsible for encouraging all this." She waved her arms around her and Victoria felt compelled to ask her to hold onto the chains.

"You've encouraged other people to be honest and admit their mistakes," Ruby continued. "People are sleeping better at night."

Victoria smiled. Her mother's feet had speeded up, scuttling forwards and back, sticking occasionally in the mud. Thankfully she wasn't yet airborne.

"You've helped to liberate an out-pouring and real happiness when people have purged their guilt," Ruby said.

"Mum, stop now!"

"You encouraged people to cope with difficult situations without blaming somebody else."

Victoria brought the swing to a halt. She got to her feet, approached her mother's swing and brought it to a gentle stop. "You need to know that any share of the profits from the book would go to Doug," she said. "I owe it to him because the money from the letter to the newspapers wasn't mine to give away."

Ruby lowered herself gingerly down from the swing and they both wandered out of the park as if the other had suggested it.

"Besides," Victoria said, "the whole book thing hinges on whether the Pickerings will agree to it."

Ruby guided Victoria's arm through hers as was customary these days and tapped her hand.

"Let's explain to the Pickerings that you would give up every single scrap of work on the radio and television." She chewed her lip. "Tell them you'll steer clear of making any statements which get your photo in the newspaper but that the book will have to stay because it's going to change the world."

Victoria stumbled slightly. She apologised as Ruby helped her restore equilibrium. "I should be helping you, Mum."

Everybody seemed to think that Victoria's life was a simple series of choices: ham or eggs; trousers or skirt; new life or old. Perhaps you had to have survived a high speed collision and a coma, seen your life smash into too many fragments to count without any instruction on how to create a copy from the few remaining pieces, to understand that most doors had swung shut firmly behind. And of the doors in front, any of those could lead to a vacuous space. If she chose to end the nightmare with a lump sum and a media blackout, she could find that with the sense of peace came a brick wall.

"I wish it was that simple," she said.

She pointed to a grey squirrel scampering over the wood floor to a spot behind a beech tree, a little way from the edge of the path. It scraped and scratched then reappeared with a crumb of food supported in its mouth with its miniscule hands. It scurried into the centre of the path in front of them, stopped and stared as if to question their trespassing. Only when Victoria smiled did it shake its tail and bound over to a hollowed tree stump.

"Might be some babies in there," Ruby said, "being February."

"Is there nothing you don't know, Mum?" Victoria asked.

Ruby patted Victoria's hand. "Today's morality question is a little tricky."

The squirrel darted to the top of another tree and propelled itself from the upper branches which swayed in the wind now it had picked up again.

"Get that hip sorted and you'll be jumping around like that," Victoria said.

Ruby's face was stern, her tongue poking out from between her lips as was usual in times of intense concentration. "I think we've exhausted the squirrel conversation," she said.

Victoria scuffed her boot in the damp peat, bringing her and her mother to a standstill.

"If I choose the pain and selfishness of continuing with the court case, I might keep a semblance of choice in the life I'd like to live." Her view landed on the crags up ahead, children and dogs zipping up and down, parents encouraging nervously.

"Last I recall, you wanted to be punished for sending that text."

"You know I'll never forgive myself."

"Then make this your punishment," Ruby said. "Lose your career in the spotlight, and show these unhappy people that you respect their loss."

But Victoria wanted to fight for her right to respond to people who sent letters asking her advice, rather than her appearance on game shows.

"What about Parliament? Don't forget its No Blame Compensation Scheme starting with the National Health Service—"

"I'm not disputing—"

"—how proud we both were when we heard the 'Tori Williams' name associated with the scheme?" Victoria heard a mother tell her child it was none of her beeswax and saw that this wasn't the only person standing still and staring. She directed her mother behind one of the many rocks which now lined the path. "Even you don't think I have the power to halt government, surely?"

"No need to be facetious," Ruby said. "Maybe that's what they write on your tombstone and maybe that will have to suffice."

Victoria pulled on her hood. The rain wasn't so refreshing this time. "And my articles in progress, Jupe, for example?"

"The deals are off."

"Doug?"

Ruby pulled her hat from her pocket. "You don't need me to

tell you that Doug would choose you and the life you had over anything financial."

"Life we had," Victoria repeated, with a terseness to her voice she didn't like. "That's the point, Mum, Tori and Doug died six months ago."

Ruby teased her hair out from beneath the hat. "You have to try to do the right thing," she said. Victoria swallowed hard. They should get inside the café. They'd had enough fresh air. She tried to lead Ruby from the rock but she stood firm.

"Instead of helping strangers it's time to help these people now," she said. "If you don't do right by the Pickerings, you won't be able to live with yourself."

SIXTY

ETTA SNATCHED HER KEYS from the table Miranda had given them for the hall when they moved in together. She said it would keep them going until they got married. Etta would have liked the keys to have left a scratch but unfortunately they left no trace on the high gloss veneer.

She took a look back. Sniffed. She despised that lonely smell which frequented her house now that Andy didn't come home from work smelling of diesel and the children were only released from Miranda's clutches for a visit once a week.

What had she expected? That a flippin' journalist would tell him the biggest secret Etta had ever held and he'd hold up his hands and say, 'Silly old me, worrying about something as trivial as a positive breath test'? If she was honest, he'd reacted as she'd feared. If Oci and Victoria Williams were to be believed, however, she had the power to alter the ending she'd anticipated.

She rubbed a smear from the door panel with her coat sleeve, nose practically tickling it in her search for a reflection. Perhaps the green eye shadow was a little stark, she didn't want to give the faintest impression that she was happy with the situation. When she looked even closer, she settled on the red rims around her eyes, sunken behind her cheekbones, the pounds she'd shed clearly registering in her face. She sighed, slapped her cheeks to give them some colour. The truth was written all over her.

She needed all her composure to get past the fortress keeper, all her strength not to cry when she saw the children and all her humility to make Andy realise that she knew she'd let everyone down and she was never going to do it again. One more chance. This breakdown in communication wasn't going to be another unsolved case for the next seventeen years. Etta wouldn't be leaving until she had the three of them in tow.

– – –

She pressed the bell so lightly it didn't even sound. So she pressed it again, twice to be sure, only to hear Miranda from behind the glass asking why in the Lord's name people didn't have any patience any more. Etta coughed, smoothed her dress, slicked her tongue over her front teeth.

"Etta," Miranda greeted her as if she'd opened the door to an ex-girlfriend freshly covered in tattoos. "You'd better come in."

Etta stepped over the raised threshold which had stubbed her toe on many a previous occasion, and flung herself into Miranda's arms. She was buffeted somewhat by the box of chocolates and the lilies from Waitrose - because she knew Miranda would check the labels - clutched to her chest. But still, not an entrance to calm nerves.

"Thank you for having me," Etta said, straightening herself, and forcing the gifts into Miranda's hand.

Miranda nodded, a stiff acknowledgement. "I can mediate," she said, patting the sides of her silver pixie cut to check for absolute equilibrium, "the offer's there if you need it." She turned on her heel with the assumption that Etta would follow and gestured through the glass panel in the stable door to the garden to alert her to Andy sitting by the fire he'd laid with the children earlier. "I'll bring out a pot of tea. You're lucky," she said, into the air in front of her, "I've been teaching Adriana to bake."

Etta leaned against the stable door so that it swung out wide. There he was, perched on one of the two wooden seats arranged around the fire pit where Johan and Adriana had spent many a happy hour watching the fire turn to embers while they toasted marshmallows. She'd never had a meeting with him before. Had Miranda set an agenda?

She took in his dark hair curling around his ears and his tongue peeping out between his lips: thinking. He was wearing the sun-bleached, orange cap he'd had since uni and it catapulted Etta's mind back to when they first met in the building society. He'd returned the next day to deposit five pounds and written his desire to take her out for a drink on the paying-in form. She'd smiled and chided him for marking the paper. They'd have to fill out another but as the first slip was spoilt, it wouldn't do any harm for him to write where and when he'd like them to meet. She'd whispered it and Andy had smiled and obliged.

And now she was standing at one of Andy's sites on the A1, delivering his forgotten sandwiches because she wanted an excuse to see him in his hard hat at work.

Forward she raced to Johan's birth, Andy crying when Johan's tiny fist rested on his cheek. And a rare moment of retaliation when he'd told Miranda that she should butt out, he didn't care if she thought it was selfish to choose a Slovak name for their son. When Adriana was first introduced, she'd said that it was a pretty name and only offered as an aside that if English people really struggled they could perhaps call her Rhianna?

All of a sudden she was standing next to Andy, taking in his smell of fresh-laid cement and bonfire smoke. A piece of paper lay in his palm. He inclined his head. There was a smile. Tiny, but evident. He crushed the paper into a ball.

Etta stood arm's distance away and said, "I lied, Andy. I'm so sorry," and before he could respond, "I don't deserve you, but it was the only lie, just the single one." Her head swayed from side to side. "But that one lie lasted so flippin' long and once I was in it, I was scared to stop."

"I know," he said, without looking at her but staring instead into the fire. He threw the ball of paper into the flames, nudging it with a stick to make it splinter and flash.

"Anything I can do to make it right, I will. Anything I can do to put the past in the past and regain your trust." She lowered herself down to the seat next to him. "Andy?" she asked, "You know?"

"No more drink near a steering wheel." Still his gaze didn't move from the fire.

"Andy, you know I don't—"

"No more beating yourself up."

Etta shook her head.

"No more feeling sorry for yourself."

"Not a becoming feature," she said, quietly.

Finally, he turned to her. "You lied," he said, but told her to 'sssh' before she could agree. "But I'm no hero." He removed his cap, gave his scalp a quick polish, realigned it, "I knew."

Etta's mouth dropped open, her fingers rushed to her lips. "Oh."

He shook his head. "Not the drink," he said. "Not the breathalyser. But I knew there was something else, knew there was more to it."

"That's not a crime," Etta whispered.

Andy held out his hands and Etta took them. "Deep down I didn't want to know. You didn't want to tell me and at first, I was happy ignoring it. So I pushed for the course in the hope it would cover the cracks."

"We both did."

"And I left the room when I thought I might hear something I didn't want to hear. I latched on to your stress being all bound up in the Texting Killer's—"

"Andy, she's not—"

"Tori's accident," he corrected, "which was sending you down this spiral of destruction. So—"

The tears Etta had refused to allow for much of the past few weeks finally burst through, one after the other, a relay of sadness and shame, but Andy had her hands in his so she had to leave them to fall. He leaned in to kiss her, their lips finally meeting until Andy gave a start and rolled his eyes. Etta turned around to see Miranda immobilised mid-stride, barely beyond the back door, the teapot and plate of biscuits sliding to one end of the tray.

"Goodness, I'll just—" She pushed open the door with her bottom and retreated to the kitchen.

Etta grabbed Andy's face and pressed her nose into his, her tears less frantic, stuttering now. He pulled away and laughed as he wiped the wetness from his face. He stared at Etta, their faces now inches apart, knees bent towards each other, hands on each other's shoulders.

"What are you thinking?"

"That you can forgive me! As easy as that?"

Andy dropped his hands so that he could pick up his jacket from the ground. "Yep," he said, throwing his coat around Etta's shoulders because, despite the fire, her teeth were chattering. "But it's worth sweet FA if you don't give yourself a break. Promise me?" he said, shuffling around in the back pocket of his jeans and producing one of Adriana's thick plastic rings.

Etta stared at Andy and back down at the ring. "Yes," she whispered.

"Fuck it if my mother thinks she's won." He reached for Etta's hand. "Marry me?"

SIXTY-ONE

VICTORIA LEANED BACK, hands behind her head. Her tiny study had always been her space, somewhere to read, to focus solely on colour schemes and ticket prices. She'd taken down the mosaic of fabric swatches, marquee designs and the odd piece of left-over silk ribbon but much of the montage of photos remained, albeit with some of the pictures of friends removed. She gazed up at Nicky with her fist in the air at the top of Scafell Pike, Victoria pretending to frown because Nicky had 'beaten' her to the top again. Next was Carly, only ten years old, hiding behind her cello and then as an adult, playing an electric violin in her band with the other four, busking in Harrogate for a packet of Marks and Spencer's sandwiches.

And there was Doug, with that smile of his, the head thrown back. He was the dishevelled headteacher at the ball who was liked by staff and respected by pupils, or so his colleagues told her. He'd have received her letter now. Whatever became of her and Doug, she would never take his photos down. She returned to the screen, stared at the four sentences enlarged to maximum capacity.

Ruby knocked on the study door and presented Victoria with her second cup of tea since she'd taken her seat that morning.

"Still typing that letter?" she said. "Can I help?"

Victoria asked if she'd stay to fold and pop it inside the card and envelope. She smiled. Her mother seemed older with her newly lolloping gait and yet she was so strong. Her love was unconditional. "Thanks Mum." She rose from the chair and kissed her on the cheek. "For everything."

She pressed print and apologised out loud for the type. She held the missive as close as possible and examined it for mistakes with the help of the magnifying sheet. It was word perfect, amazing how the simplest of activities could make her happy these days. Next, she wrote the final sentence in ink with as much of a flourish as she could muster. Of course she would be at the airport for Nicky and Kyle's arrival in a month's time. She even managed a vaguely recognisable signature - and a kiss.

She knocked one whole minute off the record for her walk to the post office. She couldn't jump up and down any more but she performed a one foot shuffle with a fist in the air before straightening herself to go inside. She handed the three envelopes to Neville, the postmaster.

"Hello Victoria, first class?" He pointed to the letters to the Pickering family and a copy to their lawyer.

She nodded and asked that delivery be guaranteed. "And that one's for Australia," she said, unnecessarily. "My daughter lives there."

— — —

Why, on the rare occasion when anyone bothered to use the telephone any more, did they always call when Ruby was upstairs? She'd coped when Victoria was in hospital and in the early days of her care at home she'd also managed to shrug off the pain of her worn hip. But now that Victoria had become much more independent, each scorching stab was a glaring reminder of her cancelled hip operation.

Damn ageing body. She'd wanted to give the house a thorough clean but wouldn't be brushing down any stairs today. Still, at least the caller hadn't hung up. How many times would it ring before BT cut them off?

"Yes?" She hadn't meant to be curt but the pain often showed itself in her voice.

"Ruby! How are we this fine morning?"

"Not as well as you by the sounds of it, Gerald, to what do we owe the pleasure?" Ruby's top lip curled as she listened to the list of all the marvellous escapades Gerald had enjoyed this week. It was when he said that he was perfecting his golf swing that she removed the phone from her ear, stared at it and eventually said,

"But you hate golf!"

"Got some time on my hands, haven't I?" he said. "Tori in?"

"She's gone for the bus."

"Oh, where's she off to?"

Of all the different guises Ruby attributed to her ex-husband, this pleasantness was the most unnerving. And she found his sudden re-kindled interest in her daughter a little unsettling, but perhaps that said more about her relationship with him than his with Victoria.

"Harrogate for a couple of errands and a meeting with the co-writers on her book," she said, her pride lending some lightness to her voice.

"Perfect. Listen love, I'd like to discuss something with her in person. Last time we spoke on the phone it didn't go too well."

"Right." Ruby lowered herself down to the chair. As soon as

she'd got rid of Gerald, she'd call the doctor, get back in the system. "She may be free tomorrow."

"Oh, you know what I'm like, impetuous sod that I am," Gerald said, with that beguiling tone which still made the hairs prickle on Ruby's arms. "Thing is, I happen to be in Harrogate today so I could join her. Like I say, I'm not busy."

Ruby suggested she give him her new mobile number, so they could arrange a meeting themselves. But Gerald laughed loudly and said that he didn't do mobile phones.

"Surprised Tori does to be honest."

Ruby bristled. "For emergencies. Large buttons. She can barely even see those, poor lamb."

"Anyway, I'd like to surprise her," Gerald said.

The discomfort was worse than Ruby had known it. She was nauseous. She exhaled, lifted the cushion from behind her and pressed it over the pain.

"Victoria's going to Charltons." She cleared her throat. "Please don't get in her way."

— — —

Etta locked her car and couldn't help smiling at her progress. For the first time in her life she was early for everything, now that the motorway was her route of choice again. She was a little nervous about today's meeting. She'd spent weeks in a perpetual spin of contact and avoidance with this man whom she'd latterly assumed was a social pariah. But she trusted Victoria's judgement. She stopped outside a flower shop, her favourite gerberas and tulips splattering colour around the entrance and orchids stretching the height of the window. It was a small token of appreciation even though nothing she could buy would be in proportion to her gratitude, but she turned on her heel. Yes, Victoria must have some flowers, it was the least she could do, but from somewhere cheaper. She twizzled Mama's single diamond ring around her finger.

— — —

"Gerald?" Victoria said, as the doors opened at the bus station. "Fancy seeing—" She caught her breath, turned gingerly to thank the driver who said it was a, 'pleasure, Victoria,' and that she should mind how she went on the slippery steps.

"Slumming it, aren't you?" Gerald said, inclining his head towards the bus. He greeted her with a hefty kiss on the cheek, dressed in skintight jeans and a pressed white shirt, the cuffs rolled over. Wasn't he cold?

"You'll want to hang on to me, no doubt," he said, hand on hip, "we're going to the same place."

"Charltons?" Her hands were wedged at her side. "Is this a coincidence?"

Gerald shook his head. "I'm coming with you to meet your co-writers. All arranged."

"Steve and Etta?" she asked. "But how do you—"

"I like Etta, nice girl. We used to chat you know."

Victoria shot him a glance. "She's fifteen years younger than me," she said. When Gerald winked, Victoria was tempted to peel off in the other direction but she refused to offend, so she hooked her arm through his. With her bag clumsily over the other shoulder, she and her stepfather took their first steps: Gerald with a definite stride and Victoria despising the disabilities which meant she had to be quite so close.

— — —

Ruby heaved her stiff leg up the stairs again but paused halfway and lowered herself down to sitting. She stared at the phone in the hall, shook her head and leaned on the bannister to pull herself back up. She was being ridiculous! She climbed the remaining steps, shaking her head so fiercely she was forced to grip the handrail. Since the first day she'd known that man, he'd got right under her skin.

She started with the bathroom. It was easier than pushing a vacuum cleaner around the house and much of the cleaning she could do sitting on the stepladder.

What exactly was the problem today? Why was his voice quite so chilling? He'd said he would never set foot in that ruddy golf club again, everyone had been so rude to him. "Got some time on my hands," she mimicked.

"Strange man," she said, and jabbed at the black silt around the base of the taps with the rejected toothbrush. She used an old T-shirt of Doug's to shine the mirror above and tutted at the bleach-free-bleach Victoria had insisted she use around the basin. Reluctantly she admitted that with a little elbow grease, it came up almost as bright. She stood at the entrance and took in her efforts as had been her ritual for the past fifty years: take a moment to appreciate the beauty of a clean space, for in a few minutes, your work will be undone.

She shook her head. Descended the steps as quickly as she was able and picked up the receiver.

"I'm so sorry to call you at work, Doug."

– – –

Gerald and Victoria made their way over the pedestrian crossing towards the town centre, passing the area where Victoria had worn the sandwich board suggesting people purge their souls of their mistakes. And purge they had. The sole piece of abuse had been Gerald's note. She looked at him; his head fixed straight ahead. His voice may have been crisp and brusque but in stature he'd shrunk. With his watery grey eyes and the drab pallor of his cheeks, he looked older than when Victoria had last seen him in the restaurant.

"You're enjoying your celebrity presumably," Gerald said, without waiting for a response. "And the book?"

"I hope it will have a positive influence on readers' lives," she said. "How did you hear—"

"There's some interest in my involvement so I said I'd come and see what it was all about. I'm fairly proficient at this media lark myself."

Victoria shook her head. "It's more of a self-help—" She halted so that she could concentrate on crossing the road. Nobody else gave junctions enough attention. Before taking the right turn into the one-way street, a narrow one with shops too close to the road and customers trip-trapping on and off the pavement without a care for the relatively slow but constant stream of traffic, Victoria pulled back on Gerald's arm.

He tutted, "What now?"

"It's strange that Steve didn't consult with me," she said. "We make all the decisions on the book together."

"Perhaps this Steve character doesn't tell you everything." He pulled forward again, squeezing his arm into his chest so that Victoria had no choice but to be dragged along. They forged ahead and the pace was a little too quick.

"I was sorry to hear about Doug," Gerald said mechanically. "I always thought he was good for you."

Victoria gulped. She hoped it might be temporary. "And Sophie?" she looked at his tense face, unswervingly fixed ahead once more. "Gerald?"

He shook his head. "Separated."

"Oh!" Victoria gasped. "Gosh. I'm sorry." Gerald's expression didn't alter, he kept on walking, down the hill and towards the main road, fast, long steps. "No chance of a reconciliation?" she asked.

"It doesn't get any easier, you know." Gerald still refused to catch her eye. "However old you are. Emotionally I feel like I've been run over by a truck."

She tried to pull back on his arm. Her left leg was dragging awfully. "I feel for you."

"It was your face everywhere, she couldn't cope with it." His step quickened, his stride lengthened. "So yet again, I'm the one who suffers."

"That isn't what I want."

"You scared her with all that stuff about marriage."

She pressed the button at the pedestrian crossing to oblige Gerald to use it. She focused on the beeps to blur the sound of the traffic as they crossed, the engines idling as they waited and the beat of intermittent wiper blades. Twenty-four beeps again. Was that standard?

"I'm making changes." She was better able to concentrate now that they were safely on the other side of the road. Charltons was a few hundred yards further down. She could almost touch it. "Big changes," she said. Cars were too close, every vehicle shaking her as it passed. It was busy, just not busy enough to slow people down.

"You're having a ball, Tori Williams, you love all this!" Gerald said, grabbing her hand and tugging it further through the triangle his arm had made.

"I do love it," she said, trying to nudge Gerald a little further towards the inside of the pavement. "And I've learnt that I can't go back to being anonymous."

"Meanwhile, I'm on my own," he spat.

"So I'm going to compromise," she said. "I'm going to become a local councillor." She knew Gerald wasn't listening but she liked the sound of the words now she'd finally voiced them out loud. "And perhaps then an MP and after that, Prime Minister," she whispered. Why not? Somebody had to.

"Shall we take a short detour through the park?"

Gerald shook his head. "Why won't anyone let me be who I am?" His step quickened again. Her arm was at full-stretch now, attached only where he held her hand through the arm lock. She was so close to the road she could feel the speed of the traffic lifting her coat.

"Gerald!" Her voice was shrill. "Please slow down." He wasn't aware of her words, of the traffic, of her reliance on him.

"Life's for living," he said. "That's how I get the most from life, and you, along with everybody else, stick your ruddy oar in and ruin it for me, time after time." A bubble of spittle dropped from the corner of his mouth into the curling grey hairs on the arm locked with hers.

"It wasn't my intention to upset Sophie." Victoria grimaced at the sight of the damp spot on his arm. "All I can do is apologise."

"Never is your intention, Tori. You never intended to kill that baby but you did. You hadn't planned to murder two people but you sent them to their coffins. Next it's my marriage. Well, congratulations, Tori Williams, on your 100% success rate in snuffing out everything around you."

Victoria retched.

"No," Gerald shook his head with so much force, Victoria thought he might pull a muscle. "Never," he hissed. "I will never forgive you."

They'd marched right past Charltons and it was only when

Victoria heard Steve call her that she realised and yanked her arm from Gerald's, relieved to walk back at her own speed without him.

"I haven't broken up any marriages," she muttered as she lumbered back up the hill. "Certainly not any of yours, Gerald."

"Your word against mine," Gerald shouted after her, catching up with her two steps before the café. "I love her!" He spun her round to face him. "Love her."

"Then tell her!" Victoria snapped.

"All OK here?" It was Steve.

Victoria smiled. "Could you give us a moment?"

Steve raised an eyebrow and said he'd get into the queue, which had filled the foyer and leaked outside.

Gerald, oblivious to the interruption, screeched, "Why doesn't anyone want me to be happy?" He grabbed her hand for emphasis. "Why?"

"Can't you see?" she asked.

He leaned into her now, his finger inches from her face. "I can see that people resent me, because women are attracted to me," he said, "so, jealousy, I see that."

"No, Gerald." Finally, she grappled her hand from his clutch. "You are in charge of your own happiness. Only you can decide who you really are."

"Mumbo jumbo!" He jabbed her chest with his finger.

"Oy!" It was Steve again. "Back off mate," he said, propelling himself between them.

"Until we recognise our mistakes we always make the same ones," Victoria said. "And Gerald there's no place for your attitude in our book, is there Steve?"

Steve looked at Victoria and then at Gerald. "Certainly not," he said. "I know this man from the hospital. He's a total charlatan."

Gerald shoved Steve, so hard that he stumbled backwards and

the small crowd queuing let out a communal gasp.

"Don't you dare hit Steve!" Victoria called and Gerald shouted that nobody was hitting anybody as he jabbed Steve in the stomach with his elbow.

"Tell that nutter to bloody apologise!" More spittle flew out with the words.

Victoria's straight leg thwarted her efforts to get close enough to stop them, luckily a member of the public wedged himself between them and said, "Gentlemen, have you any idea where you are?"

"Get back to your bloody golf club!" Gerald swung a punch to catch Steve off guard but it only reached Victoria, already unsteady and scrabbling in her bag for her walking stick.

— — —

Victoria lay on the road. She'd heard these sounds before: the banging doors; words wrapped in screams, and horror blended with sympathy. And Etta. It was Etta's voice.

"I'm here, Victoria. We know the drill. We get you to hospital and you get right back on with changing the world, OK?"

"Back off!" she heard, and the mumble of a crowd grew quieter. A louder voice explained through pants of desperation that, "the woman came from nowhere," and, "I wasn't speeding, was I?"

She could hear Gerald. She could have laughed: he was apologising. "Wake up now," she heard. Were those his lips close to her ear?

Move me away from him! she shouted, but nobody heard.

"Sophie was the only person I've ever loved, you see. You made me so cross, it hurt. It was a slight push though Tori, that's all. Wake up, love."

"You shut the fuck up!" she heard.

Hello Steve!

"I'm getting him out of the way, Etta. Just keep her still. Ambulance three minutes away."

"We're putting some coats over you, you're icy cold," Etta said. "And I've bought you some flowers, they're right here. Can you feel them? I've put them in your hand."

Victoria couldn't feel them. She smiled to say thank you but didn't know if Etta saw. She was quite comfortable, if a little chilly. Etta was right. But there was no real pain, just pins and needles in her bad arm.

She thought about the first time this had happened. What would she be thinking now, had she not plunged herself into that black hole on that day in August? Faced with the choice of the two worlds she'd known, where would she pitch herself? In the safe life of a regular income, three-hour lunches and a wholesome reputation, or a life of picking up the pieces, steered by the guilt of knowing she'd committed the worst sin? And yet the second was a world she better understood, one in which she preferred the answer to where and who she was. Gone was everyday angst because she knew where she stood.

Engines revved. There was chatter, so much chatter all around her. A siren crescendoed and then cut out. Doors banged and somebody said to Etta that she'd done a great job and did she know if the patient was breathing?

"It's Tori Williams," Gerald's voice was so formal. "Her eyes let her down, gents."

"Etta Dubcek," Victoria heard. "I saw it all."

Voices swarmed, gasps discharged:

"Tori Williams? No!"

"She changed my life!"

"My role model."

"People are so much nicer now."

— — —

Etta and Steve stood back from the road, pressed against the glass front of Charltons. In between them was Gerald, his head bent, his greasy hair fallen forward from his ears and hanging in his eyes. They gripped his arms on either side.

"What are you bloody doing? You can't arrest me!" Gerald tried to pull Etta's hand from his arm and she felt a stab of joy at the strength she found to make sure that justice was done.

A few steps away, a huddle of staff in different uniforms circled Victoria like a paper people chain. She lay on a stretcher with a cage around her head, tubes protruding from her hands, a mask over her mouth. One member of the ambulance staff clung to her side holding a bag of fluid in the air.

"They're very proficient," Steve said.

"But she's so still," Etta whispered.

Finally, two police cars juddered to a halt at the roadside just beyond them and officers jumped from all front doors. An ambulance technician pointed out the driver: a hunched figure sat on the kerb on the other side of the road, staring into nothing, as if alone in the countryside, lost in the view.

From down the hill a familiar voice was shouting, "Excuse me, yes, thank you, I appreciate, so sorry, my wife…" Doug acknowledged Etta, looked Gerald up and down and staggered into the road where he crouched down next to his wife. An open case, like a suitcase, lay on the floor and a technician took out some paddles.

"No," Doug moaned, his head lolling from side to side, "revive her! I beg you!"

"If you could move away please, Sir," a paramedic asked. But Etta called over that the patient was his wife. An arm wrapped itself around Doug's shoulder to force his back to the scene and guide him to the pavement.

A police officer freed Gerald from Etta's grasp and she rushed over to Doug. He jumped at the command to, "Stand clear!"

"I'm Victoria's friend," she said.

He looked at her. "Etta," he said, "yes." And the person assigned to look after him melted back into the hubbub.

"She sent me a letter," he said. "She's found herself a new career. Do you know about her new career?" Etta shook her head. "We were going to meet. Tomorrow. She'd also tell me about the book and I could have my say. I was going to agree," he said. "More important to have her back."

Tentatively Etta lifted her hand, gently rubbed his back. "She'll be OK. She's a survivor."

"She has to survive!" Doug turned back to the road where someone in uniform held up a hand, insisting he stay back. He ignored it and pushed past. Some of the staff who'd surrounded Victoria walked away, the paddles no longer applied.

"So sorry, Mr Williams," a lady in uniform said to Doug. "So sorry." He walked on through the middle of the ring of staff, head bowed, no words, and sank to his knees at the side of his wife.

Silence pulled and twisted around Etta as muted people drifted away from the scene, walking in huddles as if to keep themselves vertical. They arrived from all directions and wandered into Charltons where the front of house gentleman waved them all in, because nobody must be outside at a time like this.

Etta sobbed, great heaves of sound to accompany a deluge of tears. Steve hadn't spoken, simply leaned against the front wall of Charltons, but now he took a step towards Etta with his arms outstretched and said, "May I?" Etta leaned against his chest, he wrapped his arms around her and they cried together in silence.

When they finally pulled apart, Steve said that Victoria would be laughing at them now.

Still Doug knelt at Victoria's side until a police officer laid an arm across his back, whispered something in his ear and directed him to the pavement where Etta and Steve were standing.

"She'll have died in peace," Etta said when he reached them. "In peace." She bit her lip.

"She left a legacy mate," Steve said. "She saved my life, influenced a nation." He gave Doug's shoulder a squeeze. "Not many of us get to say that."

ACKNOWLEDGEMENTS

MY HEARTFELT THANKS to early readers, Liz Lavender, Antonia Banks, Emma Brennan, and fellow writers at Authonomy and Litopia, for their brilliance and encouragement when Glass Houses was still a babe in arms. Thanks also to Amanda Newman for later gems.

Special thanks to Kathy Page for her inspiring mentorship and to Debi Alper, Emma Darwin and all my self-edit course class buddies for the inspiration, expertise and very firm hand-holding.

I'm so grateful to Jane Rusbridge for the constant encouragement and many reads of Glass Houses, not least her most recent edit, setting off light bulbs like Wembley Stadium at night. I'd also like to thank the many agents who read the full manuscript and took the time to send pages of enthusiastic feedback, sprinkled with gold dust. You didn't need to do that. I'm also grateful to David Smith for his diligent proof read, not least for removing my hyphens.

To Matthew Smith of Urbane Publications, whose enthusiasm, professionalism and joie de vivre has made the reality of publishing every bit as exciting as I'd dared to hope, thank you for believing in Glass Houses from the start. Thanks also to the rest of the team for the cover design and for making a 'real book' from my words.

Many people held my hand through an exploration into coma and recovery including Fiona Rainford and Marjorie Carruthers who let me pick their brains extensively on the sensitive subject of brain trauma and disability. Thanks to Dawn Schubert for her expertise on paramedics and Road Traffic Accidents, and to Emma Treadaway for patiently answering my inane questions about Scenes Of Crime Officers. Thanks to Emma Patterson, Road Side Lawyer, for giving freely of her time and expertise, particularly for helping me achieve the punishment I wanted for Tori, and to the lovely staff at Harrogate Magistrates' Court who chaperoned me through an illuminating day in court.

I'm indebted to Jane Lapotaire's poignant account of her own experience of brain injury and recovery in 'Time Out Of Mind', and to Richard Hammond's 'On The Edge', as well as Steve Pape's 'Stepped Off'. Phew! They were some crashes. For 'lucifugous' and other bizarre and aesthetically beautiful words, thanks to Peter Bower's, 'The superior Person's Book of Words' and for 'Mesoscale Meteorology in Midlatitudes' by Paul M. Markowski and Yvette P. Richardson - you're far too intelligent for me but thank you for the title.

Whilst I endeavour to be accurate with my research, all mistakes are most certainly mine.

I've happily mentioned specific places in Glass Houses but made some adjustments to aid the story. The law court is fictitious and the hospital could be anywhere. The geography of Harrogate bears some resemblance to truth but any establishments mentioned in detail are works of my imagination. There is no village called Deepbeck that I know of and this one has certainly come from inside my head. There is a Glass Houses in North Yorkshire and I promise I'll visit one day.

To my Mum, Kate, Julia and Antonia, my larger family, my local, school and Uni friends - you know who you are - thank you for exploding with enthusiasm at every stage and for keeping the faith, even when I'm sure it waned sometimes. I get it. I swore you'd never catch me in skinny jeans, either.

And to Lissie and Rosie for counting the beeps with me at pedestrian crossings and for patiently answering my, 'Would someone young say...?' questions, and to John for knowing that dreams aren't logical sometimes and for picking me up off the floor (not just emotionally) too many times to mention. Thank you to my wonderful family.

And finally, to all those I've kept waiting while I moved around commas, I'm sorry. Things will be better now. No, really.